Razor

Thin

This is one of those books that had me staring at the wall after making a variety of faces, reading the last sentence, slowly closing the book, putting it down, and resisting the urge to scream out loud. Not to be dramatic or anything, but this had an ending I did NOT see coming. So many times, throughout this book, I thought I had the ending all figured out, but no. No, I did not. -Maddie K.

This is a must-read for any fans of Freida McFadden!!! The way the author wrote the plot twist was incredible, to say the least. This story threw me for a loop in such a good way! I love psychological thrillers so much, and Amy's writing made me love them even more! The description of this book alone was so intriguing. I'm anxiously waiting for the next book!! –Destiny I.

Razor Thin has fun wordplay, and I appreciate the nods to life in Wisconsin. The chapter titles and dates kept me thinking, and I did not guess the ending. I had the opportunity to meet Amy at an event, and she was so gracious with everyone who stopped by to meet her. Looking forward to the next part in this series! -Megan

It's rare for me to be so enamored of a book that I have a hard time putting it down. I can't recommend this book enough! I can't wait for *Double Take*! – Lana

Dedication

Madison, Memphis & Montgomery.

Word List

Bluff [bluhf]

noun

a cliff, headland, or hill with a broad, steep face*

Geologists blame erosion for carving away the Mayfair bluffs outside stately homes along Lake Michigan.

verb (used with object)

to mislead by a display of strength, self-confidence, or the like*

My ex said he's single again, but I know he's bluffing.

*www.dictionary.com

Niall [ni(a)-ll]

noun

a masculine name of Irish descent given to impoverished newborns destined to break free from societal constraints, translates to "champion," this child will debunk any nature versus nurture debates

Niall was a sprawling landscape: mountains of testosterone, valleys of emotional strength, oceanic eyes beneath a stunning twilight horizon.

The Cast

Babs: Estelle's sister and Mayfair's top real estate agent. Kate and Kylie's aunt.

Cass: Kylie's boyfriend.

Damian Deveraux: Niall and Harrison's first manager.

Estelle Vanguard: Kate and Kylie's sensible mother.

Harrison: Niall's smartass best friend.

Henry Vanguard: Kate and Kylie's doting daddy.

Jolene: The love of Niall's life?

Kate Vanguard: Irrevocably lost without her sister, Kylie.

Kylie Vanguard: Kate's perfect twin sister.

Lance Deveraux: Damian's prodigal son.

Milly Rodrigo: Kate and Kylie's childhood best friend.

Niall O'Brien: Henry Vanguard's newest team member.

Nora: Babs' daughter. Kate and Kylie's cousin.

Peaches: Triple B's manager, Kate's current boss, and self-appointed life coach.

Piper Rodrigo: Kate and Kylie's childhood best friend.

Professor Holliday: Mayfair University professor.

Roxanne (Roxy): Influencer with 50K followers.

Soo-jin: Niall's close friend.

Verity: Lance's assistant.

Zakary: Kate's perfect ex.

5

The Day of the Murder.

6

Last One to See Her
April 10th

"PERCEPTION IS REALITY," my Creative Writing professor said. "If you tell me a lie and I believe you, that lie becomes my truth. Two perceptions emerge."

Polished fingers clicked against laptop keys, off-the-shoulder sweaters hugged soft skin, and a haze of perfume drifted above the classroom. What motivated my classmates? Were they eager learners captivated by academia, or were they desperate bimbos fantasizing about the school's only PILF?

"Who's correct?" he asked. "You or me?"

Professor Holliday then rattled on about red herrings and raising the stakes. Both were equally important elements in crafting a killer mystery.

I struggled to stay engaged. I mean, how could I? I'm Kate Vanguard, Mayfair University's only currently enrolled student to have earned a perfect score on the math portion of the ACT. Give me facts. Give me reality. Absolutes? Yes, please. Professor Holliday, on the other hand, thrived in the fictional.

And yet, there I sat, but it wasn't by choice. With only three credits needed to graduate, I agreed to take the course with Milly, Piper, and

Kylie because they convinced me it would be an easy A—my goal back then was efficiency. My future was secure with no uncertainties.

"Unknowns are essential," the professor said. "We must keep the reader engaged, on their toes, racing through the chapters. It's no easy task."

With two pages of single-spaced notes already typed, I paused. Milly, to my right, had doodled bubble hearts around Holliday's name. I nudged her with my elbow and gave her a disapproving look; she drew another. To my left, Kylie arched her brows, gestured lewdly to the teacher, then whispered, "His ass is so spankable." I rolled my eyes. Seeking sanity, I checked Piper, who was sitting on the other side of Kylie. When we made eye contact, she pointed at my phone—a text notification appeared. Against my better judgment, I clicked.

Piper: Daddy is looking extra delicious in those khakis today.

Me: You are not talking about my mother's co-worker, best friend, and a man old enough to be your DAD.

Piper: What a daddy, though.

Seconds later, a *thud, thud, thud* interrupted my judgmental thoughts. Then a yellow tennis ball flew over my shoulder, hit my laptop, and pressed a mysterious series of keys, causing an untimely shutdown.

"Sorry, Kate!" Cass shouted from the back of the class.

"Mr. Biggs," Professor Holliday scolded, as he scooped the stray ball before it could crash into his podium, "save the games for recess."

"My bad," Cass said. "I was trying to get Kylie's attention."

Kylie made a groaning noise and whispered, "I am so done with him. He's twenty-two but still acts like he's twelve."

I shrugged. On, off, on, off. It was always hard to tell if those two were still dating or in the middle of a breakup.

Speaking of *ON*, after I powered on my laptop, I searched my files for today's notes, but they were gone. *What the—*

"—Plot twist!" Professor Holliday shouted and raised a fist in the air. "If you craft a plot twist so cleverly that the reader will never see it coming, you could very well have a breakout novel. Any questions so far?"

While Milly asked Professor Holliday about unreliable narrators, I restarted my computer, but with no success. My notes were unreliable.

"Before I get into the good stuff, class," Holliday said. "I wanted to touch on the topic of appreciation. Becoming a published author was difficult, and having my friends' support was important, but an equally vital factor was having a critique partner. And this is the part of the lecture where I must give credit where credit is due."

Holliday used a remote to change the presentation slide. A picture of Mother popped up on the screen.

"Estelle Vanguard is the reason this debut novel, *Kitty Jossalyn: Somewhere Beyond the Mayfair Massacre,* became Amazon's #1 True Crime biography. She had a vision, came to me for advice, and we ended up working together to create this big, beautiful story." He clutched a copy of the manuscript against his chest.

A big, beautiful story.

My life was, in fact, a big, beautiful story.

I smiled and chewed the tip of my pencil.

Daydreaming wasn't a normal hobby of mine, but lately I'd been excited. Everything appeared perfect, in order, under control. In a few weeks, I'd graduate and become a real adult.

Smiling, I opened Excel to update my personalized budget to include the new salary I'd begin earning once my dad promoted me to vice president at Vanguard Family Builders. After I hit SAVE, I nearly giggled out loud. With this promotion, not only would I be able to afford my own apartment, but maybe even a new car—and just then, an error message appeared on the screen: *Critical Files Have Been Deleted. Reach out to Microsoft Office for further support.*

Well, screw you, I thought. Not looking for anyone or anything to take my joy away, I abandoned my notes for the day.

As I lowered the screen, a feeling of unease began creeping in. The idea that perception might matter more than reality made me feel uncomfortable.

For the duration of the class, students squeezed clammy fingers against their desks while Professor Holliday spoke of an innocent girl, murdered. I politely interrupted to clarify that a massacre usually involved multiple killings. He politely asked me to wait until the end of the lecture for unnecessary commentary. While the professor urged students to stay away from the bluffs at night, I reminded myself to add a row to my spreadsheet for a bonus in my new job. No doubt, I'd earn a BIG one.

"Did the mysterious woman die at the hands of a lover?" Professor asked. "Or was it an accidental fall over the Mayfair bluffs that led to her demise? An angry ghost seeking revenge? In my novel, I've collected the facts, and I can confidently say… the death that took place exactly fifty years ago today was… murder. A massacre." As if to emphasize his point, Professor Holliday glared directly at me.

"Ghosts? Urban legends?" I asked. "Dark strangers and misty spring evenings? The lonely nineteen-year-old found herself bludgeoned to death afoot the Mayfair bluffs because she replaced logic with an over-stimulated libido."

Piper snorted. "Please. The bluffs are for booty calls. Bet it was the same fifty years ago."

The class ended with useless chatter about the best local spots for indiscreet, public sexual encounters. My group of friends collected their things and headed towards the exit.

On our way out, Professor Holliday surprised everyone by giving out signed copies of his novel. Of course, Mother had written an inscription on the inside cover as well. Sweet Estelle never missed a chance for self-promotion.

After class, Piper and Milly headed off to the cafe. Kylie went to speak with Professor Holliday about the F she had earned on her last assignment. I made my way back to my dorm. My schedule was relentless: a midterm essay due before tonight's party, plus two other worksheets for Advanced Accounting Principles.

With a twelve-pack of cola in my dorm and a basket of Easter candy stashed under my bunk, I was certain I could crank out a scholarly seven-thousand-word essay before joining my friends for a night of drunken abandonment.

But before I could crack open a single can of soda or chomp my way through a single sugary treat, the energy of campus drama crashed into my sanctuary.

Kylie's meeting with Professor Holliday was a success, sort of. As always, she was able to lobby her way to an A, but only after she caught Holliday engaging in a scandalous sexual act of his own with a Mayfair University student—a juicy bit of information she didn't know how to process, so she swore me to secrecy out of both shock and fear of consequences. She really wanted that A.

Later that very night, our friend group had the most amazing party— a red flag party. The most iconic party ever, until it wasn't. Until it ended in death. A *murder.*

And ever since then, I'm sure everyone I love—and hate—has been lying to me. Perception has not been reality. Facts have bled into fiction. Frenemies have become friendly. And those I trust the most have hidden unspeakable things from me.

But to be honest, I can't even trust myself.

How can I? I *was* the last person to see her alive.

12

13

After the Murder.

14

Group Chat
Friday, May 27th @ 1:44 p.m.

ZAKARY SHIFTS HIS Ford F-150 into park outside his Mayfair duplex, taps the send button on his phone. The group message is delivered.

Zakary: I can't stop worrying about Kate.

At a local hotel, the silenced phone in Niall's $1,200 jeans receives a notification. Miles away at Bear's Bluffs & Brewery (known as Triple B's by the locals), Peaches' Android phone plays the first few chords to "Vincent." Behind the nearby bar, Roxy's smartwatch flashes brightly. Inside the Mayfair Day Spa, two iPhones, so new they haven't even been released to the public, vibrate in the hands of partially manicured nails.

Piper: Same.
Milly: I'm really worried about Kate, too, but WHY ARE WE TEXTING?!
Zakary: We need to talk about what happened. Everything ended so badly. I can't stop reliving it. Did we do the right thing?
Piper: The red flag party?
Zakary: Yes.
Roxy: Honestly, I've been losing sleep, too.

Milly: Please, take me off this group text! I can't handle being part of whatever this is becoming.

Milly: None of us like how it ended, but it's over, and we shouldn't bring it up. Ever again.

Piper: If Kate knew we were randomly texting, she'd be suspicious. It's not like we all hang out.

Milly: We're not friends—we're accomplices. Don't you all get that?

Piper: We agreed we would do anything for Kate. Everything was for her. Don't forget that. WE AGREED.

Milly: I can't believe you're all okay with this. I never agreed. Are you hearing me?

Piper: Has something else happened, Zakary? Why do you want to talk after all these months?

Zakary: Kate's barely keeping it together, and I'm really scared for her. I just thought talking together might help us figure out how to help her.

Roxy: There's nothing wrong with talking. Honestly, she seems completely unraveling at work lately.

Zakary: Also, Niall is back in town this weekend, so…

Roxy: Niall is back?

Zakary: Yeah. I guess he's meeting with Mr. Vanguard. It appears those two have unfinished business as well.

Milly: You know what? I care deeply about Kate, but I can't be part of the lies anymore. Please remove me from this group text.

Piper: Mute us or hide the notifications… Stop being dramatic…

Milly: Dramatic? This situation is the very definition of dramatic.

Milly: Are you triple dotting me? Twice? I'm so irritated with you right now, Piper! YOU can't be irritated with me, because I'M FURIOUS WITH YOU…………

Piper: Calm down.

Zakary: Do we just tell Kate the truth?

Milly: We are not telling Kate anything. She'd be destroyed if she knew the truth. Are you all insane?

Zakary: Milly, honey, this is just a conversation.

Roxy: Zakary is right.

Milly: Wait, who else is on this group text? There's a 312-area code that's not in my contacts.

Piper: Not in mine either. 312 is a Chicago area code.

Milly: Chicago? Who is it, and why, I repeat, WHY are they on this chat?

Zakary: I added Niall. He knows too much. We have to include him.

Milly: I am so done with all of you.

At the day spa, Milly and Piper head to pedicure stations, arguing as they follow the nail technician. Zakary hops out of his truck and kicks his front tire out of frustration. From behind the bar, Roxy pours two Brandy Old-Fashioned cocktails (no Brandy, extra Sprite) and hurriedly types a private message on her smartwatch.

Roxy: Hey, Niall, I heard you were back in town. I'm a little disappointed you didn't reach out.

When Niall doesn't reply, Roxy selects a beauty filter, swipes on Candy Yum Yum Pink lip gloss, and sends a selfie. Her cleavage looks amazing. After serving Honey Bear Ale to out-of-town guests, she checks her watch. No response. She quickly messages Niall again.

Roxy: Come to the brewery? I want to see you again.

Roxy: Hi, sexy. Read your messages and get back to me.

Roxy: I really want to see you again.

Then, Roxy opens her ClickYap App and creates a group chat with Milly Rodrigo, The Pied Piper, ZakAtak, JustPeachy, and Slide_OB. She sends a message:

Fauxy Roxy: Let's text here.

A Sister's Plea
Friday, May 27th @ 1:42 p.m.

"KATE, HEARING VOICES isn't normal," Peaches says while adjusting his Fendi headband with the tip of a pencil. A whiff of mint gum floats across the table.

"Hannibal Lecter didn't whisper in my ear," I deadpan.

A breeze off Lake Michigan rustles the overhead canopy of faux maple leaves. Knobby branches jut out from the wall. Even after a busy lunch at Triple B's, Mayfair's favorite brewery and grill, Peaches' face gleams. His shirt looks fresh from the dryer. I look under the varnished oak table. His checkered jeggings are spotless, and his bold hair accessory makes me want to rethink my entire life.

Since he sat across from me, he's blinked no less than a hundred times. Something is off.

Is he finally working up the courage to fire me? My stomach tightens with dread. I snarl and grab another fruit and slice. While lemon slices pile up in front of me, I try to read his face.

A stray hair tickles my cheek. I brush the back of my hand against my face. Powdered sugar dusts my skin. I pinch the fabric, irritating my coffee-splattered thighs. How are they still wet—

"So," he says, "hearing voices is fine? As long as the voice is… familiar?"

"Yes," I say, full of confidence. But the truth is, I'm not confident at all. Thankfully, Peaches—my boss, life coach, and match-maker—will help sort out this latest dilemma. His track record is nearly flawless. Last week, I teased, twisted, and braided my hair into the humble beginnings of dreadlocks. The project took longer than expected, making me extra late for work. When Peaches spotted me in the kitchen with my new look, he ushered me outside. He said my look was too bohemian for small-town Wisconsin and demanded I go home and shower. We've played this game for seven weeks. I try to move on, move on incorrectly, and he redirects.

Suddenly, the blade I'm holding slips against the slick peel of the lemon and nicks my fingernail. I jerk my hand back and let out a 'whoops!'.

"Careful with that knife," he warns, "and slow down. We're low on garnishes, but there's no need to lose a finger trying to restock. And you know I'd be useless if you julienned your thumb. Blood makes me queasy."

He shudders.

A second later, his phone comes alive as some hippie folk singer coos about a starry, starry night. Appearing bored, he ignores the alert and sets the device on the bench.

"I'm not hearing random voices," I say, irritated with him, the phone, and the fact that I might soon be unemployed. Frustration burns in my chest. "I don't have schizophrenia either. What I'm feeling is an intense desire." I shove a ramekin of dipping sauce towards him. Gelatinous liquid sticks to my knuckle. "For the grilled cheese squares," I say, licking my finger clean. "I need your opinion."

"In my opinion, you have an obsessive personality," he says, zoning in on the platter of bite-sized morsels, "and these look yummy."

"Channeling obsessions into productive behaviors is super healthy," I offer.

"Self-diagnosing is dangerous," he counters, his pupils darken under a veil of neatly arched eyebrows, "as are obsessions."

"I wasn't self-diagnosing." I avert my eyes to the cutting board. "My, uh, doctor said that."

"Your doctor? You mean Google?" His head tilts. The napkin slides across his lips. He nods. He nods a lot lately; it's much kinder than telling me my marbles have tumbled into the lake and taken residency under muck, seaweed, and decayed fish guts.

"Peaches," I say, my voice elevates, "what I'm about to tell you is super important—"

With more poor timing, the moody singer on his phone interrupts us again.

"Can you please get that or turn it off?" I ask, irritated. "Either way, be quick."

When I arrived at work today, two orders were already impaled on the ticket holder above my workstation. Throughout the lunch hour, the dining room, giddy from the wind-swept air through open garage doors, demanded squeaky cheese curds, salty onion rings, and greasy burgers. I've been waiting all day to share my news with Peaches.

His head shakes with quick, short movements as he looks down at the screen. Seventies folk music begins to play over the restaurant speakers.

"Notifications are silenced," he says, "therapeutic music is playing. You're more important. And these are super important." The mini sandwich he's holding dips into the sauce; he takes a bite, and lets out an orgasmic moan. "Kate, you've nailed this recipe with a sexy, tasty nail gun. Mmm. Mmm. I don't know if I ever told you this, but when I promoted your pudgy, sixteen-year-old ass from dishwasher to head chef, I took a superficial leap of faith. Truly, I had no idea you could actually cook."

He pulls out his phone again. "Mind if I tweet about this and post a quick Insta?" Without waiting to hear if I mind, he wipes a cheese dribble off the side of the dish, snaps a picture of the appetizer tray, then frantically pecks his phone. "Everyone needs to know about this."

"Seriously?" I ask. "And back then, I wasn't pudgy, I was healthy—"

"Triple B's is premiering a new sauce tonight," he monologues, "come get your grilled cheese apps and dip them in heaven before dying and going there and…" He stands and takes a pic of the patio and the lake in the distance. "The outside dining area is finally open. Hashtag best patio dining, hashtag Roxy is working, hashtag what's trending, hashtag celebrity sighting near me."

"Your hashtags are misleading," I say.

"Triple B's has the best patio dining, everyone, and I mean everyone wants to know when Roxy is working, we are trending, and c'mon, Jennifer Aniston is your mother's celebrity look-alike." He steps away from the bench, then carefully walks backwards towards the bar. "Properly placed puffery is a restaurant's greatest asset." Just in time, he spins around, snags our Old-Fashioned drinks off the beverage station, and steadies them as he returns to the table. He hands me one and sits.

A minute later, Roxy magically appears and sets a bowl of almonds in front of Peaches and a heaping tumbler of cherries by me.

"Dessert is served," she says. Her shoulders shimmy. Cinnamon bun boobs nearly spill out of her lacey tank top.

"Thanks, babe," Peaches smiles and claps his hands in delight.

I squint and rest into my resting bitch face.

"Ah-hem," Peaches says, scowling at me, looking very annoyed.

"Thanks, Roxy," I say forcefully.

Roxy and Kylie met in college and quickly became friends over vibrant lipstick, tube tops, and psychosomatic case studies. Roxy's a year younger than us, and Kylie took her under her wing. At first, I was glad Kylie found a study partner. Later, when I was left out of group chats and movie nights, I took it personally. Now, since Kylie's gone, I'm just super jealous of Roxanne's banging body.

"Well," Peaches demands. "What are you waiting for? Tell me the news!"

Not wanting Roxy to hear my latest development, I wait for her to return to the bar. Once she's a safe distance away, my words spill out like a hastily opened bag of cereal. "The nightmare I've been having has nothing to do with closure. It's a message from the other side. My instinct was right all along." I grab a lime from the bowl and stab the innocent fruit. "Kylie finally spoke and needs my help. She said…" I pause for several seconds to make sure he's paying attention. "Hurry! Help, before it's too late!"

By the look on his face, he's more worried than ever about my mental state.

"Shall we alert the authorities?" His lips pucker in doubt.

"No," I say. "First, we must narrow down the suspects, locate the murder weapon, and find the killer."

"Weapon? Killer?" he asks, kindness absorbs his face. "The last time you investigated a hunch," his voice drops to a whisper, "the police got involved, and you got in trouble. So, promise me you won't investigate anything. By the way, what's up with Dr. Miracle's restraining order?"

"That was a misunderstanding, and this is different." I use the knife's tip to macerate the insides of a lemon. "I think he's overturning it."

"You should probably check on that," Peaches says, steering me down the right path. "I might be wrong, but I think employers can pass you over if you've got a record."

"I don't think that counts as a record, but I'll check…"

"Anyway, darling, Kylie's been gone for seven weeks. What can you possibly do for her now?"

"For starters," I say. "I can hurry and help her. Don't you understand? Kylie's vanished from my life, and I've done nothing. I've slept, sulked, and been useless. But now, she's asked me to find the killer before the evidence disappears. The fingerprints are wiped off the weapon. The D.N.A. washes away. Time is against us, right?" I continue angry-slicing garnishes.

"If we were living a Netflix murder mystery," he says, "where a blonde Kristina Pimenova played you—the slightly disheveled yet endearing detective—and I was the dashing personal assistant, your statement is on point."

I'm almost sure he's toying with me, but nothing will stop me now, not even his deflecting sarcasm. Kylie needs me.

"Exactly," I say, "in every crime show, there's a point when the camera zooms in on a blood-smeared wall or an abandoned car, and the voice-over says 'The clock is ticking,' or 'Time is our biggest enemy.' Well, time and the sadistic killer."

"Kate," Peaches says, but his eyes are no longer smiling, "I wasn't serious. The case is closed. Her death was natural. A heart complication. What evidence is left to discover?"

For several seconds, silence falls between us.

"Your dad told me about Doe," he says, his worried face becoming a pout. "Maybe that's why you had a bad dream?"

"Possibly," I say.

"Finding a dead cat in the kitchen is traumatizing. Poor Doe."

"It was awful. But that has nothing to do with my dream."

"I'm just saying…"

"Kylie wants me to find the murderer."

"Kate—"

"What about Cass?" My slicing slows.

Peaches shakes his head. The headband shields his eyes from dark, buoyant locks.

"Cassidy Biggs may be going through some personal stuff right now, but he has always adored your family. He's lost without Kylie. We all are."

"Mother never approved of him dating Kylie."

"Kylie didn't seem to care."

"He messaged me last night."

"Cass?"

"Yeah."

"Again?"

"Ten texts."

"What did he say?"

"I didn't open them."

"He probably just misses Kylie and wants to talk to a familiar voice."

"I always thought he was a good guy," I say, "but I've been doubting myself lately. I feel like nothing makes sense… What about me—"

"Stop," he says. "Those gossipy nurses know nothing. You may have knocked yourself out that night, but you didn't do anything nefarious. You, my dear, are an angel."

"Nefarious?"

"Criminal, devious. You didn't do anything wrong."

I pull a crumpled receipt from the plastic grocery bag on the bench, borrow Peaches' pencil, scribble 'nefarious' underneath 'innocuous', then stuff the sheet back inside my makeshift purse.

I clench my jaw.

"What about those missing hours?" I ask. "PTSD doesn't happen during happy moments. It takes something serious. Horrible, tragic things. Anything could have happened during that time. I could have done or said something terrible to hurt her. Someone I loved died, and I'm pretty sure I saw their murder."

"We told you what happened," he says, softly.

He's right. Those missing twenty-four hours were reconstructed carefully and intentionally by my friends and family. Relying on others to tell you about something you should have firsthand knowledge of is insane. Terrifying. They could have told me anything, and I would have had to believe them. What choice did I have?

The basic facts remained the same. The blood congealing scream. The tremor from the ground. The flash from the sky. Then she collapsed outside Triple B's, as if an invisible ghost attacked her organs. Everyone at the party saw it. Supposedly. Days later, after much speculation from local and national news sources, the coroner announced the official cause of death: Hypertrophic cardiomyopathy (HCM). A heart malfunction. An untimely natural death, occurring at an unnaturally young age.

"Step inside my chaos. Wouldn't you want to know the truth no matter what?"

"But a dream isn't evidence. Hearsay isn't either. And just because you lost a few memories from that night doesn't mean something awful happened."

"Kylie needs my help. I mean, that night was chaotic. Anything could have happened. Anyone could have done anything. I trust you, but what about everyone else? The more I think about that night, the more I wonder. *Whose* perception is reality? Could someone be lying?"

He bites his lip and snags another cheese square.

Although I don't like it, I understand Peaches' uncertainty. He didn't hear Kylie's plea; I did. And she's my sister. I let out a sigh. Peaches may not have the missing puzzle pieces, but Kylie's words have given me a renewed sense of purpose.

"It's a twin thing," I say. "An inexplicable connection. Haven't you ever felt there's more to a story than what you're being told?"

I allow a small smile to crawl across my lips; maintaining peace with my dear friend is essential.

"Every damn day," he says, and returns the smile. "Dear old daddy always said I'd never be successful, but look at me now. I'm a bar manager, making more money than pops ever did. So bougie, in fact, I wear my Gucci onesie when I weed my garden. Truth is relative."

"It's impractical and yellow," I say and laugh as I recall last spring when Kylie and I helped him weed his garden.

"The truth?" he asks.

"No, your onesie. How many times have you been stung?"

"Only that once."

"Only once? I doubt that. We witnessed you curse Mother Nature while an entire hive chased after you."

"Correct, and had I not been wearing a full-body onesie, things could have turned out dramatically different. Color did not matter. And no one can prevent me from doing me. All day, every day. You should feel the same way. Baby girl, it's time you dip a toe in the water of your glorious future." He pops another gooey square into his mouth. "What do you think about adding a chopped salad to the menu—"

"Salad?" I ask. Annoyance washes over my brow. "Peaches, twenty-four hours isn't a speck, and something awful did happen. I'm going to keep digging until I find the truth."

Maybe Peaches is right. The menu could do with something green. Broccoli doused in a four-cheese sauce? Bacon-wrapped Brussel sprouts?

I could also benefit from healthier choices. The end of college is the beginning of the rest of your life, right?

But I can't look forward because the past keeps dragging me back to April 10th. I'm the worst time traveler ever. Who obsesses over the details of a family member's tragic death—details that may, or may not, mean anything? May, or may not, toss me thoroughly over the edge?

Me.

That's who.

But I'm doing the right thing. I know it. And Kylie asked for my help. I can't ignore her.

Peaches quickly begins to drone on about the salad options he's been considering for the menu. Chopped, tossed, crisped, shredded. Romaine, spinach, kale.

Peaches isn't hiding anything from me. Is he? He wouldn't. He's my friend. And he wouldn't hide anything from the police. None of my friends would. That would be wild. Totally Riverdale-esque. And we don't live in fictional, crime-ridden Riverdale. We live in teeny-tiny, sweet and homey, boring-as-hell Mayfair, Wisconsin.

Even still, I can't stop until I find the truth. A sister's devotion is unending. If the roles were reversed, Kylie would do the same for me. Audible should have a novice guide for conducting a murder investigation. I'll look later.

While Peaches discusses the difference between organic and non-organic veggies, I pull out my phone and send Kylie a quick text.

Me: What do you need me to do??? How can I help?

I twirl the tungsten ring on my left hand. Kylie's ring. *Hurry! Help, before it's too late!* I stare at my phone, waiting for Kylie to respond. For a second, my heart expands as I see her avatar pop up on the screen, but just as suddenly, it's gone.

Group Chat
Friday, May 27th @ 1:56 p.m.

IN HENRY VANGUARD'S guestroom, Niall unpacks his suitcase. Exhausted after months without good sleep, he rests on a wooden chair by the tiny desk. For the first time in weeks, he pulls out his laptop. He exhales, taps the power button, and waits for Outlook to load. A 3 o'clock meeting reminder appears: *3:00 Henry Vanguard (Kate) @ Vanguard Builders.*

He closes his eyes, takes a deep breath, then snoozes the notification. The slight burning sensation he's had in his chest since he awoke is now a roaring fire. He grabs a bottle of antacids from his suitcase and chugs them like a bottle of water. He powers on his phone, opens ClickYap, and messages Harrison.

Slide_OB: O'Brien Consulting is officially back in business. Thanks for covering for me.

The Battering Ram: NO PROBLEM. IT WAS EASY PRETENDING TO BE YOU. JUST HAD TO SHOVE A STICK UP MY ASS.

Slide_OB: Thanks, I needed those couple months away.

The Battering Ram: GLAD YOU'RE BETTER. YOU MAY BE A NEUROTIC ASS, BUT I'M GLAD MY COMPETITION IS BACK. YOU'RE THE BEST CONSULTANT OUT THERE.

The Battering Ram: KILL EM BOO.

Next, Niall checks his texts. A slew of messages pops up in a group chat. Two of the names—Roxy and Zakary—are in his contacts. The other numbers are new. He quickly scans the messages.

They want to talk about the party?

This is not good.

He opens and reads Roxanne's messages.

Without thinking, he tosses his phone onto the bed; it skids across the comforter and crashes on the floor. He curses but leaves it. He changes his shirt three times, finally choosing a French button-down and denim jeans. Both were hand-sewn by his personal tailor, Gervais. The clothing arrived late last night by international mail.

His reflection in the mirror shows confidence. A false confidence. Acid builds within his stomach. He straightens his collar, flattens the front pocket, and massages his hands against his jeans. Before heading out the door, he grabs his briefcase and shuffles into his white Nikes.

After too much deliberation, he arrives at Triple B's. He parks south of the building, facing Lake Michigan. The sky overhead is pale blue. To the north, dark gray clouds gather over the bluffs. Something bigger than a spring storm is looming. To the south, a clear sky and bright sun hover over Chicago. It's almost as though the weather is telling him to go home. He has no business being here.

He checks his back pocket, scans the passenger seat, then the floor. He slams his fist on the wheel.

He forgot his phone. He checks his watch. Although he has an hour before his next meeting, he can't leave. Not now. Not when he's so close. But can he really go inside? The place is so tiny, he'd bump into Kate. What would he say then?

Hey Katie, you don't know me, but I'm fucking crazy about you. Every woman I meet reminds me of you—because they're nothing like you. I'm reminded of what I don't have. You. What I will never have. You. I thought you were an illusion, then realized you were real, then I fucked up. I want to…

He knows what he wants, but can't say it or feel it. He slumps in his seat and opens the window. Warm air slithers in. A lawnmower rumbles in the distance. A haunting, folksy guitar tune plays from the restaurant.

Everything feels wrong.

Everything feels ominous.

He shouldn't be here. Never should have left Chicago.

Before the Murder.

An Okay Business Guy
Tues, Feb 1ˢᵗ

THE SLEEP IN my eyes and lack of sunlight in the room suggest it's too early for anyone to swear and demand I do anything. And yet, an angry voice thick with a ridiculous Scottish accent crows: "Niall, ye lazy arsehole. Quit playin' wit ye willy and an'ser ye bloody phone."

I burrow under the blankets, drawing them tightly around me. A chilly February morning hovers over my comforter, making me even less inclined to leave my bed. Plus, I'm not interested in answering anything, too tired to play with anything, and not even slightly curious why my phone is speaking. Another vibration rumbles in my ear. The pretentious man repeats himself.

I sit upright.

My phone continues to buzz on the nightstand, just out of arm's reach.

Harrison.

He must have changed my ringtone. I fall back and sandwich the pillow around my ears.

Last night, Harrison said we'd chill and watch basketball at his place, but before long, we went to a friend of a friend's twenty-fifth birthday party, and an intense game of *Get Niall Laid* ensued because Harrison claimed, "Six weeks of celibacy was something to be ashamed of."

As usual, I was sober, so when Harrison introduced me to several women, I turned into meemaw selecting avocados at the market. Everything was overpriced, nothing was in season, and I already had an avocado at home.

By the third ring, I don't know how it's possible, but the man seems furious, so I reach for the noise and squint at the glaring screen. A very early morning phone call from an unknown number is never good.

"Niall O'Brien speaking." I swing my legs over the side of the bed.

"Good morning, Mr. O'Brien," a very awake man says, as though he's having a much better morning than I am. "Henry Vanguard of Vanguard Family Builders. Harrison Collymore gave me your number. He says you're a pretty okay businessman, and my company is doomed without your help." A hearty chuckle forces me to pull the speaker away from my ear.

"That's me," I reply. "An okay business guy, and the Collymores are good friends of mine."

"I'm in Chicago for the day," Mr. Vanguard says and cackles joyously. "What's your schedule? I'd love to meet and discuss your services."

I cross the room and head to the en suite bathroom. I stub my toe on a hard object. The object retaliates in a sing-song voice: *The wheels on the bus go round and round, round and round…* I hold back a curse and scoop the toy truck off the floor, fumble with the power switch, and toss it onto a nearby chair. Right now, I want nothing more than a blacked-out room, absolute silence, and to lose myself between my Egyptian silk bed sheets and luxury pillow. But I can't have any of that—can't do any of that, because my condo is currently charred to ashes, as are my sheets and everything that was inside. For now, I'm making the most out of Soo-jin's guest house, brimming with pastels, sheer curtains, drafty windows, and toddler toys.

It's tough to brood in such a brightly lit area. Technically, it's not quite a guest house; the building and main house are attached by a short hall, with a privacy door that doesn't lock. Soo-jin and Bennett are free to walk in unannounced at any time of day.

I check my watch. Six?

Who has the energy to make a business call this early? I tell Mr. Vanguard I need to check my calendar.

My schedule is packed today. Even though Mr. Vanguard's request is obnoxious, I can't say no. For a small business owner, turning down an opportunity is professional suicide. The meeting will have to be short and early, but I do my best work under pressure. Challenge accepted, Mr. Vanguard. We'll meet for coffee, and I'll earn your trust and business all within an hour.

"Mr. Vanguard," I say, "I can meet early this morning. Are you familiar with the coffee shop off La Salle?"

Turns out Buns-n-Bakery is his favorite Chicago breakfast spot. How intuitive of me. He'll meet me there at seven.

To prepare for today's meeting, I take an icy shower, shave, slam a Powerade, and toss back a couple of antacids.

Then I message Harrison.

Me: Little Dick, is Henry Vanguard insane? He just called to schedule a meeting today. The sun isn't even up yet.

I'm positive Harrison's asleep, but I send the message anyway, hoping his phone will vibrate, ding, or beep—preferably all three—and interrupt his sleep.

After ordering an Uber, I slip into my white-collared shirt, virgin-wool suit jacket, and black slacks. Expensive, quality, and comfortable. My favorite suit, now my only one, since my wardrobe went up in smoke with my belongings. And since the insurance investigators discovered a gasoline bath saturating my bedroom mattress, there has been a delay in paying my claim. Restocking my life is going to take time.

And that is unfortunate, because the truth is, proper clothing is essential to my success. When I meet a client for the first time, they judge my appearance, but I never worry because I always leave a positive initial impression. After being paid for my first consulting gig, I purchased several custom-tailored suits from a famous French clothier, Gervais. Together, they cost more than a couple of months' rent. This week, I'll have to find time to restock my wardrobe.

From the hallway, I hear a door slam and Bennett's booming giggle.

I don't have time to answer Soo-jin's twenty-one questions about last night, or the time to turn Bennett down when he asks me to 'pay'. Looks like I'll be sneaking out the back. My stomach growls, so I snag a protein bar from the cabinet, then pull my coat off the broom hook, grab the jewelry box off the nightstand, and sprint out the door.

Outside, the air is cool and still. I shrug into my jacket. A good foot of snow covers the lawn. I shovel a narrow path down the sidewalk—careful not to slip. The snowplows have already made a pass through the streets, so the roads are clear. Once I safely reach the curb, I check my phone messages.

I have one from Soo-jin. And Harrison has responded. I smile because my earlier text woke him, and since his response will be unpleasant, I tap Soo-jin's name first.

Her message will also be unpleasant, but less unpleasant. She's sent a video. She fits her twenty-one questions into thirty seconds. Why was I out so late last night? (Thanks, Ring.) Did Jolene and I finally break up? Am I avoiding her? Why did I run out the back door without saying good morning? Have I seen Bennett's favorite toy truck? Can I watch Bennett Sunday?

Me: Sorry. I have an early breakfast meeting. My man! Bennett! What's up! Sunday is clear. I'll take him to a singles mixer. Gonna teach him how to play the ladies.

Next, I open Harrison's message.

Harrison: YOUR CRABBY LITTLE BITCH ATTITUDE TELLS ME YOU'RE CRANKY AND NEED TO GET LAID. FORGET JOLENE. GET YOUR SHIT TOGETHER, SLIDE. YOU HAVE ONE SHOT WITH VANGUARD.

Harrison: WEAR ONE OF YOUR PRETTY LITTLE BITCH SUITS AND MAKE DADDY PROUD.

I chuckle to myself as I heart the message.

Harrison has never had a serious relationship, so he's clueless about women, but the amount of unsolicited relationship advice he gives suggests otherwise.

Jolene and I aren't over. Long-distance relationships, although challenging, aren't impossible. She moved to LA almost two months ago, so the physical distance is absolute. In the beginning, we spoke several times a day, but now, we only speak once or twice a week, at most. And Friday, she tossed around the idea of an open relationship.

Ouch.

A surprise visit to California and presentation of the ring may be necessary to restore our spark. When Jolene and I lived together, our relationship was simple: work, laugh, date, trust, fuck, repeat. But now everything feels complicated. When we talk, every word carries a double meaning. If she's meeting a friend for lunch, is she going on a date? If she had fun with her girlfriends at the club, did the fun include making out with some random loser? Distance has created a new, uncomfortable normal between us.

Given the two-hour time difference, Jolene won't be awake, but if I simply hear, "This is Jo, you know what to do," maybe I'll know what to do? I call her.

While I wait for an answer, I distract myself by watching the neighborhood come alive.

At the end of the driveway, Soo-jin's neighbor, Mariah, and her Pomeranian, Biscuit, walk towards me, hugging the cleared road. The glitter collar and beaded lead jingle. Mariah's stiletto winter boots click against the slushy road. She looks me up and down several times. Across the street, Mrs. Abigail Prescott, wife to a professional basketball player, rushes her four children into the family's Cadillac Escalade. She finds a reason to smile and wave—twice—before she buzzes down the courtyard.

Before Soo-jin's neighbor to the east, Claire Alexander, completely saunters down her front porch stairs wearing a microscopic cotton robe, my Uber driver, Rafael, arrives and rescues me from the visual assaults. Before he even comes to a complete stop, I hurriedly hop inside his sedan. My nerves are on fire, waiting for Jolene to answer.

The phone rings against my ear.

Jolene, I miss you so much. Can I visit soon?

What if she doesn't answer?

Hey, Jo. I've got back-to-back meetings all day, but let me know when you're free, and I'll make time to call.

After a fourth vibration, my name floats across the miles. "Hello," Jolene says. I imagine she's propping the phone between her chin and shoulder, flipping tangled, ebony hair into a messy bun. She repeats herself, "Niall?"

Relief floods my body, and I let out a heavy breath of air.

Even though I want to see Jolene, her gorgeous smile, and sexy eyes, she would never take a FaceTime call this early. Not when she hasn't had time to shower, style her hair, or apply make-up.

"Jo, you answered," I finally stammer. "Sorry, I just got in my Uber. Did I wake you up?"

"Sleeping is impossible lately," she says with a noticeable sigh. "I'm so tired. Sorry, I haven't messaged or called. I've been really busy." The apology is automatic; I may as well be a stranger she's accidentally bumped into on the sidewalk. But I can't be upset. She's exhausted, of course, she's not herself.

"Don't worry," I say. "I know you're busy. How are the auditions? I bet the agents and casting directors love you." *And all of California*, I think to myself.

"The casting director I told you about last month has an amazing opportunity for me," she says. "It's a role as a supporting actress in an

Indie film. I'll be a model." As she speaks, the excitement in her voice shows. Finally, her dreams are coming true. This is everything she's ever wanted. I feel a surge of pride for her.

"Super cliché," she says, "but don't worry, it's legit. I would have told you about it sooner, but I wanted to wait until it was solid. I think this is my chance. But I'm not sure…"

"You're hesitating?" I ask. "You know what I always say about open doors—"

"They're open for a reason," she says, letting out a playful laugh.

A flicker of hope tugs me along. She hasn't totally forgotten about me or my motivational speeches.

"Chase your dreams, Jolene," I say. "You've worked hard for this and deserve to be happy."

She's secured a future in California, and business is booming for me. Work.

I tell her the weather is out of control. Last night, Lake Michigan blasted us with snow, and we're expected to have six more weeks of arctic nose hairs. The bed is cold without her.

"Soo-jin said you've been a big baby lately," she says with a playful laugh. "She warned me you'd be on edge because she was going to visit her old college roommate. And we both know you can't sleep alone in that big, scary house." Her teasing tone is infectious. A sense of warmth surrounds me. I can almost feel her arms hugging me.

I remind Jolene that I can sleep alone, and I've done so plenty of times at the condo. The wailing sirens, rumble of dump trucks on the streets, and squall of kids running down the hall used to lull me to sleep like a fresh-diapered, milk-coma baby. Sleeping in Soo-jin's historic home, built in the 1860s, is a different story. The floorboards creak, the rooms are drafty, and there are at least three weird Harry Potter storage rooms that are totally inhabited by a ghost.

"You're convinced the salty spirit is stuck in the in-between, brooding, sulking, and terrorizing occupants," she says. "You should get along with the ghost because you're an excellent brooder. You really are a big baby." Somehow, her playful jab turns me on.

We both laugh.

She knows me so well. Another reason we're perfect for each other. Jolene asks when Soo-jin and Bennett are back in town. *Today.* She's glad. She doesn't want to worry about me being rude to Soo-jin's ghost.

Jolene says I should feel sorry for her because she's stuck rooming with a horde of VSCO girls, which is a thousand times more deadly than ghosts; someone is constantly borrowing her Olaplex shampoo, and her gold hoop earrings are still missing. Worst of all, the temperature has been in the eighties all week. She's forced to wear shorts, tank tops, sundresses, and bikinis, which means awful tan lines. Awful tan lines? Never heard of such a thing. Later, she'll send pics. A welcome warmth takes over my body. Laugh.

I compliment her courage to follow big dreams and say she's beautiful inside and out. The shortest date we've ever had, but we've connected, two thousand miles apart, and I'm getting pics later. Date. Almost.

No sex, but at least we're talking again, and everything feels... simple.

Before we say goodbye, she asks to borrow $1,500 to help her prepare for the role. Lip filler, fake spray tan, hair extensions—I tell her she's a knock-out with those things. She pouts and begs, "Please." Jolene's love is worth so much more, so I agree to wire her the money.

An actual old-fashioned wire. No one sends wires anymore, except mortgage lenders and title companies. And, apparently, me. But right now, that's my only option, because the money in my bank account is frozen. Some asshole has it out for me; someone wants to become Niall O'Brien really badly.

Three times this year, someone has tried to open credit cards in my name. Thankfully, a few years ago, on a whim, I had signed up for an identity theft monitoring service. For added protection, my financial advisor recommends that I minimize the use of my personal information online. No Venmo, eBay, or Amazon. For now, I use a prepaid VISA for small purchases, and for larger amounts, I write a check or wire funds.

Thankfully, I trust Jolene. And that's important.

A relationship is doomed without trust.

Trust.

Curiosity (Almost) Killed Kate
Friday, May 27th @ 2:16 p.m.

SOMEONE HAS KYLIE'S phone. My hands are clammy, and a ball of phlegm is stuck in my throat. Who would take her phone? And when? Have they had it all along?

"The thing is—" Peaches says, adjusting his headband. Beads of sweat have accumulated on his forehead. I had almost forgotten, he's about to fire me.

"Yes, the thing," I say, feeling an impending sense of doom. Not only for this situation, but also about Kylie's missing phone. "Tell me the thing already."

Let's get this over with, I think to myself.

"Bear reviewed current staffing needs and rated each employee on punctuality, overall customer service, teamwork, and no-shows."

I slink into my seat. My no-shows are showing up way more than their namesake would suggest.

"Scores were tallied," he says, centering the ketchup and mustard bottles in front of him. "The necessary cuts have been determined. I am so sorry, but you've become unreliable to a perilous fault."

"Is this why you had me train the Hundred brothers on the grill all week?" His guilt is obvious.

"I might replace you here," Peaches says, placing one hand flat on the table between us. "But I could never replace you here." He puts the other hand over his heart. "If I owned the place, I'd have kept you on. My love for you is blind, and nothing, and I mean nothing, can pull me away from my affair with your grilled cheese sandwiches. Don't even get me started on that new sauce."

"It's cheese and bread." My head drops, heavy with embarrassment, my forehead taps a semi-clean section of the table. "With butter." The words croak out, defeated. "I suppose I should thank you for not firing me sooner."

"There's a secret ingredient," he says. "One day, you'll tell me, and life lessons are how we become better people."

"So I'm not on the schedule next week. Is today my last day?"

"I'm sorry," he whispers.

"That's cool," I say, "because I was just telling the voices in my head I need to find a better place to plot out my neurotic plan to investigate a murderer." I slide my apron off and toss it on the bench beside me.

At this moment, the devastation in his eyes quite possibly matches the bleakness in mine.

Seconds later, the bell above the entrance rings. Needing a distraction, Peaches looks toward the door. Equally desperate for one, I follow his gaze.

"Aviator sunglasses inside a bar?" Peaches whispers, criticizing Mayfair's newest arrival. He does a double-take. "Wait, those are eyeglasses. No—nerdy transitional lenses. And look at those slacks he's wearing. They are designer. I bet he spent at least $1200 on them—Oh my!"

"What?" I half-heartedly ask.

He glides off the bench, patting my hand as he leaves. "I've got to talk with Roxy about tonight." Without a glance, he moves towards the bar.

"Tell her to put on a t-shirt," I say. Ignoring my request, he walks swiftly towards the bar.

Even though I'm fired, I'll finish my work. It's the right thing to do. I focus on moving the knife in a steady rhythm. Out of habit, I shake free a cluster of white-blond tendrils, letting them fall across my right cheek, properly covering my scar. And my shame.

I just got fired.

I'm supposed to be an overachiever. My life was together. *What have I done?* Tiny knots of uncertainty form in the pit of my stomach.

Kylie whispers, *Look on the bright side, Katie.* Given it's called the bright side, I should spot it rather quickly.

I suppose I have to accept the truth; it's time I transition to a 'real' job. Working with my dad full-time will be a well-needed distraction, but leaving Triple B's feels like losing a piece of myself.

I look around the room. Patrons perch on stools along the horseshoe-shaped bar or at high-top tables dotting the dining area. Fake birch and maple trees decorate the corners, and carved bear statues cling to each. A row of wooden picnic tables occupies the center of the party room— The Bear's Den.

Months ago, Mother reserved the space for the rehearsal dinner. Tonight's celebration will take place promptly at 6 o'clock.

My parents have been divorced not once, but twice. From each other. Tomorrow is supposed to be their wedding date. Anniversary date? Would they be getting remarried? Re-re-married? May 28th has always been their special day. Right now, a wedding seems ridiculous. Mother mailed Save-the-Date cards for both events back in March. I'm shocked everyone still wants to get together.

Apparently, a celebration is necessary.

Now that Memorial weekend is upon us, the patio facing the lake and the beer garden to the north are available for tipsy, bloated patrons in need of fresh air or a cancer-causing puff of smoke.

Even though the view from the front of the house is spectacular, I always stayed away. But when we'd be slammed, I'd be forced to leave the sanctuary of my kitchen and run food.

A couple of weeks ago, when I served Mama Bear burgers to a group of rowdy Brewers fans, one jerk commented on the scar running across my right cheek. The douchebags wanted to know if a cat had attacked me. Was I involved in a knife fight, or injured working undercover for the secret service?

I smiled along and blamed a fictional, drunken tumble on the Port Wine breakwater pathway during freshman welcome week. Inside, I wanted to whip off my apron and fling it at the idiots. After returning to the kitchen and telling Peaches about their comments, he reminded me not to quit, since I had recently spent my savings on those twenty-one stars and needed this job. But what better way to honor a twin sister's twenty-one years on this volatile earth? Necessary purchase, right?

Well, now I'm fired. The finality of this truth slams through me.

I sigh and drop the lemon slices into the dish with a soft plunk.

Peaches is still talking with Mr. Sunglasses and Roxy. The three are leaning in close. I'd say they are arguing, judging by the frown on Peaches' face and Roxy's perfect pout. Sunglasses has a clenched fist by his side. What kind of intense conversation could they possibly be having this early in the day? I must be imagining things.

Seconds later, Peaches catches me staring and waves shyly before heading back over.

"Who is that guy?" I ask, nodding towards Hollywood Hair.

"Oh," Peaches says, "just some business guy from Chicago. I've seen him here a few times."

"He and Roxy are close?" I ask.

Peaches turns a dark shade of peach. He shrugs.

"I guess. Your dad knows him, too."

"My dad knows everyone."

While I finish my slicing, Peaches switches gears and focuses on my future. He encourages me to craft a vision board, insists I write a detachment letter to Kylie, and begs me to find a better way to distract myself from my obsessive tendencies.

While Peaches rambles, my attention is pulled to that man from Chicago and Roxanne. The two are still leaning in close. Roxy has pounded her hand against the table, and he's shaken his head several times. And this could be the strangest part of the day so far, because

Roxanne's attention span usually snaps out after a minute. She doesn't hold serious discussions with anyone unless they involve critical commentary on Paris Fashion Week, so what could those two possibly be discussing?

"How does that sound?" Peaches asks.

"Perfect," I say, having no idea how that sounds.

Satisfied, Peaches continues his rant. "Your mental health and happiness are so important, Kate."

I nod, but…my curiosity can't be killed. I allow my curiosity to nag. Really hard. Super hard, so hard I must permit another teeny-tiny glance in Chicago's direction. Not even a glance, a glimpse. Is a glance less evident than a glimpse? Whatever's more discreet, I'll do that. Someone has to monitor the town for shysters, riff-raff, and no-good-doers.

And players. He's a player.

Glancing, or glimpsing, for a second time won't alter my destiny. I raise my lashes and capture a peek—a furtive glimpse lasting a millionth of a second. During my feather-light stare, my lashes flicker. As if sensing my gaze, the executive turns his head toward me.

Our eyes connect.

And in that moment, I'm sure I recognize him. A wave of unease washes over my chest. As I'm trying to place the man, something unexplainable happens. The man slowly drags his thumb across his bottom lip, eyes locked on me. I'd turn around to see if the seductive drag was directed at someone, but there's a wall immediately behind me decorated with very unsexual pinecones and honeybees.

Who is he looking at? Not me. Peaches? The tint has left the man's nerdy eyeglasses, and a black frame circles his sparkling eyes. Two thin lines form between his devastating eyebrows; radiant eyes search mine. *What is he looking for?*

I snap my head back to my work—the work I should be working on—and freeze. What could I have that belongs to him? Nothing. Clearly, I'm delirious. I dig to the bottom of my glass for a cherry. Ice cubes levitate to the surface, and liquid splashes over the edge. I stuff the sweet cherry into my mouth. With one bite, the burst of sweetened goodness fills my mouth.

Even though I'm minding my own business, I can feel the man watching me from across the room. Feeling uncomfortable and unsure what to do, my body acts on its own. In a moment of sheer madness, I do the only thing that feels right. I confidently lift my chin, lock eyes with the man, then stick out my tongue and give him my best wide-eyed crazy face.

The man nearly spits out his drink.

"What the hell just happened?" Peaches asks, frowning as though I've lost my senses. "Why did you stick your tongue out at a grown man? Have you lost your senses?"

I shake my head. A heavy French fry odor fills the vicinity. A lengthy shower and triple shampoo are necessary.

Mortified, I sit quietly while Peaches scolds me.

Frustration grows in my stomach. I saw the man's face plain as day, and I'm positive I recognize him. But from where? My heart races. My mind teleports to *that* night. That awful night. Moments from the red flag party crash through my mind. Peaches is waving a red t-shirt. Mother is standing near the bluffs, pointing at the sky. Kylie twirls, her blonde hair swirling like radiant streamers. Professor Holliday is setting up his electromagnetic field detector. Cass is slamming another beer.

And that man is standing in front of me. *Why am I seeing that man?*

Dizziness swirls around the zigs and the zags. I feel woozy.

"Careful," Peaches urges. "Don't cut yourself with that knife. Your chopping is a little sloppy. Are you okay?"

I grip the edge of the table for mental support, my left arm flails and bumps into my fizzy soda, and my slippery fingers fumble with the glass. The damn thing tips. I swipe my hand to catch the teetering drink but miss, and somehow my palm strikes the immobile knife's blade. Intense pain spreads between the soft flesh of my thumb and index finger. Blood rapidly spews onto the table. The cup clanks. A swirl of grenadine-laden fizz, cherries, and ice spreads across the table.

"You cut yourself!" Peaches chirps. "Blood!" He cries and pushes himself out of the seat.

A ton of blood.

So. Much. Blood.

"Shoot, sorry," I say and pluck the remaining napkins from the dispenser and toss them over the carnage.

Lemon juice sets fire to my palm. A needling pain catches my breath. I press my hand against the wound to slow the gush. Liquid lava worms through the creases and trickles down my forearm. Droplets pelt the table. A splattering of blood and juice decorates the bottom of my untucked shirt, and I'm confident I look as though I've murdered someone.

"Oh my, I may faint," Peaches says and slides onto a neighboring chair. His head tucks between his knees. "If I pass out, catch me. I promised baby Gucci I'd never let her touch a filthy floor." He groans. "You know I'm a straight-up Gucci hoochi."

The stinging red intensifies, and Peaches' voice fades. The lights hanging throughout the bar become more vibrant. The walls of the room and the air in my lungs seem to shrink. My brain thumps in time with the pulse of my finger.

A voice cries, *Katie.*

The room darkens. A maroon flood replaces the wooden floor. Lake Michigan's frigid waters lash at my sneakers. The space in front of me is the dark sky. I pivot, sinking into the damp sand. Now I'm facing the bluffs. The moon above illuminates the beach. In front of me, a small, dark mound, surrounded by a pool of oozing liquid. Black water? No. Blood. I take a step closer.

A splayed yellow crown frames the heap. A lifeless body lies in the sand. A familiar sound calls again, but before I can answer or place the voice, the insides of my bones dissolve, the floor lifts, and the smell of lake water is replaced by a rich aromatic scent. Something warm wraps around my waist. As dizziness consumes me, I wonder why the brilliant white shoes in the sand are splattered with blood, and my red t-shirt is sticky and wet.

Then…
I fall.

Open Doors
Tuesday, Feb 1

AFTER JOLENE ENDED the call, I slid the ring case from my front pocket. The box sprang open as the vehicle sped through a red light onto La Salle. At the intersection, the sunrise over Lake Michigan released blinding rays, filling the backseat with a thousand panels of light.

"Sorry for the acceleration, sir," Rafael apologizes, "but I know punctuality is important to you."

And a big tip for getting me to my destination on time is essential to him. I thank him for remembering.

Apart from my condo, the engagement ring is my biggest purchase. I bought it for Jolene two years ago for our anniversary, but I haven't found the right opportunity to propose.

The vehicle rolls to a stop outside our destination with fifteen minutes to spare. I stuff the case back inside my coat and hand my driver a fifty-dollar bill.

"Forty-five minutes?" he asks.

"That should do it," I say.

Inside the bakery, a line stretches from the counter to the door. Aromatic coffee fills the room, and caffeinated guests crowd tables. I text my client, hoping he arrived earlier. In response, my phone rings; Mr.

Vanguard says texting is tricky. He's near the back of the café, sporting a Brewers' baseball jersey, and has coffee and breakfast sandwiches. Food, yes. I like him already… minus the fan gear. He's in rival territory. The glare from Henry's gold and navy-blue super-fan stocking hat makes him easy to spot. After I weave through the tables, he stands to shake hands. Mr. Vanguard is a short, round man. Gray, slicked back hair tops a face that had been handsome, twenty years earlier, and forty—no, closer to twenty—pounds lighter. Compared to the pictures online, he's lost a little weight. Good for him.

"Mr. O'Brien," he says, "to show appreciation for your eagerness to meet." The white tablecloth is overflowing with breakfast bagels, sugary pastries, and two cups of steaming coffee.

"I appreciate the opportunity, sir," I say and shake his hand. I slip into the empty chair and eye the food. "And your generosity."

"Best bakery in all of Chicago," he says. A healthy belly presses against the table. He bites a half-eaten jelly donut, swallows, then adds, "Man, I haven't changed my diet, but I've lost quite a bit of weight this winter. The sweets have finally decided that fighting with me was useless." The donut disappears. He taps his watch. "This fancy thing counts my steps. 10,000 every day."

"I've been here several times," I say, "and you're right. No one can beat Geo's homemade donuts. And it sounds like you've found a new diet hack?"

He massages his belly and laughs.

"Yesterday," Henry says, "Harrison said you boys were going out. I wager you had a memorable evening then?"

"Every moment with Harrison is memorable," I say.

Henry's round cheeks shine; his blue eyes are barely visible. He produces a mischievous grin, like that of a pirate who specializes in commandeering ships.

"Man, oh man," he says and slides sandwiches and a coffee towards me. "Better believe I had my share of those days. This breakfast will cure the most memorable night."

"I bet you did, Mr. Vanguard, and thank you." He's generous and chill, a pleasant surprise. Most successful business owners are the opposite.

"Call me Henry," he says. "Now eat while I tell you why I'm doomed."

He says he has two daughters in college and jokingly adds that's why he's doomed. More than once, the girls have nearly given him a heart attack. He's raised a family and achieved a level of professional success that most only dream of. For thirty years, he worked in the carpentry trade. Being an independent contractor was cutthroat. Business was either booming or stagnant. His income varied from season to season. At one point, he hit rock bottom when a previous client sued him. Henry refused to give up, though.

Instead, he took a break and enrolled in an interior design course at the university in his hometown. He felt content and looked forward to a new future. One night, after he and his friend Dale had drunk too many shots, Dale called Henry a knick-knack pansy, fabric-swatch lover, and challenged Henry to elevate his creativity by designing and building a home. They made a bet: if Henry built a ranch, Dale would buy the finished house at market value. They shook hands. Sixteen months later, Dale purchased Henry's first custom-built home.

Since then, Henry has built four to five homes each year. Last summer, he broke ground on Weeping Willow Estates, an 18-lot residential development on the shores of Lake Michigan, with a private pathway leading down the bluffs to the lake. The two-million-dollar homes are an easy 30-minute drive north of Milwaukee and will be completed by the fall.

In the last twelve years, Henry says he's never worked; instead, he spends his days making dreams come true. But he admits that accounting and marketing trick him up. He believes that with my help, his company's profits will skyrocket. He has an upcoming project—twice the size of this one—and needs an ambitious and trustworthy business consultant to ensure there are no hiccups.

Harrison will be happy to know my shit is not only together but pristine. A one-page document outlines my services. My fee—which is large both visibly and quantitatively—is highlighted at the bottom of the page. A person's value should never be hidden, and clients appreciate financial transparency. The proposal shares a few opportunities I've uncovered for the company. He reviews the document.

"The testimonials on your website are outstanding," he says. Skimming my website and reviewing references from prior clients is normal.

"And I hired a private investigator," he says. I stop mid-chew and sip my coffee. Hiring an expert to snoop is not. Thankfully, I've hidden most of my secrets in the past or in my head. Even so, entrepreneurs are a quirky group, so I'm not entirely surprised by Henry's precautions. Over half of small businesses fail within the first five years, so a person must be a little crazy to abandon a salary and risk losing personal savings, assets, livelihood, and relationships to shoot for the moon. It seems Henry and I have that in common.

"The distant past doesn't define us," he says, "especially when a younger, more immature self made the mistakes." His pause is slight, the message is clear: He knows something.

Henry's smile is wide like the Joker's, but has a softer, more playful edge to it. "Dedication is rare in your field," he says, "and clearly professionalism. But you answered my early-morning call, and I appreciate it. You agreed to a same-day meeting. Now, that's intense dedication. I have a question for you. What experience do you have with difficult employees or peers? Even clients? And do you have any interest in mentoring or coaching?"

His first question isn't so weird, but I avoid speaking negatively about former co-workers. Plus, idle chatter is unprofessional. Instead, I share a struggle from my first job as a teenager.

"My extended family is quite large," I say. "Growing up, there were a ton of kids in my neighborhood. My family thought it would be an excellent experience for me to babysit rather than work in a restaurant or in customer service. I thought I was taking the easy route. Babysitting? No problem. I agreed and watched my brothers and sisters and the neighborhood kids. I soon realized I had made a mistake: I should have taken a fast-food job.

"The kids were awful. They colored my white Nikes with Sharpies. A four-year-old stuffed chocolate kisses in the pocket of my North Face hoodie. You can imagine how excited I was when I did laundry later that week. I had to wash that thing five times before it was clean. The worst was when two brothers buzzed off a chunk of my hair after I fell asleep one night. With each interaction, I had a choice. Respond with humor? That only encouraged the inappropriate behavior. Tolerance? They walked all over me. Anger? They hated me.

"I tried something different. After an... incident, I stayed silent, letting the kids consider what they'd done and giving myself a moment to breathe. Even though they didn't deserve it, I showed them respect. Eventually, I earned their admiration. From the age of twelve to sixteen, I made money by working with some of the most disagreeable people on the block. I learned diplomacy and how to handle trying customers. Also, not to brag, but I can make an epic peanut butter and jelly sandwich. And my boxed mac and cheese? World-class."

Henry grins, deliberates for a moment, then says, "Dealing with children is difficult, especially if they're not your own, but your actions speak volumes. Not too many young men would accept that responsibility. It shows you have compassion and patience."

"The best lesson I learned from those years," I say, "wasn't how to get others to do what I wanted, but to understand the motive behind their actions. For example, the little girl who stuffed chocolate kisses in my pocket had a crush on me. The boys who buzzed my hair? They were trying to help. Earlier that day, I had said I needed a haircut. And the kids who marked up my shoes? They knew I was obsessed with the Cubbies, so they wanted to draw the logo on my sneakers."

"Amazing," Henry says, "truly. The more I get to know you, Niall, the more I'm convinced you're essential for this role. Now, what about mentoring?"

"I feel confident in my role as a consultant," I say, "but I haven't managed or coached others."

"I appreciate your personal assessment," he says. "You know where you excel and where you can improve. There's no doubt you'd be an asset to my company." He rubs his chin. "My daughters are growing up fast. In May, one will graduate summa cum laude with a double major in accounting and finance. She wants to work with me… her frumpy old dad." Pride fills his expression, and his eyes grow misty. "My youngest is studying psychology, but she wants nothing to do with a small-town business. She has her sights set on New York or Chicago. But she's… going through some things. No matter what, I'll always be their dad. I'll always want the best for them."

"They sound like overachievers," I say, but I'm not sure what his daughters have to do with my services. "Congrats to you for raising successful children. I imagine there were highs and lows, especially raising girls, now women."

Parents love it when you compliment their children, so I never miss the opportunity to plump a future client's ego, when appropriate. Plus, I've never had the privilege of being a father, but I imagine it's like nothing else in the world, and the love and pride for your child is unending. Soo-jin's son, Bennett, has transformed many of my weekends from late-night parties to quiet afternoons falling asleep with a toddler glued to my chest. I never thought, at twenty-five, I'd be content spending a Saturday afternoon watching The Disney Channel.

"My oldest is passionate and dedicated," he says. "She's a genius with numbers and smart with technology. But man, when she gets excited, she may go off on a tangent and forget other responsibilities. She's smarter than I am but has my spirited personality." He twirls his coffee cup. "If she works with Vanguard, I'll need a middleman."

I'm unable to follow Henry's logic. He has an intelligent and passionate daughter who's graduating from college with honors and desires to carry on the family's legacy. She could fill in the gaps where Henry lacks, and he could pay her a quarter of what he'd be paying me.

"Harrison said you're direct," he says. "No BS. Tell me what you're thinking?"

"I don't want to insult you, Mr. Vanguard—"

"Henry," he insists. "And insult away."

"I'm not qualified to be your daughter's mentor or boss."

He laughs.

I'm glad he thinks our conversation is amusing.

"You'd be a team," he says, "discuss ideas and solutions, implement the best. But of course, you'd have the final say and…." He stretches back and pats his shirt. "When necessary, make sure she's prompt, follows a dress code, and plays well with others. She also volunteers as a part-time dance instructor and works at a local restaurant, so she'd have to juggle three part-time jobs."

It sounds like his busy, book-smart daughter requires a life coach or a nanny, not a boss. My interest in Henry's proposal disappears faster than his donut. The answer is clear, but my experience in consulting has shown that those involved rarely see the solution sitting right in front of their face. I decide to be so straightforward, it may hurt.

"How can your daughter utilize her assets and help your company if she's working two other jobs?" I ask. "No offense, but that other work is trivial. Nothing that would advance her professional career."

"You're right," he says. "She enjoys following recipes, cooking for others, and teaching dance, which is her stress reliever. But man, I can't make her give those up."

"You want her to work for Vanguard, right?"

"Absolutely. She handles my bookkeeping now, but once she graduates, she could be a big help in other areas. She has the skillset, but she won't have the time."

"Give her an ultimatum. If she wants to work at Vanguard, she must quit her other jobs."

"She won't listen to me," he says. "She's bull-headed."

"Decide for her."

"What do you mean?"

"Talk to her bosses. Blame downsizing, budget cuts, whatever. They can let her go."

"I can't do that," he murmurs.

"Even if it's in her best interest?" I press.

"That's the problem with parenting," he says, "children rarely take advice from their parents. Ever. They learn better when you allow them to make their own mistakes." Worry lines form above his brows. His chortle has disappeared.

For a moment, I worry I may have overstepped a boundary. I'm rarely privy to the backstory of familial relationships. But Henry is an intelligent man, and I'm a well-paid, successful consultant. He needs to hear the truth; I'm here to help his company financially, not to line my pockets.

"Henry, hire your daughter." I drum my fingers on the table and silently count the thousands of dollars I'm setting ablaze. "You don't need me."

Once he realizes my services are no longer required, we'll shake hands and part ways. I await Henry's "nice to meet you" speech. My suggestion is for the best, and working with a loose cannon like his daughter would be a nightmare. Vanguard Family Builders can remain a family company.

"Truth be told, your ideas are unexpected," he says, "but brilliant. You're already thinking outside the box, but your last statement concerns me." He runs a plump finger over the form. "Whether you see it or not, you're a necessary part of this equation. How about I double your fee to show I'm serious. You'd start in June."

He reaches into his briefcase and pulls out a pen. "I'll make you the new temporary VP for Vanguard. I'm prepared to write a check today for half as a retainer, and I'll take your suggestions about my daughter." He pauses and then begs, "Please, Niall. I need you."

For a business transaction, Henry's face is full of emotion. I don't know the man at all, but it almost feels as though he's about to completely break down right in front of me. I feel sorry for him.

But that's not a reason to take on a new client.

Plus, Henry's kid sounds like a mess, and I'm still not sure why he feels doomed without my help. The offer is unexpected and generous. The position, pay, and opportunity for new experience seem perfect. Money is important, and Henry is offering a lot of it. But something feels off. Henry doesn't have to pay an outsider a ton of money for work his daughter can do. If she's academically successful, he could teach her. The company is profitable and well-managed. There isn't any negative publicity or drama associated with Vanguard. His company isn't doomed. Even though open doors are open for a reason, I won't take advantage of Henry.

Plus, I'm not interested in babysitting a spoiled, feisty, college graduate. She'd probably do worse than ruin my shoes, maul me in the middle of the night, or wreck my clothes.

Sorry, Henry, I'm not down. I decline.

Henry pleads.

I assure him he doesn't need me and wish him the best of luck. I thank him for the food, coffee, and opportunity, and leave.

As I wait for Rafael outside, I contemplate the future. Although expanding my business across state lines would be impressive, I shouldn't overextend myself. Jolene is a priority. I can't ruin my relationship with her by taking on an out-of-state contract, which would only consume more of my free time.

I grip the ring case in my pocket. It's time this band is given a proper home. I smile as a sense of calm washes over me.

Jolene comes first.

Lemons into First Aid
Friday, May 27th @ 2:33 p.m.

I NEVER FALL.

Growing up, I've never tumbled out of a tree, down a flight of stairs, nor been prone to stumbling, tripping, or slipping. I'm a dancer. No student of Juilliard. Just locally trained at Miss Christie's School for Dance.

But lately, I've been a clumsy sleeper; I lose the control I always had when awake. My nightmares have become so violent that I often roll off my bed in the middle of the night, only to wake up the next day on the floor.

In my recent dreams, the moon is high, the air is damp and mossy. Kylie is present, and for a few seconds, everything feels normal. Until a gust of cold wind slithers down my spine.

The night becomes eerily quiet.

My sister sits on a nearby rock, blackness behind her. Dread lingers between us. Mere inches away, the bluffs drop one hundred feet below to Lake Michigan's sandy shores. A voice softly echoes 'Sheepish' along the banks, but I can't tell if it's Kylie or me saying it.

Sheepish!

Sheepish!

Sheepish!

Over and over until the noise becomes so loud that it shatters my ears. Pulled by "Sheepish," I'm drawn to the switchback path. My feet start moving—first slowly, then faster. Before I realize it, I'm running, running, running. I'm out of breath. I stumble down the trail, struggling to stay upright. The shore below calls to me. Suddenly, my feet leave the ground, and I'm falling, air rushing past me. Fear grows in my stomach, and my fingers tingle. I expect to hit the ground with a deadly thud, but I always wake before anything bad happens. Too bad life doesn't work that way.

Often after my nightmare, I realize I've rolled completely under the bed frame. The space beneath the mattress was already filled with dirty clothes and misplaced shoes. I'm amazed I even fit. I've always wondered how I managed to fall out of bed and slide underneath without waking up.

Now, I find myself lying on a floor. The world around me blurs as reality drifts back in, shifting from nightmare to waking confusion.

A voice whispers: "Katie." An affectionate finger traces my jawline, my scar. A shiver of insecurity spreads across my cheek. That voice… I want the person to speak again, but I'm afraid to respond. Afraid to say anything. Afraid to open my eyes. Because my chest—and palm—both ache, and I'm slightly worried about what kind of crazy shit I've gotten myself into. I squint and inhale. Where am I? Peaches' apartment? Dad's? The area smells of stale beer. Glasses clink in the distance.

No doubt, I'm at Triple B's.

I adjust my head; I'm lying against a soft and sturdy… something. "Karma Chameleon" plays in the background. *You're my lover, not my rival.* I tap the floor with my hand that isn't throbbing. Something soggy sticks to my palm.

A French fry.

Karma, any insight into what just happened?

No?

Nothing?

Karma, you're such a bitch.

Seconds later, my conversation with Peaches floats to the surface. I'm lying on the floor of my former workplace. Eyelids raised; a distant fuzzy peach comes into focus. My quirky friend is rocking in a chair and moaning. Roxanne is rubbing his shoulders. She coaxes him to drink from a cup.

Peaches looks up, our eyes connect. "Kate! I'm so sorry! Can you forgive me? I totally—"

"She's fine," Roxanne shushes him, "she's in good hands."

Peaches moans a dramatic, "No!" He makes a theatrical attempt to escape Roxanne's nurturing hold.

If he's the damsel stressing out, and she's the knight. Am I the court jester? *Am I fine?* In whose good hands am I in? I curse to myself. A laugh comes from above and behind. The sound makes me smile.

I feel quite light. Airy even. What is this feeling?

What is light and airy? Hmmm… The air is airy. Popcorn is light. So are potato chips. No, no, no.

What feeling is light and airy?

Hope.

Possibilities.

Am I feeling hopeful about a possibility?

Interesting…

Someone applies pressure to my hand. I stop smiling. The cut stings like hell. When I sliced that knife through my skin, it probably hit a few veins. A stupid accident, all because I was distracted by the vision across the bar, and losing my job. The image was… memorable, but getting fired?

Expected and unfortunate.

And right before I fell… my memory flickers. I was by the lake, at the bottom of the bluffs. The red t-shirt. A woman's body was lying on the shoreline. Blood splattered shoes. The night of the red flag party.

Are these new memories, or am I hallucinating?

"You're safe," a pleasant male voice says.

I tilt my head. A carved set of black paws sits to the left, and an oversized bear in a Packers' football jersey stands to my right. The floor is wooden again, scattered with stray appetizers and napkins.

I urge the thoughts running through my brain to slow down so I can concentrate on the man's words.

You're safe.

The words are more delightful than his laugh. Maybe the laugh was better? I'd need to hear the laugh again to compare properly.

While I comfortably lie on the floor and shush the horde of questions milling over my tongue, his two words flutter above my chest like wind-blown dandelion seeds.

Each seed brushes against my skin, then gently permeates it. My body warms. Even though my very non-Gucci shirt is very much on the floor and my palm aches, I do feel safe.

I finally get a partial glimpse of my rescuer's feet.

My savior is the sneaker-wearing 'he'.

The blood loss must be extreme because I feel giddy from his cologne. I've never actually smoked or snorted anything—Mother would kill me if I did—but I'm confident this is what euphoria smells like. I breathe deeply. He smells like cherry Pop-Tarts and success. A winning combination.

The 'he' says he'll help me up if I'm ready. I'd rather lounge here and listen to him say over and over, "You're safe," but I know that's not really an option, so I murmur an "Okay". He helps me to my feet. Once upright, my legs become al dente noodles, so I lean against his solid ten structure and breathe in his woody scent. He steadies, then guides me to an unsullied bench. I sit.

Strong, hesitant fingers touch my shoulder.

He's touching my body.

Oh my, the man who stared at me after I barely peeked at him is touching a part of my body. My unsexy shoulder, but still, a part of me.

"You passed out," he says, "but I caught you before you hit the floor. I had to use the rest of your napkins to stop the bleeding. Sorry." He sounds truly apologetic. "Do you have a first aid kit in the back? Oh, and have you ever had a tetanus shot?"

Passed out? A tetanus shot? Why is this person asking me questions? Does he expect answers? Passing out is not my thing, and yet this is the second time I've done so in as many months. Is fainting my new thing?

Not wanting to make eye contact because I'm so embarrassed, I stare at my throbbing hand. "Your assistance is appreciated but unnecessary," I say. "I'm outstanding. Leave me here, alone, to bleed out."

"I'm not leaving you," he says. A soft rumble of laughter accompanies his words. His laugh sends a shudder through my chest. The movement buries his kind words. Somewhere deep inside, they latch on and take root.

"Rest against the table," he says, "but don't get up. Hey buddy." His voice is louder, authoritative, and in control. But still very pleasant. "Can you grab a first aid kit and a glass of water for us?"

Buddy is our busboy, Andy. No doubt, Andy is thoroughly enjoying this spectacle. I wouldn't be surprised if the boy recorded my episode with his phone.

A stray tater tot under the neighboring chair captures my attention. Then I wince because Chicago has had a front-row seat to the scar on my cheek this entire time.

Suddenly, the lonesome tot disappears when the man sits on the chair in front of me. Now, I've nothing but a knee covered by $1200 pants to observe. The knee bounces slightly. I want to think it was a nervous movement, but what could make this man uncomfortable? A second later, his hand covers mine; I flinch and pull away.

"Don't—"

Blood splatters on his shirt, pants, or shoes would not complement his attire—too late. A bright red speckling decorates the hem of his jeans and the tip of his sneaker.

"It's okay," he says, calmly.

"But I got blood on you," I say, looking down at the guilty stains.

"Relax," he says, unbothered. "I'm going to help you."

"Relaxing isn't possible. I think I just sliced off my finger."

Relax? How am I supposed to relax when the sound of my pounding heart is louder than George Michael's "Careless Whisper" playing over the speakers? I wonder if this man can hear the thumping? I hold still, the closest I can do to relax, and stare at his pants. They don't appear any fancier than those at Macy's. I'm about to tell him $1200 is excessive when something thuds onto the table.

Andy asks if I'm okay.

With my good hand, I offer a feeble thumbs-up. "I've never been worse."

Andy adamantly states, "That was wild," and begs for a close-up pic of my bloody hand.

Chicago sternly tells Andy no.

Andy pleads, but Chicago must give him a look of death, because our busboy relents with a meek, "Yes, Sir," and leaves. This knight in shining Armani appears trustworthy. I suppose I'll let him rescue me. Plus, my hand is stinging and still gushing blood. I'm worried I'll pass out again if I try to stand.

My personal medic scoots closer. His hand slides underneath mine.

"You don't have—"

"I don't mind at all. Please sit still." He gently swabs each finger, then carefully cleans under and around Kylie's ring. A sterile antiseptic odor replaces the fryer basket perfume I'm wearing. Next, a bandage is secured.

"All better," he says, satisfied with his work.

I feel as though he's my babysitter, and he's rescued me after a spill off my bicycle. A child would sit in place and stare at the table, but I'm a grown woman. What should I say? Plus, if I don't say something soon, he'll think I'm concussed without even hitting my head. I can't be funny or witty right now.

Kylie, what should I do?

State a fact, she whispers back.

"I have an interview soon." My voice cracks as I stare at my coffee-stained jeans. "I can't be late." What else? Another fact. "That's the last lemon I'll ever cut."

"Admitting defeat?" he asks. "The lemons won?" His voice is certainly lovely. Even familiar.

The restaurant has become stuffy. What happened to the breeze? My neck is hot, my face is on fire. My nerves are on fire with wonder. Where are my senses?

"I guess," I say.

"What if you're the best lemon cutter at work, and no one can cut lemons like you?" His finger traces my palm.

"I, ah… I nearly sliced off my hand and just got fired, so that's not the case." He's quiet for several seconds. It feels like minutes. Why isn't he responding?

"Maybe you're too good for prep work?" he asks. "And there's something better in store for you?"

"I'm too bad for it," I counter. "I can't believe I passed out."

"Do you have hemophobia?" he asks.

"What?" Even though I want to vanish into thin air, I'm stuck to the bench like a dried splotch of ketchup, and I can't look any further down unless I crawl under the table. "No. One of my best friends is gay."

He lets out a cadence worthy of heaven's ears. The laugh. It's glorious.

"Not homophobic," he says. "Hemophobia. Are you afraid of blood?" He's laughing at me. A concussion might be beneficial at this point, because apparently, my brain can't process the English language anymore.

"No, uh," I say, "not that I know of."

"Your shirt is stained," he says. "Is that blood?" The chair screeches, and his thighs inch forward. On a high and burning from the inside out, I stare at the dark splatter.

"A little," I say. "I think most of it's cherry juice from an Old Fashioned. Actually, it's an Old Fashioned without whiskey or brandy. Really a Shirley Temple."

"A kiddie cocktail? Of course." He chuckles again. "Nice drink choice. I love the way the carbonated lime flavor teases the sweetness of the cherries."

Why is he having so much fun at my expense, and why hasn't he returned to his cozy bar stool?

"But seriously," he says, "your shirt will be ruined if you don't wash it soon."

I examine the grungy material.

"This is my only good work shirt."

"You can't wear that to an interview."

For some reason, he genuinely seems to care. Little does he know, my prior statement wasn't out of concern; I've no issue wearing this precise outfit. I was merely stating a fact. Logic calms me.

"I'll grab some wet paper towels from the bathroom," he says, quickly standing. "I'll be right back."

Once his pants are out of sight, I finally lift my eyes and follow his movements—graceful and deliberate. He walks with purpose, as if on a mission. What is he searching for?

Chaos?

The day can't get any weirder.

The table has been wiped clean; my savior was productive and efficient. Peaches has moved to the bar, and Roxanne is massaging his back. When Peaches makes eye contact, he mouths "I'm sorry." Roxanne has her other hand propped on her hip, and she's smiling. We don't smile at each other.

Before things get any weirder, and the chivalrous man can reappear, I exit the restaurant with my bloodied wound and overflowing curiosity about a know-it-all man who went out of his way to help a frazzled fry cook.

Ex-cook.

Group Chat
Friday, May 27th @ 2:43 p.m.

A CROWD ENTERS Triple B's. Peaches inhales deeply, anxiety flickering in his eyes as he re-tucks his Gucci shirt inside his slacks, forcing cheer into his shout: "Welcome to Triple B's! What can I get you all to drink?"

Roxy waits patiently for Niall outside the bathroom hall. When he returns, his movements are restless, desperate as he scans the packed restaurant for Katie—only to realize she's vanished.

Roxy corners him in a nearby booth, their whispered argument sharp and strained. After several tense minutes, Niall insists he must leave— frustration shadowing his face.

Left stewing, Roxy heads to the bar, masks her bruised pride, and uses her cleavage to help pay for next semester's tuition. The restaurant is back to normal.

JustPeachy: That did not go well.
ZakAtak: What do you mean?
JustPeachy: She did NOT take the news well. I feel like an ass.
ZakAtak: What happened?

JustPeachy: Niall showed up and she almost cut her finger after I let her go. Niall, I'm really upset with you. Explain yourself! Why did you come?

Fauxy Roxy: I invited him.

JustPeachy: Roxy, don't start drama.

Fauxy Roxy: Babe, I would never.

ZakAtak: HOW IS KATE?

JustPeachy: She's seeing ghosts again, spiraling, and I'm scared for her.

ZakAtak: What?

Milly Rodrigo: I think this is when I can confidently say 'I told you so'. Kate needs to know the truth.

Slide_OB: Hey everyone, it's Niall O'Brien. The owner of the 312-area code.

Slide_OB: I agree with Peaches. I think Kate's experiencing mental trauma from that night. We need to do something.

Slide_OB: Her memories are coming back.

The Pied Piper: How do you know?

Slide_OB: She recognized me.

ZakAtak: That is not good.

JustPeachy: She dreamt about Kylie last night, and this time Kylie gave her a message. "Hurry help, before it's too late." We all know Kate has an obsessive personality. She really seems dead-set on finding the truth.

Milly Rodrigo: Did you tell her anything?

JustPeachy: Nothing.

The Pied Piper: We need to stick to the original plan.

Milly Rodrigo: I'm tired of lying.

Fauxy Roxy: She's coming unraveled. I've never seen her like this. She needs counseling. The truth could be what she needs, guys.

JustPeachy: Careful what you ask for.

Fauxy Roxy: Why?

JustPeachy: Um, she thinks one of us is a murderer.

A Broken Heartache
Friday, Feb 4th

HENRY VANGUARD IS persistent. Within twenty-four hours of the Buns-n-Bakery meeting, he left me six lengthy voicemails. In the last message, he quadrupled his prior offer. I didn't respond.

The man must be crazy.

Unless he really thinks I'm essential to his company's success?

But why?

Even if I had a better understanding of Henry's thought process, I couldn't accept his offer. Hiring his daughter is the right option. He can't see the answer because he's too close. He should take a step back and consider the big picture.

Luckily, I have a new distraction. Harrison has arranged a prospect meeting for me this afternoon in Wisconsin. After lunch, I pack my overnight bag and drive the two hours. Traffic is light, so I stay focused. I practice my elevator pitch and think about my expanding business. Harrison has played a big role in its success.

To this day, I'm still shocked that we are friends; we did not start that way. Harrison and I met in high school while playing on rival baseball teams. Senior year, after my team whipped his team's ass in a regional tournament, a bunch of us finished the night at a sixteen-and-over club.

Harrison was performing on stage for Open Mic Night. At first, I didn't recognize his voice, but when I saw him, I knew it was him. Bleached hair stands out.

By midnight, Harrison and I realized a stunning brunette had been flirting with both of us. We took our fists and pride outside. The cockfight ended with a broken cheekbone and a bruised rib. The brunette went home alone, which was for the best.

In college, we were enemies until sophomore year, when we both unknowingly accepted internships at Damian Deveraux Consulting. Amid insults about each other's work and character, we made copies, filed documents, cleaned the office, and made too many coffee runs to count.

Although Harrison and I were hired as part-time interns, we often worked until midnight. Harrison refused to leave until the project was finished, and I couldn't let him outdo me, so I worked harder and stayed later.

Soon, Harrison and I realized our boss was overcharging and underserving clients. Quickly, our mutual dislike for Damian replaced our hatred for each other.

The tipping point came a month before graduation when Damian introduced the staff to his son, Lance, who would soon become the co-owner of Deveraux Consulting. To celebrate, Lance treated the team to dinner. Over fried chicken and mashed potatoes, Lance said he wanted to rebrand Deveraux and create a fierce marketing plan. And to save money, either Harrison or I would be laid off.

I'm not one to leave my future in someone else's hands, so a week later, I created O'Brien Consulting. Then I gave Lance my notice. Now, whenever the Devereaux's disappoint a client, Harrison apologizes and suggests they get a second opinion. Lucky for me, I'm the second opinion.

It seems Damian screwed over another business owner—Yuhr Mahm. The poor soul is begging for a proposal from a competing firm.

I've got an address, a time, and a name. Expanding my business to the north seems inevitable.

The sun is high, the sky clear. Wisconsin seems happy to see me. Jolene, on the other hand, hasn't spoken to me since I sent the money. She's left my ClickYap messages unopened. My texts, on 'read'. Not even a 'Sorry, busy. Call you back later', or a meaningless string of emojis.

Nothing.

For four days.

Is she really that busy? My spirits are low, my heart a heavy brick. She's cheating on me. That must be it. Why else would she ignore me?

I pat my chest.

The ring pushes back.

Tonight, after my meeting, I'll buy a plane ticket to California. I'll surprise Jolene. Arrive Sunday. Leave Sunday. But all I need is a minute to give her the world. Before the weekend is over, our future will be finalized.

At the Mayfair exit, I merge off the freeway and head east. Snow-covered barns and farmhouses speckle barren fields. A sign alerts me, '5 Miles to Mayfair'. Frosted-tip pine trees line the roads. A winter storm off Lake Michigan visited yesterday. And a few minutes ago, a black ice warning popped up on my phone. Another heavy snowfall is expected tonight.

In the small town, cobblestone sidewalks hug the road. An antique store, quirky cafe, and several specialty shops line the town, each decorated with bright signs or twinkle lights. The village is a tourist's dream. A tourist's trap.

If Soo-jin were with me, she'd be tangled up in Wisconsin-themed merchandise, noosed by a string of brats, drowning head-to-toe in cow t-shirts, and sweatpants with cheesy sayings like, 'Holy cow, it's cold out'.

On the way to the hotel, slushy white stuff begins to fall, blocking my view. My janky Volkswagen is a death heap on slippery roads, so I decide to give my car a break and take an Uber to my meeting. Lately, I've noticed my vision falters at night. Car lights blind me, and reading road signs is nearly impossible. Soo-jin worries that I need glasses for astigmatism. Eyeglasses? No way. Contact lenses would be even worse. The thought of purposefully poking myself in the eye makes me queasy.

I'll never wear either. I see fine during the day. At night, when I need to go somewhere, I Uber.

At the hotel, I unpack and change my shirt. Yesterday, I purchased several off-the-rack suit jackets, shirts, and slacks. The fit is either too tight in some areas—my legs—or too loose in others—my waist. I've messaged Gervais, asking him to duplicate my previous wardrobe, but he said it could take months.

A notification pops up on my screen: *4:00 Yuhr Mahm @ Bear's, Bluffs & Brewery.* Not wanting to be late, I schedule an Uber and hurry back outside. My ride arrives quickly, and I comfortably settle in the backseat. During the drive, I enjoy the Hallmark card views of the lake and the city of trees out each window.

Living in Chicago never gave me forest-savory views like these. With the snowstorm pelting the area, the scenery is both breathtaking and haunting. Thanks to my skilled driver, I arrived on time. On my way inside the restaurant, my phone dings.

JoJo: Have time to talk?

Fuck yeah. I immediately FaceTime her and rush towards the building. Before I make it under the awning, she answers. Standing in slush, snowflakes showering me, I watch the screen. California's orange skyline pops up, surrounding her in a personal halo. She's sitting on her patio. She looks more stunning than ever. Is it possible she's glowing? I stop breathing. An anxious feeling builds inside my chest.

"Wow, that was quick," she says.

Worried, I misread her message, I backpedal, "You asked if I could talk. I thought you meant now."

"I didn't think you'd call right away," she says.

"Should I call later?" I ask, my nerves beginning to fray. Why do I feel like I've been walking on eggshells around her lately?

"No," she says. "It's fine."

Calm down, Niall.

"What's wrong?" I ask. "You seem upset."

She shifts the phone slightly. The new angle reveals red eyelids and blotchy cheeks.

"This long-distance isn't working," she says. "I miss us." She sniffles and takes several shaky breaths.

"I understand," I say. "You're making sacrifices to follow your dreams. I'm so proud of you."

"Thank you." She finally smiles. "The role is going to be amazing. We start shooting next month. But…"

If the job is going well, why is she sad? Did she meet someone? I want to ask, but the words are lost in my throat.

"Have you made more friends?" I ask, knowing my jealousy shows.

"There's no one else, Niall. Promise."

"What's bothering you then?"

"The days are long," she says. "I'm exhausted. I have no one to come home to at night. The stress from moving, leaving everything behind, and making new friends… I—uh, wasn't feeling well yesterday, and went to urgent care… I'm better now, but… It might have been a bad reaction to the lip filler. Or maybe just anxiety…"

My heart aches for her. California is tearing us apart, but what can I do? I can't surprise her with flowers, give her an amazing back rub, or shower her with love. The distance is our enemy.

"That's awful," I say, "I feel like I should be there with you. We need time together. I want to come as soon as possible. What do you think?"

Her sniffles grow louder. In our six years together, Jolene has never cried in front of me. *What is going on?*

"Or maybe I can catch a flight tonight?"

Tears spill down her cheeks. I want to make her laugh.

"How are the pick me girls?" I ask. "Did you pick one?"

"That's not how it works." She half-smiles. "Pick me girls… never mind." Her smile fades.

"I was teasing."

"The place I'm renting has a 'pick me' actress in every apartment," she says. "They're all pretty nice, and supportive, but I need… physical affection."

"The loneliness is real," I say. "I think that's why I stay so busy during the day. But at night it's a lot harder to ignore." I hope my words somehow comfort her. The sound of her sobs catches inside my chest.

"Jo?"

I'm not a kiss-ass, but I know the importance of treasuring what you have. I give her words of encouragement and tell her I would do anything for her. Anything. She wipes the tears with the back of her hand. She wants to know if I'm serious. Of course. Anything for you, Jolene.

"I do want something from you," she says and raises her head with newfound confidence.

"Anything, Jo."

"I want to break up," she says. "I want to break up completely. No texting or calling. A complete break. I just can't." Her words become shaky, conviction flickering behind the tears.

"Did I do something wrong?" I ask. I tell her I'll support her and love her anyway possible. If that means giving her space… My body is on autopilot. I'm saying what she wants to hear because her happiness means everything.

"… for taking this so well," she says. "This is for the best, for both of us."

If I agree, she's happy, happy without me. If I disagree… she's unhappy? Unhappy with being my girlfriend? She talks about freedom, the future, and her happiness. My consulting business.

She says long-distance relationships are impossible. It's not you. It's me. Everything she's supposed to say. But her voice grows lighter, her words come more easily.

The more she convinces me we need to break up, the happier she becomes. My head, face, and hands are frozen and wet. Shivering, I duck underneath the awning and side-step a group of teenagers as they exit the building.

I listen to Jolene, intently nodding. What else can I do? She's already made her decision. She says she loves me, wishes me the best, and she'll never forget me. She's a better person because of me.

A heaviness in my chest pulls me forward. I step back to steady myself, pressing my spine into the brick wall for support. The ring in my pocket feels unbearably heavy. Before I can say what I feel, she ends the call. Too late, I stammer a quiet, "Wait," reaching for her halo on the darkened screen. I'm left asking why I didn't fight for us.

Better yet, why wasn't I more considerate? Starting a new career in another state is overwhelming, and I wasn't there to support her. I should have moved to California and worked remotely for a while. Or, I could have flown to California every other weekend, but the job I've worked so hard to build kept me too busy to travel and brought out my selfish side. The distance wasn't the problem. I was.

Should I call her back? Beg her to give me another chance? Tell her about the ring? The right words are impossible to find, hidden under a bubble of emotion. If I open my mouth, nothing comprehensible will come out. Sleet has seeped into my loafers. My feet are frozen, nearly numb. My jacket is drenched in a layer of heavy snow. I brush the slush off my coat and stand. A beep from my phone reminds me: *4:00 Yuhr Mahm @ Bear's, Bluffs & Brewery.*

The walk inside the restaurant is a blur of wet snow.

Jolene.

How did I fuck everything up so quickly?

I text Harrison. He won't give me anything close to helpful advice or encouragement. But when I tell him, "Jolene and I broke up," his response will piss me off. Feeling pissed is better than feeling like a failure. I send the message, then silence my phone.

Inside, the warmth from an electric fireplace, friendly chatter, and smoky barbecue aroma remind me why I'm here. A client is waiting to meet over dinner and cocktails. The only future I have control over is here and now. I brush shaking hands through frozen hair, adjust my collar, and scan the room.

Yuhr Mahm.

Usually, I spend hours researching potential clients before I meet them. But I didn't have time today. Harrison scheduled this meeting at the last minute and said Yuhr was a 'good dude'.

I'm guessing Yuhr is a tall, self-absorbed man. Probably a workaholic. Drinks too much. Yuhr… I wonder what nationality he is? Yuhr, sounds like 'your'. Or the contraction 'you're'.

Different.

An elderly couple at a nearby bench holds hands. Nope. A hostess with a wild head of teased hair and big blue eyes stands in the corner holding menus. Not her either. Next to her, a stocky man rests a plump hand on the hostess station. His back is to me.

Mahm is an unusual surname. Sounds like mom.

Yuhr. Your?

Mahm. Mom?

Your mom… Weird-sounding name.

The possible Yuhr is wearing a glaring navy blue and gold stocking hat and a Brewers jacket. This is Wisconsin. Everyone's a Brewers fan. When the man slowly turns around, with only a glimpse of his smile, I recognize him. His shoulders rise in an upward shrug and fall. His smile is innocent, mischievous.

Henry fucking Vanguard.

I've been commandeered.

Fucking Harrison. That meddling—

The Crumb-free Intruder
Friday, May 27th @ 3:07 p.m.

HENRY VANGUARD IS a terrible father. Upon entering the office, his dewy forehead and creasy brow indicated his irritation level was as elevated as his blood pressure. But I wasn't surprised, because the same erratic temperament that runs through his veins runs through mine.

Although I showed up early, in my best dress shirt, toting a 46-page proposal, sadly, my grocery bag proved faulty before even reaching the door. The wind hijacked six sheets, whisking them across the parking lot. A rescue attempt was unsuccessful, leaving me seven minutes late for my meeting.

After I entered the office, my dad criticized my unprofessional attire; I shot back, assured him I've learned from the best, as I pointed out the flaky frosting bits on his shirt.

Irritation spiked again as I scolded him for the empty box of donuts sitting on his desk, only for my embarrassment to surface when he reminded me of my own sugary habits.

He questioned my bandage and suggested I slow down and pay attention. I blamed my overall lackadaisical behavior on missing Kylie and eagerly shared her cryptic early morning message. Of course, Daddy knows all, so he said I should hurry and help myself, forget the past, and focus on my future, because I'm an adult with a college degree.

Sort of.

My diploma is currently on hold, but he doesn't know that. (More about that later.)

I assured him I'd help myself once I investigated the murder and untangled the truth from the lies. He then pulled a few hairs out of his head. At this point, I was so frustrated that I just wanted to make my dad as angry as I was.

So, I asked him what he was doing the night of April 10th. He went completely still. That's when I discovered what falling over the edge of what really felt like. What kind of daughter am I? How could I suggest he's hiding something? Embarrassed and ashamed by my actions, I cussed a few times. Well, three times. I agree; that was out of line and nothing I'd be proud for anyone to witness.

Then he got really quiet and said he was disappointed in me for being late for the meeting today. And that's when I realized he was right about everything, but I wasn't ready to tell him that.

The interaction was highly unprofessional, lacked an agenda, but was entirely normal. Unfortunately, we didn't even discuss the VP role. Since it was clear we both needed to cool down, he advised that I step into the waiting room. At the perfect moment, his landline rang. He waved me out—said he needed to take the call in private. I respectfully slammed the door.

Now, here I sit, outside his office door, in a heap, crisscross applesauce, next to my depleted confidence and shaky future. Anxiety and desperation overwhelm me. At best, I'm a mediocre Catholic, but I beg the powers above to give me a break. I shut my eyes and whisper a quick prayer, "Don't let me lose this job."

This 'interview' is not off to a great start. Worry builds in my stomach. I've already lost one job today; I can't afford to lose another. I suppose I've lost two jobs. I used to teach dance at Miss Christie's studio, but she let me go last month. But that wasn't because I'm a terrible worker—or was it? Is there a pattern forming? Am I losing everything?

Although Henry Vanguard is rich, there are no freebies 'just because you're my daughter'. Instead, he believes in working hard, striving, failing, hitting rock bottom, achieving mediocre success, then making it big. Just like he did.

Apparently, Dad's lesson today involves striving.

Do I deserve a promotion from part-time envelope licker, check writer, and donut gatekeeper?

Maybe.

But I'm his daughter—heiress to the Vanguard fortune—a week (or two) shy from graduating college (fingers crossed) with double majors in both finance and accounting, who else would he hire?

I never saw this coming.

Honestly, my internal radar feels off lately. Dad took a construction job in Chicago, even though he has always despised anyone living just south of Wisconsin's border. He claims a true Wisconsinite never associates with FIBs (fucking Illinois bastards). Lately, he's been sweating unexpectedly, blaming it on hormonal changes at sixty-eight, but he also seems uneasy and distracted. He has no reason to lie, but… Chicago? Seriously?

Milly cries nearly every time we're together—which isn't unusual—but lately, her tears seem tinged with worry she can't voice, not just her usual sadness. Piper has become bossier than ever, but now, when she gives orders, she covers her mouth and avoids eye contact, as if anxious about my reactions. Peaches and I still laugh, but he constantly worries about my future, shifts the topic when I mention the past, and blames his frequent blinking on seasonal allergies, although his tense expression suggests deeper concern. Mother is still Mother, but she's more intrusive than ever. Zakary, obsessed with his family, missed his great-grandmother's 100th birthday last month—because he refused to leave me alone while Dad was in Chicago. Chicago? Ugh!

Out of frustration, I tap the back of my head against the office door. Anger quickly takes over, flooding my thoughts and body, pushing aside reason. I have an overwhelming urge to throw something. I snatch the useless edition of *Untamed* from my bag and hurl it across the room, hoping it'll shatter something—maybe the vase, maybe my pride. After a second in the air, I hear a loud thud followed by: "Whoa."

An obscenity escapes my lips; my eyelids snap open.

The book didn't hit the lamp.

Someone's here.

The intruder is sitting on my dad's waiting room couch, facing away from me, and I'm certain I hit him with my paperback. From my place against the wall, I realize my escape routes are limited. I can either sit like a child in a time-out, confront the guest, or yell like a lady. I choose to yell. After all, I am Henry Vanguard's daughter. I stand and march toward the unwanted visitor. But once I round the couch, I halt, because the visitor is more than unwanted.

"Looking for this?" He holds up my book. "Yours, I believe."

My heart tailspins, crashes, and sets my chest on fire because it's him. The 'dark-rimmed spectacles-wearing, I'll buy whatever you're selling' salesman from the restaurant.

Chicago Hollywood Hair.

"What are you doing here?" I blurt.

He doesn't respond, so I stare back. I give him the once-over of all once-overs. His core occupies the entire loveseat, but not the way Dale, my dad's carpenter, does. After Dale sits on the sofa, he leaves sweat stains imprinted on the backrest and a trail of cracker crumbs in the cushion creases. This man is crumb-free. Of that, I'm certain. He's nothing like the normal visitors my dad has—no beer belly, no unruly beard or paint-stained arms, and the air near him is fragrant, not dusty.

His athletic legs crowd behind the end table, leaving little room for anything else, while his arms span across the couch's length. And to my dismay, the book I threw is resting on his lap. I hit him. Hard. That book sailed—

"Ahem," he says and hands me the book.

"You found my book, thank you," I say, reaching forward and exuding a Midwest smile. Before I throw in a Southern curtsy, I stop myself. My brain sends conflicting signals to my body. Should I bow?

The novel is a foot away, but I don't retrieve it. Instead, I stare. But I'm not zoning in on the colorful front cover or the shiny spine. Instead, I discover the stretch in his $1200 slacks. My eyes latch on as though they've found the world's eighth wonder.

I imagine receiving a scolding from my dad, but this time, he's justified. "Kate, I hear you objectified my payroll rep today. He says you stared at his crotch. Now he's raising my fees!"

I dart my line of sight upward and, for the first time, make eye contact. Once again, I seem to be gawking, but his eyes are truly remarkable. The left one silver-gray, while the right glows with amber flakes. Heterochromia. A genetic trait creating multicolored irises.

So unique, but also so familiar…

I didn't notice this anomaly at Triple B's.

"Finished?" he asks, grinning like a buffoon.

Horrified, I blink repeatedly and question how long I've been staring. He quickly fills me in on what I've missed.

"Hopefully, a full minute has given you enough time to take me all in?" he says. "I see you've washed and pressed your top, looking brilliant for your meeting." His gaze drops to my clenched fist at my side. "How's your hand?"

I'm too busy remembering how to breathe to tell him my shirt requires an intense regimen of palm pressing and air drying on a car floor, and a partial amputation is unnecessary.

I release a lengthy, descriptive "Ummm."

"Before we continue," he interrupts my important explanation. "I should confess."

My cheeks burn, my hands sweat, and I've begun to fluff my hair.

"Let's both acknowledge I heard your conversation," he says, pointing towards my dad's office. "More of a disagreement, but don't be embarrassed, because I'm not here to judge."

Too late, I'm feeling judged.

After a few moments, he says, "I agree."

I lift my chin and engage. "Agree with whom?"

"Oh, him," he says without hesitation, pointing towards the closed door. "But his delivery needs improvement." The man settles into his seat.

The neurons in my brain lose their ability to function as my glutinous vision follows his movements. I'm speechless. Even though Kylie says I'm quick-witted, darn near scintillating, and never at a loss for spot-on comebacks, inappropriate thoughts about a stranger fill my mind. Seconds pass; words form in my head. I've created a sentence.

"My conversation was private, and eavesdropping is rude," I say. Unoriginal and lacking wit, but at least his crotch isn't holding me captive anymore. He shrugs; my life falling apart before his eyes is a minor inconvenience. "Who are you?" I ask. "And what are you doing here?"

The man's expression becomes puzzled.

"I'm here to see Henry," he says.

"*I'm* here to see my dad."

"You're here to meet with your father? And you were late."

"He's my dad, he doesn't care."

"Behaviors, even small ones, create who you are."

"What?" Piping anger fills my chest.

"Do you want to be known as unreliable?"

"It doesn't matter. I'm his daughter."

"You can treat him poorly, because you're related?"

"Yes!" I squeal, more irritated than ever.

"I suppose you believe in nepotism, too?"

"It's worked for centuries."

"But it's unrealistic unless you're a princess?"

I sneer.

"Are you?" he asks. The corners of his mouth twitch into another slow smile, his pupils' glow.

"I'm sorry," I say. "Who are you? And what are you doing here? Did you follow me?"

He seems to deliberate. My question is simple. His answer should be easy. Why is he taking so long to respond?

"I don't think you want to know," he says, his playful tone has vanished. "I'm working. And no."

"I asked. That means I do." The words come out slow and clipped. "What work? And I think you did."

"Are you sure?" He rubs his chin. "Wait—I want to keep my answers straight… I'm the one who's going to be working with your father, and I have an appointment."

He must be a new breed of contractor or a Swarovski chandelier salesman, and I've completely lost track of my questions. "Are you one of my dad's out-of-town workers?"

His eyes twinkle. "It's hard to say…."

What a strange answer, and what's wrong with his eyes again?

My irritation level and blood pressure are at an all-time high, and I might need to give the table a ladylike kick.

Before I do, the man stands and towers over me. I quickly take a step back and crack my calf into the end table. Even though it hurts, I clench my jaw and reach my hand out to balance the shaky vase. Unfortunately, now is an inopportune time for it to crash to the floor.

In a swift movement, he kneels and picks up a scrap of paper off the ground. But he doesn't return to his comfy seat on the couch; instead, he takes a step forward, and now he's only inches away.

He's trying to intimidate me. Little does he know, intimidation won't work. I take a small, arthritic step forward and hold my shoulders rigid, head high.

Even though I try to maintain something close to composure, I lose my senses—thank you, Peaches, for that intuitive foreshadowing. The man's cologne carries hints of cedar, a pinch of mystery, and gallons of testosterone. All I can do is imagine him standing in front of me. His hands tangled in my hair. My fingers tugging his pearly buttons, releasing each. My palms following closely behind, exploring every inch of his exposed skin.

"Ahem," he says.

He's staring at me. Did he ask me a question? I retreat to my former standing place and request clarification, "What?"

"I didn't say anything," he confirms.

"Oh."

"Is this yours?" he asks. He lifts the paper in the air.

The word list. After propelling through the air, the damn sheet must have fallen out of the book. Unable to speak logically, I nod and spin Kylie's ring. He examines the slip, longer than a stranger should analyze someone else's personal property.

"Isn't a word of the day list more appropriately suited for a middle schooler?" he asks. "Possibly a high school student? Certainly not a college grad?"

I've no desire to explain myself, but my only other option involves physical violence, so I calmly respond with a fact. "Successful writers," I say, "should have a robust vocabulary. And using a thesaurus when you need a unique word leaves your work feeling inauthentic. The words should already be part of your daily vocabulary. The list is my reminder." I add, "My mother taught me that."

"You're a writer?" he asks, as though he already knows I'm not.

I respond with as much irritation as I can muster, "No… um, my mother writes. It's her list… I carry it with me as a reminder to learn a new word every day."

"Oh," he says, as though he wished he hadn't asked.

I shrug and reach for the sheet.

He brings it towards his chest, and a crooked smile replaces his earlier confusion. "Use one in a sentence."

"Give it to me," I demand. My foot stomps the floor. Unmoved, his eyebrow raises, and a permanent marker of determination absorbs his face.

"Innocuous," he reads from the sheet.

I press my lips together and shake my head from side to side.

"You're in the challenge round, now." He smiles and holds up two fingers. "You have to use two now, and the sentence must tie to something in this room."

I frown so hard the muscles between my eyes hurt.

"Make it creative," he adds.

If I don't play his stupid game, he'll never leave.

"The nefarious guest asked the innocuous girl questions about her stupid word list."

His lips barely part, his eyebrows playfully raise.

"The sentence isn't accurate. I'm not nefarious, and you're not innocuous."

Dumbfounded at his brazen statement, my mouth opens.

"Lastly, you're in your early twenties," he says. His arms cross, and he steps backward. His gaze lingers on my hair, eyes, and nose, shifts slightly to my lips, stays there for far too long, and passes down my chest. Stops again at my waist, slides past my thighs, and completes the entire slow and easy attack on the return. His journey ends on my mouth. Time is lost; my confidence is gone. A scorching fire is left in his wake.

He waits several moments, then glides his tongue across his bottom lip. "Therefore, a woman."

I'm unaware if he's asked the time or requested directions to the nearest sushi restaurant. I can only recall that his delicious invasion ended with the tip of his tongue… and something about a woman.

"Are you going to faint again?" he asks.

I flap the front of my blouse with my hand that isn't stinging. I'm overheating, and this damn oven of a room keeps getting hotter. I should call out his lewd behavior, but I set this ridiculous tone minutes before when I gaped with zero restraint.

"I, I couldn't be better," I assure him. "I appreciate your concern."

Now I'm polite? What is wrong with me? As I fan myself, I glance down. The hem of my shirt pulls from its hiding place. The faint stain reveals itself. I should leave; I'm a mess, in appearance and in thought.

"You have a scar on your cheek," he says, breaking the silence.

My heart sinks. Spots of heat flash over my cheeks, and a burning sensation tugs at my chest. Instinctively, my hand reaches up to cover my cheek.

"Please give the list back," I stammer, "it's important to me."

Finally, he rests the sheet inside the back cover of my book and presses the novel towards me.

"I'm Niall O'Brien, from O'Brien Consulting."

"Why… why would my dad want a consulting firm here?"

"He told you about me, right?"

"Told me what?"

His playful smile transforms into a pained expression, and he takes several moments to speak.

"Mr. Vanguard—your father—and I connected a few months ago. At the time, he was seeking a consulting firm. After several discussions, your father decided to hire me for a bigger role." His voice lowers. "I'm the new Vice President of Vanguard Family Builders."

My head becomes dizzy, my vision blurs. I slither into a neighboring chair.

"Wait," he says, "this afternoon, at the restaurant, when you said you had an interview, did you mean with your dad? I thought you meant another company… to replace this job…"

His voice grows distant and becomes muffled…

Didn't realize… thought I already knew… thought my dad had told me about the change… so sorry…

A crashing thud, and blinding pain restarts my heart.

I look down.

The vase is safe, but my sister's tungsten ring lies shattered in pieces atop the indestructible oak coffee table. Fresh blood seeps through my bandage.

The Necessary Heartache
Friday, Feb 4

"NIALL, YOU PASSED the test," Henry says, outstretching a hand to shake mine.

"What's that?" I ask, trying my best to sound excited. "Falling for Harrison's asshole pranks? Or making it here alive in a severe snowstorm and choosing to wear something other than my Cubbies gear in a rival territory?"

"Both," Henry says with a laugh. "Wait—all three!" Once his chuckle fades, he apologizes for the slight deception in bringing me here for this meeting. He cups my elbow as the hostess guides us to a table.

"Next time you're in town," Henry says confidently, "you'll stay with me. It'll save you some money, give me company, and we'll be productive. Talk shop. Drink. Watch baseball. I won't take no for an answer."

Outwardly, I'm polite and say, "Thank you." Inwardly, I want to call Harrison up and cuss his ass out.

The hostess, an older woman named Babs, wears at least six visible hair clips, has a full figure, and rosy cheeks. She seats us at a small, open table. After taking our beverage order, she asks Henry if he enjoyed the powdered donuts she dropped off at the office yesterday. She says he looks handsome today; Henry's cheeks turn as pink as hers. They set a date for coffee this weekend.

Babs insists I order the grilled cheese appetizer and the Mama Bear burger. Apparently, people travel all the way from Milwaukee for Triple B's famous bar food. Henry chimes in, saying his daughter created the recipes on the menu.

Reluctantly, I stroke his ego and tell him I'm excited to try her food. He'd love to introduce me to his daughter, but unfortunately, she isn't working tonight. I ordered a double portion of grilled cheese squares and the famous Big Mama burger with everything on it.

After Babs takes Henry's order and compliments his shirt, she collects our menus and heads to the kitchen.

"Tell me about your family life and growing up in Chicago," Henry says. "How did you survive? What an awful place to live." He jokes, but he has no idea how true his statement is.

I exhale heavily.

I'm already here. The food has been ordered. I might as well make the most of my two-hour drive and see what Henry has planned. Plus, he seems like a great guy—a true family man. I hate to admit it, but I enjoy his company.

"Chicago was great," I say. "I was an honors student throughout high school and graduated third in my class. Missed earning salutatorian by one-tenth of a point. College was always my goal. I knew I wanted to own my own business someday, and my family always supported my dreams."

The fluffy, feel-good version of my past is always a crowd pleaser.

"Big goals are important," he says. "And support from loved ones, even more so. My two daughters are very different, but I have always encouraged their individual gifts. I should show you a picture of the girls." He pulls out his billfold and flips through its contents. "Shoot, they're in my other wallet."

"No pictures on your phone?" I ask, even though I'm not interested in seeing his daughters. I'm sure they're not my type. Plus, I hate lying, and I'm not in the mood to tell him his mediocre kids are beautiful.

Thankfully, the images on his phone are currently inaccessible because his fat fingers have a hard time pressing the correct buttons.

His warning comes with a chuckle: The Vanguard sisters are off-limits. He says the small town is full of busybodies, and he won't tolerate scandalous activity at Vanguard. His girls mean the world to him.

I assure him they're safe.

Honestly, my priority going forward will be to expand my company. Getting Jolene back is equally important. So, a new relationship isn't even an option. I've too much going on. Too much at stake.

Just then, Babs returns with our grilled cheese appetizer squares, and Henry forgets all about his lovely daughters.

Henry insists I take the first bite. Now, there's nothing fancy about melted cheese and butter or toasting bread, and people from Wisconsin tend to obsess over dairy products, so I have low expectations. After I bite into a crispy, hot square, an explosion of flavor bursts over my tongue. I never knew grilled cheese could be so creamy and flavorful, and there's a secret ingredient that gives the dish a little extra kick. At least his homely daughter has kitchen skills.

During dinner, the only conflict we acknowledge is rooting for opposing professional sports teams. He jokes that he feels sorry for me and laughs because my football team has been irrelevant for more years than I've been alive. I respond by saying that professional baseball is a different story. My Cubbies will beat his Brewers any day.

"This summer," he says, "I'm taking you to the Brewers-Cubs series in Milwaukee. My treat. And I'm not inviting you so you'll feel obligated to work for me. Even if you decline—we're going."

A joyous glow washes over his face. "Too many of my friends are old," he says, "It's time I start rubbing elbows with the younger generations." He crows.

"Mr. Vanguard, can we cut to the chase?" I ask. "Why are you set on hiring me for this role?"

"Your reputation is pristine. Clearly, you're the best in the business," he says. "Obviously, you know that I already met with Damian Devereaux?"

I nod.

"Horrible man," he says. "That meeting was awful. I had brought my a—well, my accountant along. She sat in the waiting area. While we were in the conference room, Lance made a suggestive comment about her—my accountant. He was so disrespectful. I got pretty upset, threw a glass vase against the wall, and stormed out. That man is a pig."

I don't tell Henry, but I know about this incident. That day, right after Henry left, Harrison texted me and said I should expect a call from Mr. Vanguard. Then Harrison told me about the super, fucking hot accountant. Curvy, but incognito, and you'd have to have an eye for asses to see through her flare leggings and oversized, red, Pink Floyd t-shirt that read, *A little sick*. Very memorable.

"The Devereauxs can come across a little rough," I say.

"That's an understatement. From what Harrison told me, I'm surprised you aren't running his name into the ground."

"Not my style."

"So, Devereaux hates you because clients are leaving him and coming to you?"

"That's correct."

"But you charge more."

"I do."

"And your service is better?"

"It is."

"Harrison told me Damian has sent you all kinds of 'Congrats on the new business' gifts."

"I don't know for certain who is sending me the 'gifts'."

I can tell Henry is the kind of man who loves some good gossip, but I have a feeling that he will keep this to himself.

So, I tell Henry that the mass exodus of prospects and clients from Deveraux to O'Brien Consulting has my former boss and his prodigy behaving strangely. Over the past year, FedEx delivered a bird skull to my condo. A courier dropped off an empty black envelope via certified mail, and a bouquet of chrysanthemums arrived at my door. A lovely card accompanied each gift, affectionately signed DYE. Two weeks ago, my condo went up in flames. And just last Wednesday, a fun-size Niall voodoo doll was left on Soo-jin's back porch. The thing creeped me the fuck out. Thankfully, Harrison was with me when I found it and promised to discard the effigy. The polite me wants to send the Deverauxs a thank-you card for all the thoughtful gifts and then sue them for arson.

But I don't have any proof.

"Well, I have all the proof I need." Henry winks. He retrieves a document from his briefcase.

He's updated the terms of my proposal. Effective immediately, he wants me to become the company's Vice President. If I sign tonight, he'll give me a 25% ownership stake in Vanguard Family Builders. Tomorrow, his attorney will meet us at the Vanguard office to finalize the paperwork. Henry keeps listing all the benefits of this partnership, but I stop listening.

Twenty-five percent?

Based on my previous assessment of the company, this new contract would put hundreds of thousands of dollars in my pocket. Henry says the agreement needs to stay quiet because he'd rather his daughter graduate before he announces me as the newest member of Team Vanguard.

From my phone, I open the contract Henry sent me Tuesday night. The one that outlines my services as an independent contractor, where I would earn a few thousand dollars to consult with Henry. I agree to E-sign that agreement.

Henry shakes his head.

If I don't sign, Henry warns it's unlikely I'll do business in Wisconsin again. The verbal threat, along with the fact that everyone who was already in the restaurant before we arrived has waved hello to Henry or patted him on the shoulder as they walked by, underscores his influence. Henry is a well-known businessman in this town. His reach runs deep, and I can't risk damaging my reputation before I even get a chance to succeed in Wisconsin. I can't afford to lose potential clients.

Plus, I'm worried Henry will follow me to Chicago and stalk me until I agree. Because that's exactly what Henry promises he'll do.

I've always believed that open doors are open for a reason, and the door to Vanguard Builders won't close. I carefully re-read Henry's new document. Henry and I will start working together next week.

And there's been another update.

Once his daughter graduates, he'll make her quit the other jobs—or ensure she's fired—and then she can focus on working underneath me.

For now, Henry says I can work remotely. My presence in Mayfair isn't necessary, but would be appreciated occasionally.

The contract details are ideal, as I'll be traveling to Germany in June for several months to work with another residential development company. Having back-to-back jobs is every small business owner's dream, and these two opportunities would give me the extra operating cash needed to hire my first staff member and finally rent office space. Suddenly, I can't seem to remember any of my previous concerns, and I'm finding every reason to say yes. My professional career is expanding rapidly.

My personal life, on the other hand, has fallen to pieces.

Henry and I shake hands and agree to meet at his office tomorrow morning at eight to finalize the contract. I check my watch; it's already nine, and I haven't even had time to process the break-up with Jolene. I'm wide awake but somehow also exhausted. Henry notices the restless look in my eye as we walk towards the entrance.

"You staying out then?" he asks.

"Long day, long drive, and there's a blizzard outside. I'll stick out the storm here for a while."

"Behave tonight," he says.

"I assure you, I won't." A hand smacks my back, and Henry gives another joyous laugh.

Before Henry steps outside, he whispers, "Remember, we'll keep this arrangement quiet until I have time to talk with my girl."

Given Henry's Santa Claus white beard and expansive mid-section, I'm not concerned with noticing, then approaching his daughter in a crowded room. I'm positive I wouldn't give her a second glance.

Group Chat
Friday, May 27th @ 3:10 p.m.

ZAKATAK: MURDERER? WHAT?

JustPeachy: She's having nightmares about that night and is adamant that there's more to the story than what she's been told. She thinks everyone is a suspect.

Fauxy Roxy: She's not wrong for questioning us.

Milly Rodrigo: Of course, she's not wrong. Kate is way too intuitive for this charade. She's going to find out the truth eventually.

Slide_OB: Perhaps we should change our strategy.

JustPeachy: Let's noodle on this. I don't want to make a rash decision. For now, let's stay vigilant, people. Let's talk later.

Mirror's Reflection
Friday, May 27th @ 5:05 p.m.

"OH, MY GOODNESS. You are kidding me. This is not real." Mother's voice is as sweet as sugar; her face puckers as if she's tasted vinegar. I'm standing here, Mother. Of course, I'm real. You're the fake one, I think to myself. "Did you wear that shirt to your interview?" she asks. Her passive-aggressive tone is much better than, "What the fuck are you wearing?" Her perfect posture falters for a moment as her body, too, becomes disappointed.

Coffee-stained slacks? Seriously, Kate? You work in a kitchen, but that doesn't mean you give up. Powdered sugar dust in your hair? Of all the things to get stuck in your hair? A bandage on your hand? What did you do to yourself this time? No apron? Did you leave it at work? (A hand moves to cover a perfect pout. Clarity sets in.) *Oh, no. Did you get fired?*

A writer catches even the smallest detail. But great details—like a twelfth birthday— often go unnoticed.

Red platform heels crush the sidewalk; harsh words sting my heart. Estelle's entrances are never forgettable. I plaster a smile on my face, walk up the newly poured concrete sidewalk, and admire the weeds overtaking the yard. The ground's job is simple: just be. No deadlines or demands. It sits and waits. Once landscapers till, seed, and cover, and the homeowner waters, fertilizes, and waters some more, a spectacle blossoms. Even if left alone, weeds and grass will eventually sprout from the dirt, at least in Wisconsin's fertile farmland. Midwest dirt has it made. It can do nothing, and seeds take root, things grow. People cheer. Spring is here! Look at the first buds! Hooray, nature! The dirt isn't pressured. The soil needs more water and less sun. It's not the ground's fault. Sprinkle the seed. Add more fertilizer. Oh, to be dirt.

"How will you succeed in the real world if you can't even dress professionally for an interview with your father?" Her question is my question. On the ride home, as I drove down unnecessary side roads for nearly two hours, I reflected on that thought repeatedly. The truth is, I've become hopeless. I swing my hands behind my back and say nothing because no one will hear me; no one's listening. I spin around my own merry-go-round of differences. My eyes blink rapidly with vacant interest.

"You've so little fashion sense," she says. (She's not wrong.) "I swear, Kylie absorbed it all in the womb." (A scientific experiment could probably verify such a theory.)

Bright red lips land on my cheek. A hazy cloud of Chanel No. 5 surrounds me. I use the back of my hand to wipe away the lipstick— there isn't any—and unfortunately, the hazy cloud never disappears. I'll deal with the ache in a minute.

Eager to change the subject to something positive, I blurt: "I can't believe summer is almost here. And May 28th is tomorrow. Only a day away. Time is going so fast… but then sometimes I think it's dragging."

My parents' wedding day. Anniversary. I'm not sure what the term would be.

They first divorced when Kylie and I were eleven. Mother said they lost touch with each other, whatever that means. They remarried when Kylie and I were freshmen in high school. A year ago, they divorced again. Mother said Dad had a wandering eye and enjoyed the company of other women. I know what that means. I never confronted my dad about the infidelity because I couldn't bear the truth.

Even with their issues, Mother always said that she and my dad were destined to be together. And 'Til death do us part' was wrong because even after death, they'd be together. That's the whole point of soulmates.

When my parents fell in love this past March, Mother wanted a posh black, white, and rose-red ceremony—on May 28th. She didn't care what Kylie and I wore as long as we attended and matched. Kylie and I didn't mind matching, but we definitely didn't want to attend. Who marries the same person three times? Since Kylie and I opposed the union and had no interest in choosing a dress, Piper shopped online and insisted, "A Bright Red Tie-Strap Pleated Midi would be to die for, and we'd both look divine." With one click, Piper ordered two size eights, next-day delivery.

I think both dresses are still hanging in the bedroom closet inside a dry-cleaning bag. I should check.

Honestly, I never thought Mother would consider marrying again. But I imagine her tune changed when Dad's financial situation improved and he moved into a new house in a fancy subdivision. Mother was never especially motivated by wealth, but she wouldn't object to a rise in socio-economic status, which caused some jealousy among the volunteer committee members along the way.

"It's forever this time," Mother insists. A teased head full of hair shakes but remains unmoved, courtesy of a shield of hairspray. She traces a symbolic cross over her body. She's a vision of beauty. A mirage of a masterpiece. "Through space, time, even death."

"I think you lovebirds are meant to be," I say.

"Lovebirds," she says. Her smile is heavenly, as though she floated down from the heavens with the sole purpose of gracing me with her presence. "Tonight is a big night. *A celebration not to be missed.*" She eyes me as she walks towards the car. "Don't dig in your… bags for an outfit." She winks and lowers her voice, "I want you to wear the dress from Piper. There's a nice pair of heels hanging next to the dress, too." She glows with the idea of me wearing a beautiful little dress and heels.

Lately, my fashion sense rivals that of an overweight, middle-aged, divorced dad. My staples include comfortable sweatpants, baggy t-shirts, and mismatched socks. Anyway, it would be highly inappropriate for me to show up tonight wearing the dress.

The red Midi was supposed to be for tomorrow.

"Mother, what…" I say, but stall. I need to ask her about April 10th, but when she turns, her eyes pierce mine, and her head lifts subtly. *A celebration not to be missed, wear the dress from Piper.* Her words twist my heart.

"Well, what is it?" she says and impatiently tosses heavy locks over her shoulder. Her normally stick-straight hair barely moves. Even with outdated, ratted blonde waves, she's reminiscent of any famous '80s actress. A true dame where it counts: on the outside. The faint crow's feet around her eyes disappear.

Kylie materializes in front of me.

I can't ask the question I need to ask.

Not today. My vision becomes blurry, and Mother vanishes down the sidewalk. She's too busy for my nonsense questions.

Tonight is her celebration. Plus, she can only handle my shortcomings for short periods. I suddenly miss her and wish I weren't so angry with her lately.

I'm startled out of my wits when the front door slams shut, and those same platform heels click against the sidewalk. I spin around.

Cousin Nora walks towards me, carrying a small wooden box in one hand and her extra-large purse in the other.

I mumble to myself, "Why is she here?"

Nora is Auntie Babs' newest real estate assistant—my cousin— and is still overwhelmed by the 'big' city. Nora is talking to me, but I have difficulty concentrating on her words because Nora's curly, dirty-blond hair is teased, her lips are red, and she's donning a sensible black dress and pop-of-color heels. She smells like Mother.

"Kate," she says. "I was wondering where you were. Are you okay?"

"Are you wearing my mother's perfume?" I ask.

"Her perfume is so divine," Nora says. "I couldn't resist." She bites her lip in apology.

I frown, my lips pout.

"Were you talking to yourself?" she hesitantly asks.

"No."

I was.

"Can we give you a ride to Triple B's?" She asks with so much pity; it drips off her tongue. She clutches the cardboard box to her chest and adds cautiously, "Your dad suggested we drive together." She eyes my bloody shirt and my bandaged hand. "Sure, you're, okay?"

"Piper and Milly are picking me up."

"That's perfect," she says. "I have to make a quick stop at Triple B's, then collect the lockbox from Professor Holliday's house. The closing is Tuesday." She crosses her fingers.

"Holliday?" I ask, surprised.

"Yeah, he's back in town for the weekend. It's going to be so nice to catch up with him tonight."

"He's coming to Triple B's tonight?" I ask. It's taking me a few moments to process this information.

"I mean, he was so close to the family. I think it's nice of him."

Perhaps I can confront Holliday? What else does he know about that night? He's clearly not the man we all thought him to be. Besides the scandalous sexual incident, what else is he hiding?

Is perception reality?

A sudden wave of excitement passes through my body. With renewed energy, I brush past Nora towards the front door. I certainly can't tell Nora about my suspicions or about my strange Kylie dream. But I can figure out a plan of action for tonight.

"Careful," she says, holding the box tighter.

My eyes flick to the box and then back to Nora. All at once, emotion washes over me. Fear swells in my chest. My future is uncertain. Anger burns across my face. Niall O'Brien received my promotion. I'm embarrassed that I let Peaches down. And I'm so, so very sad.

What is wrong with me?

Holding back tears, I ask Nora if she's driving Mother. Emotions overwhelm me. I can't cry in front of Nora. She'll never leave. And I need time to figure out my next move.

Nora nods and exhales a heavy dose of pity. The pity turns to worry. "You sure you're okay? I can stay, if you like—"

"No," I say and head towards the front door.

"Wait," she says.

I turn around.

She fishes inside her handbag. "I guess I'm Uncle Henry's assistant, too, now. He asked me to pick up the mail." She passes an envelope from her purse. "This… has me worried…"

"What?" I eye her, then notice what she's holding. "You opened my mail?" My cheeks flush, but only a little. I reach forward and yank the mail out of her hand. Kylie's cell phone bill. I shove it in my back pocket.

Henry's assistant? This day is getting worse by the minute.

"You're still messaging her?" Nora asks. Her whisper is flat and urgent, "Stop messaging her."

Nora sounds like Mother, too. An invisible piece of lint is flicked off her dress, and her smile returns. "It's not good for you," Nora says. "You need to create your own future. That bill shows you've been messaging her daily, sometimes 20 or 30 times. Why, Kate? Just stop. Tomorrow is your priority, and the next day, and the next."

My future is none of her business. But… I should ask her… now that she's been nosing around my parents' things, she may have come across other personal items.

"Have you seen Kylie's phone?" I ask.

Nora jerks back, as though my words carry the weight of an anchor.

"Phone?" she asks. "Why?"

"I want to know."

"I haven't seen it." She tips her head to the side. "Please let her go. Focus on your future."

"I have an amazing future," I lie.

"She's never going to respond. You do know that?"

My face grows hard. "Was there any other mail today?"

"For goodness' sake, why are you so morbid? Let go—"

"Well, obviously, you got the mail. Was it in there? Yes, or no?"

"Why do you keep asking?"

"I want to frame it on my wall."

"You're so crass."

"Well… did it come?"

"The death certificate did not come," she says, now nearly as frustrated as I am. "You need to leave the past in the past."

"Nora, I'm an adult. Trust me, I'm doing what's best for… me." My smile doesn't fade. I could be dying inside, and perhaps I am. Would anyone notice?

She shakes her head and walks towards Mother's car.

"Wait." I raise my voice. "Do you think Mother knows what happened to Doe?"

Nora doesn't answer. Instead, she slams the car door. The vehicle hums eerily down the drive.

Damn it, Doe.

Everyone probably thinks I killed the damn cat. But I didn't. I'm like 99% sure. I stopped by Mother's place last night. Cat-sitting has its perks. Doe usually snuggles on my chest and keeps me company.

Snuggles-ed.

Keeps-ept.

Prior tense. (A made-up tense used when referring to the prior actions of a deceased person. A deceased person you can't seem to let go of. Also, it can refer to the feelings towards a deceased Felis catus.)

Last night, when I walked into Mother's kitchen, I'd been awake for nearly twenty-four hours, and the room was dark except for the glow of a nightlight by the toaster. So, at first, I thought the clump lying in the middle of Mother's mahogany floor was a hoodie. On my way to the pantry to grab a package of Pop-Tarts, I briefly stepped on the mirage and freaked out because my sockless foot grazed a squishy, silky object. Mid-step, I hurdled over the blob. Once a safe distance away, I spun around and gripped the counter. (As though the Formica could protect me.)

Upon closer inspection, the non-shirt thing had a shiny coat. The thing was indeed Doe, Mother's beloved cat. I immediately panicked because Doe doesn't sleep on the floor; she's too refined. She sleeps on goose down, oversized pet beds strategically placed in the sunniest part of every room or at the head of Mother's Posturepedic mattress. Doe was not mindlessly basking in the sun or flippantly leaving cat litter prints on the bed.

Mother's precious Doe was very much dead before I even walked into the room—I'm ninety-nine percent sure. One percent of me is terrified I might have done more than lightly touch her fluffy body. Did I accidentally crush her? Surely, she would have balked or hissed first?

I kick a pile of dirt and stub my toe on a hidden rock. Debris flies against the house. I wince and hop in place. Dirt really doesn't do anything, yet it still manages to kick up a fuss. I curse at the ground. A fat June bug crawls out from a crack in the sidewalk. I leap back. June bugs—with their bloated bodies and crunchy shells—gross me out. How do their impossibly tiny legs support such a hefty body?

So creepy. Unnatural.

A heavy thud startles me. My hand goes to my racing heart, and I spin around. On the other side of the road, the lone porta-potty's door slams as the wind picks up. In the distance, the sun touches the tree line, casting shadows over milkweed-filled fields. The air has turned colder. I shudder. Tonight, Weeping Willow Estates is empty except for me, and I start to wonder if I even matter.

The construction workers are gone for the day, and with the long holiday weekend ahead, they won't return until Tuesday. Dad, being the kind-hearted boss he is, gave the crew a full four days off, knowing they'd be back next week, ready to work overtime. For now, rusty cranes frozen mid-lift, plastic wrappings blown into the field, dumpsters overflowing with cardboard boxes, and a quiet, secluded space fill the emptiness.

And the lowering sun in the distance.

And me.

If I'm empty and I'm occupying an empty space, is the area still empty?

I believe so. Yes.

0 x 0 = 0

0 + 0 = 0

Mathematically, it checks out.

My dad's two-story contemporary home sits in the farthest corner of the subdivision. A thick family of bushy red maples and prickly pine trees line the perimeter. Future Weeping Willow residents will enjoy a level of privacy rarely available to owners of new construction homes. The fields are solemn. The skies are clear, apart from a territorial hawk sailing above.

If I were to scream right now, no one would hear me for miles. I cup my hands around my mouth, ready to test out a killer scream, but first scan the fields to the right and left, then settle my vision on Halyn Court leading out of the subdivision. I'm very much alone.

"Ahh!" I belt.

The sound echoes through the field and softens at the woods' edge.

Faintly, at first, but then louder, a response comes from the woods.

"Sweetie!"

I start to smile. Is that a chickadee calling to me?

This time I whistle, "Sweetie!"

The response is louder and closer, "Sweetie!"

I scan into the woods. Part of me wants to check out the sound, but the logical side of my brain reminds me I'm alone, pretty much in the middle of nowhere, while a murderer is on the loose.

"Sweetie! Sweetie! Sweetie!" Although the chickadee really wants to get my attention, thankfully, I'm not one of those blonde bimbos in every thriller movie, so I wisely scramble into my dad's custom-built house and lock the heavy French door behind me.

I crank the door handle and pull as hard as I can.

Locked.

An enormous bouquet of red flowers sits on my dad's console table. Roses, tulips, carnations. The smell of paint is briefly masked by the resinous, tree-sap luster emanating from the real tree branches nestled among the flowers. A card lies next to the vase. I pick it up and read: *Estelle, through it all, you are my forever. Here's to eternity. Love, Henry.*

I gag slightly at the sentimental note, then rush to the kitchen, after I drop my dirty shirt next to the vase. Thirty minutes means no time for dilly-dallying.

Snowy marbled counters, bleached hand towels, white soap pumps, silver wall hangings, and a disinfected detachment complete my welcome home. The white room is always clean but never cozy. And there's a difference. Auntie Babs is an expert at reading the energy in a room. Kitchens should always have clean energy. They don't need to be cozy. Who knew? Babs, she knew. She's a real estate agent. She has an uncanny ability to assess a home, gauge its energy level, and fill it with air fresheners—all in under fifteen minutes. If you choose to list with her— or Nora—and follow their *32-Point Seller Marketing Guide*, you're guaranteed to get top-dollar for your home.

I grab a glass from the cabinet and pause, breathing in the shelf's earthy scent. When my parents were divorced, we'd stay with my dad every other weekend. He'd often bring Kylie and me along to construction sites. After he spent hours chiseling, sawing, sanding, and drilling, and following blueprints to measure, mark, and frame the walls of a home or hang kitchen cabinets, he'd save discarded sections of wood for Kylie and me. The pieces were perfectly crafted doll beds, tables, and furniture. And they smelled earthy and sweet, like him.

As I'm about to grab the bottle of vitamins, the doorbell rings. I freeze. When it rings for a second time, my heart quickens, and for some reason, I feel the need to crouch to the floor.

The bell rings again.

My heart feels as though it's about to burst out of my chest.

I lose count of how many times it rings.

Why am I so scared? I should answer the door like a normal person. But… something's stopping me. Intuition? Foresight? The feeling that doom is on the horizon?

Yep. I'd say all three.

Who could it be?

My dad won't be home anytime soon. No doubt he's several beers deep at Triple B's right now—telling Peaches how disappointed he is in me. Piper and Milly are picking me up tonight. For some reason, they don't trust me to arrive on time. I don't think they'd be here this early. Just to be safe, I text them.

Me: Sexy ladies, are you almost here?
The Pied Piper: Be outside in 30 minutes!
Milly: Make it 25, you know how crabby Pipe gets if she has to wait.
The Pied Piper: What? I'm never crabby.
Milly: You're always crabby.
The Pied Piper: You're always critical.

A giggle escapes my lips, and a feeling of normalcy replaces my fear. Glad to be feeling something other than sadness or fear, I let out a heavy sigh. The doorbell hasn't rang in minutes. Certain I am alone again, I leave the lights on, rush upstairs, then squint as I prepare to enter my room.

The pink room.

A mouthful of fuchsia bubble gum might have burst open in here. From the lampshade to decorative pillows, throw rugs, and curtains, every accent has a pink tint. It was my favorite color growing up. Kylie's too. I walk to the window and push aside the heavy pink polka-dot blackout curtains. The bird feeder is ten feet from the house, surrounded by patches of green grass and muddy clay. Hundreds, maybe thousands, of seeds scatter across the dirt. I went overboard. When Kylie and I were young, hearing the first Black-capped chickadees outside our bedroom window in spring, we believed the birds were calling us to come out and play.

"Hey, sweetie! Hey sweetie!" they would sing.

Since Kylie's been gone, I haven't seen any chickadees at the feeder. I jerk the curtains shut. I slip Kylie's cell bill out of my back pocket and walk to my dresser. The top drawer is partly open. Lonely socks, half-empty lotion bottles, and hair clips scatter inside. The gift Kylie gave me for our twenty-first birthday pokes out from underneath an empty Target bag.

I lift the framed picture of Kylie and me. The photo was taken last summer. The four of us: Piper, Milly, Kylie, and me, straightened our hair, layered flannels over tank tops, slid on short shorts, and wore plastic sandals. Kylie applied our makeup, just enough to highlight our natural beauty. Then we crowded into Piper's Audi and drove to the Port Wine Marina.

And I was… happy. Is that the right word? It's been so long; I think it was. I think I was.

That day, on the breakwater path leading to the abandoned lighthouse, we took turns taking sister pics, selfies, and group shots. Afterward, I forgot all about the photo session. But then the morning of our birthday, which happened to land on the summer solstice—June 20th—Kylie surprised me with the framed pic. The two of us were holding hands, wide smiles, wind swirling around us, beams of sunlight bouncing off our cheeks, her eyes were shining. Under the photo, she had drawn a thin, straight line. On the left, there was a 'play' and a 'pause' emoji button. To the right, a 'repeat' emoji. The track playing was "My Best Friend" by Queen. The song was paused at 1:20.

I carefully set Kylie's cell phone bill in the top drawer. I brush a layer of garbage off the dresser. Empty cups, gum wrappers, and junk mail fall to the carpet. I display the picture frame on the clean section of the bureau.

Now that my room is in order, I can get ready. I take a warm shower, and for Mother's sake, shave my legs. Next, I apply antiseptic to my cut and use an old gauze roll from the bathroom drawer to re-wrap. Wearing my towel, I check the bird feeder again—still empty—then I crash on top of my rumpled comforter and pink throw pillows.

Feeling accomplished, I stretch my arms and steamroll a department store bag on my bed. What should I wear tonight? Something sensible. Nothing flashy. No sweatpants. Even though my projected success rate is zero, I dig through the piles on the floor, searching for a wrinkle-free article of clothing. In my small closet, a black dress hangs from the rod. It reminds me of a funeral. Not wearing that.

Tonight is a celebration.

After a few minutes of searching, I realize that most of my clothes haven't been washed, and I don't own any other dresses.

Ho hum, ho hum.

Except…

The red dress.

No.

I can't.

That would be inappropriate.

Last year, before checking out of the dorms, Kylie and I cleaned our room. Well, she cleaned. I shuffled totes from one side of the room to the other.

Before boxing up her clothes, Kylie washed and pressed each item according to its label's instructions. Suffice to say, I didn't follow the same laundering protocol. I cleverly eliminated the need for boxes or suitcases. Instead, I stuffed my clothes into a series of easy-to-haul garbage bags.

This year, I followed the same technique. So, now most of my clothes are stored in trash bags, piled against my wall or in my car.

My favorites have already been worn and tossed to the floor. Could I show up naked? Mother would die and haunt me from her grave, but there isn't enough alcohol in my dad's liquor cabinet to catapult me to a state making that plausible.

Desperation seeps in. I crawl to the smaller of the two closets in my room and yank down the dry-cleaning bag. The dress cascades to the floor in a rush of red. It's blinding, sexy, and not my style. A pair of lace panties, a matching bra, and heels lay at the bottom of the bag, completing the disaster. I'll try on the dress, but the coaster-size doilies and 'may I please have a broken ankle' stilettos can stay in the bag. I stuff the undergarments into the empty department store bag on my bed. I remove the tags, drop my towel to the floor, and slip into the Midi. I find a pair of clean biker shorts. I squeeze into those. After adjusting the straps, I review the reflection in the mirror.

The fabric hugs, curves, stretches, and wraps tight around a silhouette that's not mine. A glow up, carrying enough cleavage to pay for next semester's tuition installment, smiles back at me. A cool draft enters the room. My skin tingles. Goosebumps travel up my arms. I turn to the right, flip my hair in a high pony, pop my ass, and make a kissy face.

Kylie stares back. Mother hovers. The two plead.

Katie, wear the dress. You look stunning.

Kate, you look so grown-up.

The dress is flattering. It's also uncomfortable and totally inappropriate.

Katie, puh-uh-lease?

Please, baby girl?

My only other option is the black funeral dress, and I'm not wearing that. *Tonight is a celebration!*

Ugh.

I can't wear the atrocity. I stretch my arm behind my back, but can't reach the zipper.

The dress is stuck.

I'm stuck.

Once again, the decision is made for me. But tonight no one needs to be reminded of Kylie, so I'll bring my favorite work shirt along and use it as a cover-up. I fling the heels onto the bed. Given my agenda for tonight, sneakers are more sensible. I thoroughly blow-dry, then use violent strokes to straighten my hair. When finished, it looks moderate to okay. Best of all, nothing like Mother's.

Since I've moved back home, I can't recall where I placed my mascara or lip gloss. They're probably tucked next to my dishware in one of the garbage bags. I'll be all-natural tonight, and no one will care or notice, except Mother. My near-white eyebrows and almost invisible eyelashes make me appear ghostly. I'm an apparition. Thankfully, yesterday's extra sun mixed a little color into my iridescence.

At the front door, I slip on my Vans. As I tie the laces, fuzzy bubbles begin to form in the pit of my stomach.

Today was surprising. Well, getting fired, not so much, but my dad choosing Mr. O'Brien? How did I not see this coming? He never spoke a word to me about this, Mr. O'Brien, and yet, supposedly, they've been talking for months? Did they connect before April 10th? No, that's not possible. My dad wouldn't do that to me. Wouldn't keep a secret from me.

What should I do now?

Make amends with team Vanguard and take on a half-assed role at the company? Succumb to Mr. O'Brien's reign? Search for another job?

Truth be told, I have been searching. Maybe part of me knew this was coming? I've applied for hundreds of decent-paying 'college grad' jobs, but turns out you need a degree to be classified as a grad, so I'm stuck right now. But I'll need a better job—soon—because I can't live at home forever.

A month ago, a consulting firm in Chicago posted for an intern with an accounting or finance degree. On a whim, I applied for the job. I told the HR woman, Miss Verity, that I had been through a family tragedy and that, because my homework due dates had been extended, my diploma wouldn't be awarded until mid-June. She didn't seem to mind and wanted to schedule an interview with her boss. Lance? Lancelot? Anyway, I never went forward with it. Maybe I should now?

My stomach begins to ache.

The thought of moving away from my hometown makes me feel like I'm deserting Kylie. Can I really move to a city? Two hours away from my family? I'm used to living in a tiny town with trees, deer, and birds— no chickadees, but every other fucking kind of bird. Could I live in a forest of cement and brick? With people everywhere? And my loved ones so far away?

But can I stay here?

Living in Mayfair is like walking inside a ticking time bomb. Memories of Kylie are the explosive powder. And I'm afraid, once I finally remember those missing twenty-four hours, one of those memories is going to explode in my face.

And now, Mr. O'Brien is working for my dad.

And he's stolen my job.

What if he never showed up?

What if he left?

Even better, what if my dad kicked our new VP out of the equation? Maybe that's the answer? What if I were to discover Mr. O'Brien's Achilles' heel? There must be something that keeps the man up at night.

Once I uncover his secrets and share them with my dad, O'Brien will be fired, and I'll be promoted.

Then and only then will I be able to stay in Mayfair and learn to live with Kylie's memories.

It looks as though I've got another mission: destroy Mr. O'Brien.

Kylie
Saturday, February 5th

A BARTENDER WEARING a neatly pressed designer shirt and a flashy tie approaches. The nametag pinned against the Gucci shirt says 'Peaches'. Feminine features, but the fine print under the name says he/him. Being observant and respectful in any interaction, whether business or personal, is important to me. The pillar of my success.

"Fresh face among the locals, love the shirt," Peaches says, wiping down the counter. "Armani is a dear friend of mine. What are ya drinking?"

Henry and I spent a long day together. Our morning started with a tour of Weeping Willow Estates and a pot of black coffee. At his office, we watched the sports channel for a couple of hours. And we ended the night with another dinner at Triple B's. I can see that working with Henry is going to involve a lot of eating out and coffee, and not much work.

Exhausted after a long day, I'm looking forward to sipping a beer, and then I'll order an Uber back to the hotel.

I ordered a Grizzly Black draft beer. Then check my messages. Over the course of the day, Harrison has sent me several sympathetic texts and is mildly pleased I'm officially single again.

Harrison: FREEDOM FUCKER! TONIGHT'S HOMEWORK: FIND A REPLACEMENT AND TEXT ME HER BRA SIZE.

I respond politely, saying Jolene was the one, and I need to win her back. Harrison calls me a pussy and insists I finish my homework before midnight. He asks if I enjoyed meeting with Yuhr Mahm. I refuse to give him the satisfaction of an answer.

Frustrated with Harrison's immaturity, I open my Uber app to request a ride, but before I complete it, the bell above the restaurant door rings, and a group of women walks in.

I hunch over my phone while watching them. They chat near the door and point in different directions. Apparently, picking a table is crucial for a successful night out. From afar, they seem like copies of the same person: sleek hair framing shiny faces, semi-clothed bodies under puffy coats, high heels supporting curvy and slender figures. One is so beautiful it's obscene-she's a cliché.

A presence in pink catches my attention. She tosses her coat onto a chair. Skin-tight jeans and a rosy sweater cover her. Most of her. A thin strip of waistline shows from underneath. She turns. Denim fabric clings to an amazing ass. When she swings her long, white-blonde hair over her shoulder, a vibrant energy takes over the room.

Vibrant energy? What does that even mean? I don't know, but it's real, and I can feel her—her confidence, her sensuality, her presence. While the girls talk over each other, her face stays serious until the gorgeous one makes her laugh. That smile is rare, and the sound hits my core. My core of what? All the women have their own charm. She's nothing special, just another potential to add to my list of one-night stands. And I just broke up with Jolene, who was the love of my life and the woman I hoped to marry someday. What am I thinking? I knock back the rest of my drink and loosen the top button of my shirt. I should call Jolene. Now. But my hands won't move. What am I waiting for? I stare at the empty glass, yet the woman across the room pulls at my heart.

Peaches kindly offers to pour me another drink. Even though I'm leaving, and never drink more than one, I say yes.

While the group of females heads to a table in the back, the woman wearing pink bravely breaks from the crowd and walks toward the bar. I pretend to be busy with my empty glass but watch her out of the corner of my eye. Her smile reaches only a few. Babs receives kind words and a wild grin. A busboy is playfully jabbed in the chest. His face turns twelve shades of red. I immediately feel jealous of a blushing teenager. As she walks, she doesn't scan the crowd; she ignores strangers. She keeps her radiant smile for those close to her. She shows no interest in bystanders, but something inside urges me to keep watching. I focus on her. As she draws nearer, my attraction to her becomes magnetic.

The bar is horseshoe-shaped, and I'm on the wrong side. She stops at the opposite end and elbows her way between two men. Nope, I'm on the right side. From my seat, I have the perfect view. The creep's eye her. Jealousy fills my lungs, and I want to scream it out.

Why?

She's just…

She's nothing…

She's beautiful.

But.

She's more than beautiful. Beautiful is cliché. Breath-taking?

No.

Not even breathtaking, because my heart has strangely stopped.

Heart-stopping?

No.

Now my heart's taken over, pounding a thousand beats per minute as blood surges through my veins. Even though I keep my ball of foot steady on the footrest, my knee trembles. A shiver runs through the floor and reverberates through my body.

The men are frozen. Even though she ignores their prying eyes, I can't. I feel the urge to knock them both out. What? Hours after becoming single, I'm ready to fight some drunks over a piece of ass? Am I about to make a move? This is nuts. I've always been super picky. How have I already forgotten Jolene? I don't know, but the woman across the bar feels like a volcanic eruption branding fiery ash into my skin.

She calls the bartender by name. Peaches lights up when she waves. Damn, even the bartender seems to be in her circle. When she pinches his cheek, my heart swells, then crashes into my chest and shatters. A heartbreak. I lose sight of her as she places an order. A longing builds inside me. My broken heart pounds, then aches. My breathing becomes ragged, my chest feels like it might burst.

When I leave tonight, I'll never see this woman again. A new kind of ache begins to form—a longing. The pain feels unfamiliar. Jolene's been gone for nearly two months, and I've missed her presence, but now that we've broken up, I don't miss her as much. I feel somewhat broken inside. Mostly, I miss her being there. Something is missing when I come home at night. Just having her around was… nice. Convenient. But these feelings I'm experiencing now are new. The thought of never seeing her again is... agonizing. The woman across from me is causing a different kind of pain. The ache is constant and endless. It's a persistent, all-over-body hurt that grips my heart.

The two slobbering drunks crowd in closer, likely relying on liquid courage to muster enough bravery to make a move. Losers. They don't stand a chance. Not with her. But what if she says yes? What if she says no, only because she already has a boyfriend? The man to the left throws a cheesy pickup line. I wince; it's terrible. The poor guy was destined to fail. She turns him down. Of course, she turned him down. I exhale. She says he reminds her of her grandpa—not when he was alive, but when he was lying in a coffin. Original. I smile, not because I'm glad she said no, but because she's funny.

That's what I tell myself.

The man to her right leans in. I sip my beer. The ache intensifies. Before he speaks, she mentions she's recovering from major surgery—big, glorious breast implants—and has to wait another five weeks before sex. Can he wait that long? His face is priceless, and I almost spit out my drink. She's quick-witted, fearless, and has excellent instincts.

The ache deepens.

The men around the bar, old and young, become her audience, but my heartache remains unnoticed by strangers. She's unaware of the attention, but not in a ditzy way. Strangers are a waste of her time. How do I become important? The ache is nearly unbearable.

The pain persists. A heart attack? No. A heartache. She's a heartache. A heartache waiting to happen. I remind myself that this weekend is for business. O'Brien Consulting is the only thing that matters. Heartaches aren't allowed.

When her drink order is ready, she carefully stabilizes the glasses and bottles on a large serving tray. A bottle tips. Peaches teases her, but jokingly. He replaces the drink and offers to carry the unstable tray. She accepts. As they leave, I casually spin my stool. A small tattoo peeks out from under her sweater, above her hip. An unsexy beep from my phone ends my stalker vibe.

The Battering Ram: NAME? SIZE?

Me: I'm not hooking up with anyone, and you're weird.

The Battering Ram: Y

Me: I'm working, and you're weird because who asks a woman their bra size?

The Battering Ram: YOU DON'T ASK. YOU PERFORM AN INTENSE VISUAL INSPECTION. OH WAIT, DOES JOLENE STILL HAVE YOUR DICK IN HER PURSE?

Me: Ask your mother about my dick.

The Battering Ram: OK. TEXTING HER NOW. MEET A GIRL AND GET HER NAME. NO FUCKING CUDDLE SESSIONS. GET LAID.

Me: Too busy working.

The Battering Ram: WEAK. A NAME.

I should leave.

Now.

Jolene is the one.

Until I get her back, O'Brien Consulting is my only interest.

The roads should be clear by now, so I request an Uber. In ten minutes, this ridiculous ache will be gone forever. When the bartender returns, I wave him over. My random desire to socialize has everything to do with killing time, and nothing to do with learning more about the pain in my chest. At least that's what I tell myself. First, I ask Peaches about the bar's unique name. Apparently, the owner's nickname is Bear. He's six five, three hundred pounds, has a beard rivaling that of an 1800s lumberjack, and a heart of gold. That explains the restaurant's forest decor and wildlife. And since Bear opened a brewery on the bluffs, the name is both descriptive and geographically accurate. Then I ask Peaches about his unique name. His real name is Jess. When he was fourteen, his little cousins would chase after him and yell, "Hey Jess." At the time, his sister was only two and misunderstood the shouts. She yelled along, "Peaches!" Although he hated the nickname at the time, now he fondly adores it. She passed away five years ago.

I apologize for his loss.

He says she's finally free from pain, so it was really for the best. Now that we're acquaintances, I ask Peaches if he knows Fuzzy Sweater's favorite drink. He laughs and asks me to confirm if I'm referring to Pink Fuzzy Sweater. I say, "Yes." He laughs. I'm not sure what's so funny, but then he says the woman doesn't drink. She's not twenty-one yet? He adds that she doesn't like drinking unless she's really upset or depressed. He's only seen her wasted once, when she failed a midterm last year. She prefers kiddie cocktails with extra cherries. Then I laugh. For twenty dollars, I ask him to deliver that exact order. I also ask him to add a shot of vodka to it. She can give it to a friend.

He would be happy to.

And when he asks, "Who shall I say it's from?", without thinking, I say, "The one."

I wince.

He says I'm cringey as hell but loves it.

He fills a glass with ice, pours in grenadine, and tops the drink with a splash of Sprite, then nods to the women in the back. He says the girls are celebrating tonight. The squealing one is mourning; she broke up with her boyfriend. He rests a stick of cherries on the rim of the glass; I slide another twenty onto the ledge and ask him to add an extra plastic cup of cherries to the order. An exaggerated pout spreads across his face, and he says, "How romantic," then he carries the drinks to the back. Knowing that Peaches is talking to her and possibly about me, the pain in my chest grows. When Peaches returns, he gives me a double thumbs-up. I want to speak to him, but a herd of drunk college guys has taken over the bar. Peaches gets busy filling their requests.

Uber will be here in a minute. The ache has only gotten stronger. What do I do? My face and chest grow hot. Do I leave? Find her? I grab my coat and turn to go.

I should call Jolene.

I should—

I shouldn't do anything—can't.

Fuzzy Sweater is walking towards the bar.

This time, when my heartache navigates the tables, she stares at her phone and heads towards my side of the horseshoe.

The pain intensifies.

A few seats away, she claims an open space. Something feels different. Before, she carried herself with confidence and an undeniable swagger, and I've never felt more unworthy of a woman. Up close, those qualities are gone. Her curves are still incredible, and her sweater remains tight. Her pale blue sweater. I thought it was pink… soft pink? My perfect memory is never wrong; the lighting must be off. Her top is clearly blue. My phone keeps dinging. Harrison won't stop until I finish my assignment. Peaches is busy quenching the college crew, so another bartender takes Heartache's order.

A tap beer?

Another flash from my phone alerts me that my Uber ride is almost here. I approach the woman. Several feet away, I sputter an embarrassing pickup line, worse than the drunk guy from earlier.

I think I just introduced myself as "The one."

She doesn't hear me. Thank goodness. Or maybe she heard and doesn't think I'm the one? *What am I—*I collide with a chair; it screeches across the floor and nearly falls over.

This time, she notices.

The chair.

I steady the backrest and ask her for something. Her name? Number? Hopefully not her bra size... She shrugs and looks down at her device. Where's the snarky evasion? The creative rejection? No need to spit out my beer either.

She sets her phone on the counter and looks up.

"What's your ClickYap?" she asks.

"Slide underscore OB," I say.

I tell her Slide was my college nickname. I played ball. Baseball. I was pretty good. Stole a lot of bases. A few hearts. 'OB' is short for O'Brien.

She taps her phone and doesn't respond. Heavy makeup covers her lips, cheeks, and eyes. The ache has disappeared. She collects her order and walks away without a second glance. Lucky for me, the view leaves a tattoo imprint above her hip. Letters? A symbol? I can't make out the image. She rounds the corner and returns to the back dining room.

She's gone, but the ache returns.

I check my phone; the Uber driver is here. I hurry outside. A blast of frozen air pelts my face and chest. Tiny snowflakes melt against my skin. I rush to the car. When I reach for the door handle, my phone dings.

The ache grows.

I fumble with my passcode and stumble into the backseat.

The driver asks if I'm okay.

Silence is my answer, because a girl named Kylie with a kiss emoji next to her name just added me on ClickYap. I smile, exhale, and text Harrison.

Me: Kylie. A full D.

"I've never been better," I say aloud.

The Pied Piper and her Accomplice
Friday, May 27th @ 5:27 p.m.

THE PROBLEM WITH rarely drinking alcohol is the uncertainty of how fucked up you may or may not become when you mix fruity shots and fermented beers. The last time I drank was the night of the red flag party… and the horrible murder.

The one certainty?

Tonight's not going to go well. My nerves twist tight in my stomach. I peek out the front window. The sun sets beyond the maple trees at the forest's edge. Knotty shadows spill from the trees and reach toward our house. My phone beeps, and I startle.

Milly: Piper is in one of her moods.
The Pied Piper: Warning: Milly is a mess.
Milly: I am not.
The Pied Piper: Yes, you are.
The Pied Piper: You're always a mess after you break up with Mark.
Milly: He broke up with me.
The Pied Piper: Don't be late, Kate!

Even though I'm on time and ready, Piper scolds me with teacher-like authority. Soon, thanks to her degree in physical education, she'll get paid to intimidate people. This spring, she finally graduated after a year as a super senior. And in August, she'll be moving to nearby Madison to teach hopscotch and kickball to privileged elementary students at State Street Prep.

Me: But it's what I do best.

From the downstairs hall, I snap a close-up selfie of my cartoon-widened eyes, hit send, and push aside the lingering worry about tonight.

Since Kylie's gone, Piper has taken over as our friend group's mother hen. I'm her wandering baby chick. And I'm not surprised Milly is a mess. Today, Milly has a valid reason to be upset because a freshman said her boyfriend, Mark, cheated on her.

At the bottom of the stairs, I give my reflection one last look.

Looking good, sister.

Too good, I think. I grab my bloody shirt off the end table. It's mostly dry. I smile and step outside just as Piper's vehicle pulls up the driveway.

The window slides down, revealing Piper's thick, black hair in a low pony. Her petite nose still makes me jealous, and her perfect, round, doll-like eyes make me want to down a bottle of Nyquil, to sleep away my under-eye bags and worry.

And she's not even the prettiest Rodrigo sister—sometimes the envy stings more than I want to admit. Self-consciously, I adjust my cleavage.

"That's an interesting selection," Piper says, eyeing me.

The red dress. I know, I know. Not my normal look. "I'm trying," I say. I awkwardly smooth the fabric while shifting my weight on the driveway. For once, I wanted to look pretty. Plus, Mother will be elated. It's time I make things right with her.

"What happened?" Piper squeaks when she spots the bandage.

"The lemons won today," I say, as I open the door and plop into the seat.

Her eyes soften. She knows today has been hard for me… and tonight is going to be even worse.

Once I'm seated, the engine revs, and we speed down the road.

"You know I've gotten pulled over a million times," she says, "but for some reason, I just never get a ticket." She sings, 'Never get a ticket'. I smirk. Piper cannot sing.

Milly sings from the backseat, "Worst driver ever."

The two start bickering over whose a better singer.

Milly is not only a model on the outside; she has a beautiful voice. But she's too shy to take the stage. She prefers giving private vocal lessons to tone-deaf kids.

I peek into the backseat. Milly is curled into a ball, small and broken, her wavy, strawberry blond hair cascading onto the carpet. A t-shirt covers her face, muffling her sobs.

Kylie and I met Piper and Milly Rodrigo in Middle School. The week before school started, Kylie and I received our 6th-grade class schedules and realized we didn't have a single class together. I begged Mother to call the principal and ask to change our schedules. Mother said it was time we learned to live as individuals. Kylie and I cried.

During my first three classes, Milly Rodrigo sat next to me.

I was in awe of her. There was no way she was an actual sixth grader.

She could easily pass for an eighth grader, maybe even a freshman. Her skin was creamy ivory, and shiny golden ringlets hung from her head. She wore snug, white socks in scuff-free Vans. Her green sweatshirt highlighted emerald eyes. Could a sixth grader's sweatshirt be sophisticated? If Milly Rodrigo wore it, yes. And white pants too.

Twelve-year-old girls don't wear white pants. They can't, because there's always an imminent threat of a sticky-fingered friend or a nearby drippy ice cream cone. And what about the foreboding scarlet river? I gasped. Was Milly so mature that she had already gotten her first period? And was also responsible enough to track her monthly cycle, giving her the freedom to plan out pastels?

Inconceivable.

The crowds parted everywhere Milly went. And when she walked through the 8th-grade wing, no one pulled on her braids or called her a nerd. In class, no one snickered when she gave the wrong answer. She was… untouchable. Mesmerizing. She was…

Popular.

Even though I was thoroughly annoyed with Milly's presence, she kept saying, "Hey," to me at the beginning of each class. After the fourth, "Hey," a breeze of roses drifted across the aisle and masked the sour onion stench radiating off the boy in front of me. I've always been a sucker for roses, so I reluctantly said hello.

Maybe she wasn't the worst person in the world after all? And maybe us having so many of the same classes and assigned seats next to each other was a sign?

Within a week, Kylie and I were invited to the Rodrigo family home for a sleepover. Before long, the four of us were eating lunch together every day. The summer after sixth grade, the Rodrigo family brought Kylie and me along on their family trip to Italy.

"Mark is an ass," I say to Milly. "Put on your seatbelt."

"Can't. I'm dying a slow and painful death." She gags as though she really is dying. "Mark is a cheater, and guess what? I deserve it." In between sobs and hiccups, Milly's startling green eyes flash to meet mine. "Worst girlfriend ever," she adds in a Mary Poppins sing-song voice.

"You may die anyway because your sister's driving is terrible, so buckle up," I say and click my own seatbelt into place.

"Mark cheated," Piper says. "He's the worst. Is this his fourth or fifth time? Don't you dare blame yourself." The two argue. Milly is positive she's to blame for Mark's unfaithfulness, and Piper is confident Mark's head has been up his ass for years.

After a few anxious brake taps, Piper curses under her breath. The gas pedal hits the floor, and we swerve around a slow driver.

"So, uh," Piper says. "How was your day?"

I sigh. I'm surprised Peaches hasn't told them already.

"Today was my last day," I announce.

"Flipping meat and toasting bread?" She gasps and opens a protein bar while using her knees to steer.

"And my dad kind of blew me off for the VP role," I say, staring out the window.

"Oh no, Kate," Piper says.

Milly comes alive and leans her head forward. She pats my shoulder. "Why would he do that?"

Shame heats my cheeks. She has a great question. I take a deep breath.

"My dad kind of wants me to get my shit together," I say.

"One day, you'll be a successful business entrepreneur, and we'll all say, geez, remember when Kate was that sugar-obsessed, lost soul who slept the day away?" Piper tries hard to make light of the situation, and I appreciate her support more than she knows.

"Your words are too thoughtful," I say. "Yep, I'm destined to succeed." Slowly, her words give me a boost of hope that I direly need.

"Are you going to work with your dad?"

"I hope so."

"Well, we need to get you a new wardrobe."

"Ok, Piper," I say.

"Suits and heels for the elevated status," Piper hollers at Milly, "babe, a shopping spree is in order."

Milly's sobs are suddenly loud, snot-filled, and growing more intense by the minute. She yells something that can't be understood. Piper tells Milly to stop overreacting. Milly retaliates with a foghorn-style nose blow into a shirt. She then tosses a crumpled napkin and an empty fast-food bag. More words are exchanged. The Rodrigo sisters fight much more often than Kylie and I ever did. Kylie and I have only fought twice. The first time was on family photo day in third grade. The weekend before Easter, Mother tried to win the title of Parent of the Year. She dressed her precious daughters in matching outfits of different colors.

A sky-blue dress for Kylie. Mine was blush pink. To Mother's dismay, Kylie and I fought like wild children over the silky pink dress. In the end, Kylie walked away with an unraveled braid, lace torn from her sleeve, and a missing shoe. During the scuffle, Kylie's rhinestone shoe buckle scraped against my face, leaving a deep cut along my jawline. Afterwards, my parents abandoned their previous way of telling us apart.

A polished pinky nail. *Oh, that's Kate.*

Disgusting facial scar? *Oh, that's Kate.*

Milly and Piper's sisterly banter continues, but now I'm thinking of Kylie again. Usually, my messages are positive and uplifting or stupid-funny. Today, I'm not feeling any of that. I tilt the screen away from Piper. She thinks messaging Kylie is unhealthy. She may have said it's a little creepy. After snapping a selfie and typing, my finger hovers over the send arrow, and I tap before I can change my mind.

Me: I'm so mad at you. I COULD SCREAM! Everything is ruined since you left.

What kind of monster am I? Sending a text in all caps?

Me: Sorry. Why would I be mad at you? This is not your fault. It's just… Today has not been a good day. I got fired! I still do love you schoo much. Nothing will ever change that. And I'm going to do everything I can to help you.

Even though I know Kylie won't reply, I watch for her avatar. *Will I see it again?* Or was I imagining things? I bite my lip and watch. Eventually, I set my phone on my lap and pick at an annoying hangnail.

"Kate, yes, or no?" Piper asks.

We're stopped at a red light, and Piper's hawklike stare transforms me into a nervous field mouse.

"Sorry, it's an enthusiastic yes for me," I reply, lacking enthusiasm or understanding of what she's talking about. Still, I figure I have a fifty-fifty chance of responding correctly.

"You've invited someone, or you've found someone to invite? Which is it? I need to know because, based on your answer, my meddling style will change."

A blank stare is my only response.

"The grad party? Do you have a date?" Piper asks, apparently for a second time.

"Leave her alone," Milly says, finally coming to life. She pokes her head forward, tissue in hand, and wipes black streaks off her face. "If you don't want to bring a date, don't."

This Sunday, the Rodrigo family is hosting a combined graduation party for Milly, Piper, and me at their home. Over the past few weeks, Piper has been bothering me daily, hoping I've found someone willing to be my escort for the event.

"Well, um, I was thinking..." The truth is, I haven't been thinking much because I've had no time for male disruptions. Hello, everyone— I've been too busy running into ghosts. Now I need to confirm and verify alibis. I have to hurry and help my sister before it's too late.

Piper must sense my cornered cat hesitation, because she places a maternal pat upon my leg. "Milly and I will think of something."

That's what worries me. I scrape the bottom of my feelings barrel and find a small spark of excitement. "Tell me more about the party. Who else is coming?" I ask cautiously, adding, "Will Cass be there?"

The sisters exchange a quick glance in the mirror. Then Milly digs into her makeup bag and flips her hair into a perfect messy bun. Piper stares at the road.

In a rush, Piper says, "I think he's still in Alaska," and at the same time, Milly quietly says, "Europe must be lovely this time of year."

I press my lips and stare at the cloud-stained sky. Stringy hair swirls in the wind and pokes my eyes. Either they think I'm clueless or wish I would detach from Kylie's past. More than likely, though, they know more about Cass than they're letting on. Probably all three. This lack of honesty and support is exactly why I can't share my mysterious Kylie dream with either of them or my more recent lakefront vision on the floor of Triple B's.

"There's something strange about that guy," I say. "Why did he and Kylie break up? Kylie never told me. And I know she didn't tell you guys. And did you notice how controlling he was with Kylie? If he couldn't get a hold of her, he'd often call me. Like, bro. Chill out and let your girl have a life of her own. Also, can we agree that Cass has a type? Kellie and Kiki looked just like Kylie. And their names all started with a K." I can feel myself rambling, and I'm sure Piper and Milly think I've lost my mind, but I have to get these feelings out. Someone must know something. Kylie needs my help. "And ever since Kylie's been gone," I add, "Cass has sent me random ClickYaps I've left unopened—always in groups of ten—and it gives off a super creepy vibe I can't shake. And why has he been MIA since the red flag party?"

Piper has ignored my questions about Cass, and now she's carrying on about the party playlist and demanding to know if I have a date yet.

As she nags, an ache forms in my stomach. The girls still don't know my diploma is on hold. So, celebrating my graduation is a bit premature.

Piper slaps the steering wheel and says, "We're setting you up with our cousin, Bert."

"Piper," Milly says, "Bert's kind of a mess. Find anyone else—"

"Wait," I ask," Your British cousin Bert? Wasn't he caught peeping in your neighbor's window last year?"

"Yeah, but it was a misunderstanding," Piper says. "Turns out a neighbor saw Bert shimmy from the second story via the downspout and thought he was a burglar, but burglars usually aren't naked—"

"Hard pass," I say and cross my arms. I have zero desire to hang out with bare-bottom Bert.

"Kate," Piper whines.

"What?" I whine back. "How about instead of you questioning me, I question you?"

Piper gives me a curious look, then eyes the road; Milly grips the seatback and leans forward.

"Absolutely," Piper says.

"Sure," Milly says cheerfully.

Both appear pleased I'm interacting with them. I turn in my seat. I'm facing Piper and can see Milly from the corner of my eye.

"What do you remember about that night of the mur—death?" I ask.

"What do you mean?" Piper asks and touches a finger to her lips.

Milly slides backward, out of my line of sight, and begins to sniffle again.

"Details about that night," I say. "My memory is still foggy, and I want to fill in the blanks."

"We've already told you," Piper says slowly. "The red flag party. Everyone was there. The stars. The scream. The light. The tremor. And then…"

"And then is right," I say, "That is exactly what I need to know. What happened next?"

"Why relive it?" Piper asks. "We have more important things to discuss. Like the party. The party that is *this* weekend." She rolls her shoulders. "So, Kate, are you coming alone? I mean, come on, it's time you had some fun."

Today, Piper will not share. Although she's normally shrewd and determined, the graduation party will be different. She's that girl in every friend group who has no off switch. Usually, after a night out, she ends up puking in the elevator or face-down in a row of bushes while everyone else patiently waits for the Uber. On Sunday, I will come for her after she's had a few drinks. Dammit, I'm now looking forward to Sunday.

Everything is slowly coming together. This weekend I'll get my life back in order. I'll help Kylie, destroy Niall, and find the murderer.

Ignoring their irrelevant party-planning talk, I press on. "What about Professor Holliday?"

"What about him?" the sisters respond in unison.

"I don't think he'll be at the grad party," Piper says.

"He's in town this weekend," I say.

"That makes sense."

"What if I told you both that he has something to hide?"

"Like what?"

I hesitate for a moment because Kylie swore me to secrecy, but sharing this news with my best friends can't hurt. In fact, it might very well help me get closer to the truth. This scandalous news could be important to my investigation. Piper and Milly might be able to help solve this mystery.

"Right before the red flag party," I say, "Kylie caught Holliday having sex with a student."

"What?" they shriek.

"Like that afternoon."

"No way."

"She told me every detail," I say in a rush of excitement. "She went to speak with him right after class, but his door was closed, so she called his name. She was going to leave, but then she smelled a candle burning, so she pushed her way in. Then she saw—with her own eyes—Holliday giving a personalized tour of the university."

I use air quotes when I say 'tour'.

"The 'tour' took place against Holliday's bookshelf, slightly to the right of his first edition Plato, directly above his unzipped khakis."

Piper and Milly shake their heads in disbelief.

"Kate, I really don't think Holliday would have sex with a student," Milly says. "He may be hot, but he's a gentleman."

Piper shrugs. "He's the hottest professor I've ever met, but I don't trust what Kylie might have said back then."

"Why would she lie?" I ask.

"Kate," Milly says, "let it go."

"I agree with Milly," Piper says. "Let it go. What you need this weekend, Miss Kate Vanguard, is a distraction."

She carries on for several minutes, offering up potential dates.

I barely pay attention, because the more I think about Professor Holliday, the more I wonder… is perception reality?

Over summer break, the professor posted a photo on his Instagram of steaming homemade lasagna and chilled arugula salad, complete with edible flowers. October showcased a panoramic shot of his yacht, the Twisted Sister. Scroll to his spring break photo collage featuring a rescued pup, Wally, at the Mayfair Animal Shelter. If your inner fangirl is begging to be let out, click on his author page. You'll find bright, white smiles and photogenic, non-sexual poses with his co-author, Estelle Vanguard.

The week after the murder, Auntie Babs listed his Kensington model, six-bedroom home for sale. In a fury of silk ties, vacuum-sealed lasagna, and haphazardly packed suitcases, the professor disappeared with his anxious Aussie doodle to neighboring Minnesota.

Why did he leave so suddenly? Was it because he couldn't handle the death? Or was it because Kylie was right all along and he had been giving A's for lays and B's for blows? Or was he part of something more malicious?

Which perception is reality?

I'm yanked back to the conversation when Piper pounds the steering wheel, completes a slow nod, and squeals. "I've got it!"

By the intensity in her pupils, her meddling style's amped to the highest degree possible. Critical. The vehicle slows to a stop outside Triple B's. She cuts the engine. Anxious to leave the cross-examination room, I quickly unbuckle my seatbelt. Before I can yank the door handle, the lock clicks.

Piper smiles deviously.

"I'm pulling the Pied Piper card. Opening ClickYap." She taps her phone and sings like a drunken songbird, "Scrolling."

"Oh, hell no," I say. I flick the unlock button.

Piper locks it with vampire-like speed.

"Scrolling!" Piper belts. "The connection is secured when I tap on a guy, and he'll be tapping on you Sunday evening."

"Piper, enough," Milly says.

"Baby, I'm the Pied Piper, and Kate will do as I say."

Curse my clever wit. In high school, I jokingly called Piper a Pied Piper one evening after she led Kylie, Milly, and me to a party filled with underage drinking and stoners. The four of us stood in the living room, surrounded by drunk, high teenagers. Milly refused any 'party favors,' but Kylie and Piper snuck off and did something—something they never admitted to. Anyway, at the time, I explained that a Pied Piper is someone who persuades people to follow them, often with a flute, but usually to their ruin. The nickname was, and still is, perfectly fitting.

Milly leans forward and grabs Piper's phone, but Piper yanks harder and wins.

"The man I choose," Piper says, "will enjoy an evening with the lovely Miss Kate." She eyes me. "There'll be a hundred percent chance of heavy petting, hands on your tits, tongue in your mouth, and possibly d—."

"Not playing your crazy dating roulette game," I say.

"Leave. Her. Alone," Milly says.

"We… are… landing… on…"

I rack my brain. How do I end the torture? A date. I need a date. Zakary would be the easiest choice because everyone, except Peaches, assumes we'll get back together someday. And as far as I know, Zakary's not dating anyone. Piper won't stop until a match is made, and today, Milly is too weak and sad to act as my relationship bodyguard. I'll throw a Hail Mary and hope Zakary is free this weekend and willing to play pretend with me on Sunday.

"Sorry, you said date?" I ask. "Totally forgot to tell you girls. Zakary's coming. We're hanging out again."

"Love that," Milly says.

"Sunday is going to be so much fun," Piper adds. "This grad party is going to be the party of the year. And, shockingly, for once I agree with Milly. Take it easy tonight, because we have a lot to do tomorrow. The decorators are coming over at nine. You'll be able to come over around then, right?"

"Okay," I say. "But I'm busy in the afternoon…."

Piper and Milly are quiet. "The wedding is tomorrow," I say. "Remember? May 28th. The big day. Wedding, anniversary, whatever you want to call it. Whatever they're calling it."

I purposefully miss their visual exchange because I look down too quickly. The sisters whisper to each other.

The wedding…

The anniversary…

She shouldn't be left alone tonight…

Or tomorrow…

Piper and Milly are terrible at talking about me behind my back, in front of me.

"I'm staying by my dad's tonight," I say, hoping to ease their worries.

They still look very worried.

"Girls," I say, "I'm fine. I'll help you in the morning and leave for Mother's around one. Plenty of time for all the things."

"Think of this weekend as the kick off to the rest of your life," Milly says, "College is over. We've graduated. We're contributing members to society."

"Right," I say, not feeling right at all.

We arrive at Triple B's precisely at six o'clock. The invite on the fridge says this is the rehearsal dinner, but for many reasons—one of which is that the entire wedding party has attended this charade twice before—no one will rehearse anything.

Inside the restaurant, Piper and Milly hug me and make their rounds. They can only stay for half an hour, then it's back to their house to decorate for the grad party. After they leave me alone, I wonder how quickly a person my size can get drop-down drunk. I Google, 'How to get drunk fast'. I find a drunk app calculator. Very scientific. As it downloads, I scan the crowd. At large gatherings, I prefer to blend into the crowd. But the sleepy-eyed barflies suddenly come alive upon the arrival of a blood-red dress. Sticky glances hit me from multiple directions, and the hum from a nearby group of vultures grows deafening. The dress, venue, and surprised glances all remind me of April 10th.

The red flag party.

"We are Young" plays in my mind.

Kylie had picked out my outfit, put on my makeup, and straightened my hair. She finished with a simple comment. 'Beautiful.' When I said she was even more beautiful, she responded as she always did. 'Not a chance.' Kylie claimed my unpredictable personality made me intriguing in a way she could never imagine.

The idea for the party started when Bear gave Peaches permission to host a small 'team builder' for the restaurant staff. Due to the short notice, only Roxy, Peaches, Babs, and I could make it. The other staff and servers were out of town. So, the get-together would be chill and harmless—just 4 guests. But when Piper heard about the empty bar party and saw the weather forecast for crazy warm temperatures, the night grew into something bigger, like the blob from Stranger Things—expanding into the most iconic party. The teambuilder fell over the bluffs, replaced by a wind-whipped red flag party inspired by a TikTok trend.

On Wednesday, April 6th, Peaches shared a video in a group text called 'Show me your flags!' Outside the restaurant, Peaches wore a red muscle tank top turned inside out. On it, in black Sharpie, it said: 'I'm a hoe for gardeners'. A stylish black headband completed his look. Using a selfie stick, he recorded the video invite.

"Who? Peaches here, live at the bluffs. What? The most epic party, crusty, dusty, and busty, Mayfair has ever seen. Time to celebrate, in true small-town freaky fashion, the fiftieth anniversary of the Mayfair Massacre. When? April 10th, of course. Shenanigans begin at 7 pm sharp. Where? Triple B's. Let's ring in the fiftieth anniversary of the Mayfair Massacre! Dress code? Bottoms can be whatever. But! You must wear a red top—T-shirt, sweatshirt, tube top, nipple patches—pick your poison! Additional rules? Glad you asked! Upon arrival, you'll be greeted at the front of Triple B's. Rule number one: wardrobe check! Violators won't get in! Number two: your Red Flag must be displayed on your shirt. Bold and clear, people! If you forget this, I will have a black Sharpie ready. What is a red flag? It's a statement—short, up to five words—that warns others about you. Here are some examples…"

The screen fills with fake blood, and vibrating words flash across: Allergic to Tacos, Kiss Me I'm Drunk, Free Booty Rubs, Would Rather be Sleeping. The camera zooms in on Peaches; he's spun around, with Triple B's as his backdrop.

"It's your party tagline," Peaches says. "What everyone thinks about you, but maybe doesn't say. Or perhaps, no one knows about you, but you're ready to reveal. Get ready, Mayfair, April 10th is going to be a night that goes down in history."

At the end of the video, words scroll upward, like a low-budget prescription marketing campaign:

Party is by invitation only.

BYOB (bring your own blanket). We WILL be star gazing.

Twenty-dollar cover (to cover my ass, and pay Bear back for unlimited drinkies).

Kylie, ZakAtak, The Pied Piper, Milly Rodrigo, and Cassidy viewed the message.

5 additional guests.

Since it was April 10th, Mother and Professor Holliday were camped on the bluffs, monitoring for paranormal activity. Mother ran the high-end tripod audio and visual recording device. Holliday carried the EMF equipment.

2 additional guests by proximity.

Kitty—as her closest friends called her—always made an appearance near Lake Michigan on April 10th. Sometimes Kitty appeared holding a baby or pushing a stroller.

1 ghostly guest.

12 suspects in total attended the red flag party.

 I mean guests.

Later that same night, Kylie and I had our second and worst fight ever. To this day, I can't remember what it was about—that memory is lost along with many others from that night—I only recall an intense pain filling my chest and tears streaming down Kylie's face.

By 11:58 pm that night, I believe one of our 12 guests committed murder.

One of the *11* guests.

I certainly didn't do it.

Standing inside the door to where Kylie and I had our big fight—our last fight—I slip on my dingy work shirt and wrap my arms around my stomach. Triple B's is alive tonight. Time for me to join in the fun.

Time to do some math. After the app downloads, I fill out the necessary fields. Considering my weight, the current time, and my light cherry-and-orange lunch, I'll need six shots—and no more. A bold notice at the bottom of the screen warns me that some people react more strongly to alcohol's hops than others, so I should use the app with caution. I'm not sure what to make of that, but I definitely need to be completely numb by seven forty-five, or eight at the latest.

I chew the inside of my lip and pinch the flesh on my arm. Suddenly, that overwhelming sense of doom is stronger. Something bad is going to happen tonight.

Group Chat
Friday, May 27th @ 5:44 p.m.

JUSTPEACHY: CAN someone keep an eye on her? I'm going to be busy at the bar. She's gonna be a mess tonight.

The Pied Piper: Milly and I can only stay for a little bit. We have so much to do for the grad party.

ZakAtak: I can.

Slide_OB: I respect the hell out of Mr. Vanguard, but the meeting this afternoon did not go well. Kate was pretty upset.

JustPeachy: And WHY are you the new VP?

Fauxy Roxy: Henry is spiraling, too.

ZakAtak: Peaches, please be nice.

Milly Rodrigo: We need to keep these text messages short. Please get to the point.

ZakAtak: How did the ride to Triple B's go?

The Pied Piper: Not good. Peaches is right. Kate thinks that one of us is the murderer. She drilled us about Cass.

Milly Rodrigo: Now Professor Holliday is a suspect.

JustPeachy: This is getting out of hand.

The Pied Piper: She said Holliday was fucking a college student.

ZakAtak: Holliday did what?

Fauxy Roxy: He's a grown-ass fuck boy. Are we surprised?
The Pied Piper: Not really.
JustPeachy: I don't believe it.
Milly Rodrigo: This is going to blow up in our faces.
Just Peachy: Please, everyone, just keep an eye on her tonight.
Slide_OB: I'll take care of her.

T&A

Friday, May 27ᵗʰ @ 6:03 p.m.

MY DESTINATION IS clear. Across the room, my dad is propped up at the bar, chatting with Peaches. After weaving through the crowd, I hop on the stool next to my dad. Peaches gives wide eyes as he stares at my outfit.

"Is that your bloody shirt from today?"

"I'm cold."

"You're in a funk."

"We're both in a funk," my dad chimes in.

Relief floods over me. Maybe he and I can get along tonight?

"You two need to talk," Peaches says. "I'll be back, because I have words for you, Kate." He gawks at my dress while walking towards the other side of the bar.

After Peaches attends to other thirsty patrons, my dad sputters out a quick compliment and says I'm as beautiful as Estelle. He requests to share a celebratory shot of Jameson with me. I concede. It's definitely the something stronger I need to save myself tonight.

After we clink our shot glasses and toss our heads back, the fiery liquid stings my throat. Suddenly, I can feel Mother glaring at me. I swear I won't drink much more tonight. Mother says that would be smart. Not much more than six. One down, five more to go.

My dad's face grows serious. My chest tightens in anticipation of his disappointment. Here comes the scolding. He clears his throat and fake coughs.

"Niall's taking over my job duties for several months," he says, staring at his empty glass. "I need to travel to Chicago for work. I…uh, I was worried you'd be overwhelmed on your own."

He assures me this is for my own good and promises it will all work out. I stop listening—I can't listen—my ears are filled with fresh dishonesty and betrayal.

I would expect this kind of strategy from Mother, but from my dad? This job—the VP role—was supposed to be a fresh start, my reason to try harder, an escape from living at home. Once my dad is finished, I ask the question I already know the answer to. I grip the counter to steady myself. "You don't believe in me?"

"That's not true. It's just these last few months. They have been hard on us all. Vanguard is a big responsibility. Too big to handle alone," he claims.

"I'm responsible," I say, hoping he'll agree, and the last few hours were merely a test in failing.

"This month," he says, "you slept through at least four shifts at the restaurant. The only reason I know is that you work Saturdays, and when you're still sleeping at noon, I know you're not where you're supposed to be. Last week, I asked you to check on the floor install for the navy-blue ranch, but you forgot, and now we're behind schedule." His belly heaves, and the weight of my deficiencies wears his spirit. "We need to stick together, Kate. Don't let this tragedy tear you apart… or us."

Dad examines the counter and says he hopes I'll continue working at the office because he'd be bored and far too level-headed if I weren't there to disagree with him regularly. He claims I keep his heart beating and calls me his natural pacemaker. He doesn't apologize, but I know he feels bad about today. And, although I should still be piping angry, I'm not mad at him. That anger has shifted toward the newest member of Vanguard Family Builders.

My dad's words are thoughtful—but I'm not ready to agree to anything. Yet. First, I must try to eliminate Mr. O'Brien. No—destroy him. Plus, my dad has been here since early this afternoon and is buzzed, so the alcohol is doing most of the talking.

Suddenly, Dad's rowdy groomsmen join us, and the celebration must continue. The group welcomes me with awkward hugs, manly pats on the shoulder, and they jokingly call me 'boss lady'. Suddenly, my mood brightens as I feel part of the group. A team player. I let out a breath of air I didn't realize I had been holding. It's time to relax and enjoy the night. If not for even just a few minutes.

The brood of construction workers includes cracker crumb Dale, two of Dad's high school friends, and Tomas, who owns a handyman business. They each wish to celebrate this special occasion in the same way Daddy does. Four more shots? It would be rude of me to say no, plus my deadline will be here before I know it.

I celebrate.

The shots of Kessler's tingle my lips. As expected, my sliced fruit lunch today turned out to be barely sustainable, so the booze hits me like a punch from a heavyweight champion. After our celebration, Dad and his buddies set off to join the bridesmaids and leave me wobbling on the edge of my stool, the edge of you know what, and the cusp of Mother's disappointment.

Mother hovers in my ear and says, "You shouldn't drink so much. It's very dangerous."

"Do you care?" I wonder, but already know the answer. She cares, but only because public drunkenness is sinful.

I grab an unattended beer from the bar and slam its hoppy contents. The amber lager, I think this one is 'The Call of the Wild'. It tastes like piss and has a lower alcohol content than my shots, but if I drink the whole glass… Several splashes miss my mouth.

When I lean back to steady myself, my shoe slips on a spill—the spill I just created—I overcompensate, careen forward, and douse red pumps with the mug of beer.

As Mother pours out her acid-coated concern, my blood sizzles, and the alcohol sliding through my veins births an amped-up Kate.

"…disappointed in you. You're drinking way too much," she says. "And now, I hear you won't be moving out. I do hope you get your act together. You're too young to be this flustered." I listen but not very closely, because I've had this conversation with myself many times tonight.

Everyone remembers the moment they first fell in love. They recall the color of the sky, the song playing on the radio, and the wine they sipped at the restaurant.

I've yet to experience such a euphoric moment. I do, however, recall the moment someone fell out of love with me. The sky was gray and rainy, a mid-afternoon spring day, and OutKast played "Hey Ya!" over the speakers at the mall. Kylie and I sat in the portrait studio's waiting room, staring at the purple and blue striped carpet. The photographer had just placed several large Band-Aids over my cheek and jawline. A smear of blood covered Kylie's white, ruffled sock. A scarlet line branded me imperfect. After that day, Mother never looked at me the same.

Disappearing eyes slice through my already fractured heart. And just as quickly as she appeared, Mother vanishes.

I congratulate my performance, the worst of the show for the evening. Time for my trophy.

"Hey, sexy," I shout to Peaches. "Double vodka on the rocks."

He holds up his index finger, finishes his current order, and then joins me. When he shakes his head, I reply with a fish face.

"You're drinking?" he asks with scolding eyes.

"Tonight I am. A little." I pinch the air and squint.

"I see," he replies.

"I don't," I say. "Please, don't judge me."

"Wouldn't think of it," he says. "Not tonight."

"Thank you," I say. "This celebration is lame. A bar? Everyone's getting drunk. We have entered the land of the lame."

"It may be lame to you," he says, "but everyone else is glad to be here."

"You think?" I ask.

He shrugs.

I shrug.

We both shrug.

He smirks.

I smirk.

He giggles.

I giggle.

"I love you," he says.

"I love you, too."

"I texted," he says, his brow wrinkling. "What gives?"

"Chicago tended my wound." I show him the bandage. "And you were right. He reeks of success."

"I'm sorry he had to be the one to help you," Peaches says. "I knew I hated blood, but I didn't realize the mere sight would paralyze me."

"To be fair," I say, "you did warn me. Did you faint?"

His shoulders relax, and he grins. "Yep, for all the shit we give Roxanne and her tits, I'm lucky they're so huge. When I blacked out, I landed right on top of her cozy melons. Almost took a nap. But seriously, if it weren't for her, Gucci would have landed right next to the discarded appys."

I laugh.

"Was Chicago a jerk?" he asks.

"Not at all, he was super nice. Annoyingly so."

Peaches hums.

"So," he says, "I'm glad neither of us has any permanent damage from this afternoon."

"I'm ready for my drink," I say. "Gimme… now. One extra-large Brandy Old-Fashioned cocktail. Hold the Brandy, extra Sprite… A straw. One of the big ones. And a bunch of shots, or beers. You pick." Words have become wet cotton balls, and I have difficulty unsticking them from my tongue. I check the clock behind the bar. For once, I appear to be ahead of schedule.

"Based upon your sloppy drunk behavior," Peaches says, "I may have to cut you off. You're acting aggressively, and you know Bear's policy on mean alcoholics. Not a good look on you, Kate. And no one orders 'a bunch of beers or shots'."

With a loud sigh, he pours me a sugary non-alcoholic beverage.

My body is heating up like an oven, so I unbutton my cover-up.

"Peaches, you're such a bore," I say. "Will you hire me again?" I shake my chest. The shirt slithers off my shoulders.

"First of all, that dress is insane on you. Wear it every day." He whistles. "But probably not an appropriate look for tonight. And you've got the wrong audience for those delightful mounds."

I try to look extra sad.

"I can't hire you back," he whispers.

"Henry double-crossed me." I slump in my chair. "Chicago is actually Mr. Niall O'Brien, and Mr. Niall O'Brien hijacked my job."

"What is Henry thinking?" Peaches asks as he wipes the counter.

I scowl.

"I want you to stay away from Mr. Niall O'Brien," Peaches warns.

"Apparently," I say, "Chicago knows all about business, business things, things related to business. Consequently…" I stumble on the word and take several seconds to spit it out. "Henry demoted me to Chicago's assistant. Can I puh-lease have my job back?"

"You know I have no control over that," he says, "but if you've had enough parental supervision, you can stay by me. Or I can cheer you up and kiss you on the cheek now?" He smiles.

"I'll take the kiss." I tap my cheek. "But if things get worse, can I be the big spoon?"

"You know I love you so much, right?" He looks as though he's going to burp or be sick. "I know a lot of terrible things have happened lately, but what if you were the hero in this story?"

"What?"

"What if the fire-breathing dragon was already dead, and you were free to ride off into the sunset?" His hand rainbows the air.

"Are you crazy?" I ask. "Dragons are everywhere, and the best heroines are all brunettes. Bella, Katniss, Hermione, and Elizabeth from *Pirates of the Caribbean*. Jess from *New Girl*. Even Pam from *The Office*." I point at the disarray atop my head. "Have you ever seen a platinum blonde save the day? Ever since Cinderella tumbled into Prince Charming's arms, through no effort of her own, the world has considered all blondes to be clueless. You've seen *Clueless*, right?"

"Well, the world is in for a surprise with this curvy blonde." He points at me.

"What if I'm not the hero. What if I'm the opposite?"

I tap into my long-term memory. Lately, I trust those memories more than I do my recent ones. But this time, I go way back. Back to when Kylie and I were still in Elementary School.

It was the summer Kylie convinced a boy she was me, and got him to kiss her. The summer I discovered that if I used enough of Mother's cream concealer and pouted, I could look like Kylie. The summer our dad realized he had two daughters and the summer Mother disappeared.

The summer my parents separated for the first time.

The day after my dad moved out of our two-bedroom home, Mother called in sick to work and spent the entire morning in our drafty, spider-web-infested basement. At lunch time, when I peered down the darkly lit stairs and called for her, she called back, "Found it! Kate, my sweet, baby girl! I found it!" She ran up the stairs and brushed a soft hand smelling of roses and stale cardboard against my cheek.

I watched as she ran across the street to Bear's house. A few minutes later, she returned, the helpful neighbor towering behind her. Bear shyly lifted a hand to me as he followed Mother to the basement.

The old stairs creaked and moaned, then there was a screech of metal against the concrete floor, then more creaks and groans. I spotted Mother's ratted head of hair first, then her stunning smile as she climbed the stairs. Behind her, Bear cradled a massive brown trunk in his arms.

Shiny metal accents and cursive lettering decorated the box. It was magical.

The two disappeared outside. From the bathroom window, I saw them enter the garage. I didn't know for certain, but I was pretty sure they moved the trunk to Mother's writing room, above the garage attic.

After that day, when Kylie and I weren't spending the night at Dad's apartment, we only saw glimpses of Mother at breakfast, a curve of her smile during lunch, and occasionally her bright silhouette at night through the window of her writing room.

One night that summer, Kylie and I pretended to be sleeping when Mother entered our room for a later-than-usual peck on the cheek. Mother's phone was on speaker as she talked to Auntie Babs.

Mother had found a breakthrough story. Part fiction, part fact. The story of a century! The one that every author hoped to write one day. The one avid reader pre-ordered on Amazon and paid full price for the hardcover copy. Full-price!

Mother had to get the story out of her head and onto paper. Her finished work would have romance, thrills, paranormal activity, and exaggerated details. And only a little fact.

She came to a new conclusion. The truth was not indestructible. The truth wasn't what would make her successful—quite the opposite.

Drama, partial truths, and lies sold. Fiction was king! But most interesting of all? The truth was rarely much different than a lie. The difference between the two was so thin that it could be sliced with a razor.

It should be sliced with a razor.

Until it was razor thin and the real and perceived truths could be extracted and examined, because both were equally important.

Soon after, she and Professor Holliday became very close. They worked together every weekend on their manuscript. With his creative writing background and her attention to detail, the novel was bound to be a success.

Later that summer, I remember Mother holding an advanced reader's copy of *Kitty Jossalyn Somewhere Beyond the Mayfair Massacre*. Professor Holliday came over to celebrate. He spent the afternoon explaining creative writing concepts to Kylie and me. The protagonist needed to exude spirit. Be likable. Rise above all odds. The antagonist worked against the protagonist. In their book, Kitty was the protagonist, and her lover was her opposition. Or, was he?

Peaches clears his throat. "Were you listening?"

"I'm the lover in my own story," I say.

"What?" Peaches asks, looking befuddled.

"I mean… What if I'm not the hero? What if I'm my own antagonist? My own worst enemy."

"I'm cutting you off as of right now," he says. "You have lost your mind."

Nora calls his name from the other side of the bar. I groan.

"What beef do you have with Nora?" Peaches asks.

"She's annoying."

"She's sweet and harmless."

"I think she killed Doe."

"What?"

"Mother's cat."

"I know who Doe is—was."

"Peaches," I say, gripping the counter. "Nora is obsessed with my parents. She acts like my dad is her dad and Mother is her mother. Nora would do anything to look good in front of my dad. She knows my dad hates cats. And yet, the day Nora is supposed to transport Mother's stupid cat to my dad's house, the cat dies mysteriously? The facts are pointing to a murder."

"Doe ate rat poison," Peaches states.

"That was put in her dish."

"Your dad said Doe Houdini-ed her way into his basement and clawed through a bag of rat poisoning, died on the kitchen floor, and that's how you found her."

"Everyone has secrets."

"You were the last one to see her alive," Peaches says. His accusation is playful, and I know he wants to make light of the situation, but his words sting.

"I wouldn't hurt a fly," I say aggressively. And I'm not sure who I need to convince. Peaches. Or myself?

"Enough," Peaches says. "Doe's death was unfortunate. I have to get back to work. Now, promise me you'll discard that filthy shirt. And try not to drink anything but water for a while. If you're in this condition tonight, I'm worried about how you'll be feeling tomorrow. And now that Niall is here… this is not good."

"What do you mean, Niall is here?"

"Oh, um, I saw him walk in like two seconds ago."

Feeling more annoyed than ever, I clench my jaw. Why would my dad invite a near-stranger to Triple B's tonight? This is supposed to be a celebration for close family and friends. Before I know it, hot anger replaces annoyance. If I see him, I will confront him and destroy him. Who does he think he is? He's not a Vanguard. He has no right to be part of my family's business or this stupid celebration.

"Who else is coming that I need to know about?" I ask.

"Everyone who loves your family—"

Just then, I notice that Professor Holliday has walked into the restaurant. I haven't seen him since that night. After the murder, he left Mayfair in the middle of the night. Everyone thought he was just shaken up. When I finally felt well enough to attend classes, a new teacher was leading his Creative Writing class. I didn't think anything of it at the time.

But now that Kylie has asked me to hurry and help, I can't leave any stone unturned.

As I watch Holliday make his way through the crowd, memories from that night come flooding back— the black sky, the cool breeze off the bluffs. He and Mother were checking the area for paranormal activity.

My heart stops.

Mother was with Holliday all night, and although Kylie swore me to secrecy about Holliday's activities, Kylie would have told Mother. She told Mother everything. Perhaps…

Professor Holliday had a motive to kill after all? This makes sense.

A heavy wave of fear rises in my belly.

"What about Professor Holliday?" I ask, fear forcing me to say things I might not normally say.

"What do you mean?"

"Maybe he's not the man we think he is."

"He has nothing to hide."

"Who actually saw it happen? I mean, it was dark, and we were all scattered."

"I'm not sure—"

"Exactly. No one really knows—"

"Holliday caught everything on video."

"You saw it?" I ask.

"I didn't, but some of the others did."

"Did they?"

"Are you suggesting Holliday would lie?"

"Maybe."

"Your mother's best friend and respected professor?"

"But that's just it," I say, stalling because Kylie swore me to secrecy. But I've already told Piper and Milly, so... I bite my lip and then whisper, "Professor Holliday has a dark side."

"You mean tall, dark, and handsome side?" he asks, smirking.

"Kylie caught him having sex with a student," I say. "Maybe he was worried she'd tell on him—"

"What?" Peaches asks, bewildered. "He doesn't have anything to hide. Secondly, there's nothing to investigate. And let's say there was a murder. What's the motive? Without a motive, there's no crime. That's blood and gore one-oh-one, gorgeous. Time to leave the past where it belongs."

"But Kylie needs me to help her," I plead.

Peaches leans forward. "After everything that happened... do you really trust what Kylie might have said *before*?"

I know Peaches cares about me. Maybe he's right? Could Kylie have been mistaken? Nothing makes sense lately. I let out a sigh. The bar is full, and Peaches can't keep me company all night. Plus, I have a busy agenda: find Niall, destroy Niall, find Professor Holliday, and confront Professor Holliday. Look at me being productive.

To appease Peaches, I promise to behave. He playfully rolls his eyes and says he'll be right back.

I blink. The alcohol has had time to run through my blood, and now I'm feeling quite calm. My prior fears and frustrations seem unnecessary. I spin on my barstool several times. Blink a few more times.

Suddenly, I'm surrounded by three ogling college students. One has his thumb tucked underneath my thigh, clutching the seat; I think he's the reason the chair stopped spinning. I recognize the other two guys. Juniors with permed brown hair. They're on Mayfair University's basketball team. The one who's touching me—let's call him 'perma-blush'—has moved his thumb so that it's just under my ass cheek. And he's… interesting. I don't recognize him, but his smile is deadly, and he can't keep his eyes off me, so I don't let him. I mean, I should be nice to him. He is the reason I didn't fall off the stool.

No doubt the sexy golf pro look has captured their attention. I adjust my sexy cover-up so that my shoulders are showing.

Within minutes, the alcohol transforms me into a friendly flatbed trucker, and before long, I'm telling my buddies 'your mama' jokes and dodging hideous pick-up lines. The three beg to buy me a drink, and I'd hate to appear rude, so I accept.

The room's center has shifted; it's under my feet. The galaxy around me thrusts into motion. Wait, the chair is twirling again. I spin in circles and giggle.

The smiling one stops the chair, grips my waist, and catches me before I tumble off. His boyish face and perma-blush cheeks make me wonder if he's even twenty-one, but he saved me from toppling to the floor and has asked me on a date, three, maybe four times, so I soak in the moment.

His two friends not-so-discreetly jab at each other in hopes of touching the soft red fabric. Perma-blush is winning, because he's not only gripping my waist, but his hand is currently on my thigh, and it's hot. Sexy hot. The jealous friends pry in between us and demand a group selfie. They're more interested in pics of my cleavage, but I don't mind that either. On Instagram, I add our pic. We exchange ClickYaps. Finally, I upload a stellar boob shot to my private ClickYap story. Piper immediately comments. Sexy AF. Milly saves the pic. Ari from my Calculus 3 class comments, "Look who's finally out! The girl who puts the T & A in Kate!"

'Finally, out?'

What's that supposed to mean?

Have I unknowingly maxed out my allotted time to grieve? Ari can fuck off. Roxanne loves the pic and says, 'Iconic'. Why is she commenting on my pic? She can fuck off too. Why are strangers commenting anyway?

Upon closer examination of my phone, it appears I accidentally uploaded the pic to my *public* ClickYap story.

Opps.

Before I can delete it, my newest, very best friends in the whole world beg that I thoroughly insult each of their mothers for a second time. After I'm done, we promise to stay in touch. Forever.

Peaches' digitally synthesized eighties pop music serenades the throng of impatient guests waiting for a table near the hostess station. Hall & Oates plays over the speakers; I can hear Mother singing along off-key. Her singing used to embarrass me. Time has softened many of my strong negative feelings towards her. Tonight I'm also feeling an overwhelming urge to apologize to her.

The restaurant is busy, even without the Vanguard party crowd. With the arrival of summer, patrons can enjoy outdoor dining for 2.5 more hours until sunset. The air is warm, the sky zebra-striped with blues and pinks. The garage doors raised. Outdoor tabletop fire-pits waiting to be lit at sundown. The air off the bluffs is fresh and fishy. In The Bear's Den, Mother's friends sip Chardonnay. Dad's groomsmen, including cracker crumb Dale, slam more shots. Reminiscing about the prior two weddings and the good old days.

Suddenly, I feel uh-may-zing.

Like on top of the world.

Why can't I feel this way every day? The boundaries of happiness are lifted, the air feels wispy. I grab my cherry drink off the counter. Together, we bob through the crowd in search of a bathroom. The bathrooms? My kiddie cocktail spills, leaving sticky juice running down my thigh. I've forgotten how many lavatories are in this fine establishment. To make matters worse, I can't recall its or their location. Tonight they're hiding from me. While I seek, I worry I may have an accident, but my spirit is coasting on a cloud of joy, so what do I care?

Finally, after what feels like a century, I run into my favorite and only ex of all time. Zakary. He bumps into me; I bump into him? Something liquid-y spills on my hand and makes my bandage wet.

"There she is," Zakary says. "And what have we here?" He looks me up and down.

"Bathroom. Pee. Now," I murmur and bounce from side to side. He removes the glasses from my hands and sets them somewhere. Zakary and I are somewhere on the tiny dance floor. The 80s sensation Wham! and the crowd of voices overpower my request.

"What?" he asks and leans in close. "You're mumbling, I can't understand you. And what happened to your hand?"

Okay, so I was mumbling quietly, and that's why he didn't hear me, but I have to pee so bad, and now he's stalling me and making me repeat myself.

For a second time, I shout my request. Zakary, with his caring hands, steers me in the opposite direction from where I was headed. Nothing new. I'm down; he picks me up. Lost, he organizes a search party. Hungry, he feeds me sugar-based treats.

The day after April 10th, when I awoke at the hospital, Zakary was at my side. He shared every known detail about that night. The truth destroyed me.

Could she really be gone?

He said no one could have saved her. It happened so quickly.

Silently.

A murderous thief in the night. Nothing could have saved her. Nothing. Nothing. Nothing.

Then my dad came into the room and told Zakary to stop bringing up the past. My dad said I needed to move on. We had each other and a bright future. But when I begged my dad to go to the morgue, he refused.

When I asked why, he said over and over, "I love you, honey. We'll get through this together. Can I get you some water?"

But I had to make sense of what happened.

There was zero substance to his coddling. When I pressed for details and facts, the answer was always the same.

Can I see the body?

No. We'll get through this together.

Can I see her autopsy?

No. I love you, honey.

Can I see the death certificate?

No. But would you like some water?

He assured me that all I needed to know was that she died of natural causes and was in a better place.

That evening, after he left me alone in the hospital, I sat on the cold, scratchy sheets and stared at the gray-speckled floor. Seventy-eight visible floor tiles. The wall held fourteen cabinets. The ceiling cradled twelve LED, recessed lights. One cobweb hung between the northeastern corner of the room and the first cabinet. Two monitors beeped next to my bed.

When my third shift nurse, Crystal, walked into my room—big hazel eyes, eyeing my chart—I complimented her pretty black hair and petite figure. Did she work out? Could she share her hairdresser's name with me? I'd simply die if she said no. What brand of adorable shoes was she wearing? And what an angel she was for bringing me a second dinner, after—in my distraught state—my tray accidentally slipped, sending a landslide of steaming meatloaf and jiggly Jello onto the floor. Oh, and her ombré nail polish was so chic. So… meta.

She blushed and said she had no idea what that meant but was flattered beyond words. Truth be told, I had no idea what that meant. I was totally winging it. And I'm pretty sure I was still a little loopy from hitting my head. She then went about nursing me. Adjusting my pillow, refilling my water, and gossiping about me outside the door with another nurse.

It wasn't an accident.

Or natural.

Do you think she did it?

Maybe.

Affluent families like hers have the darkest secrets.

You know what else I heard…

After nurse Crystal had been clocked in for two hours, I got down to business.

"Oh, nurse Crystal," I said, as I gripped the sheets, holding them close to my chest. "Could you pretty please walk me down to the morgue? My daddy wanted me to say a final good-night—"

At first, the tears came like a leaky faucet, then a waterfall. I told Crystal I needed closure… No one understood my loss… No one felt my pain… Could she do this for me? Please, please, please…

"Oh, sugar," the understanding nurse said and took my hand, "let me walk you down there. If you need to say your final goodbye, who am I to say no?"

The elevator ride to the subfloor seemed to go both lightning-fast and take forever. When the doors screeched open, the hallway wasn't eerily dark. There wasn't a faulty, flickering light loosely hanging from the ceiling. Not like in the movies. No cramped stretchers covered with sea foam mattresses. No model-esque medical examiner holding a scalpel.

The hall was brightly lit and carried a summer floral fragrance thanks to several plug-in fresheners tucked into the wall sockets. And the space was very tidy. Not a single dust bunny on the floorboards. Nurse Crystal held the door open and quietly said, "I'll give you privacy."

The attendant on duty was "Assistant Evers." His face was solemn. He wore a clean but worn white medical coat. A stark contrast to his father, Dale, my dad's lifelong, blue-collar friend. A man who has dirt in at least one crevice on any given day.

The room was silent, apart from the hum of a nearby floor-to-ceiling stack of doors. The freezer, I imagined.

In a kaleidoscope of grays and whites, the truth lay in the middle of the room. Her face appeared swollen but clean. Her pink lips had never looked so pale. Her bleached-white skin had never looked so white. A sleek head of blonde hair had never been so severely pressed against her scalp. A dusting of white powder makeup covered her skin. A thin cloth lay over her breasts and waist. She looked nothing like the vibrant woman I remembered.

Next to her body, on a metallic tray, was a sheet of paper. On it was scribbled: HCM? A harsh line slashed through the letters. When I peered forward to get a better look at the smaller writing underneath, Assistant Evers' nails caterwauled against the table as he scooped the page up in his hand. Frightened by the piercing screech, I staggered backward and bolted to the elevator.

After that day, nothing seemed possible. My future came to a halt. I was frozen in time. The past was incomprehensible. The present? Unreal. The future? Non-existent.

My family was broken beyond repair.

I had to understand more. But since my dad was unwilling to share the private details from the autopsy or death certificate, I would need to complete my own research. Back in my hospital room, I googled HCM on my phone.

Hypertrophic cardiomyopathy...

A rare genetic heart condition…

Hardening of the heart…

Often goes unnoticed…

Kills instantly…

Suddenly…

Without warning.

What did it all mean? The articles only left me with more questions. In the weeks after April 10th, I became obsessed with learning about her final moments. Was she in pain? Did she know she was dying? Could someone have saved her?

I couldn't answer any of these questions, but an expert could. So, I searched online for the best heart doctor in southeastern Wisconsin and found Dr. Miracle. His profile picture showed a middle-aged, African American man with kind eyes. I had always wondered what it meant for someone to have kind eyes. Dr. Miracle cleared that up for me. Plus, I had hoped his last name was foretelling.

Then I called his clinic and asked the receptionist to have the good doctor call me regarding an urgent matter. Even though I left my information several times, I never received a call.

Eventually, I scoured the internet and found the doctor's contact information. I sent him a Facebook friend request, added him on ClickYap, and even left a 5-star Google Business review for his practice. Ridiculous, I know, because he wasn't my primary.

Nevertheless, it was only when I showed up at his beautiful colonial home in Bayview while he and his grandchildren played catch in the backyard that I captured his attention… and a restraining order.

But he misunderstood my intent; I wasn't trying to murder him. I wanted his medical expertise. Although looking back, my networking method was questionable. I should have connected with him via LinkedIn instead.

The alcohol slugging through my veins suddenly gives me a strange sense of clarity. *I need to leave the past in the past.* Maybe everyone is right?

I'm pulled back to reality as Zakary rubs his thumb against my palm. During our trip through the busy restaurant, Zakary asks if I'm feeling okay. I close my eyes tightly and nod. If I move too abruptly, the water's going to get really warm.

"What's with this music selection?" he asks. "Is this song on an eternal loop? Every time I walk in here, I feel like Lionel Richie is saying 'Hello' to me."

"Peaches is flexing his 80s playlist tonight," I say, "hoping to win over Mother."

And I have to pee really badly now.

We arrived at our destination, although the trip was a little bumpy. When we stop moving, I feel carsick. To prevent the vehicle from shaking anymore, I neck-hug Zakary and keep my arms wrapped for longer than I would sober. I blame the alcohol; it couldn't have been the kiddie cocktail's fault. His neck reminds me of Irish Spring bar soap, and his warm shoulder supports my woozy head.

"Is your shirt made from a down comforter?" I ask and rub my cheek against his chest. "Or a baby blanket? It's super snuggly."

"Look at you, Kate." He unwraps my arms and cups my shoulders. "You're so wasted, and it's still so early." He chuckles. "This is exactly why you can't drink."

I should scold him for making fun of me. I'm not the one who was driving carelessly. It's his fault I'm nauseous.

"Do you want a ride home?" he asks.

"Nope, you were swerving a second ago. I don't trust your driving."

A buzzing noise comes from his ass. "I have to take this." He points behind me. "Bathroom doors at the end of the hall, in case you forgot."

He smiles, and I hate him and love him all at once.

"I'll wait over here," he says.

After telling him not to treat me like a child, I spent the next minute struggling with the door handle, like a child. I pull as hard as I can, but it won't budge. Then the door swings inward, and someone walks out. I tip forward. More caring hands catch me, and although I resist the help, my struggle is useless because this person won't budge.

The sturdy person blocks the pathway. The sturdy man. *A Man?* I'm very drunk, but a man in the women's restroom is still unexpected. But as my dad says, times have changed. I contemplate whether I should share this scandalous news with Mother. She'd simply die. Before I can decide, the blurry, solid figure fades, clears, then transforms into a familiar face. Angelic. Devilish. Delicious. Bossy.

The face of a job-stealing thief.

It's my sworn enemy. Mr. Niall O'Brien. With my good hand, I make a fist and slug him.

Velcro Balls
Mon, Feb 7th

HARRISON'S LOUISVILLE SLUGGER cracks the baseball.

"Slide," Harrison says, "you're a fucking idiot." The ball clips the bat and swerves out of control.

"Damn, Battering Ram," I say. "You're failing today."

The scary thing is, I'm starting to wonder if Harrison's right. A week ago, I was ready to propose to my long-term girlfriend. Now, Jolene and I are over; I did not see that coming. A week ago, I was adamant I wouldn't work for Henry. Now, I have a twenty-five percent stake in Vanguard Family Builders; I didn't see that coming either. Said I wouldn't consider pursuing a new relationship, but here I am. Obsessed with Kylie.

"C'mon," Harrison says, "that was a wonky pitch. And it's *The* Battering Ram. As in *The* Ohio State."

"I'm playing it cool," I say and hang my fingers on the diamond-netting.

"And that's exactly your problem." He pivots and points the bat at me. "You're playing it way too cool. Kylie is a fucking hot name." He turns around just in time as the pitching machine launches another fastball.

"You don't keep a girl like her waiting," he adds. With a crack, the cowhide sphere sails straight across the gym and bounces against the netting.

"You failed a little less on that one," I say. "It's only been three days. I'll text her tonight after my call."

"How did the Oxford meeting go?" he asks.

"I signed with them yesterday." I smile, the smile of a winner.

"Pretty soon you can afford me," Harrison says and takes a practice swing, "and that company car… for me."

"Work together again? Nah, you're too much of an ass."

He swings. Another ball sails. "So, when you finally Velcro your balls back on, what are you going to say to this hot Kylie?" He props his Slugger against the bat rack and holds open the cage door. "You're up."

"I'm in town and want to meet for dinner." I enter the cage; he tosses me my Marucci bat.

"By the way, you can thank me anytime," he says and takes my place outside the cage.

"For what?"

"If it weren't for me, you'd still be obsessed with Jolene."

"If it weren't for you, my personal life would be much less chaotic." At the plate, I align my feet with my shoulders. My foot closest to the pitching machine inches forward. I shift my weight to my back foot. "Kylie was different."

"If the girl is different, maybe you should act differently? Considering your last girl was closely related to the devil, we both know your judgment sucks. Listen to me; I'm your voice of reason."

"Voice of insanity," I correct him. I take several practice swings. The muscles in my back stretch and strain. Endorphins kick in. "Jolene didn't do anything wrong." I reset my stance. A ball projects towards me; my bat collides with it.

"You getting weak?" he asks. "Maybe you should work out more? Wait, did you forget to wear your gay necklace? And that's a damn lie. You were so caught up in the idea of her that you refused to see the reality of who she really was."

I focus on the next pitch and tighten my stance. "It's not the gay necklace that gives me my good luck. It's the super cool ring attached to the gay necklace. That's my charm." A crack echoes throughout the gymnasium.

"So, this Kylie?" he asks. "What's with her? I've been begging you to ditch Jolene ever since she moved to L.A. Well, really—how long have you two been together? And by the way, the ring is gay as fuck. What's it called? A Claddagh ring? Listen. Claaaa-duh. It sounds gay."

"How could you forget?" I ask. "Remember that client party Damian threw at his downtown penthouse?"

"Which one?" Harrison asks.

"When Mrs. Deveraux tried to get me in bed?"

Harrison shakes his head no.

"Lance was doing coke in the bathroom," I say, trying to refresh his memory.

"Bruh, that was every penthouse party."

"Same night you fucked Deveraux's pastry chef?"

"Oh, yeah. That night. What can I say? When I told her my nickname was 'The Battering Ram', she went wild. What a fucking, crazy night. I was scrubbing sugar granules off my skin for days. Somehow that shit got stuck in the crack—"

"Same night Jolene and I met," I interrupt him.

He grins. "I remember now. After you declined Mrs. Deveraux's hand job, Jolene showed up with Lance."

"Their entrance was timely."

"So, were Lance and Jolene like together? If they were, I totally missed that."

"They weren't," I say. "Don't you remember Damien introduced Jolene to the group? He gave that whole speech about how Jolene's family and his had been longtime friends. Lance and Jolene grew up together…"

"Might have missed that."

"Really?"

"Must've been when I was banging the pastry chef in the pantry."

"To answer your original question," I say, "you have been a dick about Jolene for six years."

"Six? Dang," he says, then pauses. "I've been begging you to drop her for six years, but you've never listened to my wisdom. And now, suddenly, within minutes of Jolene kicking your ass to the curb, you ask a girl out?"

"It was closer to two hours, and I didn't ask her out, yet… technically."

"But," he says, "you fantasized about her, stared at her, approached her, had a very short and awkward interaction, got her contact info, and intend to fuck her?"

"She actually got my info… but your summary is semi-correct." I shrug. "I'd like to get to know her first," I smirk.

"Of course, of course. Chivalry is your damn middle name."

I smile.

"Even so," he says, "the ultimate goal is to fuck."

"I guess," I say, "ultimately, after I get to know her."

"I still don't get it." He shakes his head. "I've introduced you to at least a hundred women in the past few months, and you didn't even flinch. What's so great about this girl?"

I take two more swings.

Harrison's question is valid because I can't put into words what's so great.

"She's… different," I say.

Harrison asks me about Kylie's hair color. Blonde. Electric. He says electric isn't a color and calls me an idiot. What was she wearing? Everything was tight. And girly. And pink, maybe blue? Maybe blue? What the fuck does that even mean? I think she changed her shirt. This time, he calls me a fucking idiot. What did she say? Actually, nothing. Nothing significant. She asked for my ClickYap. He says I have no game, then asks me to confirm her bra size. D. He pumps a fist in the air and howls.

I can easily answer his questions—I'm still confused about the shirt color—but her personality is a mystery. When Kylie walked into the bar for the first time, her interactions with the staff and those losers captivated me. Reminiscing about those few minutes brings the dull ache back to life. And I want more. More of that pain. But with Kylie's second appearance, her mysterious, kryptonite-like hold over me vanished. Maybe she was drunk at first, and during that short time, lost her buzz? Or was she sober, and then got totally wasted off the drink I bought her? But in a matter of minutes? Not possible. It's like she had two separate personalities, as though she were two different people.

Was I hallucinating?

But I can't tell Harrison any of this. He'll call me an idiot again.

Before Jolene and I dated, when I'd connect with a beautiful woman at a party or through a friend, I'd always wait several days before calling or messaging. That was my rule. No matter how much I was into her. And usually during those few days, I'd completely forget about the girl. None were memorable. And most I never ended up calling or messaging.

But I can't seem to shake Kylie.

No one could possibly be sexier or more intelligent than her.

"Talking to a woman for two minutes in a crowded bar gives you a fuckability factor, nothing else," Harrison says. "That's perfect for you, because you need a good fuck. And, even better, you and Jolene are over, so hopefully the fucking will happen sooner than later."

I turn my head and destroy the last ball.

The truth is, I wish I had spoken to Kylie for two minutes. I barely said a few sentences; I can't even remember exactly what I said or asked.

Harrison collects his bat and our bags and hands them to me when I walk out of the cage. Our gym—Pinnacle Success—is also Chicago's largest gymnasium and fitness center. Harrison and I usually come here daily to let off some steam.

"Text Kylie now," Harrison says, and turns so that he's walking backwards towards the exit. "Must I reiterate? You need to get laid."

"I'm not messaging her yet." I toss the bags over my shoulders. "Plus, my hands are full." I shrug. "You're making me haul everything. Can your lazy ass do anything?"

A mischievous grin suddenly replaces his annoyance.

Seconds later, he sprints behind me. I spin, hoping to dodge whatever asshole prank he has in mind, but the gear weighs me down, so I stumble.

"What the fuck," I say, as he reaches around my waist.

Before I can react, he yanks at the pocket of my sweatpants. With my hands full, I'm unable to stop whatever he's doing.

"Get your gay hands off me," I growl.

Once his attack is over, he sprints several feet away. He smiles triumphantly as he holds my phone in the air.

"Dude," I say. The duffel bags drop to the ground.

He hunches over, ready. "If you don't agree to text her right now," he says, "I'll message her for you."

I charge. "How do you always know my passcode?"

Upon impact, we topple to the turf. Wrestling ensues. He gets one good jab in my side; I plant a fist in his stomach. Just because we're friends now doesn't mean we don't fight anymore. It simply means we don't send each other to the emergency room anymore. We grapple. The phone is the prize.

"You have gotten weak," he says. "How am I still hanging onto this phone?"

"Give it back."

I wince as he twists my arm. In return, I twist his harder. After what feels like too long, I begin to wonder. Maybe he's right? Why am I waiting?

"I can't be held accountable for what I might say or send," he says.

"Fuck off," I say and tug harder on the device. "I'll message her."

"You better."

Finally, Harrison lets go. I push off the ground. Like animals, we slowly circle each other. Like prideful men, we hurl more insults. After catching my breath and before Harrison does something stupid, I type a message to Kylie. I show him the message.

Me: Hey, Kylie. It's Slide. From Triple B's Brewery the other night.

He reads the message, then looks at me, disgusted. I hit send.

"You didn't even ask her out," he says. "And isn't it called Triple B's or Bear's Bluffs and Brewery? It's not Triple B's Brewery. And she already knows your name." He rakes his hands over his face. "It's worse than I imagined. You have absolutely no game. You're clueless when it comes to women."

Once again—and I'm shocked to agree—Harrison's right. I fucked up the restaurant's name, but the text is already sent. See, this is what happens when I text under duress. I curse to myself.

"Girls like a little mystery," I say, rationalizing. "My technique is proven."

"What kind of technique is that?" he asks. "Vague and boring? And when did you ever prove it? Jolene is the only girl you've dated since we met. Your technique has never been proven."

"During that time," I counter, "you've never even had a long-term relationship."

"I won't waste my time or lead women on," he says. "That's the difference. When I meet the right one, I'll know."

"So, one day you're going to meet a girl and instantly know she's the one?"

"Yep."

"That makes zero sense."

"It's no different than how you feel about this Kylie girl."

How is Harrison able to spin pure nonsense into logic?

In the gym's parking lot, Harrison pops open his trunk, and we toss our bats and bags into the back of his black Suburban. A small cardboard box gets crushed under his backpack.

"Shit," he says, "I forgot to give this to my dad." He leans forward and pulls the box towards him.

"What's in the box?" I ask.

"Your shit."

"What shit?"

"Your fucking voodoo death shit."

"What the fuck are you talking about?" I yank the box from his hands and slide it closer. Written on the top in black Sharpie are the words: 'Niall's Voodoo Death Shit'.

"What the hell?"

"Your voodoo death shit," Harrison repeats himself. He flips the cardboard flaps open. He tips the box so I can see.

At the bottom of the box lies the bird skull, a bouquet of black chrysanthemums, an envelope, and a tiny Niall replica voodoo doll. I quickly back away.

"Why'd you keep it?" I ask.

"Evidence."

"What?"

"Obviously, someone has it out for you," he closes the box and shoves it back into the trunk. "I'll have my parents take a look at it to see if they can figure out who sent it. They're private detectives; maybe they can make sense of it."

"Damien and fucking Lance," I say. "They're responsible."

"Maybe. But maybe not. What if someone else has it out for you? You still don't know who was trying to steal your identity. All of this may be related. And someone other than Damian's family is responsible."

"Well, whatever," I say and walk towards the passenger's door. "Keep that demonic shit away from me."

"You're too superstitious," he hollers. "There's a logical explanation for this, and you'll thank me once I figure it out."

✳✳✳

On the ride home, Harrison says he's concerned Jolene has my balls in her purse. He says if Kylie hasn't replied to my weak message by Friday, he's taking me out, and I will get laid. He has a secret fishing spot that never fails. Lots of needy, horny, available piranhas. And no, it's not the grocery store.

After Harrison drops me off at Soo-jin's, I head to the living room and collapse on her leather couch. Painter's tape lines the walls and floorboards. Soo-jin is in the midst of renovating a three-story, seven-bedroom Victorian home. Until the insurance company completes their due diligence on my destroyed condo—and pays me—this is my home.

Stretched out on the sofa, I get lost reading an article about baseball spring training on my phone, then get bounced into a news flash warning the locals about a thief breaking into high-end homes. At some point, I find myself taking a quiz called 'Is she the one?'. When I'm about to click submit, my arms begin to tingle and feel numb. I look at my watch. An hour has passed. *What am I doing?*

I have proposals to finish and meetings to prepare for.

I reluctantly hop off the couch and head to the kitchen—I guess I'll never know if Kylie is the one. Inside the refrigerator, Soo-jin has a plastic container with a post-it note stuck to the top: 'Dinner - microwave 2 minutes'. I open the container. Homemade enchiladas and orange rice. Soo-jin loves to cook and is a sensational chef.

I love to eat, so this new living arrangement is working in my favor. But it's truly been beneficial for both of us. In return for Soo-jin's hospitality, I've been watching Bennett more on weeknights. If Soo-jin goes into the office, she won't arrive home until well after seven o'clock, so Bennet and I enjoy a few hours of bro time.

While I'm devouring the enchiladas, I text Soo-jin and thank her for the meal. She writes back and says she and Bennet will be late. She's visiting with Zoey, her babysitter.

Full and tired, I head into the guest room. I slink out of my hoodie and sweatpants. After showering, I prop my device against a glass of water on my nightstand. I roll onto my side and watch for Kylie's name to flash on the screen. After what feels like forever, I finally fall asleep. Tuesday comes and goes; Kylie doesn't respond. Wednesday passes, still no response. On Thursday, I haven't given up on Kylie, but Harrison has.

Friday morning, Harrison shows up at my door and says the outing is on, promising I will get laid before midnight. He barely gives me time to toss on a sweatshirt and joggers before he drags me out the door. On the way, he won't give up any details. He says the anticipation will be worth the wait.

At our gym, we head upstairs to the second floor. I follow Harrison into a rectangular, mirrored room. At least twenty women are milling about. Stretching and chattering. Harrison whips off his heavy sweatshirt and track pants, revealing nothing underneath but tiny gym shorts. He closes his eyes and jogs in place. When we walked into the room, the women gave us a quick glance. But now they're blatantly gawking at Harrison. Within seconds, every pair of eyes is staring expectantly at me.

I want to follow Harrison's lead and toss off my shirt too, but I feel as though I'm at the zoo *inside* the lion's cage. Plus, I didn't bring shorts. Large beads of perspiration collect on my forehead and lower back. The instructor—plain, vanilla, skinny, but strong and authoritative, rocking a buzz cut—reminds us to fill our water bottles. She says the room temperature is elevated to ensure optimal results. And if anyone needs to leave the room for a moment, she won't judge.

It's hot. Super fucking hot. Standing still, I'm sweating profusely.

Hairston stops hopping in place like a moron and hands me a pink mat. He's smiling and totally enjoying my discomfort. I reluctantly toss off my shirt. But keep my sweatpants on.

The women form two lines in front of Harrison and me. We are in an ocean of sports bras, tight shorts, leggings, panty-lines, thongs, biker shorts… oh, hello white, booty shorts. And… no panties. Good morning to you. Hot asses are everywhere.

"Namaste, class. Welcome," the instructor says. "I'm Meredith, and I'm so excited to be with you all today. As many of you know, today's Bikram yoga session…"

Meredith shares the benefits of sixty, uninterrupted minutes of stress-relieving heaven.

We are fucking doing yoga.

Meredith softly commands, "Half-moon… awkward pose… eagle pose…"

Within minutes, sweat is pouring down my face and back.

During the session, I copied White Booty Shorts. The view is decent. The stretches loosen me up, and I begin to feel relaxed. The workout isn't terrible. While lunging and stretching, Harrison points out several options for me, but I decline each. I don't say it aloud, but the women don't compare to Kylie.

"You met this girl, big deal," Harrison whispers in the middle of us sitting and stretching forward. "Kylie is not interested; she hasn't responded. Move on."

"She was the quality of Jolene, though," I whisper. "I felt it. But better."

"Better is… better," he says. "Jolene fucked you up. You almost lost out on that opportunity with Wolfgang because of her. Then, after you spent all your time pouring into her, she dumps you. That's the girl you run from. And I know you still don't believe me, but she's evil."

Before the class is over, Harrison earns wingman of the year, proving I don't need Kylie. He connects me with three available women. Within minutes of leaving the studio, they each sent eager messages and pleasing attachments.

The morning session strengthens my confidence and kills my hamstrings. But by Friday afternoon, I have a massive hangover. Kylie consumes my mind, so I block the hot asses. I'm holding out for my heartache.

172

Unrequited Anger
Friday, May 27th @ 7:14 p.m.

MR. O'BRIEN DIDN'T budge after my fist collided with his bicep, not even a fraction of a centimeter. Instead, he steadied me with his stupid, supportive hands while I swayed. Worried I'd have an accident if I punched him again, I jerked away and hurried inside the bathroom.

Now safe in the restroom, I get furious because the bee paintings on the walls and honey pot vases lining the counter are gone. They've been replaced with sleepy, drunk bear statues. The new decor is a disaster. In just a few hours of getting fired, the place falls apart.

Frenzied, I lather up, wash vigorously, then wince as pain spreads across my left palm. The soggy bandage hangs from my hand. I carefully peel off the gauze. At least the cut isn't bleeding anymore, just throbbing and raw.

I carefully dry my hands with a paper towel, then glance at the mirror's reflection. The cover-up has ruined the dress's enchantment. Kylie has disappeared, and chaos stares back. I finger-comb the crown of my head and rake a clump of hair forward. My cheeks are an unnatural shade of embarrassment, my chest is ghostly pale, and my mind is overcast with a chance of rain.

The devastation looking back at me from the mirror is Mr. O'Brien's fault. He had no consideration when he stole my future. My life would be glorious without that man. Wait. Mr. O'Brien is no mister at all. No gentleman, either. He's just an ordinary O'Brien. And that's even too much. Brien will do.

Before I leave, I drink rusty water straight from the faucet. After gulping for several seconds, I wipe my chin and start to panic. What if Brien is waiting for me in the hall? I did physically attack him; he might want to press charges.

Does it matter if he does?

Can my life get any worse?

Why is he even here? Why would my dad invite him? Tonight was supposed to be a private gathering for close family and friends.

Oh, that's right.

Brien is now an 'integral' part of Vanguard. I groan loudly. I've already embarrassed myself in front of Brien several times today. I guess if I walk outside this door and he's standing right there, ready to reprimand me, it won't matter.

On my way out, I remember to pull the door inward. In the hall, Zakary and Brien stand next to each other, talking. As if they sense my dagger-like glare or are more likely to hear the door thud and my audible curse, they look in my direction. Practiced, sympathetic smiles greet me. Have they become best friends while I was gone? No, they've formed a club—a group whose main goal is to pity me. A 'Feel Sorry for Kate' club.

I ignore the dream stealer and snap at Zakary, "Really? Talking to him? About me?"

While the sweet man walks toward me, he fumbles out an "Um," "Ah," and "Well." Zakary's warm hands settle on my shoulders.

Once in front of me, he becomes a barricade. Now my least favorite person—Brien—stands behind Zakary, and I can glare as much as I want.

"My current situation is Henry's fault," I hiss into Zakary's ear. "And that guy behind you, so don't become his friend. That meanie stole my job."

"Niall and I just met, uh, in the hall," Zakary says, cheeks turning pink. "Kate, he can hear you."

The fog of confusion around us isn't Zakary's fault. He's as innocent as they come. "Sorry," I say, resting my forehead on his shoulder. "I'm not mad at you."

"Kate," he says, "you don't have to apologize. I'm sorry your dad didn't give you the job." His comforting hand strokes my back. It's time for a better apology; I look into Zakary's hazel eyes.

"I'm truly sorry, Zakary," I say. "Thanks for trying to save me, though. Turns out, I'm un-save-able. A bull? I have no idea if that's a word. But my point is… don't bother. I'm helpless. Hopeless. Here's to Kate Vanguard," I say, lifting my hand in a mock toast, "the girl who can turn possible into impossible. Success into failure. Co-workers into enemies. Give her five minutes, and she'll undo years of progress."

A light punch hits his chest; he doesn't deserve a forceful jab. Plus, he'd probably cry if I did. "I need another drink," I say. Tender fingertips brush my shoulders.

"Let's hold off on that for now," Zakary says. "You know, I've been thinking. We really need to catch up."

"Did you get all of Mother's stuff moved out today?" I ask, then quickly peer past Zakary. My nemesis is leaning against the wall. Cozy. Chill. Not a worry in the world.

"Everything but the recliner," Zakary says, "the living room TV, and the master bedroom set. We'll take one last trip to get those. But yeah, the rest is at your dad's now." He rubs my shoulders. "And I hope you don't mind, we put a few things in your bedroom closet. Keepsakes and—"

"That's fine. Thanks for helping my parents."

"Anytime. I love your family. Hey…." His tone turns serious. "Piper and Milly were looking for you. They wanted to say goodbye, but I told them you were in the bathroom. They had to leave. They're worried about you. I am too. Do you want me to stay with you tonight?"

I adjust my beer goggles and ruffle Zakary's sun-kissed hair. Why did we break up? He's insanely attractive, considerate, and best of all, I could easily wrestle him to the ground if he were ever to steal my job.

"I'm fine," I say. "I don't need anything."

Wait—Sunday. The grad party.

"What are you doing Sunday?" I ask. "Piper's hosting the grad party, and if you don't mind escorting me, that would be helpful. Otherwise, I'll probably end up like this." I fan unsteady hands over my wrinkled top and dazzle him with a smile.

"That smile of yours," he says and laughs. "Of course, I can't say no to you." His finger brushes my cheek. "Have I ever said no to you?"

His eyes scan mine and search for the old me. Keep looking, Zakary, and once you find her, let me know where she is.

Apart from a few intoxicated nights in high school, Zakary and I never open-mouthed kissed or made out. So, my first week as a freshman at Mayfair University, Zakary and I officially became just friends, and still are. As I reflect on our time together, Zakary was more like the brother I never had. In fact, for Junior Prom, Zakary joined Kylie and me when we browsed dresses at the Port Wine Boutique. The saleswomen at the store thought we were triplets. Siblings? And asked if we would be interested in modeling for their petite clothing line?

"A date then?" I ask.

"For you? Anything."

It's final. I'm taking my brother, look-alike, ex-boyfriend to my pretend graduation party. This could be rock bottom for me.

My annoyance peaks when I remember that the big fat meanie is still hovering behind Zakary. I peer over Zakary's shoulder. Double damn. Brien put on his dumb eyeglasses again.

Is he planning to hypnotize me?

"Oh," I say loudly to Zakary, "now he's a nerd again."

"C'mon, Kate," Zakary says and hugs me tightly; his arms politely asking me to behave.

I think I'm slowly losing my mind. No. Brien's making me lose my mind. Frustration builds with every glance.

"Check out his kicks," I say, letting my guard down. I pull two cherries from my pocket. "White sneakers. There's something oddly sexual about a man wearing athletic shoes outside the gym." Chewing, I mutter, "Something feels off about him."

"What do you mean?" he asks, "And what did you just put in your mouth?"

"He's missing something."

"Where did you get those cherries from?" He is clearly appalled by my late-night snack.

"Look." I nod.

Zakary gives Niall a once-over. Smirking, he asks, "A smartly accessorized blazer?"

"Confidence."

"You're confident he could use a blazer?"

"No, that's what he's missing. Or lost. It's all over his face. I mean— it's missing from his face."

"Kate, Girl," Zakary says, "you got cherry schmutz on your face." He brushes the back of his hand against my cheek.

I suck my fingers clean and glare over Zakary's shoulder.

Zakary whispers in my ear. Something about, "Afraid to tell you… Guilt… Lies…." And something else, but I can't pay attention, because I'm too busy trying to find my mind—and my shit. I lost both today. Multiple times. Brien is to blame.

My eyes lock with Brien's.

Brien is brooding.

I brood back.

Brien.

The man stands over half a foot taller than Zakary. Most men do. Of course, Brien is ridiculously taller. But unlike most men, Brien is dark, intrusive, and prone to theft. Zakary is like other men, because he's prone to kissing my ass, but unlike Brien, he's uniquely compact, colorful, and reminds me of a Care Bear. A sexy, ripped Care Bear.

A tight line has replaced Brien's smile. What happened to his triumphant grin? He's scored a fuck-tastic job today. He should be doing cartwheels. And his eyes? Oh, they're on alright, and putting on another magnificent performance, but this time a thunderbolt of lightning has replaced the sparkle. His hands fidget in his front pockets. Why would he fidget? And how do his caring mitts even fit inside those snug pockets, let alone have room to fidget?

Before I can ask Zakary if I can borrow his car's travel sewing kit for a spool of thread—would a tiny string fit between Brien's thigh and the fabric of his jeans?—I regain control of my senses.

Sort of.

After I give Brien's pants several intense glares, my curiosity returns to Brien's stupid, nerdy face. Now my curiosity wants to know why Brien's sparkle is missing. I consider a theory. Not the thread test—I already know a snippet of thread wouldn't stand a chance between Brien's thigh and his designer jeans—I'm considering a theory. I should analyze this theory. Now.

Brien's gaze cautiously latches onto mine.

I brush my lips against Zakary's neck. And watch.

Tortured curves replace Brien's shadowy brow. His head slowly tilts from one side to the other. A shake of disappointment? Disagreement? A sore muscle?

It's hard to tell. More data is required.

I brush my lips against Zakary's ear. And wait.

Zakary chuckles and says I'm wild.

Brien's lips stiffen, his eyes expand into a full-blown summer storm, and the muscles in his biceps throb as his fists clench tighter. His mood has certainly been altered. One final piece of data should be considered…
I slowly and as seductively as my poached body can muster lick Zakary's neck.

I barely notice Zakary's yelp because a category five hurricane replaces Brien's temperate climate. The gale-force winds send me adrift on an imaginary cloud propelled by Brien's fictional jealousy. I roll in it. It's soft, real soft. My theory that Brien is in love with me has been proven through a very complicated series of scientific experiments. No—wait. Am *I* crushing on Brien?

Fuck me.

I'm completely drunk. Brien *is* 100% fuckable. And I want him. Bad. I look at the clock on the wall. It's not even eight. Congratulations, Kate. For once, you're ahead of schedule.

Zakary, thoroughly confused by my behavior, gently unlatches my death grip.

"So drunk," he says and chuckles loudly. "I can't wait to tease you on Sunday about how you acted tonight." He cradles my face. Brien vanishes.

"Pick me up at three?" I ask and squeeze his hands.

"Doesn't it start at one?"

"Probably…"

"I'm picking you up a little before noon. You're a guest of honor, so we should get there early."

I shrug.

"Be careful tonight," he says and steps away from me, then glances at my blouse. "What's with the shirt?"

"A choice." I shrug into the sleeves, gather one side of the shirt in each hand, and tie the sections into an elegant knot above my midsection.

"It's you," Zakary says, "I like it." He pats my cheek and gives Brien a friendly tap as he walks by.

I scowl at Brien and boldly move closer to him. When his chest is only inches from my lips, I lift my eyes to his.

"Brien," I say. "I was brought up to love my neighbor, even the terrible ones who don't return Tupperware, but I literally loathe you right now. I hate you so much, I want to punch you again."

"Brien?" he asks, amused. "Whose Brien and why do you hate him? Are you talking about me?" His shoulder braces the wall. "It's Niall, and I thought we were cordial co-workers. Excited employees. A tenacious team?" His breath smells like sweet citrus and barley. The Honey Bear brew. His head cocks to the side. "A diverse duo?"

"Too soon, Brien, too soon," I say angrily, taking a step back. "Why are you here?"

"Your dad invited me." He takes a step forward.

"Why?"

"He enjoys my company."

"Leave," I say through gritted teeth. "Leave Mayfair and never come back."

I've had enough of this 'everyone loves Brien', 'give Brien everything' love. Afraid I'll punch him again, I shove past him and trudge into the belly of the restaurant. After a few "pardons" and a severe detour I blame on the spinning room, I find The Bear's Den.

Black, white, and red balloons frame the entryway. The oversized picnic table is covered with a white cloth and sprinkled with rose petals. Against the wall, an end table draped in black lace displays a collage of silver-framed Vanguard family photos. The previous two weddings, my parents on Port Wine Beach, and our first family photo—me with a large bandage on my cheek. Some pictures don't include Kylie or me. All feature Mother front and center. In each photo, my dad stands right next to Mother or nearby, looking fondly at her.

The members of the wedding party chat away at the table with mugs of cold ale and carbonated sodas. As expected, the only two empty seats are at the farthest side from the door. Farthest from the grown-ups. Nora is my neighbor. She and I are in the children's section. I wave hello to the now somber faces.

They've all had time to see me in my red, inappropriate dress, acting inappropriately. I plop into my seat. Nora pours me a glass of water and slides two pain relievers into my palm. She says I'm flushed, and although she loves my cover-up, she convinces me to toss the garment over the neighboring chair.

After I'm comfortably situated and I've gulped several cool sips of water, I observe the room. Andy comes around the corner carrying a tray of family-style bowls of coleslaw and baked beans, along with baskets of rye bread. He begins setting platters at the end of the table. When he passes me, I ask him if he served my homemade donuts yet.

This morning, I arrived at work early—shocking, I know—to make fifty of my dad's favorite deep-fried treats. The recipe was a copycat of his favorite Buns-n-Bakery treat. The sugary desserts were the reason for the powdered specs in my hair earlier.

Andy looks confused by my question. He drops a basket of rye bread on the floor, apologizes, and quickly leaves the room. Clearly, he has no idea what I'm talking about. I ask Nora about the donuts. She also has no idea what I'm talking about. Maybe I don't know what I'm talking about? I ask Nora if she killed Doe. Her face turns bright red, and she excuses herself from the table.

Looks as though I may have uncovered one killer.

Moments later, while I'm frowning at my folded hands in my lap, a warm, stupid, caring hand brushes my shoulder, and by my skin's reaction, and the hint of cologne in the air, I know Brien is standing behind me. From the other side of the room, my dad welcomes the intruder. I ignore the chatter, but imagine Mother's bridesmaids oohing and aahing over Brien's hair. Feeling like I might be sick, I sink further into the seat. Everyone is watching me; maybe no one is. Either way, I won't embarrass my dad and ruin the fake rehearsal dinner.

Then, without warning, Brien sits next to me, and I'm ready to embarrass someone. Anyone.

"Is this seat taken?" Brien asks.

"Brien," I say with severe irritation, while staring at a delicate petal. "My cover-up was sitting there."

"The shirt is on the floor where it belongs, and my name is Niall."

"What?" I push my chair back, looking for the accessory.

"Hello, Niall." Nora has returned. She takes the free seat next to me. Once settled, she reaches over my place setting to shake Brien's hand. Her arm becomes my seatbelt strap. "So nice to finally meet you," she says. "The Vanguards adore you."

For the next several minutes, Nora monopolizes the conversation. She's worried about low real estate inventory, rising mortgage rates, and whether her business cards make her look older than nineteen.

Brien listens carefully.

The red rose petals on the table sway with the ceiling fan's movement; they begin to blur into one another. A pool of blood collects and rushes towards me. I jerk backward in my seat, and the wooden legs of the table screech against the floor. My water glass wobbles atop the table. The scattered flowers bob and move as the overhead fan spins.

Nora asks if I'm okay.

I tell her I'm not.

Feeling useless, I try to act bored, but I can't because Brien's knee has grazed mine. Twice. And he smells divine, better than divine. He smells like a winner. And his irritating patience with Nora's ridiculously boring life story is beyond admirable.

As my fried brain returns to the conversation, Nora gushes over Brien's gorgeous eyes. Brien denies any knowledge of being gorgeous. While Nora and Brien argue, I examine Brien's eyes. They aren't sparkling; they aren't doing anything. They're off.

Nora stands, says she needs another root beer, and asks if she can get us anything. Brien politely declines. I need to pull myself together and get classy, so I politely ask for two shots of Hennessy, then think twice.

Does one order Hennessy by the shot glass? Two shots could be a lot. And I'm already pretty drunk. I changed my order to a large plastic cup.

Before Nora obediently leaves, she whispers in my ear, "Your dad never let on how attractive Niall was. Did he say anything to you?"

"A sixty-eight-year-old heterosexual male wouldn't notice Brien is attractive," I say loud enough for everyone at the table to hear. "Only every woman and gay man alive would think him undeniably sexy."

Nora leaves a sympathetic pat on my arm and walks away.

"So," Brien leans in close and whispers, "you think I'm undeniably sexy?" He stares at me, searching me again, but this time I know what he's looking for. He wants the truth. No more games. He wants my truth.

What do I think about him?

What do I see when I look at him?

The universe stops spinning long enough for me to take him all in. The crease above his brows, the tiny laugh lines framing his lips. His lips. Perfect in size and slightly chapped from the summer sun. His strong chin. Broad shoulders. He suddenly breaks eye contact and takes a sip of water. With the movement of his arm, his shirt strains against his bicep.

Looks like I won the staring contest this time, though not entirely by my own doing. The performance-enhancing alcohol gave me an advantage. My mind is gone—lost in space, caught up in endless possibilities. Everything feels possible right now. Could I be attracted to Brien? Is it possible he's interested in me? I look into his eyes. That damn sparkle is back. His eyes are on. So uncommon.

"In a super common way," I finally say, scanning the room for a strobe light or some sudden appearance of the setting sun sneaking in at an odd angle to cause the shimmer. His knee brushes mine again. His leg bobs just slightly. "Too many squats at the gym?" I ask.

"What?" he responds, curious.

"Never mind," I reply, frowning. If he didn't overdo his leg workout, then why would he—?

"Do you mind coming outside with me?" His hand reaches toward mine. Firecrackers explode in his eyes.

"I do mind," I whisper, trying to convince myself that I'm still angry and actually do mind. My attempts to insult him fall flat. He's glowing—practically shining. It's the fucking Fourth of July in Brien's world. And he wants to spend even more time with me. The scent of his cologne continues to cloud my thoughts, leaving me with no logical reason to refuse. Without waiting for my quick retort, he stands and offers a welcoming hand.

"Let's find somewhere quiet."

184

Don't Call me Katie
Friday, May 27th @ 7:37 p.m.

THE SUMMER AFTER our first Vanguard family photo, or maybe several years later—it was definitely *after*—Mother was selected as a chaperone for our class field trip to the Milwaukee County Zoo. The memory comes back to me now, years later, on this emotional night.

Once the buses were parked, we pooled into the parking lot. The air brimmed with excitement, freshly mowed grass, and a rancid penguin poop smell. Mother was 'in charge' of Kylie, me, and three other kids. I didn't care that Colten and Lucas were in our group, even though they kept making farting noises with their armpits while the teacher divided up the remaining students. At least they smelled better than the penguins. But I did not like that Wren was in our group. After our teacher—Miss Jackie—separated the class, Kylie grabbed Mother's right hand, and Wren clung to her left. Without a hand to hold, I screamed.

Mother shushed me, laughed, and said I was too old to hold her hand anymore. I asked her why Kylie could. She said I was the older twin, and

Kylie was still a baby. Then we entered the Aviary building, and the park worker asked the class to quiet down.

All day, I kept trying to slide my hand into Mother's warm palm. When we walked through the spider monkey exhibit, she couldn't because she was holding Colten and Lucas's lunch boxes. When we visited the elephants, her hands were busy holding water bottles. After lunch, Kylie finally offered me her open palm, so I clasped my fingers tightly around hers, but it wasn't the same as Mother's. Her hand was bony and cold. On the way back to the bus, Wren said she'd hold my hand, but her fingers were worse. Sticky with cotton candy. And her jagged nails dug into my skin.

That afternoon, I decided holding that hands was gross.

But tonight the feeling is different.

Many things are different tonight.

For one, Brien has ruined everything; he needs to leave. Secondly, he's everywhere; he needs to leave. Third… he's pulled my hand into his. It's not sticky—his skin is warm, and his hands are strong.

I want my throbbing hand in his. My wound seems to absorb something good from him. His nails don't dig into me. I catch myself rubbing his thick calluses—I want to massage them. I hate that urge. The part that scares me the most is that now that we're connected, I never want to let go.

He guides me to the corner of the Bear's Den, away from the guest table. Standing next to the array of family photos, he faces me. I can't bear to see his truth, so I stare at his chest, unwilling to lift my head any higher.

I can't.

Not now. Not when I finally know *my* truth. I'm certain it's written all over my face.

But he's not interested in me. He's less than not interested. The truth is, he's probably bored with me. Perhaps ambivalent? Annoyed? What if he's disgusted with my behavior?

I catch a glimpse of my dad from across the room. His eyes are red, and Dale just gave him a manly pat on the back.

What if… what if something worse came of my bad behavior? What if the hold Niall has on my dad is stronger than *my* connection to my own father? Could this rift between Niall and me cause my dad to completely give up on me? Of all nights for me to fall off the deep end. On this special night. What have I done?

"How's your cut?" Niall asks softly.

I can feel him looking down at me.

I raise my hand and show him the inflamed skin.

He cups his hand beneath mine and examines the wound. He says the cut will heal quickly if I apply Neosporin and keep it covered. I nod in agreement. He explains the benefits of proper wound care, but I've stopped listening, because he's a stranger, and my new potential boss, who's touching me and acting as though he has a vested interest in my well-being.

He gently releases my hand, retrieves his cell from his front pocket, then types something into his phone.

While he's messaging his girlfriend or wife, I scan for my dad. Likely, he'll be in worse condition than I am by the end of the night. I find him at the bar. Dale just handed him another beer. Good. My dad is experiencing all the emotions tonight. In his other hand, he's holding a sheet of paper. I think those are the vows. He really is a wonderful man. I need to be kinder to him.

"Niall," I say, stepping towards the door. "I don't want to be here now."

"I figured you might need some fresh air." His tone turns playful. He's doing an excellent job of handling my roller-coaster emotions. "Now's your chance. Wanna get out of here?" He nods towards the beer garden. "It's really beautiful out tonight."

I must appear surprised at his suggestion, so he hurriedly adds, "We're not totally ditching. Earlier, I gave your dad a heads-up that I'd keep you company during the speeches, so technically we have permission."

Why didn't I think of it? Instead of getting wasted to avoid this part of the night, I could have just left for fifteen minutes.

I think I'm smiling, but my face is numb, so it's hard to tell. Brien tucks my hand in his and, with one word, "Come," he leads me through the restaurant.

My stomach flutters while the solar system whirls around the room. Somehow, Brien has replaced me at the center, and his gravitational pull steadies my orbit.

Today, I've lacked common sense, but now I'm drunk, and life is simple. Listen to Henry, collaborate with Brien, show up for work, stop whining, and forget about the past. This insight eluded me earlier.

For now, I'll shamelessly enjoy this heightened acceptance of everything unacceptable.

I've lost all authority over my movements. Like my desire to punch Brien or sabotage his business. Both are missing. We've reached the door to the beer garden. For a moment, he releases our connection and pushes the screened door. The cool night air rushes against my bare shoulders. My heart pounds. I hold my breath.

Brien reclaims my hand.

I exhale.

His other hand circles my lower back and leads me to a small wicker love seat next to a heated outdoor lamp. The couch is the same length as the one at my dad's office. I calculate Brien's size, add my chaos-filled frame, divide by six (seven?) shots, and prepare to sit somewhere else.

Before I can escape, he pushes the drink table forward and quickly pulls me beside him. Once seated, I let go of his hand and try to slide away, but it's useless. There's nowhere to go.

Outside, intimate couples laugh and whisper near the fire pit. A goth couple kisses in the corner. In the distance, the gray moon's reflection illuminates the lake. Peaches' playlist, and the guests, have loosened up as the night has progressed. A slow, sexual vibe oozes through the speakers and hovers in the air.

I should counteract the erotic music. I pat my shoulders and neck, then suck in a breath of air. My fancy cover-up thing is over by Nora. No. Brien tossed it to the floor. What an intrusive brat. I puff my mouth and clench my teeth. To cover more skin, I pull the fabric down my thighs, yank the top over my chest, and curse Piper. The dress's design is only proper for standing alone, upright, in a dark room.

While I suffer, Brien makes a noise remarkably similar to a sexy, husky laugh.

A cacophony of chickadees may as well be courting me from the sky. From the corner of my eye, Brien's crooked smile becomes visible.

"Something funny?" I ask.

"Need help?"

I shake my head because I've already determined I'm helpless.

"Did you name your dress, Piper?"

Oh no. Instead of laughing, I grunt and exhale more air. Clearly, I've forgotten how to express joy through my vocal cords. Anyway, I'm neither amused nor happy. I'm drunk and irritated.

Worse, his magical thighs are encroaching on my bubble of personal space. As I press my dress down, the back of my hand touches the cottony fabric of his denim jeans and tingles.

"My friend, Piper, gave me the dress," I explain. "It's not my style, and I've been fighting with it all night. The matching cover-up is missing."

His surprised, open-mouthed grin makes me forget my question.

"Burn that ugly shirt," he says. "What you're wearing now is stunning. I would even say... pulchritudinous." The twinkle is back in his eyes.

"Who even knows what pulchritudinous means?" After the words leave my mouth, I stiffen. My alcohol-soaked brain processes his statement. Pulchritudinous means beautiful. The word was on my Middle School vocab list.

Did he say I'm beautiful? He didn't, or did he?

The alcohol emboldens me. I watch the man sitting next to me taking up more space in my life than he should. From his Hollywood hair to his fly kicks, I complete another tour de Brien. A sprawling landscape. One arm stretches across the couch, the other rests in his lap. One leg propped over his knee. The stretch of fabric is the same. No. Better. A thread wouldn't stand a chance.

He is physically beautiful.

And the shoes. Still white, but not the sneakers he was wearing earlier today. Then I remember: I splattered them with blood.

"Your Nikes," I gasp. "I ruined them."

"Sticky and blood splattered," he says and smirks, unfazed. "No worries, I have several pairs. And my Tom Fords are my favorite." The toes of his shoes lift off the ground.

And then reality punches me in the arm. This isn't a date. Brien's on a very specific mission to place me on formal warning for my earlier display of workplace violence. He's the equivalent of my boss. That's why we're sitting alone. Outside.

A private reprimand is mandatory. Oh, and he's probably going to invoice me for destroying the shoes. What have I been thinking? I'm not Kylie or Roxanne. I don't have spider-leg-long eyelashes, pink, glossy lips, or an impeccable manicure. I'm the girl who prefers to hide under layers and wears blood-stained shirts to an interview.

"I'm glad you left your weapons on your bookshelf," he says.

I frown ever so slightly.

"Books… sorry, that was a bad joke." A hint of a smile tugs at the corners of his mouth.

Kate, get yourself together.

Why have I been floating around like a mindless jellyfish tonight? What happened to my investigation? My future is at stake. I must find Brien's Achilles heel. Now that we're alone, I'll ask him questions about his company, college days, shady relatives, former lovers, and current lovers. Every nook and cranny must be overturned.

Subtlety is key.

"I have a covert plan to destroy you," I say.

"Any plan involving taking someone down should be secretive," he agrees. Electric eyes bore into my soul, demanding that I share the ingenious plan. Strength is my friend. He can quiz me all he wants with his savory words and mystic eyes. I'm a steel door. A pirate's treasure chest. Brien's jeans.

"I'm not telling you anything," I say.

"You shouldn't," he agrees.

"I won't."

"Although," he says, massaging his neck, "I could help. That's what I do. I review confidential plans, reveal loopholes, suggest variations, and win."

He's right, and I'm positive he's an excellent reviewer and revealer, but I'm a door full of pirates' jeans. No. Wait. A steel door. A pirate's chest. A pirate's chest full of Brien's jeans? Something impenetrable.

"The details are private," I say.

"Agreed," he says, "because if they weren't, your plan wouldn't be a secret."

"We're on the same page."

"Same line, same sentence."

"Once I find your dark secrets," I say. "I'm telling my dad, and he's going to fire you." My arms cross tightly against my chest.

His eyes leave mine and graze the top of my dress.

"Creative," he says.

Did he eye my chest? My mouth opens. Did I just reveal the plan? My mouth clamps shut.

"What secrets do you expect to find?" he asks, seemingly bored beyond belief. I'm as threatening to him as my red flag suggests. Antisocial caterpillar.

"Tax evasion," I say. "Money laundering. Blatant corruption. A dead body."

"Well, I wish you the best of luck. Dig away." His arms spread wide. "What if you come up empty?"

"Everyone's hiding something."

"What are you hiding?"

"Nothing I'm willing to share."

"Have a few secrets, Katie?"

"Absolutely."

"What if there's nothing you can do to make me leave?"

Did he call me Katie?

"Then I'll die," I say.

"Why?"

"The VP role should stay in the family. It's called Vanguard Family Builders. Plus, I need the money so I can move."

"Why can't you live at home? Free rent is fantastic."

"Because a twenty-two-year-old shouldn't live at home."

"I thought you were twenty-one?"

"How would you know?"

"Your dad."

"Why is my dad telling you things about me?"

"He loves to brag about you."

Hmm. This is not going well.

"You and your dad have a great relationship," he says.

"It's dysfunctional at best." My cheeks flush as I recall this afternoon's outburst at my dad's office.

"He loves you a lot," Brien says. "You're lucky."

"I appreciate him, but Mother's a big fat meanie."

"A bit of your mean side came out today."

"You deserved it."

"Did I?"

He didn't. And in this moment, his professional side gleams brighter than his faultless smile. He's paving the way to a fresh start. What other options does he have? He's an expert at finding common ground in difficult situations. He has every reason to show frustration, because he's stuck babysitting me, but he's smiling. He must be getting paid really well. But Brien's right. I've been a bratty child today and treated him and my dad poorly.

A sincere apology is necessary.

Ever since I was young, I've believed a request for forgiveness only counts if you look the person in the eyes, use heartfelt words, and admit your error.

Dammit.

I must fixate on his heterochromia, silver-gray, yellow-amber, pulchritudinous eyes. And they are on, like never before.

I fixate.

"Brien, I want to apologize for how I behaved this afternoon. You didn't deserve my anger, and you've done nothing wrong. You and my dad have a legitimate business relationship. I truly hope you can forgive me for my childish behavior today."

When his amber eye flickers with the intensity of a firefly, I'm more than tempted to stare over his shoulder, but apologies are my thing, and I do them right.

"I'm sorry for being rude when you rescued me and bandaged my cut. You were being helpful. I'm sorry I disappeared on you… twice. Oh, and the book. Sorry for throwing it at you."

The couch creaks when Brien squirms in the seat and breaks eye contact. I lower my lashes to the fire's brilliant glow. A second later, I startle when Niall tips my chin towards him. A warm hand covers mine.

"Apology accepted, Katie." He grins. "I look forward to learning how to stay on your good side. Please, call me Niall."

I cringe, but my expression quickly becomes a smile. One small smile.

"Kate Vanguard," I say. "Pleased to meet you, Brien." To my surprise, I shake his hand.

He pulls my arm closer, and my body follows.

"Just Niall," he says.

"Just Kate."

"Not Katie?"

In Middle School, I forbade anyone from calling me Katie. I was a mature sixth grader, and Katie was a baby's name. To the public, I would only be known as Kate. Of course, Kylie refused to honor my request, but she was my best friend, my sister. Now that she's gone, no one has called me *Katie* in nearly two months. And it needs to stay that way, because when Niall just called me Katie, he released a tidal wave of memories. *Katie, I'm scared. Turn on the light. Katie, let's play on the swings. Katie, Daddy's taking us out for ice cream. Katie, Katie, Katie…*

"Katie?" Niall asks.

I can't allow this.

I should feel sad and mourn Kylie's memory when I hear my childhood name, but I don't. I feel something else. A less-sad feeling? A happy feeling? Worry consumes me. If I don't become sad when someone calls me Katie, doesn't that mean I'm losing my sister's memory?

"My family called me Katie when I was little," I say. "It's a childish name."

Niall begins to speak, "Ka—"

A shrill noise interrupts him. "Niall!"

Brien glances beyond my shoulder and produces a weak smile. He stands, but before leaving, his eyes penetrate mine.

"I'll be right back. Don't go anywhere… Katie."

The Real Kylie
Friday, Feb 11th

THIS WEEK, I met with six new clients—all in person—hosted five Zoom calls, and did a 2 a.m. Skype call with Wolfgang Hahn, owner of Wolf's Development in Germany. That meeting solidified our partnership. This summer, I will be flying first class to Frankfurt, Germany.

Open doors are open for a reason.

To be honest, when the international opportunity originally presented itself, I considered turning it down. That was back in November. Jolene didn't want me to leave the country. She said our relationship would suffer and long-distance romances were destined to fail. But then, a few weeks later, she had a complete change of heart and moved across the country.

Good thing I held off on giving Wolfgang an answer. Now with Jolene gone, I'm free to follow my dreams.

After my busy work week, I was hoping to relax today, but Harrison has been blowing up my phone. He wants to know if I got limber with any of the hot asses. All of them?

The yoga session was the last irritating straw. It's Friday afternoon, and I'm packing. Leaving town for the weekend. Soo-jin's ghost-inhabited colonial, the non-stop business meetings, and the pieces of Jolene left on my mind are too much. Anyway, Soo-jin's new kitchen cabinets and appliances are being installed this weekend, so she and Bennett will be getting a hotel and relaxing in five-star accommodations. She invited me to come along, but I need my own getaway.

Harrison said I could crash by him, but that's not happening. I'm not even going to tell him where I'm headed. But that's mostly because I'm not quite sure where I'm going. Maybe I'll waste some time and money at the Potawatomi Casino in Milwaukee or at a secluded cabin in Door County? Madison has some nice hotels and nightlife.

Why am I thinking of places in Wisconsin?

There are hundreds of decent places I could visit in the Chicago area. Truth be told, Wisconsin is calling for me.

I grab my coat. Mid-reach for the door, my phone buzzes. I'm about to turn my phone on silent when 'Kylie' flashes across the top of the screen. She's sent me a message. With a hurried movement, I tap.

Kylie: Hey, Slide! I remember you. Wyd?

I quickly type a bold message and hit send. Kylie is different, and I should act differently.

Me: I'll be near Mayfair tonight. Wanna meet up?

I was headed somewhere; Mayfair works. Mayfair definitely works. Given her prior response time, I don't hold my breath, but I do stare at the screen. If she turns me down, I can still travel to Mayfair. I know Henry will happily take me in.

But this time I don't have to wonder for long, because her response is instantaneous.

Kylie: My friends and I are going out later tonight, but I can meet u for dinner?

I check my watch and account for rush hour traffic.

Me: Triple B's at 6?
Kylie: For sure. Just a warning, my sister may want to meet u. She's very protective. lol

I wouldn't care if Kylie brought her dad. Everyone loves me. Mothers, fathers, aunts, uncles. Sisters love me, too, but I bet a million bucks her sister isn't as hot as she is. I change my clothes. Twice. I settle on an Adidas hoodie, jeans, and my white Nikes. More casual than I'm used to, but it's my first date in six years, and I don't want to look like a dweeb.

During the ride to Mayfair, I wonder if Kylie will show her charismatic side? What will she wear? Will she be different? Bold? Blow me in my car? Play hard-to-get? Tease me with jokes? Drive me crazy with her laugh? Each scenario releases a pounding jackhammer inside my heart.

In record time and fifteen minutes early—thanks to snow-free roads and little traffic—I arrive at Triple B's. Once inside, to kill time and calm my nerves, I sit by the bar and order a Wild Cub mug of beer. Hoping the nostalgia from last weekend reappears, I claim the same seat. Peaches isn't working tonight, and the current bartender is busy washing glasses, so I watch the minutes take their sweet time. I'm dizzy with anticipation, worse than a teenager on a first date. Each time my phone lights up, I leer at the screen. Kylie could cancel. Or she could ghost me.

At six o'clock, I recognize her flawless profile at the door. The ache returns. Will she remember me? Should I walk up to her, or let her find me? I message her.

Me: Hey, Kylie. I'm here. Left side of the bar. I'm wearing a gray sweatshirt in case you forgot what I look like.
Me: Your left.
Me: Your left when you walk in.

What a dumb message, but it's too late for me to change it. The message is sent. A nervous tremor takes over my leg; I prop my foot on the stool's footrest and sip my beer.

Kylie: Here.

I spin the seat towards the front door. She's looking my way, so I raise a hand. She spots me. When I lower my arm, I nearly elbow the guy sitting next to me in the head.

I toss a ten-dollar bill onto the bar, then snake my way through the tables. I meet Kylie in the middle of the dining area, between an older couple eating onion rings and a family of five, the mother mopping up her child's spilled milk.

Kylie stops a few feet away. She's beautiful, like I remember, wearing a mini skirt and a cut-off top with a plunging neckline. I'm not complaining—her tits look fucking amazing—but her clothes are more suitable for a dance club, not a supper club. Or a hotel room, not a dining room. The floor of a hotel room. The same goes for her make-up, which is heavy and dark. And I feel… lust. The heartache is gone. The joyous pain is a distant memory, replaced by a meaningless primal urge.

Kylie keeps her distance and clutches her purse with a death grip. Given her stance, we won't be shaking hands or hugging.

"Hey," she says and tilts her head to the side. "Slide?" She nods.

"Hey, back." I do the nod. "The one, er—the one and only."

Why did I say that? It was awful the first time. The sweet couple next to us and the busy family to my right have begun to stare at our awkward interaction. I don't blame them.

"Let's get a table," I say, and wave a hand towards the hostess stand.

Kylie doesn't move, so I abandon the direct route, circle the smaller table, and hope she follows. I glance over my shoulder; she's walking several lengths behind me.

"Is your sister coming?" I ask once we reach the entryway. "Wondering how many people for our table?"

"Oh, no," Kylie says. "She's stuck working on a project." Kylie reaches into her purse and pulls out a slender container. "My sister sent this along, in case you turn out to be a serial killer."

"If I'm a serial killer," I say, "now I know you have pepper spray. Maybe don't advertise that to your dates?" I wink.

Kylie's eyes become saucers. She looks at the can and returns it to her purse.

"I'm kidding," I say and apologetically reach for her arm.

She takes a slight step back and looks around. "I know," she says. A stifled laugh confirms she thinks I'm going to murder her.

I give my nickname to the hostess, Slide. She's the same woman who sat Henry and me at our table a week ago. It feels like good luck. But she's so frazzled crossing out names and scratching on her notepad that she doesn't recognize me.

"Hey, Babs," Kylie says.

"You look beautiful tonight, darling," Babs says and pats Kylie's shoulder. "Gimme a couple minutes."

Then Kylie's quiet. Why is she so quiet? Last week, she was so… alive. She was energetic. Vibrant. Colorful.

Colorful?

She was everything, all at once.

I allow an elderly couple to pass between Kylie and me, but they don't pass; they form a barrier between us.

Now that I'm standing five feet away from my date—my date who thinks I'm a murderer—we wait in silence for our table. Kylie plays on her phone; I stare at the guests coming in and out.

After the hostess calls my name, I get Kylie's attention, and we are led to a quiet table in the corner. With the extra privacy, I hope Kylie will relax and open up.

Once seated, Kylie and I discuss the menu, gas prices, and the fucking weather. There are too many awkward conversations and silences to count, and with each passing moment, Kylie clings tighter to her phone for support. After cuddling her device several times, she says she has to leave soon because her sister needs help with that project; it's due at midnight. Kylie's disappointed that she'll have to cut our date short, and now her friend group won't be going out either. Kylie says her sister would be lost without her.

I ask Kylie if she'd like a Sprite with cherries?

She quickly looks up from her menu and tilts her head.

"Why would you ask that?" she says.

"Well, I know you really like them." I frown. "Well, I guess you wouldn't know. But the night I asked you out, Peaches had told me earlier that you liked cherries. So, I was the one who…"

Kylie tosses the menu onto the table. It slides underneath the ketchup bottle. She stares at me, but she's not looking at me; she's looking through me.

Feeling uncomfortable, I stop rambling and concentrate on the list of à la carte items.

Babs returns, and we place our order.

Kylie fills the silence and tells me about a movie she had recently watched for one of her psychology classes. *Sybil.* The movie followed a case study which analyzed a mental health patient – Sybil – who had multiple personalities and suffered from dissociative identity disorder. Kylie shares some of the movie's more disturbing elements with me. I'm all about learning more about my date, but the girl sitting across from me is nothing like the woman I saw last Friday.

Where is the bubbly, adorably klutzy, but altogether perfect woman I remember?

After Kylie answers a phone call, interrupting her detailed description of a psychotic mother who punished her daughter with water enemas, I excuse myself to the restroom, because I can't wrap my mind around Kylie's personality, let alone Sybil's sixteen.

From the restroom hall, I message Harrison.

Me: I drove to Mayfair and finally met Kylie. No longer a mystery. She's killing me.

The Battering Ram: KILLING YOU? AS IN FUCKING YOU TO DEATH? LIKE SHE BROKE YOUR DICK?

Me: No. She's boring. Not what I thought.

The Battering Ram: FOR REAL?! I WAS HOPING YOU'D GET LAID.

Me: Not all dreams come true, but I appreciate the encouragement.

The Battering Ram: THAT'S WHY THEY'RE CALLED DREAMS, MY BOY. FIND A CLOSER AND FORGET KYLIE.

I stand outside the bathroom and bang the back of my head against the wall. When I don't respond to Harrison's text, he calls me.

"Yeah," I say.

"Forget my last text," he says.

"I did, before I even read it."

"I was thinking," he says, "you've been obsessing about Kylie for a week. This type of behavior is unusual, even for your neurotic ass. And I'm not about to spend the rest of my life listening to you wonder what might have happened. There's obviously something more to this girl. Give her a chance. Trust your instincts. Maybe get to know her first, then decide. There's more to a person than what's on the outside. Plus, regrets are a bitch."

"Harrison, that's way too deep. Are you on something?"

"Yep," he says, "the girl I met last night." A woman giggles in the background.

The woman squeals.

I end the call.

What if I dig deeper and find out that there's more to Kylie? What if I find the woman from last week? What if I find nothing? At least I'll know. And Harrison is right. Regrets are a bitch. What do I have to lose?

Back at the table, the food has arrived. Kylie waits for me to sit, then immediately begins eating. She says the burgers are good, but she likes the food better when her sister's working. I wait for a sign, a word, something interesting to ignite me. Then she reaches for her phone as she takes a sip of water. The device topples off the table and smashes onto the floor.

"Oh no," she says and scoops it off the floor. "Yup, the screen cracked."

"Oh, dang," I say, "no screen protector?"

"No, I hate how they feel."

She then tells me she's had the same phone for almost 2 years and dropped it countless times. She thought it was indestructible. Once, it flew off the car dashboard and out the open window while her friend was going 55 in a 25. After they stopped to retrieve her phone, they discovered it was completely intact.

It's then that I realize you *can* die from boredom.

Unfortunately, the date ends as it began. Uncomfortable.

I pay the bill. Kylie thanks me for the meal and says she had a very nice time and would love to go out again. Well, I wasn't interested in a nice time. I wanted her to blow my mind, so I say, "Oh, for sure," unenthusiastically as we walk to the exit.

Harrison was wrong; there's nothing to dig into. The surface is so shallow, it's near non-existent. The night is a waste, and I'm not sure whether I should drive back to Chicago, to the casino, or over the bluffs.

But then, something interesting happens.

At the entrance, a stunning woman with honey-toned skin and large breasts waves at Kylie. She's a knockout and keeps smiling at me. Kylie hugs the girl and introduces us. Roxanne. Absolutely. She's a total Roxanne, and she's one of Kylie's closest friends. Before Roxanne walks away, she kisses my cheek and whispers in my ear, "Find me." Kylie leaves: she must rescue her sister. I stay: I need to find Roxanne.

Thankfully, the night ended better than it began. Roxanne doesn't think I'm a serial killer, and she blows my mind—four times—in the backseat of my car.

The Center of the Universe
Friday, May 27th @ 8:42 p.m.

KYLIE, WHAT SHOULD I do? Brien—Niall—has no right to call me by my nickname, but even after I've demanded he stop, he continues.

Every time he laughs, every glance at his thighs, his damn jeans, and those maddeningly sparkling eyes, my heart pounds harder, rattling my resolve. Everything about him keeps dragging me away from my careful, desperate plan. I feel like I'm losing the battle before I've even started.

Ka-tie.

How can I concentrate on anything other than those two syllables?

Katie.

The symphony in my head is momentarily muffled when the curvaceous figure standing in front of Niall squeals and snakes her arms around him. A banging body conceals a solid ten build.

Roxanne.

She plants a kiss on his cheek. I curse, and as usual, it wasn't under my breath, and everyone within ten feet probably heard.

Roxanne swivels toward me and offers an overly friendly smile. Niall spares me further embarrassment and only raises an eyebrow. I watch as he slowly peels Roxanne's hands from his body, but she presses in closer; their bodies nearly mold into one. One picture, putrid union. I've never envied Roxanne, but tonight I'm disgusted to acknowledge I want to crawl inside her skin and become her. Not because she's gorgeous, in a Nicki Minaj video sex symbol way, but because her fingers are digging into Niall's forearms and slithering down the exposed 'V' between the open buttons of his shirt.

Then her lips…

I need to look away.

They're—she's…

How can her pursed pout be so close to his bare bicep? In public. Are they together?

If I continue watching Roxanne molest Niall, I might fling my shoe. Surprisingly, I'd rather not hit Niall again, so I remove my Vans and tuck my feet under my thighs, trembling with the effort to hold back.

I busy myself repositioning Piper. She's hiked up to my thighs. I groan at the sight of my iridescent legs; I literally pale in comparison to Roxanne. Niall and Roxanne are probably making plans to go home together tonight. Every second, a pang of inadequacy twists in my stomach as I watch the two. I try to focus on anything but them, grateful I can't hear their conversation. Even so, bitterness tugs through me: Niall owes me nothing. But it still hurts.

A vibration on the cushion interrupts my yanking and aching.

Niall's phone.

Mother's voice whispers in my ear, "Curiosity killed Kate." Growing up, Mother created several catchy parenting phrases, hoping they would either motivate Kylie and me to act a certain way or prevent us from doing something stupid. Now that I'm older, I realize how morbid that particular one sounds. The phone vibrates again. Phones are private, and snooping causes trouble. I fidget in my seat and imitate a stretch. Why am I so paranoid? I could totally scan the couch and accidentally glance at the phone. No one would notice.

I totally scan.

I accidentally glance.

A Coca-Cola-haired beauty hugging an adorable toddler appears on the screen.

Soo-jin.

Is this Niall's girlfriend? His wife? Lover?

The woman is very clearly not Niall's sister nor his mother, but she is the most exotic woman I've ever seen. If Niall were married, he would choose a goddess, and together they would make a Gerber baby.

Maybe I've discovered one of Niall's secrets?

The afternoon's events replay in my mind. As the day went on, I gradually fell apart, while Niall's steady composure matched that of a visiting dignitary, but I'm not fooled. Everyone has destructive secrets, and I'm sure Niall keeps his well hidden.

After I pout for a few more minutes, icy fingers tap my shoulder.

"Hey, lonely!" A peppy new server with fishtail braids holding a tray of shots stares at me.

"So, there's a group of old guys inside," she says, "and one of them, Don, or Dean, bought shots for like the whole bar. Want one?" She makes an obvious glance at the open seat next to me. "You look really sad. Drink a couple. Don really wants everyone to be happy tonight."

The wisdom of a waitress. Although I haven't taken anyone's advice in a while, maybe I should? And *Dale's* right, everyone should be happy.

"Bottoms up," I say, and down two fruity shots of happiness.

The waitress insists I'm too pretty to be alone, so she sets a third drink on the table, then a fourth, 'to keep me company'. After she leaves, I gulp both.

A second, or an hour later, a calming presence settles around me, and warm fingertips graze my leg. Niall slides into his seat at the center of my universe and sets a first aid kit on the table.

He didn't leave with Roxanne? He came back to this stupid couch, carrying supplies to re-wrap my cut, grinning like a circus clown. Why?

I stare. Frowning, questioning, wondering.

Thoroughly confused.

Why is he—

"You know," he says as he pops open the container, "her name's Roxanne, not mother fuck—"

"Sorry." My palm plants against my face. The air around me has become hot, my thoughts are floating in fruity lava. "Roxanne and my sister are good friends—were. Roxanne works here too. Well, you know that…"

No matter Niall's relationship with Roxanne, an apology is necessary. Niall has nothing to do with my current dislike for his current like.

I peel my face from my hand and apologize.

"I'm so sorry for reacting like that," I say. "She's just not my favorite person." I cram myself into the backrest. "I should probably apologize to her, too."

"To be clear," he whispers and leans forward, "she's not into mothers—"

"Please," I say, more direct than I mean to, "can we change the subject?"

He's silent for a moment, his eyes hold mine.

"Did you bring friends tonight?" he asks and steadies the kit on his knee.

"Friends?" I ask.

"When I walked in, you… You were at the bar. With friends?" His lips form a wary line.

Perma-blush? I snort.

"The guys at the bar?" I ask. "Not at all. I was entertaining them. Wasting time."

Getting wasted, I think to myself.

"And Zakary?" he asks.

The glowing fire casts scarlet flames across Niall's pupils. He seems very interested in my activities tonight. Although, in hindsight, I was acting like a fool around those college guys. What if Mother saw? It had to be quite the show. And then Zakary. In the hall. And the Theory. Not to be confused with The Thread Test. During my very scientific experiment, The Theory, I imagined Niall was jealous, and I licked Zakary's neck. How do I explain my behavior? I can't, so I share a series of murky facts.

"My ex wants me to move in with him. Actually, not with him, on top of him. Ugh. Not on top. I mean his upper unit. Gosh, that sounds super sexual, too. What I mean is, I'm renting the upper apartment of Zakary's duplex. Nothing romantic. Not that it matters, because I was *going* to move in. Now, as you know, I can't…"

"Zakary's just a friend? I thought he was with you—"

"No, we're definitely not together."

Zakary was my high school sweetheart. Junior year, we spent every weekend together studying for the math portion of the ACT test.

One night, when Zakary and I were discussing the dual-aspect concept of accounting, I thought our relationship was comfortable and fine, but when Kylie and Cass tumbled into the room—her hands frantically unbuttoning his flannel shirt, his planted firmly underneath her hiked, jean skirt, revealing seemingly bare ass cheeks—I realized Cass and Kylie weren't comfortable or fine. They had a 'bite marks on the bunk bed', 'picture frames crashing to the floor' kind of chemistry. After one of Cass's airborne cowboy boots knocked our Keurig off the counter, shattering the water reservoir, I realized the affection I felt for Zakary was vanilla and brotherly-like.

"Cool."

"I guess it's cool."

"The coolest."

My smile is nearly as wide as his. Why am I smiling and agreeing with him? I should be angry. He's the main reason my future is on hold.

"I have a question," I say. "Why were you in the women's restroom earlier?"

"Why did you use the men's room?" he responds.

The updated decor was a surprise, and the newly installed urinals seemed unnecessary. Oh shit, I was in the wrong bathroom. His smile is radiant, his eyes shine. The wicker seat engulfs me.

"I'm such an idiot," I say.

"No, you're… dealing with life. And life has been… tough for you lately."

I squeeze my eyes shut. He's wrong. I'm ridiculously foolish.

"I wanted to talk to you about something," he says. "That's why I asked to speak in private, but maybe I should wait until you're feeling better?"

Great, time for my punishment. Accepting harsh words is going to be easier drunk, so I open my eyes and welcome his criticism. "By all means."

"Vanguard Family Builders is very important to your dad," he says, "and your dad wants the business to continue to succeed. Right now, he's overwhelmed and thinks I can help. That's all. If I've offended you, I apologize. Your dad was supposed to tell you about the change to the VP role right after your graduation. So when we met at the office today, I had assumed you already knew."

"At the restaurant," I say, "did you know I was Henry's daughter?"

"I did."

I bite the inside of my top lip. When Chicago rescued me off the floor, he wasn't doing so because he was interested in me. He was, no doubt, following daddy's orders to keep me out of trouble. Now I can appropriately wallow in a valley of self-pity. I'll have to ask Niall if I can join the 'Feel Sorry for Kate Club'.

"So, this afternoon," I say, "that's why you were staring at me when I was sitting with Peaches? You recognized me and felt sorry for me?"

He looks confused for a moment.

"I recognized you," he says, "but I wasn't feeling sorry for you."

Hmm.

"Why did you stick your tongue out at me?" he asks, the corners of his mouth lifting mischievously.

"I thought you were… um…you, well…" I fumble.

"That's logical." He catches me.

"Why did you eye me up and down and call me a woman at the office?" I ask.

A full smile joins his twinkling eyes.

"You are a woman," he says. "That was a straightforward observation, and I was merely commenting on your unoriginal sentence. Why did you gawk at my pants when I was sitting on your dad's couch?"

"Peaches claimed you probably spent over a thousand on them, and I didn't believe him… so I was examining them—closely… for gold thread. Why did you stare at my chest before?"

"What are we doing?" he asks, his shoulders shaking as he laughs. The melody distracts me for a moment.

What are we doing?

"Getting everything out in the open?" I suggest.

"Is there anything else you'd like to… get out?"

"Have we met before?" I ask. "I mean, before today?"

His cunning eyelids blink, he looks down at his hands, then he answers, "Why do you ask?"

"You seem familiar."

"We've only officially met today."

"Officially?" I ask.

"May I?" he asks, and reaches for my wounded hand. He flips open the cover of the kit and faces me.

I twist my body towards his, my knee bumps into his pants, and my dress rides up. While I sit frozen—my hand in his—he works quietly and as skillfully as before. In seconds, a new bandage is secure, and I've completely forgotten my question.

"Careful this time," he warns, holding my hand longer than necessary.

"Right." I pull my hand from the safety of his.

"Your dad has told me so much about you. He really does love to brag about his daughters." Niall's smile is genuine. "But I know you don't know much about me," he says, and shuts the kit's cover. "Do you care if I share a little about myself?"

I concentrate on his words, not the sensational heat raging over my body.

"Okay," I say and cross my arms over my chest.

"Good," he says. "Plus, if you decide to continue working with your dad, you'll understand a little more about my background and experience."

I bob my head in agreement.

"I went to college at Loyola University in Chicago." Niall leans against the backrest and stretches his legs out. "Freshman year, I interned at a consulting firm and worked way more than part-time, in addition to carrying eighteen credits. I also played on a semi-pro baseball team. Exhausted doesn't even begin to explain how I felt during that period of my life, but even in that chaos, I found that learning the craft of consulting became my addiction. If I wasn't working or studying, I wished I were working or studying. I graduated with a double major in Economics and Business Management."

He waits for my reaction.

Even though I'd prefer to frown, I'm smiling.

Satisfied with my friendly disposition, he continues.

"While working there, I volunteered on special projects, shadowed my boss on appointments, and quickly learned I didn't care for my boss's management style."

His hand stretches against the backrest of the couch. For a second, I can feel his warmth, barely a sliver away from my skin. Not minutes before, I was ready to plot this man's demise. Now, I'm melting in his presence, clinging to his every word.

"One day, after my manager bailed on a client meeting, because he said he'd rather play golf than help some idiot find obvious solutions for their business problems, I realized I wanted to open a consulting firm of my own, be a boss, and always put the client first. I had saved enough money to start my own company, so I did. But don't become too star-struck. I'm the sole owner and sole employee. Eventually, I hope to grow the business and hire on staff, but until then, it's just me."

His voice has become my personal lullaby.

Just me, he says.

He's all that's needed.

I agree.

'The very first company that hired me was similar to your dad's. A growing construction business outside of Chicago. I look back on that first meeting, and I was so nervous. Even though I had been meeting clients weekly, there was something terrifying about being on my own. I arrived fifteen minutes late, forgot my laptop, and had to do the entire presentation from memory."

He beams.

"Since then, business has been steady, and I've never been late to a meeting."

Anyone else might sound boastful, but Niall is genuinely proud of his accomplishments and rightfully so. He's worked hard to achieve his success. No nepotism required.

"I even picked up my first foreign business," he says. "A construction company out of Germany."

"Germany?" I ask, surprised. "You speak German?"

"Yes."

"You're fluent?"

"Ja," he says. "I took German throughout high school and studied abroad my junior year. Haven't stopped speaking it since."

Of course, he's bilingual. I believe him, but earlier he challenged me with my Middle School word list, so I feel compelled to do the same. Plus, I suddenly remember my purpose tonight. Brien needs to fail at something. And if I play my cards right, I will be the catalyst to his demise.

"Can you translate something for me?" I ask.

"Sure." His smile broadens.

"How do you say 'your business plan sucks and you should be fired'?"

He pauses, then laughs as he taps his thumb against the couch.

"You don't know any German?" he asks.

"No."

The fire burns a deep red shadow upon his cheeks. "Es tut mir so leid. Ich liebe dich."

I repeat his words, "Es tut mir so leid. Ich liebe."

He grins, examines the fire, and corrects me, "Ich liebe dich."

"Ich liebe dich," I say, and I'm positive my cheeks match the glow from the fire. "Finally, I can say exactly how I feel."

"Same," he says, but doesn't look up.

"You think my business plan sucks?" I ask.

He shakes his head. He's grinning from ear to ear. Flames dance within his eyes. What else ignites him? His secrets? Taking down others? Lovers? Or is there something else?

"So, getting back to my connection with Vanguard," he says. "I met your dad several months ago. Right after the Super Bowl. Early February. Your dad was in Chicago and invited me to breakfast. He wanted to discuss hiring me for a role at Vanguard. We really hit it off, and the relationship evolved from there. The plan was to tell you—"

The hypnotic lullaby screeches to a halt.

"Wait," I say, "you've known my dad since February? And *he* approached you?"

"Yes, and yes." Niall slowly tips his head to the side.

The two met well before April 10th? Back when I was fully capable and my dad had no reason to deny me the role? Hot tears fill my eyes, and I feel as though I've been punched in the stomach. A worried Niall scans my face.

"What's wrong?" he asks, trying to understand my sudden change in demeanor. Before he can ask me more, I quickly slip on my shoes and rush into the crowd. I leave Niall the best way I know how: without a proper goodbye or acknowledgment for his kindness. He calls out to me, but I ignore him.

Katie is not my name.

The Slutty Professor
Friday, May 27ᵗʰ @ 9:18 p.m.

I SQUEEZE BETWEEN drunk bodies and slip away to the corner of the patio. At the edge of the garden, a hidden service door leads outside. Vines cover the fence. I dig behind brittle stems, searching for the latch. My fingers peel away leaves and finally find the handle. I yank, but it sticks. I pound the latch until it opens. I slip out. Before shutting the door, I scan the crowd. Niall's back is to me. Manicured nails circle his neck.

I slam the door.

Alone, I round the corner of the building and slide against the cold wall. As relief mixes with exhaustion, the voices fade into murmurs, and the sensual music becomes a series of echoes. My palm burns. Burgundy seeps through my bandage.

Away from Niall, I should feel weightless and free, but the empty lot and sudden cold make me vulnerable. I lift my hand and wipe wet streaks from my cheeks. My vision blurs.

What do I do now?

I need an escape from this people overload.

I peer straight ahead. Lake Michigan. At twilight, intense blue, purple, and orange hues scatter across the horizon. I'm drawn toward the glorious, yet haunting sight. My feet move. My body turns cold. The brilliant stars are my flashlight; they lead me to water but can't help me think.

What kind of sick, twisted life plan is this? What lesson am I supposed to learn from this mess? My memory has become so flimsy lately. Will I ever recover from this disaster? Feel normal again? Laugh again?

Have you ever felt so emotionally overwhelmed that nothing seems to matter? Like you think, "If I drove off this bridge right now, no one would care." Or "If someone kidnapped me, I wouldn't even put up a fight." It's a dark mindset, but one that's easy to slip into.

The tips of my sneakers reach the edge of the bluff. A sharp, earthy breeze rises from the lake. My heart races. I inch closer. I wobble. Usually, I'm afraid of heights. Normally, I'd never stand this close to the spot where death struck so suddenly.

Doesn't history tend to repeat itself? What's that saying?

The best way to predict the future is to look at the past.

"Kate?" A masculine voice calls from the darkness, and reality—and the natural instinct to survive kicks in. I step back several paces.

Although I'm alone at the edge of the bluff, I don't startle or panic because I've been waiting to face this person all night. I'm already squinting, but I turn and squint even harder. Gravel crunches as the man makes his way through the parking lot.

"It's me." The man waves. "Professor Holliday."

Relief cascades over my body. The investigation is back on track. Although I'm quite woozy, now's my chance to interrogate a criminal.

"Professor Holliday," I say, in as curt a voice as I can muster. "I'm surprised you're here." His blurry body becomes clear. As he nears, his arms open wide.

"Of course I'd come. Your family is like family to me." Confusion washes over his brow when I step away from his hug. Sensing my unfriendly tone, he stops short and stuffs his hands in his pants' pockets.

He's nervous.

Good.

He needs to feel the pressure.

It's time someone holds him accountable.

"The party really turned out—"

"Why did you leave Mayfair so suddenly?"

"I—I couldn't be here. I needed space."

"I know your little secret," I spit.

Even in the dark, I see his face turn crimson.

"What?"

I'm not holding back. I have to say what I need to say. This desperate urge to uncover the truth fuels my boldness.

"Kylie told me about what you did."

"Kate, I—"

"You were having sex with a student," I hiss. "And she caught you."

His eyes widen, and his mouth drops open. "I promise you that never happened."

A surge of anger rushes through me. "The day of the red flag party, Kylie found you having sex with a student. Is that when you decided to add murder to your syllabus?"

"I would never jeopardize my career. Teaching is my passion. And murder? What are you talking—"

"You're saying Kylie lied to me?"

"Just trust me," he says. He's lifted his chin, and sincerity pours from his eyes.

"I can't."

"Perception is not always reality, Kate."

"What's that supposed to mean?"

"I'm embarrassed about what happened, but I assure you, I did nothing wrong."

"I'm going to ruin you for this," I say through clenched teeth.

"Kate, please trust me. I don't want to make things worse."

"Things can't get any worse."

"They could," he says. "I don't want you to think less of Kylie."

"What is that supposed to mean?"

He sighs deeply. He looks torn. "I didn't want to tell you."

"I can't take the secrets anymore. Just say what you need to say."

"Kylie…she came on to me."

"What?"

"That day, after class, she came into my office and said that if I didn't give her an A, she would tell everyone that I demanded she have sex with me to get a better grade."

"I don't believe you."

"I have proof."

"No, you don't."

"Kate, I was on a Zoom call with your mom when it happened. Estelle heard the entire conversation."

Group Chat
Friday, May 27th @ 9:38 p.m.

SLIDE_OB: KATIE is missing. Is she with one of you?

Niall stands outside the restaurant and sends the message only after he's spoken to Dale, Nora, the shot girl, and Henry and Estelle's friends. No one seems worried that Kate hasn't been seen in a while.

She's probably taking a nap somewhere; those shots get away from you real quick. Insert drunken, raspy giggle.

Tonight is a lot for her to handle. Maybe she's getting some fresh air? Followed by a root beer slurp from a straw.

I bet she's barfing outside; she had like four melon balls, back-to-back. I mean, c'mon, girl, breathe in between. Empty shot glasses clank together.

Tonight is *emotional, but we still can't believe she left before the speeches.* Layer on a condescending tone.

While waiting for his phone to light up, Niall canvases the area for a second time. The beer garden, although still packed, feels empty without Katie's heartfelt apology. The restaurant dining area, brewing with drunk locals, has suddenly lost its bubbly carbonation without Katie's flirty presence. The party room, cluttered with empty appetizer trays and half-filled mugs, feels more like a funeral without Katie's ridiculously inappropriate—but so, so sexy—red dress.

Now, Niall stands near the bluffs. Above the lake, the sky is charcoal gray. The waters below are barely audible. The branches from a nearby maple tree crack and break.

The screen on Niall's phone remains black. He paces, scrapes his hands through his hair, and paces some more, closer to the black nothingness of the bluffs. Closer. Closer. The tip of his sneaker touches nothingness. The ground disappears. An indiscernible tremor shakes the immediate area. He leaps backward, shifting his weight onto his stable foot, but stumbles. Not two feet away, the black, solid ground dissolves into a grayish-green haze.

The bluffs.

He could have fallen to the ground, a hundred feet below, certainly to his death. And where did that vibration come from?

A faint screeching noise ricochets off the embankment. Then again. He strains to hear, looks down, looks back at the restaurant, and to the woods. The thump from the restaurant speakers is dull and consistent with any late-night bar music. The sound coming from the lake was unnatural. A wounded bird? Wild animal? Something else?

"Watch out for the ghost," a raspy male voice says.

Niall startles and jerks his head in the direction of the man.

"Boo," Dale snickers. Dale wobbles.

"Dale," Niall says, "you scared me."

"Careful," Dale says, pointing behind Niall. "Don't wanna take a tumble, now. Do ya?" Dale nearly takes a tumble.

"Not particularly," Niall says and rushes to Dales's aide.

"You of all people should know about the legend," Dale says, clinging to Niall's shoulder for support.

"Oh, Estelle told me. I've got a signed copy of her novel if I ever need a refresher."

"Damn fruity shots," Dale says and leans against Niall. "I always get myself into trouble with those."

"What can I say," Niall says, "sometimes trouble finds you even when you're not looking for it."

"I agree with you on that."

An Uber car pulls into the parking lot.

"And I've gotten smarter over the years," Dale says. "No need to drink and drive. I drink and ride." He lets go of Niall and wavers when he opens the car door. "Found Kate yet?"

Niall checks his phone for a reply, but his screen is black. "Not yet."

"Death does something to people," Dale says as he slinks into the backseat. "Never anything good. Life can teach you a lot of lessons. But death don't teach ya a damn thing. It takes, it's all it does. It takes and never gives back."

With a heave, Dale slams the car door shut. Red taillights disappear into the distance.

Niall's phone glows. He presses the notification bar. Two messages suddenly appear. There must be a few dead zones nearby.

The Pied Piper: WTF?

Milly Rodrigo: Have you asked Peaches? Maybe he took her home. I tried calling and texting her, but she didn't answer.

The Pied Piper: You lost her?

Slide_OB: Peaches is on this chat too. He hasn't seen her either. I just asked him.

Slide_OB: Katie's phone is still by Nora, but Nora hasn't seen Katie in a while.

Fauxy Roxy: She probably went and got some fresh air check behind the restaurant. Sometimes, when she's pissed or frustrated at work, she chills by the dumpster

ZakAtak: Hey, Niall, I haven't seen her since I was with you both in the hall. Was she upset? Or did she wander off?

Niall, feeling horrible for whatever he said to make Katie bolt, paces the parking lot.

Slide_OB: I'm not sure what happened. We were talking in the beer garden, and everything was going fine, and then she ran off.

The Pied Piper: Maybe drive around? She may have tried to walk home.

The Pied Piper: Check the switchback path.

Milly Rodrigo: How long has she been missing? Should we call the police? Let's call the police.

Milly Rodrigo: She's seeing ghosts, talking to dead people, and now she's physically lost????? We need to tell her the truth.

In the next instant, a man shouts, "Help!" Niall spins around. On the narrow road flanking the restaurant, a man walks out of the shadows, into the parking lot, carrying a limp woman in a stunning red dress.

Killer Cowboy
Friday, May 27th @ 9:28 p.m.

KYLIE WOULD NEVER? Would she? I don't believe it. Without a word to the professor, I stumble into the dark. More tears stream down my cheeks. I run across the parking lot—I can't stay here any longer. The more I'm here and the more I learn, the worse things become. I'll order an Uber. Where is my phone? Think, think, Kate.

Nora. I left it by Nora.

I can return to the bar through the beer garden and risk running into any number of guests or skirt around the back of the building, where I could possibly be viciously murdered in the alley. Considering there hasn't been a homicide in Mayfair in fifty years, the decision seems easy— wait, there hasn't been a homicide in two months. Have I forgotten so quickly? A lunatic is living among us.

I hopscotch potholes down the service road. Streetlamps light my way to the main entrance. My head throbs. Exhaustion and liquor slow me. I want to lie down and never wake up.

I wrap my arms around myself. Blood soaks my palm, warm at first, then cold. Maybe hypothermia is setting in. I should keep moving, but my heart is ready to give up.

A crate sits beside the dumpsters. The perfect place for a break. I stop. I sit in the darkness and find comfort next to the rancid dumpster I usually hate. I start up a one-sided conversation.

Countless failed recipes have landed at the bottom of this bin. I thank the dumpster for always being there. I stand and nearly trip, but my trusty friend catches me. My hand rests on the plastic lid. I should say goodbye; it's the polite thing to do. I open it; a fly buzzes by. I peer inside, mumbling something heartfelt. After we reminisce about my first batch of burnt homemade mozzarella sticks, I spot a stack of white pastry boxes atop the rubbish.

Donut containers.

My donuts?

For my dad.

The delicious, doughy pastries that I spent hours perfecting lie in the trash. I ask the dumpster who did this, but he stays silent, sworn to secrecy.

A crunch of gravel startles me. The dumpster cover crashes shut; I wobble in a partial circle. A figure as tall as Niall, but leaner, rounds the corner. A hand drags through curly hair. The other hangs at his side, holding a bulky object. The man…

A monster?

A killer?

A killer holding a cowboy hat.

I tumble over the crate and shuffle backward into the darkness. My palms find the prickly wall, my eyes squeeze shut. Fear fills my chest.

"Who's there?" the voice calls.

The footsteps stop.

In an instant, I'm taken back to the summer after my parents divorced—for the first time—the same summer Mother began ignoring her precious girls, and my dad suddenly remembered he had two daughters.

Kylie and I, out of breath, crouched behind the bushy shrubs behind the garage. Branches poked through our t-shirts; mulch stuck to our bare shins. Our hearts pounded in unison.

"Who's there?" Daddy called from the driveway. "Dammit, if you're trespassing, I will call the police. This is private property."

Kylie and I muffled our giggles.

Daddy called out again.

Kylie and I huddled closer. I held my hand over her mouth; she held hers over mine. The giggling continued.

As soon as his boots hit the asphalt, Kylie and I shared wide-eyed gapes. Once the car door creaked open, we scurried across the yard and yelled in unison, "Daddy, it's us! It's us!"

Earlier in the day, Mother had left for the bluffs. "More research, girls!" she had shouted, as Kylie and I opened sleepy eyes. Before either Kylie or I were fully awake, Mother and her car were gone down the driveway and out of sight.

After dressing, Kylie suggested an adventure for our birthday. Mother wasn't home—too busy writing—so we needed to find the fun ourselves. I followed Kylie to the back of the garage. She spun the old metal service door handle. Together, we entered. The room smelled of oil, damp wood, and sawdust. I loved it.

In the corner, the brand-new wood staircase that Daddy had built over winter break led upstairs. We crossed the paint-splattered floor. Kylie climbed first, I followed. The railing felt like silk. At the top, a brightly painted purple door stood between us and a mystery.

Since Kylie had opened the service door, she let me open this door.

I pushed slowly.

We held our breath.

The door swung inward.

In the small room, dried lilacs hung from the ceiling in each corner, and fresh wildflower bouquets sat on the three end tables. Tattered, colorful, woven rugs decorated the floor.

Although we had been inside this room many times, it still felt magical.

A small electric fireplace in the far corner, next to Mother's antique writing desk, held a stained-glass lamp. It glowed. I loved the room a thousand times more than the dark garage. Two windows—one on each side of the room—cracked open, inviting the early morning breeze inside. On the wall, Mother's favorite quote in a brass frame:

It is a great mystery that, though the human heart longs for Truth, in which alone it finds liberation and delight, the first reaction of human beings to Truth is one of hostility and fear! – Anthony de Mello

"Let the adventure begin!" Kylie said, oblivious to the beauty surrounding her.

We ran about the room, opening drawers, lifting rugs, moving piles of paper, peering inside decorative cases, binders, and purses. Being thorough is essential when searching for hidden treasures, because valuables are never left out in the open for just anyone to find.

We were on a mission to discover why Mother had chosen this isolated, beautiful space over us. Why had she left so quickly this morning? Without remembering that today was our twelfth birthday?

After ten minutes, we found a golden writing pen, a purple notebook, and a stack of printed sheets of paper littered with slashes and notes. 'Robust Vocabulary/Word of the Day List' scribbled across the pad, and below it, a series of words:

**Pulchritudinous [puhl-kri-tood-n-uhs, -tyood-] Physically beautiful*

**Innocuous [ih-nok-yoo-uhs] not harmful or injurious; harmless. not likely to irritate or offend. not interesting, stimulating or significant*

**Limerence [li-mer-uhns] the state of being obsessively infatuated with someone, usually accompanied by delusions of or a desire for an intense romantic relationship with that person*

To me, everything was special. Everything was out of the ordinary. An abundance of treasures filled the room. To Kylie, the room was boring and smelled like mothballs. Kylie determined that nothing in the space would warrant Mother hiding away from us for hours at a time.

And yet, I understood.

Assuming the search was over, I turned towards the door, but Kylie didn't follow. Instead, she giggled and began spinning. This was a thing. Her thing.

Anytime we lost something. A favorite shirt, a shoe, or felt as though we needed guidance from above, we'd close our eyes and twirl in a circle. Then, we'd abruptly stop, open our eyes, and allow the universe, God, or a presence from beyond to guide us to the missing item.

When Kylie stopped, her head was tilted back, her arms spread wide. After she opened her eyes, she squealed. I followed her line of sight. Above our heads hung a tiny cloth cord secured to the ceiling.

I squealed.

All along, the secret door to the secret chamber was hanging directly above us. Kylie and I played rock, paper, scissors to determine who would pull the rope. She won. But I didn't mind, because when she clutched the rope, the smile on her face was priceless.

Kylie yanked. With a screech and a thud, a folded ladder toppled downward. A haze of dust particles surrounded us. She coughed. I sneezed.

Before I could object, Kylie climbed up first. Not wanting to be left alone in the writing room, and not wanting Kylie to be alone in the secret chamber, I quickly scurried behind her. Inside the make-shift attic, a small window facing the driveway let in a clouded stream of light. The attic was empty except for an antique chest, large and made from a heavy-duty material.

Nothing like our toy chest at our dad's apartment, which was plastic and flimsy, and housed Kylie's American Girl dolls. I was pretty sure this chest was the same one that Bear had removed from our basement. As I walked closer, it looked more magical than ever.

The chest was so enormous that it could fit both Kylie and me inside. A perfect hiding space for hide and seek when our cousin Nora comes to visit next week. Before we could lift the brassy latch, we heard a crunch of gravel outside. Kylie bolted to the window and tippy-toed to peer over the sill. I hid behind her, clinging to the soft fabric of her t-shirt.

"Daddy's here!" Kylie squealed. "He didn't forget our birthday!"

As fast as our little legs could move, we scampered down the ladder. Giggling even more, our hearts pounding even faster, descending the wooden staircase, stumbling into each other, over our feet. Finally, toppling behind the hedges against the garage, Kylie squeezed my arm and whispered, "Don't tell!"

The cool air and smell of fryer grease remind me that I'm not safely tucked away in Mother's backyard, hiding from my dad.

Nope.

I'm very unsafe, tucked next to the dumpster, hiding from a killer.

"Kylie?" a hoarse voice asks.

I dig my fingers into the back of the rusty box.

The thud of cowboy boots nears. The figure stops several feet away.

"Is that you?" the voice asks again.

That voice.

"Kylie?"

I search the alley for help. A group of smokers, or a couple leaving for the night, but there's no one. Except me.

And Cass.

I cling to the trash bin.

"I thought I killed you," Cass says, and suddenly he's next to me. Pulling me towards him. Hugging me.

My fingers grip the jagged bricks behind my back. "No," I croak.

In a last-ditch effort, I slam the heels of my palms against his chest and push. My movements are useless. He squeezes, then lifts me off the ground. Liquor oozes from his breath. I pull back; his grip grows stronger. He bites the straps of my dress. Wet saliva trails down my shoulder.

"You're freezing," he says, holding me prisoner. "Dang, Kylie. You look fucking amazing." His body shakes against mine. Unsure if he's about to puke or cry, a scream forms within my throat, but all I can do is whisper another, "No."

Fearful that if I fight, he'll hold me down or strangle me, I pray an angel saves me from a killer cowboy.

Group Chat
Friday, May 27th @ 9:59 p.m.

AN AMBULANCE SIREN wails in the parking lot outside Triple B's. Red flashing lights illuminate the lake. For a second time tonight, Niall helplessly stands near the bluffs.

Slide_OB: I know how fast news travels in this town. I have a favor to ask. If any of you saw or heard what just happened, please don't say anything to Katie. I want to tell her in person. I have to explain myself.

The Second Ambulance
Saturday, May 28th @ 3:08 a.m.

AN AMBULANCE CAREENS through Mayfair's streets. This time, the EMTs stop outside Estelle Vanguard's colonial home.

Eight minutes ago, a 911 call was placed from the residence.

Six minutes ago, the same 911 caller dialed Kate, but couldn't get through. Kate's phone was dead. Anyway, Kate was too busy tossing, turning, and sweating profusely. Nightmares often accompany night sweats.

A third call was made to Peaches, but he didn't answer; his iPhone was on silent.

The fourth call awoke Niall. He was sitting on the hard, wooden chair in Henry Vanguard's bedroom, watching over Kate, as she tossed, turned, and sweated. After Niall speaks to the caller, he sends a message to the group chat.

Slide_OB: The ambulance left Estelle's. I hate to ask again, but can you all keep this quiet? I don't want Katie to find out in a text message. I'll tell her in person.

Slide_OB: Thanks.

The Bacon Made Me
Saturday, May 28th @ 8:21 a.m.

MY T-SHIRT IS wet. Matted hair clings to my cheek. The purple lampshade in the corner confirms I'm in my dad's room, so the lumpy rock I'm lying on must be his lavender ottoman. I look under the comforter; I'm wearing Kylie's red t-shirt. The black Sharpie lettering on the front, *A Little Sick*, worn and washed. I'm wearing biker shorts. Normal. The television is on. Netflix wants to know if I want to replay *Pretty Woman*. Normal.

A fresh bandage is wrapped around my hand. New normal.

The room isn't noisy with snoring, and my dad's bed is neatly made. That's unusual. The hard wooden chair that usually sits in the corner of the bedroom has been moved; it's now right next to my bed. That's not normal.

When Kylie and I lived at home, we always shared a bedroom and naturally kept that habit through college. I've never slept alone in a room. Ever. Since Kylie's been gone, I mostly fall asleep on my dad's bedroom lounge chair and a few times at Peaches' place, because my dad was out of town. After nightfall, the rooms are too silent, my thoughts too loud, and waking up alone in a dark room is too frightening.

And yet, I'm alone right now.

But at least it's morning.

My dad's sweatpants are hanging—unworn—over the side table, his water glass is missing from the nightstand, his slippers are neatly tucked underneath his bed—patiently waiting for him to slip them on before heading to the kitchen for a morning cup of coffee.

Where is he?

Last night, we were at the restaurant together. Dad and Dale were at the bar, and I was… all over the place. By nosey Nora, the college fuck boys, Zakary, and Mr. Niall O'Brien. Now, as I reflect in the morning light, everything seems disjointed, the night slipping away into confusion.

Brien.

He was everywhere. Standing in the hall outside the bathrooms, sitting at our reserved table, questioning me in the beer garden. In my business.

Niall.

We're on a first-name basis now.

We're also on a 'Kate, do everything possible to embarrass yourself' basis. I punched Niall. Licked Zakary. Did I really tell Nora that Niall was attractive? Did I accuse Nora of killing Doe? Did she? Did Niall hold my hand? Touch my leg? Ugh! Ugh! Ugh!

What kind of crazy reality am I living in?

My life is far from a romantic comedy with a happily-ever-after.

It feels more like a psychological thriller with an unreliable narrator who sees ghosts, witnesses a murder, and is probably suffering from post-traumatic stress disorder. And I'm beginning to think the season finale will have a plot twist even I don't see coming.

I need to start piecing this puzzle together.

What really happened the night of April 10th? Why is my dad making so many trips to Chicago lately? Why do I think my friends are lying to me? What's up with Cass? And what about Doe? Did I accidentally kill her? Was she murdered? And how does Niall fit into all of this?

The last memory I have is of enjoying the company of Dale's extra-fruity shots. After that, there appears to be a slight gap in my memory. Did I run into Professor Holliday? Or was that in my dream? I did see him last night! As I recall our conversation, I'm left with more questions than answers. I feel further from the truth than ever. Would Kylie really threaten a teacher—a family friend—all for a better grade?

I groan. This investigation is not going well.

And why can't I recall the rest of the evening? This is why I never drink. But I made it home safely and slept through the night. I never sleep through the night. Last night, I slept very well. Dreaming a lovely dream.

A vivid dream involving a close-up slideshow of Niall. A flash of his lips, jawline, and neck, a super close shot of his… pants. They were very nice pants.

My hands running the length of his muscular thighs, yanking on his belt buckle. My fingers fumbling against his zipper, searching for an access point. Finding an access point.

A very personal, private show.

An enjoyable show with laughter.

Mine. His.

Such a lovely laugh.

His laugh.

That was lovely.

Overall, a solid dream. Much better than my cryptic Kylie nightmares. Of course, warm lips across my neck, breasts… bare thighs, would be better than blurry memories involving a family member's murder.

Oh, but to be clear, not just anyone's lips.

His.

Mr. Niall O'Brien's.

They were so…

So, life-like.

Es tut mir so leid. Ich liebe dich.

I smooth the smile off my face and release an irritated sigh; that pleasant dream helped me sleep through the night. Dammit. Niall's being helpful again.

Maybe Peaches is right, and I'm developing an unsavory mental health condition? My superb ability to self-diagnose says I'm experiencing a delusion of grandeur. Right, like Niall is into me, and we made out. Maybe I finally fell over the edge last night?

I lick my lips and drag my tongue across my teeth.

Minty toothpaste? I never have the required fine motor skills to brush my teeth after a night out.

And Pop-Tarts…

Why do I remember Pop-Tarts?

I throw a pillow across the room; mid-flight, it loses momentum and plops to the carpet. The images of Niall were a dream; nothing more than an alcohol induced vision. Mother is right, I shouldn't drink.

I pound the purple throw pillow and stretch against the woven ridges lined with discomfort. When my dad and Peaches painted this room, I questioned the color selection. Periwinkle? To me, it feels as though Barney, or possibly a Muppet, threw up in here, or Prince hosted a televised charity event. The sun's rays pour through the sheer violet and white striped curtains.

A bird chirps outside.

I'm smiling as I leap off my bed and race to the window. I fling the lace coverings open. My heart immediately drops like a heavy anchor. The birdfeeder is empty. Not a chickadee in sight. I yank the curtains shut and sulk back to my makeshift bed. The chickadees are ignoring me. They've moved on to a better house, with better seeds; I wish I could do the same.

When I plop down on the cushion, a wave of nausea sweeps across my brow. As expected, the alcohol hasn't worn off yet.

I wrap my blanket tight underneath my chin. A stillness passes over me. My comforter is damp. It's normal for my nightmares to cause night sweats and my shirt to dampen, but perspiring through my comforter? This is a first.

Last night, I had another dream about Kylie. Once again, she said, "Hurry! Help, before it's too late!" But this time, she urged, "Don't tell."

Don't tell what?

What is Kylie trying to tell me… not to tell?

Perhaps I have new evidence.

I bolt upright and pad the nightstand, the floor, the couch's creases. I must tell Peaches. Kylie needs me more than ever. My search comes up empty-handed. During my adventures at Triple B's, I must have misplaced my phone.

My phone…

I was looking for it last night.

Suddenly, more bits of the nightmare come rushing back to me. Cass. He was in my dream and admitted to killing Kylie. Holy bejesus. He's the murderer.

My insides bubble, and I begin spinning through the galaxy again. I'm going to be sick. I toss the blankets to the floor and bolt to the bathroom. Kneeling on the ceramic tiles, I grip both sides of the porcelain bowl. After several retching heaves, nothing comes up. And this is strange, because the few times after I've drunk, I've always thrown up. What gives?

As I return to my sanctuary, a voice calls from the hall.

"…"

My dad.

Thank goodness he's here.

"Dad, I'm fine!" I shout and tuck myself under the covers. "But I am dying, and it's all your fault. And Dale's."

I shove my face into the pillow.

"Katie, it's me." The voice is louder this time.

I freeze before I can adequately suffocate myself. That is not my dad.

"To be clear," the man says. "I came to your rescue last night and had no part in your current condition."

I curse. Who rescued me? Zakary? Cass? Dale?

"Katie?" The voice is closer now, laughing. "You swear a lot."

I gasp.

"It's me," the man says, "Niall."

Niall? Wait. What? Why is Niall here?

Not that I need to explain myself, I loudly explain myself, "I was swearing privately, in my own home, to myself. A comment meant for my ears alone. Barely above a whisper."

"Your whispers could drown out the sound of a dump truck backing up."

"What are you doing here?" I shout.

"Waking you up."

"Why? Where's my dad?"

Silence.

"You were… You had a lot of fun last night," Niall says. "I'd let you sleep longer, but I was told to make sure you didn't sleep too late."

"Who are you working with?" I ask.

"What?"

"Who sent you?"

More chuckling.

Piper… she must be involved. And my dad. Oh, and Peaches. All three. I swear extra loud this time and peek out from underneath the comforter.

"Why. Are. You. Here?" I demand.

"I just told you."

"If my dad asked you to babysit me, I'll have you know he won't pay; he's as frugal as they come. You should probably leave."

"Do you remember being upset with me last night?"

"Yes," I say. I was angry with him all night. Of course, I remember that. But why do I remember his skin? My lips on his neck. Rubbing against day-old beard stubble? His lips? Warm and wet on my chest… His tongue? My thighs?

"If you don't remember," he says, "I can—"

"Nope!" I shout.

"You don't want me to tell you?"

"Not now," I say, annoyed. Why can't I recall my own memories? I don't need Niall's help. "Can you… Can you tell me how I got home?"

"Your dad asked if I could drive you home. He said he was going to spend the night at your mother's. You know, last night in the house and all before the place sold. Your dad thought you'd sleep better if someone else was here, so I stayed." He pauses. "You slept in there. And I slept on the chair… next to you."

His words register, and he speaks clearly, but I cannot process his sentences because he *slept in here*. By me?

At least I know how I got home, but still no recollection of the restaurant after I left Niall.

I hurl another pillow towards the door.

"I'm not getting up," I say. "Es tut mir so leid. Ich liebe dich."

A moment of silence follows my insult.

"What does my business plan have to do with anything?" he asks.

"Your plans in general suck."

"Piper said you might be difficult," he says, "and if you were, I should threaten to toss you over my shoulder and carry you in your present state. It makes sense for you to cooperate."

I knew it. Piper is involved.

"No response?" he asks. "I'll give you sixty seconds to get decent, then I'm coming in. Sixty, fifty-nine, fifty-eight—"

"You are not timing me!" I leap upright.

"Fifty-five…"

He's totally timing me. I pull the covers tighter around my neck.

"Fifty-four—"

"Stop counting!" I shout. "Can you wait in the kitchen? I—I have to shower, and my clothes are upstairs."

"Do you have your phone?" he asks.

"I have no idea where it is, and it's probably dead. Why?"

"No reason. Hey, how's your hand?"

My civilized side emerges, and I formulate an "Okay." My fist opens then closes. The bandage is crisp, white. My hand feels fantastic, but I'm not telling him that.

"Katie?" he asks. "I'll make you breakfast while you're getting ready."

"Kate!" I shout.

Before I can yell louder, and for a second time, his feet pad down the hallway, leaving a rumble of laughter at the door. I allow enough time for him to walk to the kitchen—twice—then gather the sheet around my body like a robe. I peek out the bedroom door. When I'm certain Niall is nowhere near the staircase, I haul ass up to my room.

Safely in my bathroom, the mirror's reflection is pitiful. I've dark circles under my eyes, my lips are chapped, and a scrunchie is stuck in my ratted hair. I yank at the tangled mess, and a clump of platinum hair, along with the tie, releases. My fingers run through the frazzled mess. Inside the wreckage, I find another hidden scrunchie. I carefully free that one. What did I do to my poor head last night?

I stare ahead.

Why didn't I demand that Niall leave? I'm under a spell, or I've been roofied into a docile state of aloof indifference. In a moment of panic, I wonder if it's a self-induced altered state? I hastily open Mother's other Zoloft container; the contents spill onto the granite. One, two, three… I count every pill. All accounted for. I didn't accidentally overdose.

Why then am I accommodating Niall?

Gah!

I'm off the charts.

In the shower, I turn on the cold water tap and stand underneath the freezing downpour for several seconds. Once fully awake, I twist the handle to warm and spend a long time shampooing and conditioning my hair. Outside the shower, I find another bandage and wrap my cut.

My twenty minutes of cleaning leaves me looking better on the outside, but pressure fills my skull, and my stomach churns and gurgles. Today, and possibly forever, I will drink nothing that resembles alcohol, not even root beer. I open my vanity, push aside empty bottles, and stand on my tiptoes.

The aspirin bottle is missing.

Feeling defeated, I return to my room. Surrounded by trash bags and heaps of laundry, I curse myself for my inability to wash clothes regularly. I complete the smell test on several shirts and find one resembling something clean… cleaner.

A simple aqua blue tank top. I hit a goldmine when I snag a pair of white, cotton shorts off the floor, carrying a whiff of fresh linen. To my dismay, I'm at a loss for clean underwear. If Mother only knew, I'd be breakfasting with Niall commando.

When I open my bedroom door, sizzling bacon tempts me from the first floor. My brain mulls over the events from last night; I've yet to piece together the time with Niall here.

Before I can convince myself otherwise, my survival instincts kick in and scream for food. I hurry down the stairs. In the kitchen, Niall's facing the stove, flipping bacon in a pan.

I pause in the entryway.

My shorts suddenly feel two sizes too small, and I think they're riding up my ass. My top no longer fits properly either. I tug at the front and realize I forgot to put on a bra. No—couldn't find one. I contemplate running back upstairs to change, but into what?

Plus, platters containing sausage, bacon, scrambled eggs, and pancakes cover the counter. I'm half ready to leap onto the table and shovel handfuls of food into my mouth like a feral child, but instead I wait patiently for Niall to invite me into my dad's kitchen.

My heart somersaults when Niall pivots. Our eyes connect; the plate he's holding wobbles. I fidget with my damp hair and curse myself for not using the blow-dryer. I should know better; slick hair provides non-existent coverage over my scar.

"Neither of us had time to eat last night." He seems to be explaining away the abundance of food.

No food last night?

Niall should have enjoyed heaping plates of deep-fried goodness at dinner, but instead, he was stuck babysitting my drunk ass. I cross my arms and eye the buffet on the kitchen island. The food looks amazing.

"When you make breakfast," I say, "you really make breakfast."

"Don't be fooled." He sets the bacon on the paper-towel-covered plate. "I can flip, scramble, and toast, but that's the extent of my culinary magic."

Niall appears well-rested and dreamy in a white t-shirt and dark jeans. The same clothes as yesterday, minus the button-down. The t shirt is wrinkle-free. His jeans are those jeans. Clearly, he had to sleep in his clothes because of me. But he still looks scrumptious, even in his current 'state'. No eyeglasses, but I imagine he's wearing his divine sneakers. I'm completely underdressed.

Clearly, neither of us knows what to say; I'm intermittently gawking at him. The food. Him.

He…

Wait.

While I was staring at the syrup, did he complete a credit card scan? An unauthorized scan? That quick, subtle eye movement up and down the length of an object. The look a man gives you at a bar or the gym when he notices you for the first time and takes you all in, but it happens so quickly, you think it never happened at all.

He totally scanned me.

"Have a seat, Katie." His eyes land on mine. "You must be starving."

The crispy bacon has my attention now, but not so much that I miss the fact that he called me Katie. I reprimand the bacon, "You shouldn't call me that."

"You're more of a Katie. Sorry, you'll have to get used to it."

My eyes hesitantly challenge his.

"I can't."

"You'll come around."

"Please, call me Kate."

"Kate's are stuck up and fade away in crowds," he says, and scoops a spoonful of each mouth-watering item onto a plate.

"Yours," he says. The temptation slides to what must be my side of the counter.

I fluff my hair with my right hand, and my bandaged hand hides my chest. I skirt to the stool.

"Katie's," he says, setting a fork next to my plate, "on the other hand, are…"

"What?" I audibly gulp and look at him.

His glorious smile plants an ache deep within, as though something is growing inside my core.

"Fun," he answers.

Fun? What does that even mean? Like fun, funny to laugh at? Or, fun, as in I'm enjoyable company? The answer is a mystery, and I'm frozen because his earlier scan depleted my bank of pointed questions. Two heaping plates rest in front of his chair. He pours two glasses of orange juice, slides one to me, and sets two coffee cups by my plate.

"You went to the Caffeine Café?" I eagerly sample both, keep one—the one with extra cream and sugar—and return the black one to his side. "That was really… thoughtful." I sip. The hot liquid burns my throat, but I don't mind; a distraction is a good thing right now.

His response is a crooked smile, followed by a playful wink.

I nearly knock over my drink. My eyes dart to the smorgasbord. I stuff a large spoonful of scrambled eggs into my mouth and concentrate on the plate's disappearing contents.

We eat in silence. He doesn't seem phased by the quiet; he must be as hungry as I am.

"This is really good," I finally say with a mouthful of pancakes. The rich, buttery syrup tingles my taste buds. "So. Good."

"Thanks," he says. "I'm glad you like it. And thanks for not kicking me out."

I shift in my seat, unstick my shorts from my ass. Why didn't I kick him out?

"You're a businessman," I say. "You have a job to complete, a boss to impress. Of course, you're going to follow orders. My dad told you to 'put up with me', right?"

"Not at all," Niall says. "No one is making me do anything."

Hmmm… not sure that I believe him.

I rub my temples and gulp the now room-temperature coffee. Today, caffeine is not giving me instant gratification.

The toaster pops. Four Pop-Tarts eject from the heating coils on the counter behind Niall. My eyes fire towards his.

"That's an odd breakfast addition," I say.

"You like Pop-Tarts, right?" He slides off his chair and sets the breakfast goodies onto a paper plate.

"Um, yeah…"

"You don't remember?" he asks. The Pop-Tarts arrive next to my pancakes.

My coffee cup becomes a shield, I duck, then shake my head nervously. "Remember what?" I ask.

But that's just it —I do finally remember something—a very urgent desire to eat Pop-Tarts last night.

A Pop-Tart kiss?

That's not a thing.

Could it be a thing?

A thing I manifested?

"You fell asleep in the car on the way home," Niall says, eager to fill in the gaps. "I thought you were out for the night, so I was going to carry you to bed."

He pauses—takes a super long time to wipe his mouth with a paper towel—and I think he does so on purpose. He wants me to squirm. Is he sadistic? Does he truly enjoy watching me embarrass myself, and now he's going to make me relive that moment, or maybe many? Slowly, torturously?

A second later, my senses unhinge as I imagine him cradling my back, cupping my knees, my head resting against his chest. He carried me, I remember. Heat spreads across my neck. My mouth becomes a sun-dried sock. Niall's eyes shine as though the recessed light above has become his spotlight. He is on again.

"But," he says, "as soon as I pulled into the driveway, you woke up and said you were starving and wanted Pop-Tarts."

To formulate an excuse for why he's stalling, I say, "I don't remember anything after the beer garden." I set my cup down and hold my head high.

His belt buckle? His neck? A dream… or a memory?

Please, please, please let it be a lovely dream.

"I was so drunk," I say, honestly. "I'm beyond embarrassed for whatever I did."

"You were surprisingly alert when I helped you inside," he says, his voice skipping joyously. "Do you remember earlier in the night? You wanted to discover my dirty secrets. See if I had a shady past? You wanted your dad to fire me."

He awaits my recollection.

"I do remember plotting against you," I say.

"In the foyer," he says, "you wanted to investigate. 'Let the adventure begin!' Your words. 'A treasure hunt.' Again, your words. Your first stop, you claimed, was… my pants. You said it was the perfect place to start."

"You're joking."

His mischievous smile kickstarts my heart like a higher-than-recommended dosage.

"Nope," he says, "but I did stop you before you made your way to your…" He clears his throat. "Ultimate destination."

I sit taller in my seat; I need to own this. Whatever this is. Although my head is raised, my eyes are directed at the space above his thick, Hollywood Hair. Even his hair is perfection at… however early it is. I imagine running my fingers through that—as though I've overdosed, my heart stops. I don't have to imagine, because I know the feeling. Last night, I ran my fingers through that hair. Thick, clean, silky—

"To prevent you from searching," he says, "I had to wrestle you to the ground. Well, to the stairs. I kind of fell backwards and landed on the staircase."

My eyes snap to his.

"Do you work out?" he asks. "You seem a little on the small side, but dang, you were strong. Determined."

"That's not true," I say.

"After that," he says, "you stood in front of me and demanded I kiss you, because you had to find out, and I quote, 'If I tasted like cherry Pop-Tarts.'"

Yep, that was totally me. There's no way he could make that up.

"I assured you I didn't—"

"Let's skip that," I say.

"You sure?"

I nod.

"So, you really don't remember?" He leans back and crosses his arms.

I bite my lower lip and shake my head no.

He looks off to the side, nods his head, purses his lips. "Really? That's a first," he says. "Normally, my lovers remember—"

"Lovers?" I squeak.

"Let me explain," he says and settles into his chair as though he's about to offer an alternative business solution to a struggling company.

I might get sick after all.

"It's really nothing to be embarrassed of," he says, "we made out on the stairs."

I'm positive my face has lost all its color.

"No biggie," he assures me.

"We kissed?" I ask.

"Not on the lips," he says and stares at my lips.

"Well… what did we do?"

"Our activities were really limited because of the location. The stairs." He nods towards 'the location'. "As they say in business: location, location, location. It'll make or break ya. I sat at the bottom of the stairs, and you… I'm trying to think of the best word. Straddled? Mounted? You were on me. I wouldn't say it was uncomfortable. Quite the contrary. But it was limiting."

"Did I hurt you?" I ridiculously ask. I can't imagine being so forward. That's not me at all.

"Hurt me?" He laughs. "No way. While your hands were in my hair, you kissed my neck, so I did the same."

As though the memory comes slamming against me—like a kiss from the sun—my skin burns; I touch the side of my neck.

"I kissed," he says, "your chest." He sips his juice.

I cover my heart in response; it pounds.

"The stairs were digging into my back," he continues, "so for a second I flipped you over and… you were lying on your back… so, I kissed your thigh."

My thighs ignite.

"Then your inner thigh." His eyes bore into my soul.

I may as well be sitting on molten lava right now.

"Funny enough," he says, "you tasted like cherries. Did you happen to spill cherry juice on yourself last night?"

I know my mouth is gaping open. Any response is lost. The evidence against me is mounting. No pun intended. A hysterical giggle escapes my lips. It's official; I've fallen over the edge.

"You were fully dressed," he says and smiles curiously. "Totally comparable to a Middle School make-out session. Nothing to be ashamed of." His hands prop comfortably on the counter. "Thanks to my clever defense, we stayed on first base. You kept trying to unzip my pants, but I stopped you. No sex."

"I know that," I sputter.

Does he think I'm some kind of idiot college girl? Of course, we didn't have sex. I would remember that. At least now I know the images were real and not a dream. I have so many other questions, but one screams louder than the others. "Did I change in front of you?"

He thinks for much longer than seems necessary and finally says, "No. But I did help with the zipper. The top part."

I slouch in my chair. How do I not remember?

"I brushed my teeth?" I ask.

"After our make-out sesh," he says, "you bolted to the toilet." He pauses and makes a gesture with his hand; I can confidently say it's a puking gesture.

"I... I threw up in front of you?"

He nods.

"When you got sick," he says, "you struggled putting your hair up in a ponytail, so I helped you tie your hair back—you asked me to help. Sorry if it was knotted this morning, I've never had to...." His fingers fumble above his head. "Do the hair thing for a woman before."

I'm sure I look horrified.

"I'll be honest," he says, "I've never experienced anything like that. My ex wouldn't let me see her without full makeup and hair. Anytime she was sick, she'd go by her mom's."

He stares into the platters of food, deep in thought. I'm positive he's completely repulsed by me.

"Big difference," he finally says. "After you were done, you asked me to grab your toothbrush from upstairs. So, I did. You brushed your teeth. No help needed from me. After that, you said you were starving, so I made Pop-Tarts, but when I came back to the bedroom, you were sleeping. Oh." He pounds a fist on the table. "Does your phone have a pink case?"

"Yeah."

"It's above your dad's toilet."

"Intact?"

"Yeah, even though you accidentally dropped it a couple of times, it survived the evening. No cracks or dings."

My body folds into itself. My forehead nearly lands on my now-cold scrambled eggs. The legs of Niall's stool screech against the floor.

"Katie," he says, "I'm sorry, I totally dragged that out. Much longer than I should have. I'm sorry for teasing you."

"You have every right," I say. "I was out of control."

"I don't have that right," he says, speaking softly. "And the whole VP role with your dad, that was tough, even from my perspective. I honestly thought you knew about the change." His ease is smooth and layers over me like warm butter. "And about me," he adds.

He's acting cool; I can be cool. But he won't stop calling me Katie. I scowl. He did make me a huge breakfast, which was nice, so I won't complain. Not now.

I sit upright.

Our eyes connect over the sausage platter. I offer a hesitant smile; his grin is twice the size as before. I pretend my cheeks aren't ablaze and ask him to please pass the bacon.

"Do you remember what I said last night about this partnership with your dad?" he asks and refills my plate, then loads an additional scoop of everything onto his.

I nod.

"I never intended to hurt you, Katie. I'm strictly here to help your dad's business. He's a great guy and very intelligent. Trust his judgement; he knows what's best for your family. He deserves to succeed."

I nod.

"You deserve all of that too," his voice grows quieter.

Niall's statement slams a surge of belief against my walls of uncertainty. Do I? After all that's happened.

"If there's anything I can do to help you realize that," he says, "let me know."

"Over winter break," I say, "I overheard Mother say my nickname should be chaotic Kate." A fake laugh dots my tagline.

"Negative labels are damning," he says. "You have the power to create your own destiny."

"I'm not that great at steering my own destiny," I say. "I was fired from Triple B's and wasn't even considered for the VP role." I wallow extra-hard. "And I used to teach dance, but Ms. Christie let me go a few weeks ago." I stare into his multi-colored eyes. "I've failed at everything."

Niall lightly taps his fingers against the marble counter.

"You're a great cook," he says.

"How would you know?" I frown.

"I've eaten at Triple B's a few times." His expression brightens. "And your dad brags about you every chance he gets."

My frown deepens.

"Keeping a job requires being responsible and showing up on time. I used to be much better about that before… everything happened. Since then, I feel as though I've forgotten how to do basic human tasks."

"You should give yourself more credit for your accomplishments and what you've been through."

"My dad took the VP role from me before I could mess it up. If Kylie were here, things would be different. Having her around made me a better person."

"Possibly, but you don't need others to create your own value. That's fully under your control. Your life isn't over; you have time to reset and start again. Every sunrise holds opportunity."

"I hate mornings, and nights aren't any better," I say. "When the sun sets, my insomnia kicks in, and recently nightmares have been added to the mix. When the sun rises… I'm one day farther from the past and how things used to be."

He sets his fork down.

"It's hard to lose someone you love," he says. "Can I ask you something?"

"Sure."

"When was the last time you tried really hard at something?"

"Honestly? Based on what you told me this morning. Trying to undo your zipper." I grin.

"It was intense," he says, and smirks.

We're adults. It was an innocent make-out session. Nothing more. A drunk, barely dressed woman threw herself at a gorgeous specimen. He's a man, of course, he'd momentarily lose control and forget it was me.

His face grows serious. "What if you try that hard at your future?" He allows me time to think. "Look, I'm not trying to tell you what to do, but you have so much potential. I hate for you to let all the remaining good fall apart around you."

"Did my dad tell you to say that?"

"No."

My shoulders settle. Maybe today won't be such a terrible day after all?

"I suppose I should get going," I say and stack my plate on top of two empty trays. I carry the dishes to the sink. "Another busy day. Shoot— what time is it? I have to get going. Piper is going to start harassing me if I'm late." I freeze when I reach the sink.

A see-through container of donuts sits next to the windowsill. Donuts.

"Katie?" Niall asks. "I need—"

"Donuts," I say, confused.

"I picked them up at the cafe. I know you like sweets."

Donuts.

I have fifty homemade donuts at the restaurant. But they weren't at the restaurant; they were in the trash. Who put them in the garbage?

"Katie," Niall says. "I'm stuck in the middle of a tricky situation."

I set the dishes in the sink and face him. With a wave of my hand, I brush away his concern. His tricky situation is trivial compared to my heartbreaking discovery. *Who ruined my donuts?*

"If my dad really wanted you to babysit me overnight," I say, "you can feel proud. Task complete. You are free to leave." I bow, salute, and curtsy. "Thanks to your help, I survived another night."

I stack more empty platters and carry them to the sink.

"Katie, there's something else," he says.

"What?" I turn towards Niall and playfully let my guard down. "Don't tell me you bought a Kringle for dessert. Tell me you didn't get apple? Cause I will literally devour the entire thing."

Niall's face has become closed off.

"No one died," he says, abruptly.

"What?" My heart stops. The look he's giving me is the same one my dad gave me at the hospital right before he told me someone died.

"Niall, you're scaring me." The plates I'm holding rattle. Niall rushes to my side and steadies them before they can crash to the floor.

Kylie, what terrible thing has happened now?

The Game
Friday, March 20th

OVER THE LAST month and a half, when I travel to Mayfair, Henry has insisted that I stay at his place. "Save money," he says, "keep me company, and we'll talk business."

During the day, Henry and I often walk through Weeping Willow Estates. Construction is progressing well, with the skeletal outlines of homes popping up everywhere. Henry introduces me to the workers on-site. Leo, Henry's electrician, doesn't start work until nine each morning because his wife works third shift, and they have a new baby at home. On Wednesdays and Fridays, Canter, Henry's plumber, leaves early to pick up his daughter from daycare. Eloise, the only female crew member, has an aging mother in a nursing home. She finishes her day at three so she can make the hour drive to Racine to have dinner with her mom. Henry's team of contractors has flexibility, yet produces higher-quality results within tighter timelines than any other residential development firm I've consulted.

On most afternoons, Henry and I end the day at his office. Henry says we work, but we usually talk baseball, and he reminisces about his younger years and marriages.

I like it when we go to the office, because that's when I can prove to myself that I'm worth every penny Henry is paying me.

The latest business enhancement I've created is a new website for Vanguard. Clients can add home-improvement design elements to their shopping cart. Two-story? Four bedrooms? First-floor master? Crown molding? Two-panel doors? Cedar shakes? Mullen green siding? As wishful homeowners add items to the cart, the home's estimated price is adjusted. The client can view a virtual mock-up of the build on the left-hand side of the page. Almost as easy as placing a customized sub sandwich order online. I came up with the idea while ordering an Italian special foot-long via a mobile app. Soo-jin helped bring my creative vision alive. She's a genius with technology. Henry was blown away by the state-of-the-art technology. The web version will go live sometime this fall. A mobile app will launch next summer. We've patented the technology, so if another development firm wishes to use a version of his app, Henry will make money.

Vanguard Family Builders is officially diversified.

When night rolls around, Henry and I shift gears, watching basketball games and ordering take-out from Triple B's. Twice, Henry has grilled brats and burgers for Dale, Tomas, and me. Yesterday, Henry bought tickets for the four of us to go to the Cubs-Brewers game in June. One weekend, I had to cancel my trip to Mayfair. Zoey, her babysitter, had come down with the flu. So, Bennett and I lined up some serious bro time. When I called Henry to cancel, he understood, and before I hung up, he said, "Take care, son."

Even as my days and nights in Mayfair take on new routines, Roxanne lingers on the edges of my thoughts. Since my night with her, she's texted me and sent ClickYaps. She wants to meet up again, but I keep telling her I'm busy. Which is partly true, because when I come to Mayfair, I'm really busy keeping Henry company, but the real truth is, I regret the one-night stand I had with her.

I'm ashamed. Embarrassed. When I slept with Roxy, I imagined I was fucking Kylie 1.0. When Roxy removed her bra and panties—her face disappeared too—Kylie's took her place. Roxanne became an extension of Kylie. Fucking Roxy made me feel closer to Kylie. Warped, I know, but this thing I have for Kylie has corrupted my brain.

Plus, Harrison was right again. Seven weeks of celibacy were ball-busting, and I needed a good lay. If I'm being honest, I would have rather spent that night with Jolene. My love life is a wreck right now.

Jolene…

Thinking back, the last time Jolene and I made love was the morning of her flight to California. The flight she almost missed. A quick 'see you soon' kiss at the door became a tornado of tossed clothing, ass cheeks sliding against the dinette table, and a bruise on my fucking forehead from the damn chandelier. The sex was worth it. I'd say it was the best sex Jolene and I had ever had. Soulful, touching, passionate. Honest. The kind that makes babies.

Babies.

Afterwards, I realized how something so small could bring up such contention between a couple. Who knew two people could feel so differently about a single topic? I'd have proposed to Jolene the same evening I bought the ring, but she doesn't want kids. Ever. Over time, I had hoped she'd change her mind. But she hasn't. She's set on a career in the spotlight, and she's said that when she's a washed-up actress at fifty who suddenly feels the need to nurture, she'll adopt.

A dog.

So, why did I stay with her as long as I did? Why did I bother buying the ring?

Jolene's gorgeous. She's smart, motivated, loyal, honest…

The night Mrs. Deveraux introduced me to Jolene, my life changed for the better. After Jolene and I exchanged ClickYaps, minutes later, she sent me nudes from the bathroom. We made love on the first date. She moved in a month later and… it's been easy ever since. Until it wasn't. Over these past few months, I've realized a lot. Jolene was as selfish as I was. Harrison was right. The image of her was way better than the reality.

Lately, Harrison's advice about Jolene has been astonishingly accurate, but when it comes to Kylie, things are different. I've dug deep and found nothing. Kylie and I've gone on two additional dates. A dinner at Carne in downtown Milwaukee, and a Lumineers concert at the Riverside. After each date, I wanted to fashion a flux capacitor, go back in time, and cancel. Her lack of personality is frustrating.

Kylie messages me a lot.

Kylie: Hey, Slide, looking forward to hanging out again.
Me: Me too.
Kylie: Did that snowstorm hit Chicago?
Me: Nope, just missed us.
Kylie: Do these jeans make my ass look good?
Me: Yes.
Kylie: Sure?
Me: Positive.
Kylie: You're just being nice.

I've begun to play a game. How vague and boring can I be before she breaks it off with me?

Kylie: Wanna hang this weekend?
Me: OK. What do you want to do?
Kylie: idk
Me: Me either.
Kylie: Dinner?
Me: Dinner would be fine.
Kylie: Great.
Me: Super.

Sometimes she sends selfies. I see parts of the girl from that first night. A sexy shadow. A smile that looks similar but different. A playfulness across her cheek. I reply to her with shots of the Chicago skyline if I'm in an Uber. Or pictures of Soo-jin's backyard when I'm at home.

Our connection feels strictly platonic. Every time I go in for a kiss—twice now—Kylie turns away at the last moment, and I end up with her cheek. She giggles, saying she's not ready for 'that'. Each time, my confidence plummets further. I feel awkward and stripped of my usual charisma—like an outsider looking in. Harrison's right. I need to rethink my entire approach to dating.

Today, when Kylie texted, she got a little deep. She explained her hesitation on our first date. She wasn't sure if she'd be around after college, so that's why she was so quiet at the bar. She didn't want to be tied down to Mayfair. I asked her if she was planning on moving; she didn't know.

Kylie: wyd
Me: Not much.
Kylie: It might rain here tonight.
Me: Really?
Kylie: Is it going to rain by you?
Me: Maybe.

I draft a message with what I really want to say, but don't have the balls to send it.

Me: Kylie, you are literally the most boring person I've ever met. I may die if I spend another second with you. Can we at least fuck and see if there's a spark?

I'm a major jackass. I erase it.

Me: Just checked the forecast, it's going to rain here too.
Kylie: Cool. Love rain.
Me: For sure.
Kylie: I almost forgot to tell you. I've got four tix for the Cubbies opener on April 7th. My dad got them from one of his Chicago buddies as a thank you for some work he did. But my dad hates the Cubbies. Would you wanna come? We could each bring a friend. A double-date. It'd be fun!

Baseball is fun.
Opening day?
Very fun.

Of course, I want to go. But… with Kylie?

Me: Sure.
Me: I appreciate you asking.
Kylie: To make it extra-fun, I won't say who I'm bringing, and you can't say who you're bringing.
Kylie: So, fun!

It won't be so fun.

Fun isn't even part of my vocabulary lately.

The most exciting thing to happen to me lately was another delivery from the Deveraux family. This time, the present was accompanied by a note: 'Gotcha', and a return address: Lance Deveraux's home. The padded, yellow envelope held a jump drive. Mysterious. And childish.

I'm running a legit business, and the Deveraux's are losing clients because they're dicks, not because I sought out their prospects. I haven't opened the friendly files yet. Inside, I'm sure I'll find a death threat from Lance. Or, his dad. Probably both. They need to move on.

I need to move on.

But not quite yet.

I'll give Kylie one more chance. If the double date doesn't go well, I'll break up with her at the game. A face-to-face conversation is necessary. Only assholes break up over text. At least I have a deadline now and a few weeks to come up with a great break-up speech.

Then I'll finally release Kylie's memory.

The original one.

Hidden Treasure
Saturday, May 28th @ 9:05 a.m.

MY DAD HAS the most genuine smile of anyone I know—a knowing smile that stretches from ear to ear. I've always wished I'd inherited his grin, but I wasn't so lucky. Kylie did. That is the only subtle difference between my sister and me. When she's happy, her smile is exactly like his.

A joker's smile.

Not only is my dad's smile big and bold, but he's always in a fantastic mood—unless I've annoyed him. He laughs a lot. Very little alters his disposition. At sunrise, he's as happy as when the sun sets. The constant joy he carries is matched by his attentive personality. His smile can lift the mood of a room.

But today, May 28th, the wedding day, the anniversary, the anniversary of the wedding day—my dad didn't wake up smiling. No. Henry Vanguard, who doesn't hesitate to work eighty hours a week in summer heat or freezing winter or answer a middle-of-the-night call from a friend in need, woke at three this morning with a tingling sensation in his face and a severe headache.

Believing he was experiencing the aftereffects of Dale's fruity shots, he went into his mother's living room to watch TV. After turning on *Grey's Anatomy*, he began having difficulty swallowing.

Thanks to Mother's constant health reminders and nagging sessions, my dad knew something was wrong. For safety reasons, Mother has always kept landline phones in every room of her house. My dad used the phone next to her recliner to call 911. And then Mother held his hand while he waited for the ambulance.

And that makes me sick. The grief hits me hard, churning alongside fear and guilt.

What if my dad had taken his drunk daughter home last night? His house doesn't have a phone in every room. That dark scenario presses in, fear twisting tighter. If he had been home with me, he would have died slowly, holding no one's hand, watching another episode of *Grey's Anatomy*.

Once the ambulance arrived, my dad called me, but—to no one's surprise—I was asleep, so he tried Peaches, then Niall.

And now, it's late morning, and Niall has known about my dad's condition for hours but has held back on telling me. The thoughtful man let me sleep in, fed me a big breakfast, then shared the news.

Niall was also being kind when he had asked about my phone earlier; he was worried I'd get a text or voicemail from a nosy neighbor. News travels quickly in our small town, and Niall wanted to share the news with me in person. After Niall assured me that my dad was recovering at the hospital, he insisted on driving with me. I agreed and quietly went upstairs to change. A step up from running away.

Now, I'm in my bedroom, recklessly digging through a stagnant pond of shirts, pants, tank tops, and sweaters, throwing all behind me in a fury.

I ask myself, "Why?"

Why is my dad so stubborn? Why can't he eat healthy? What if something horrible had happened to him? I couldn't survive another death. Why am I so afraid?

So many whys about Niall. Why did he spend the night? Why is he chaperoning me to the hospital? Cracker-crumb Dale hasn't ever been invited to babysit me. And he definitely doesn't come rapping on my bedroom door early in the morning. Why did my heart ricochet out of my chest when I recognized Niall's voice in the hall? Then he made me breakfast? Then I agreed to have him come to the hospital with me. I didn't even put up a fight. Why, why, why?

I scrape clothing off the floor and fling the trash across the room.

I pull myself onto my bed and flop face-first onto the blankets.

I ask myself another why? Why haven't I ever purchased a casually adorable outfit?

Combing through my vague resemblance to a wardrobe confirms my clothes are basic, unflattering, and should be donated to a thrift store. The truth hits me in the face as I yank a soiled shirt out from underneath my cheek. I've never matched a blouse to a pair of shoes or jewelry to a dress. My clothes aren't even fit for a charity drive.

One day, I will burn them all.

Growing up, Kylie claimed I was undiagnosed color-blind, and when we'd shop together, she'd shriek, "No!" anytime I pulled something off the rack.

Tragically, I've worn the same clothes since high school, except for when I might borrow a plain white t-shirt or a pair of gray socks from Kylie's wardrobe. Or, the very rare occasion, when Kylie would beg me to 'get cute', and I'd borrow one of her dresses or outfits so we could have a proper girls' night out.

Kylie, I need you now.

I close my eyes and spin in a circle. Faster and faster, until I'm dizzy with desperation. So dizzy that I wobble unsteadily on my feet, catch my balance, and finally stop swaying. I open my eyes and look for a sign.

In front of me is the bedroom's large walk-in closet. A room I've never entered. If I were to use a closet—and I wouldn't—I'd use the tiny one on the other side of the room where my red dress was hanging. I step forward. The door to this room has remained closed ever since I moved back home.

Kylie's cherished belongings reside just six feet from my bed. Even her chic clothes. All in my closet.

I hesitate.

What if I open the door and memories are triggered? Memories I don't want to remember? What if nothing happens? I shouldn't be nervous; it's a damn closet full of boxes. I shouldn't be afraid of a closet. I make my way towards the door. When I'm inches away, I pause. Like a long-distance runner preparing to run the race of a lifetime, I rub my hands up and down my thighs, roll my shoulders, and crack my neck. Before I lose my nerve, I snap the handle down and push. The door flings inward, collides against something solid, and bounces shut.

I jump.

It's just a closet.

Again, I jerk the handle and open the door. Slowly this time.

Dark shadows surround a windowless room stacked full of storage containers, cardboard boxes, and plastic bins. I flick on the light switch outside the door, rest both hands against the frame, and tentatively step inside. Carefully placed labels are affixed to the sides of each bin. 'Shoes', 'Summer clothes', 'Fall sweaters', 'Winter wear', 'Books'.

The scary monsters and memories stay hidden.

The closet is jam-packed. Kylie's boxes fill one side of the wall.

An oversized wooden chest sits on the other. Mothers' precious chest is here. No doubt brimming with partially finished manuscripts, word lists, books about writing, books about editing, and everything and anything Kylie and I weren't supposed to go through.

I'll go through it later.

Zakary must have moved it here yesterday while he and my dad were cleaning out Mother's place. I reach forward to touch the antique crate—the closet light flickers. It seems I've overstayed my welcome. With no need for a second nudge, I grab Kylie's 'Summer box', then rush out of the room and yank the door closed. In my hurry, the box slips from my hands and topples onto the carpet. Kylie's neatly folded clothes tumble to the floor.

Kylie's lovely treasures.

Thank you, Kylie.

"You about ready?"

I startle.

Niall is standing in my bedroom doorway, leaning against the frame. Casually curious. I can't tell if he's bored, annoyed, or interested. Casual curiosity could mean many things. He didn't barge in; he's polite. A gentleman? Or is he irritated that I'm taking so long? Maybe I'm overthinking it, and he couldn't care less?

He's watching me.

What's on his mind?

I hug my arms around my chest and survey the room. Discarded clothes cover the floor. My bright pink comforter is crumpled in a heap in the middle of the bed. Empty cups and plates line the dresser. Niall has figuratively caught me with my pants down. Embarrassment blazes as I realize how long I've been up here with nothing to show. My body warms with shame and frustration.

I search the room, but keep returning to Niall.

Niall.

A dreamboat standing in my room. Yesterday, he was an angelic vision at the restaurant, and when we bumped into each other at my dad's office, he was worth all of $1200. And now he's showered and changed into jeans and a polo looking yummy. He seems to have a very clear understanding of fashion.

He'll have to do.

I hug myself tighter and helplessly look to him. "I'm not sure what I should wear," I say.

He reviews the contents strewn about the room, the piles lining the walls, and the bed. Scans again. "Pick something from there." He points to Kylie's partially folded clothing.

I kneel next to the heap. As though I've come across an ancient burial site and must first acknowledge the items' beauty, I pass my hands over the collection. A bright pink tank top lies nearest me. I clutch the cool fabric and hold it against my face. The soft cloth caresses my cheek; I breathe deeply. Fresh and sweet, like my sister. Kylie's laundry always smelled wonderful.

"Would you mind helping me?" I ask.

Niall's still patiently standing in the doorway.

"With what?" he asks.

His facial expression doesn't change, but there's a hint of something else in his voice. As though he doesn't notice I'm a walking disaster. A lost girl asking for directions. As though everything were perfectly normal. I can't pinpoint his disposition, but I've no one else to turn to.

I need him.

He and his ability to do everything right. I gesture towards the clean section of my bed. "You can sit there while I change," I say, "and then let me know if the outfit I pick is okay. I mean—if you don't mind."

"Sure," he quickly says. When he walks to my bed, he uses unnecessary care as he steps over the piles.

He sits on my pink pillow, propping his hands behind his head, his back pressed against the headrest. Hollywood Hair is lying on my bed. His fantastic ass is pressed against my pillow. The room is hot. Dry. Like a desert. I breathe in and exhale. Cough. Doesn't help. There must be something wrong with the air ducts.

Maybe I'm catching a cold? I can't get sick; I've way too many stupid things to do. Hunt that murderer. A ghost to hide from. Twenty-ish assignments to finish. A dad to impress. A party to fake my way through. A mother to apologize to. More vitamins. Different pills. I need to Google more than shortness of breath, rapid heartbeat, dizziness, unexplained tiredness, and fainting. Later today or tomorrow, I'll expand my search to include life-like conversations with the dead and visions of the dead.

"Want to know an easy way to choose an outfit?" he asks. "It's really a life hack."

I examine Kylie's clothes and feel overwhelmed. Last month, I did nothing but binge-watch life hacks on TikTok and YouTube. My screen time was off the charts. But I learned a lot, so I didn't consider it a complete waste of time. I bet Niall's life hack could save mankind.

"Sure," I say and shrug.

"Grab a few shirts, pants, and skirts. Try on a few combinations, even if you don't think they'll match. Then, take a picture of yourself in the mirror. Not a selfie but a picture of your reflection in the mirror. After you've tried on five or six, scroll through the pics. For some reason, it's easier to get an unbiased view of a photo rather than a mirror."

Brilliance. Sheer ingenuity. I want to leap on the bed and hug him. As a thank you gesture, not because I want to lie on top of him, while he lies on top of my bed. That's definitely not what I was thinking.

"Saw it in a movie," he adds.

He settles his ass further onto my pillow, stretches, and pulls his phone out of his front pocket.

"You can't watch me change." I wipe the back of my hand against the side of my mouth. I may be drooling.

"Of course not," he says. But his amazing ass doesn't move.

I squat, grab a few tops, skirts, shorts, and pants, and stand. I frown while clutching my treasures.

"Well?" I ask. The room seems hotter than ever, and now I'm breathing too deeply through my mouth, as though I'm congested.

"The closet can be your changing room," he says. He lifts his phone and shakes it. "I'll take pics." I look at him as though a family of centipedes is crawling out of his ears. "Or," he says, "I can turn around?"

"No, the closet is fine."

"Go on," he says and nods. "I told your dad we'd be there before midnight."

"Very funny." I fumble with the handle. "Oh, hey. Can you please shut my bedroom door? I know there's zero chance anyone will show up. One time, Mother caught me and my ex on my bed—we were just studying, but she went nuts. A grown man in my room while I was changing?" I laugh, a crazy laugh. "She'd go crazy."

Since my back is to Niall, I can't see his face, but I'm certain he's lost his composure. He's realized I'm mentally unstable.

"No problem," he says. The bed creaks. The blanket rustles, and a second later, the door clicks closed.

I enter the not-so-scary closet and close the door.

Summer *is* coming, but today is a typical spring day by the lakefront. The winds won't allow the temperature to break into anything close to tank-top weather. And I hate being cold, so I pick a pair of jeans and a light-weight, soft pink, long-sleeved shirt. Maybe it's a sweater? I'm unsure if the clothes are designer or expensive, but they smell like Kylie, and that makes my heart swell. Plus, I think I wore this same top last winter.

But I still need underwear…

I slowly open the door and peek my head out.

Niall's eyes are closed.

"Hey," I say.

His eyes open, and he smiles.

I point towards the department store bag on the bed. "Can you toss me that?"

I'll have to wear Piper's damn undergarments. He tosses me the bag—I barely catch it—and retreat to my changing room. Inside the closet, I remove my shirt and shorts, slide on the lacey bra and panties. I slip Kylie's shirt over my head and pull on the denim pants.

After I'm dressed, I preview my look. The top is inside out. I remove it and put it on correctly. Everything seems to fit. I breathe deeply and step out of the closet.

Niall is sitting up now, legs crossed at the knees, hunched over his phone. He looks up and stares as though he's seen a ghost. I tilt my head to the side. The shirt feels pink enough. Maybe too pink? Does the color wash out my skin? The jeans probably don't go with the shirt. I lift my hands at my sides.

"Well…" I say.

He looks down at his phone, swipes the screen. The phone lifts, and he holds it steady. A flash blinds me; I blink.

"I wasn't ready," I say, feeling anxious.

He rises to a kneeling position while examining his phone.

"These kinds of pics don't require a smile," he claims. "Just capturing the clothes."

"I suppose." I slowly walk towards the bed. "You're the expert, right?"

"Something like that." He's an artist, working his craft: his craft of being amazing at everything. "So, the closet?" he asks and looks up.

"Is that a question?" I ask. My voice falters.

"You were swearing when I was walking up the stairs," he says, "and since I wasn't in the room, I assumed you were swearing at something in here."

"I don't know what else my dad told you about me…" I stop at the edge of the bed.

"A little," he says. His expression is quite serious. "Can you turn to the side, and all the way around? You want a 360-degree view of the clothes."

"Sure." I slowly spin.

"I'm all ears," he says. "If you want to share."

"I don't," I say and pull the sleeves down on my sweater. There's no reason to share my PTSD-like symptoms and loss of memory with a stranger. I allow the soft fabric to hug me, as though Kylie were with me now. "How do the pics look?"

He crawls towards the side of the bed and stands next to me. The first picture shows the beginnings of Kylie's frown, Mother's perfect laugh lines, a partial Joker smile, and the scar. I don't even notice if the clothes look appropriate.

"What do you think?" he asks.

"Honestly, I hate myself in pictures. Can I see the rest?"

"You've picked a winner," he says. "Perfect outfit for a hospital visit."

"What about the others?"

He scrolls back. A photo of him holding that Gerber baby pops up. "I didn't take any other pics," he says.

"What?" I ask. "You had me spin and… I thought you were taking pics. You said a 360-degree view was important."

"Correct," he says, "it was."

I make a fist and lightly graze the mattress.

"You're a brat," I say.

I stare at his fingers, the hair trailing up his arm. His nice pants. The air has been completely sucked out of the room. In hopes of finding more breathing space, I walk towards Kylie's pile.

"Mission accomplished," he says. "You're wearing a presentable outfit."

I scoop her clothes into my arms. The pile blinds my line of sight. I walk toward my dresser.

"Oh," Niall says, "steer left, there's a wall to your right."

I peek around my clothes and mumble, "Thank you."

Once I make it to the dresser—thankfully—without tripping over anything, I stand still, because I'm not sure how one 'works' a dresser.

The bed creaks. Within seconds, Niall is standing next to me. He opens the top drawer, which is full, so he opens the next one. I let the clothes from the bottom fall. He opens another drawer. I set the remaining pieces in the neighboring drawer, as neatly as my disorganized brain allows.

Niall leans against the furniture and stares at my uneven piles.

"We can take my car," I say. "You, no good Illinois drivers, are the worst. Plus, you don't know where we're going, and I need to grab something from Triple B's before we go to the hospital."

The dumpster must reveal its secrets.

He responds with a closed-mouth grin, repressing any comments, and says, "Cool, my car's kinda trashed anyway."

We walk down the stairs; I self-consciously comb my fingers through my hair and hope my scar is properly covered. Niall uses the guest bathroom while I grab my phone from my dad's bathroom. Then, I lead the way through the mudroom door to the garage.

Inside the garage, he halts.

"No way," he says.

"What?" I swivel around.

He points at my car. "This is yours?"

"Yeah... why?"

"What year?"

"2010."

"No way..." He brings a fist up and covers his gaping mouth. "You have to open the garage door."

I send him a sideways glance and do as he asks, but I was going to open the garage door anyway. I click the opener on the wall and follow him to the back of my car. His arm bumps into mine. An innocent smile fills his face, and his eyes hold a flickering gleam. My car is parked in the driveway. No, the vehicle on the road *looks* like my car.

It's his.

"The same?" I ask.

We exchange surprised smiles, although this time mine has to be ten times bigger than his, and then I outright laugh. A joyful sound. At first, I don't even realize I'm giggling. And when my sides begin to ache, I try to stop the feeling, but the feeling I'm feeling feels so good. Foreign. Like a once-in-a-lifetime trip with your best friend. You want to soak it all in and stay forever. Niall patiently waits for me to complete my uncontrollable outburst.

I attempt to catch my breath.

"Why, though?" I ask. A snort slips out, tears fall. "Why do you have a 2010 Volkswagen Golf? You're mature and have a proper job. I mean, I know why I have one, but you?"

He stuffs his hands in his pockets. "It's sensible." His shoulders lift. "I travel a lot, and it gets good gas mileage." His innocence is adorable. "Plus, my condo was expensive, and no car payment is a bonus. Chicago traffic is brutal; I usually Uber every chance I get, anyway."

Once my laughter subsides, and I clear the front passenger seat of disposable coffee cups, empty convenience store bags, and straw wrappers, we hit the road. Niall fills the silence by asking mundane questions about my car.

I share my car story.

After Kylie and I passed our driver's exam, our dad surprised us and said he'd buy us a used car to share—within a set budget—if we could agree on the same vehicle. In the best of parenting fashion, Dad tricked Kylie and me into working together towards a common goal.

Kylie picked a blue Jeep, and I chose a white tuner car. Growing up, I had zero interest in cars, but the summer before my parents divorced the first time, my dad took Kylie and me to the movie theatre to watch the Disney *Cars* movie three times. Dad's favorite part was when the tuner cars showed up and disturbed the sleepy semi. That was when I fell in love with speedy cars with personality.

Not that I'd ever speed. The car just looked really slick at the dealership, and I wanted my dad to think I was his cool daughter.

After Kylie and I test-drove both vehicles, she changed her mind and voted for the Volkswagen. This was a tactic she'd often used. I tell Niall I think she often felt guilty for scarring my cheek when we were kids, so she'd often bend over backwards to be super kind to me.

And that's when Niall clears his throat. I glance over at him; he quickly looks out the window. Out of habit, I cover my cheek. I didn't even realize it, but while I was fumbling with the car keys, I had put my hair up in a bun—all of it—so Niall had to look at my blemish the entire car ride.

"Katie." He lets out a long breath of air. "I'm sorry I mentioned your scar yesterday when we were at your dad's office. I didn't mean to embarrass you or make you feel self-conscious. I didn't notice it… before. That's all."

From my peripheral vision, I watch as he pulls at his jeans and shifts in the seat.

"Before what?" I ask.

"Well, uh, before this week—I mean, today."

Confused, I correct him, "You mean at the restaurant… yesterday. When I was lying on the floor… I felt you touch my face."

I've forgotten a few things, but I definitely remember that warm touch tracing my jawline.

"Um, yeah," he says, and looks out the window.

Niall doesn't say, "Um." His answers are confident and direct. "Yeah," isn't in his vernacular either. And last night I distinctly asked him if we had ever met before. He said no. But, just now, he said 'before this week'. Have we met before?

If so, when?

If so, why would he lie about it?

If so, why don't I remember?

Unearned Treasure
Saturday, May 28th @ 10:33 a.m.

AFTER NIALL'S STRANGE apology, his phone rings. It's some guy named Harrison. Niall calls the man a dick. The two must be pretty close, because Niall says things like, "Bruh," "Nah," and "Gonna." I've never heard Niall sound so human.

Harrison seems to know me because Niall says, "She's here now." Who is Harrison, and why would he know I'm with Niall? Harrison responds with something particularly 'dicky' because Niall quietly tells him to, "Fuck off." Now, I'm feeling more feelings, and the most prominent one is that Niall would rather be alone right now, so he can have a proper multi-word conversation with his dicky friend.

Why is Niall carting me around anyway? I should have insisted on driving myself. But Niall's right, although I'm strong, I'm pretty sure he could chase me down and throw me over his shoulder, eyes closed, in under five seconds. That solid ten build is no joke.

The ride to Triple B's is full, so full it's nearly overflowing. Full of Niall's broken conversation.

"Uh-huh."

"..."

"Not now."

"…"

"Maybe."

"…"

"Not yet."

"…"

"Bet."

I'm full of wondering why Niall may be lying to me. Full of worrying about my dad. It's overflowing now, because the closer we get to Triple B's, the more anxious I become about my stupid donuts. Thinking someone may have thrown away my hard work sickens me. Knowing would be a thousand times worse.

The wedding isn't happening this weekend. Obviously. So, I guess it doesn't matter if the donuts are ruined. But it's imperative I discover the truth.

The delicious food I ate for breakfast has had time to slosh with the remnants of alcohol in my system. The combination is making me nauseous. I open the car window.

At the restaurant, the Hundred brothers' Honda Civic is parked alongside the building. The restaurant won't open for another hour, so I park in front. After I turn off the ignition, Niall moves for the door handle, but I quickly wave for him to stay put.

Since he's still on the phone, I mouth, "Be right back." An audience is unnecessary for my Saturday morning dumpster dive. Although he's experienced a kaleidoscope of Kate over the prior twenty-four hours, this outing might be particularly depressing, so I'd rather take the trip solo. Plus, while I'm gone, he can sprinkle creative words into his conversation.

I slip out of the car.

The garage doors to the dining room are open. In case the brothers saw me park, I peek inside, and holler, "Hello!"

Sebastian pops his head over the bar counter.

"Hey, Kate!" He waves.

"Hey, Sebastian." I wave back.

"Gonna be a nice day today," he says and rounds the bar, joining me on the patio.

"Sure is."

"Gonna be packed here today."

"Memorial weekend always is."

For a moment, we soak in the sight of Lake Michigan disappearing into the horizon.

"Do you…" He points to the kitchen door. "Did you leave something?"

"Uh, yeah. Maybe," I say. "Did you happen to find a stack of pastry boxes in the dry storage closet? Underneath the bread?"

"There's nothing back there," he says. "And we used up all the buns last night. Bear's heading to the distributor right now to get more before we open."

"Oh, okay," I say. "I had made donuts for the rehearsal dinner, and they were in the back. But the wedding isn't happening. I'm not sure if you heard? My dad's in the hospital. Mother is going to be beside herself."

"I know… uh," he says, not even bothering to hide his alarming expression. "Sorry to hear that." Sebastian stares at the pavement. "I'm sorry, Kate," he says. "I'm not good with—I don't know what to say…"

"There's nothing to say."

"I'm sorry to hear you're leaving," he says. "We miss you already."

"Time to move on to bigger and better things," I say. "I'm gonna head out now. Just gotta check the dumpster real quick."

He does little to hide his surprise.

"Sure, you didn't see anyone take pastry boxes out of the kitchen last night?" I press.

"At like nine thirty," he says, "the entire Chinooks team came in. Bear said we could keep the fryers on. You know, support a local college. Their season opener is next week, so they all came in for a final night out. Peaches and Babs took food orders nonstop until midnight. Crazy busy night. I didn't see anything coming in or out of the kitchen but burgers, Babs' hair clips, and Andy's flustered ass."

I bob my head.

"Wait—" he says. "Nora came by earlier in the night. She grabbed something from the back. A white box?"

Nora?

"Yeah," I say, defeated, "that would have been it." I start walking towards the side of the restaurant.

"Later, Kate." His goodbye falls into the lake, alongside my intuition. Nothing is making sense lately.

I huff and head to the alley.

Nosey, meddling Nora. My dad's personal assistant. And now his hostile dietician. If Nora's so set on 'saving' my dad, there's a really good chance she'd murder Doe just to keep his allergies in check.

If she has it in her to kill a cat, could she kill a person? Nora is sweet. Maybe too sweet? She loves my parents. Maybe too much? Practically worships them. But could that love turn toxic?

Cass remains my top suspect, but my intuition has been unreliable lately. Clearly, I was mistaken about Professor Holliday, though I lack enough evidence to exonerate him completely. If only I could talk to Mother, but I worry she's at her wit's end with me, and I may never mend our relationship.

My mind races with wonder.

The sun is too bright, the sky too blue. I squint and massage my forehead.

I think I have another migraine coming on.

This holiday weekend signals the beginning of three short Wisconsin summer months. With warmer weather, residents have a reason to bring out lawn chairs from storage, scrape off caked charcoal from grills, and pile wood near fire pits. The town of Mayfair has 12 weekends to enjoy the sun while hosting cookouts, beer parties, and Sunday pool gatherings.

I pause at the alley entrance.

A thick wall of leafy trees and shrubs lines the drive. To my right, the possible final resting place of the desserts. A shadow above catches my attention. I look up and grin. Two chickadees fly overhead. They flutter then perch atop the dumpster. Like a small child excited to see Santa, I clap my hands and wave.

But then I'm frowning. A dumpster can attract these flighty birds, but Dad's secluded backyard, heaped with specialty bird seed, and a multi-level feeder, isn't good enough?

Hoping to hear their little song, I softly whistle, "Hey, Sweetie!"

I'm not shitting when I say this, but I swear the two birds look directly at each other, then me, and decide to fly off into the clearing.

I whimper to myself. My self-pity is at an all-time high.

As I near the trash bins, my pace slows. Rancid garbage and rotting food choke the crisp morning air. My stomach begins to churn. I stop in front of my old, smelly friend and pat the black lid.

After several seconds, I lift the cover. The hinges creak. Donuts lay scattered atop stale, half-eaten fries, canisters of day-old grease, and bags of shredded garnish peelings. When I release the cover, it slams shut with a thud. The movement jars something deep within my chest. I think something inside of me just broke.

Hope?

Hope that people value me.

That I matter.

That my kindness is received with love and acceptance.

How can someone close to me—my family—be blatantly dishonest and lead me astray? Lie to my face. How can hope exist in this environment? It can't. Any hope I had just broke, and from the jagged creases a black sludge of betrayal seeped out and hardened my chest.

I can't trust anyone.

Head down, walking slowly, I return to the front of the building. On the grass, the chickadees have returned. They're mocking me now. They've perched on an empty Miller Lite bottle.

"Really!" I lift my arms in the air and stomp my feet. The birds fly away.

A fishy breeze blows off the lake. Although no one's going to turn that scent into a wax candle melt, there's something about it that draws me closer. I walk to the edge of the bluffs. Taking some time to myself, listening to the water lap against the shore is just what I need. I stare into the horizon.

A motherly coo calls, "Kate, hun, what are you doing over there?"

Auntie Babs.

Auntie has been waitressing at Triple B's ever since she and Nora moved to Mayfair from northern Wisconsin last fall. The two relocated here after my dad offered Babs the opportunity to represent Weeping Willow Estates as the listing agent for his new construction homes. Nora is optimistic, like her mother. Around people, they both shine. Around them, I get a migraine. Babs works two part-time customer service jobs because she—no lie—loves people. I can't believe I'm related to the woman. Since Babs' shift has only begun, a single pink hair clip holds up a frosted, brunette head of hair. By the end of the night, six or seven barrettes will be scattered throughout her locks. She's an attractive older woman and attracts as many older male customers as Roxy attracts younger ones. She's Mother's twin sister. Fraternal twins. They look similar, like any sisters, but aren't identical. Bab's has dimples, and mother has wide laugh lines. Both seem to be stuck in the 80s.

Their smiles are deadly.

"Oh, hey, Aunt Babs," I say and tuck my hands further inside my pockets.

She cocks her head to the side and fusses, "You don't look so well. I heard about your dad. I knew you wouldn't be well. Come here, hun." She folds me in a hug. "You need anything? You just find me."

"I'm fine," I whisper. The sun peeks out from behind a cloud, and the sudden brightness stings my eyes. "And thank you. I will."

"Say, how is your bird feeder coming along?" she asks and steps back, but doesn't let go. She squeezes my shoulders. "I was thinking. Did your mother allow that cat of hers in the backyard?"

"Doe?" I ask.

She nods.

"Maybe the birds are afraid of a predator?" She says 'predator' as though Doe is equivalent to death itself.

"Actually, Doe's never been at my dad's," I say and shrug. "And, unfortunately, she never will." A guilty lump forms in my throat; I swallow. "She died yesterday." Whether I killed her or not—which I didn't—I can't deny I was supposed to be cat-sitting her. And it seems I was the last person to see her alive.

"Oh dear, how awful," she says and smiles. "Well, I bought some new seeds for you. Left them in your dad's garage. Fill your bird feeder tonight. By the morning, the birds will be eating away. I bet you'll have robins and red-winged blackbirds. They usually make their way back to Wisconsin in February, although this year it was March. March fifteenth, to be exact. Oh, and I was referring to red-winged blackbirds, not robins. Have you heard a cong-la-REE in the fields by your daddy's?"

Babs educates me on Soras, a marsh-loving family of birds, plump birds, white-throated sparrows, yellowlegs, killdeer, and black-bellied plovers. I want to tell her I don't give a damn about birds in general; I just want one stupid chickadee to land on my bird feeder and chirp. Just one and just once.

Instead, I smirk and say, "And what about chickadees?"

Her eyes light up. She purrs, "Chickadees are my favorite. They will adore these seeds. Did you know that when a chickadee senses danger, their precious, 'Hey, sweetie!' chirp transforms into the famous 'Ham-bur-ger'," she emphasizes each syllable. "The more 'ers' at the end, the bigger the perceived threat." She grins.

Auntie suddenly realizes she's going to be late for her shift and nearly collapses my lungs with her tight hug. "Love you so much, baby girl. Call me for anything."

Finished with my disappointing but enlightening mission, I return to the car. I open the driver's side door and plop into the seat. Niall's melodic laughter fills the vehicle. I'm glad he was able to enjoy a private conversation with Harrison.

"Find what you needed?" Niall asks.

"I did," I say and smile wider, hoping my attempt at a Joker face resembles my father's more than a disturbed clown's. Niall frowns and tells Harrison he needs to go.

The low fuel light on my dashboard flashes, so we head to the gas station just ahead. I steer into the town's only convenience store.

After I finish pumping gas, I jog inside the store. In front of the beverage section, I vacillate between carbonated beverages, flavored waters, and old-fashioned bottled water. I grab two bottles of distilled water, two bottles of cola, and two bottles of sugar-free sports drink.

Jelly donuts are on sale. I buy a pack. A terrible get-well gift for someone who's had a stroke, but food is my dad's love language. I double-bag the gift. If Mother were to spot my offering, she'd faint.

As I carry the heavy bag of drinks back to the Volkswagen, my heart skips. Niall is standing outside my vehicle, leaning into the back seat. He comes up for air with two fistfuls of plastic bags, empty paper cups, and wrappers. I stop next to the rearview mirror.

"You don't have to do that," I say. My tone comes out snippy, but I'm not mad. Just confused. Nothing this man does makes sense. He's impossible to figure out.

"Sorry," he says, "I thought I'd help." He quickly turns away from me, but then just as quickly, grabs another heap of trash from my car and tosses it into the garbage. And I can't help but shake this feeling that I just caught him doing something wrong.

Inside the car, I hand Niall the bag of goodies, and he smiles, but then quickly looks worried.

"What?" I ask. "Are you going to criticize my 'get well soon' gift for my dad?"

Niall takes his time. I know he wants to say something, and it's probably something I won't like, because he's stalling. Niall is not one to pause. He is direct and confident. What has shaken his confidence this time?

He reaches into his back pocket and hands me a phone. I stare at him, confused.

"I found that," he says and nods to the phone in his hand. "In the backseat."

Confused, I look down. The phone Niall is holding has a pink case like mine, but a spiderweb crack covers the upper-right corner. The phone is not mine.

It's Kylie's.

Chanel No. 5
Saturday, May 28th @ 11:02 a.m.

THE REST OF the ride, I feel as though my body is in a trance. Although Kylie's phone is dead, it seems to burn through my pocket.

How did the phone get in my car?

Was it here all along?

I know I'm not the cleanest person, but I've searched this vehicle countless times for her device. There's no way I could have missed it. But somehow Niall finds it during a five-minute cleaning frenzy?

Not only that, but he seemed super weird about finding my sister's cell. And I can't be certain, but did he almost try to hide it from me? If I had not caught him fumbling with my garbage, would he have kept the phone in his pocket?

What is going on?

Likely, I'm imagining things, and it's just another weird red herring, trying to distract me from my true mission.

While my mind spirals with plotting, planning, and prioritizing, Niall leaves two voicemails for his clients before calling his dry cleaner.

Once at the hospital, outside the car, Niall falls in step beside me. At the receptionist stand, a perky-breasted woman wearing a floral knitted sweater appears annoyed with our presence. Her name tag reads: Amanda. Amanda asks for the last name, then the first. She says Mr. Vanguard is in room three, oh, four. I've no idea if my dad is in the ICU or a regular room, and I'm too afraid to ask, so I nod and chew on my bottom lip.

On the way to the elevator, the back of Niall's hand brushes against mine, and our fingers intertwine. His thumb rubs above my bandage.

He's being nice again.

Nothing more.

After Amanda said my dad's room number, I sniffled.

Signs to the third floor lead us away from the first-floor intensive care wing, past the cancer unit to the west, and beyond the second-floor mental health clinic, which isn't on the second floor at all but beyond the hospital in a separate building, ridiculously named 'Second Floor Up'. The hospital's layout is like a maze.

Since I haven't spoken to my dad yet, and the only knowledge I have of his condition is from Niall—a near-stranger—I've built a flimsy dam, founded upon the belief that everything works out for the best. A heavy waterfall piles up behind the barrier.

Outside my dad's room, Niall releases my sweaty hand and asks to borrow my car keys. He claims he forgot something. I know that's a fib. Niall is not the forgetful type. He's giving me privacy.

After Niall leaves, I step forward and knock on the door. A few seconds pass, and a voice from the other side grows louder. The door opens. Chanel No. 5 seeps into the hall. And Mother's presence.

"Good, you made it," she says and gently pulls the handle closed. Her nails softly click against the metal door. "Your dad's fine. All this fuss for no reason." She flicks a wrist at the fussy hospital.

I nod and wait for more assurance; I'm afraid that if I speak, the pressure behind the dam will mount.

"Although I wasn't with your father when he started feeling uncomfortable," she says, "thanks to my adamant prayers, he's doing great. Not that I ever doubted." She sighs and measures me. "You know, your father wouldn't be in this condition if we helped him stick to a diet…" She's an angel, of course; she's the reason he's still alive. Although I'm not entirely convinced my mother saved my dad from anything. Lately, I've begun to doubt her. And our conversations. I think she's been lying to me, too.

I stare at the door. *Three-oh-four, three-oh-four, three-oh-four.* She scolds me. My thoughtless, drunken behavior could have killed her fiancé.

I should apologize.

The hall becomes silent. The air feels mystical. Mother's perfume cradles me until it crushes me.

I call for her.

"Mother?" I ask. I'm certain my voice sounds childlike. Pleading. Scared. I wish I could look into her eyes. The desire to gaze upon her beautiful face overwhelms me. But I can't. My chest inflates, like a blown-up balloon. Stretching, pulling, on the verge of exploding. *Three-oh-four, there-oh-four, three-oh-four.*

"I'm very sorry for everything," I say. "I'm just curious. Not imperfect. And I know you tried your best with us. You loved—love us. But I wasn't there for you when you needed me most… I'm so sorry."

She responds, but my hearing is muffled. I wish I could understand her, but she represents the truth, and I'm not ready to hear the truth just yet. Heels click down the hallway, and then there's a tap on my shoulder.

"Mother?" I whisper and turn around, but she's gone.

Niall is standing behind me.

"Niall," I say and push my heart back inside my chest. "You scared me."

"Sorry," he says. "I said your name, but you didn't hear me. You were talking to yourself. Oh, hey," he adds, "did you see—"

"I did." I quickly cut him off. I have no interest in talking about her. If only she would let me apologize, maybe I'd feel better? But she doesn't have time for me anymore. I've run out of time.

I raise my eyebrows and stare quizzically at the loot Niall's holding. He smiles triumphantly and holds up a bag of potato chips, cheese crackers, and a candy bar. "I stumbled across these," he says. "You hungry?" He's also grabbed my gas station treats from the car. "A hospital charcutier board." He grins.

Unable to stand Niall's curious kindness, sympathetic frown, or the hallway noises and smells, I turn from him and use more strength than necessary to shove open the door. Once inside, I abruptly stop. Niall bumps into my back.

"Sorry," I whisper.

A privacy curtain separates me from my dad. Niall is standing next to me. Our arms collide—I misjudged how close he was. I stare at the curtain and whisper another, "Sorry."

The force behind the dam grows stronger. Afraid that if I stand in place any longer, the compromised structure will burst, but knowing that if I round the privacy curtain, it will anyway, I lift my arm and slide the panel open. Metal hooks grate against the ceiling rails.

My capable father is lying underneath a glacial hospital blanket, wearing a flimsy hospital gown. Slip-resistant hospital socks poke out from underneath the sheet. Monitors beep. Lights flash. The scene is unnatural, like a bone that's been broken and twisted the wrong way.

He's sleeping peacefully. His skin is pallid. But I imagine he's awake and reaches his arms out. I run to him and climb on the bed. I make myself fit against the bed's armrest and his chest. And just like that, everything feels perfect. I scoot closer, shut my eyes, and sniffle into his arm. The hard aluminum railing jabs into my back. My dad's fragility and the fact that Niall is witnessing another of my highly personal interactions forbid me from moving. And if I were to move, the dam inside of me would collapse, and I won't let Niall see me cry. Some things should be left sacred.

Niall and his charm take a seat beside the bed in the guest chair.

My terrified squeezing must wake my dad.

"Kate," my dad says, groggily, "oh, I'm so glad you're here. So glad. No need to get emotional. The doctors say I'm fit as a second-hand, Craigslist Black and Decker jigsaw. I still need to lose a few pounds, but other than that, I'm not going anywhere today. Man, what a morning!"

He stretches and pats my back. His chuckle is weak, but his sense of humor is strong. I scoot closer and shut my eyes.

"Niall, there you are, good man," he says, "thank you for bringing my girl."

Their hands clap together, and Dad lets out another, "Man, what a morning."

"Henry," Niall says, "anything you need? Name it. It's done."

I lay quietly while my dad talks through the morning's hectic events. He'll be released tomorrow and then must rest for two weeks. But… he says he'll make a full recovery.

Dad and Niall discuss all things Weeping Willow: fixture, lighting, and fan install dates. To my surprise, Niall has already been prepped in handling the day-to-day operational tasks my dad usually monitors. Starting next week, while Dad is mending, Niall will oversee the contractors. The transition will be seamless. Seamless and uneventful for everyone but me.

Niall's phone rings; he excuses himself and leaves the room. The door clicks shut.

"If anything happens to you, Dad," I say, "I'll die. Mother is right, we need to take better care of you."

He clears his throat.

This is when most people would say, 'You just never know when your last day will be, 'Time is never promised,' or 'I love you.' Instead, my dad embraces me, and our feelings are expressed without speaking. We share a couple more squeezes, then my phone buzzes. I pull it from my back pocket.

"It's Piper," I say, sitting up. "She's going to want to talk to you."

"I had to put my phone over there," he says and points to the closet. "She's been calling all morning. One of the nurses helped me silence the dang thing. You know, she's going to scold me and you for all the sweets we eat. Go ahead and answer. Man, let's just get this over with." His Joker smile is on full display.

I answer the FaceTime call. Piper and Milly talk over each other, argue, scold, and worry. Dad lets them know he's fine. Milly worries that we should reschedule the graduation party.

"Absolutely not," my dad says, "a party to celebrate is important for you girls. Now more than ever." Piper asks if he'd like visitors tomorrow afternoon. Mr. and Mrs. Rodrigo can sneak away from the party for a few hours. I love that. Before Piper ends the call, she asks how I'm doing. I tell her everything she needs to hear. The sisters are excited; they've spent hours decorating today, and Peaches has already set up his DJ equipment.

But now… I simply want the conversation to end. Now is not the time to disappoint my dad with the next gripping chapter from *The Tales of Chaotic Kate: The Girl Who Never Graduated.*

The screeching curtain alerts us that Niall has returned. Dad and I say goodbye to the girls. Niall crosses the room and sits in the chair. His eyes capture mine and sparkle. I scoot to the bottom of the bed to give my dad space.

"Kate, I don't want you alone. Niall will keep you company tonight."

My cheeks blush. I can't knowingly spend another night with Niall.

"That's ridiculous," I say, but I know I'm being ridiculous, because I can't stay in that big house alone all night. "Anyway," I say, "I can sleep on the chair."

"That's sweet of you, honey," my dad says, "but you don't need to do that. Niall, is that chair comfortable?"

Niall shakes his head, 'no'. My dad says, "See."

"Stay with me for a few hours," my dad says. "But I won't be up late. I'm feeling beat, and I'll be zonked out early."

The man does fall asleep early and usually mid-conversation. Arguing with him when he's not feeling well truly seems wrong. I'll save our disagreement for another day.

My dad turns on the TV and flips through the channels. He settles on a Major League Baseball game that he and Niall had wanted to watch. The two talk sports stats and discuss the players out due to injury. They make a bet on which team will win. The loser has to buy drinks and burgers at Triple B's the next time they are out.

I curl up at the bottom of the bed. Niall tosses me a pillow. The room is warm with healing, my feelings are feather-light with hope. I rest my head next to my dad's toes. My worries release, my eyelids fall. A beautiful darkness surrounds me.

***

With each passing day, there seems to be less and less to smile about. But when I awake at the hospital, a familiar sound makes my recent setbacks seem inconsequential. The sound takes me back to my childhood. Warm summer nights watching the sun set, cool fall afternoons chasing wild leaves, winter evenings at home with Mother's homemade meatballs bubbling on the stovetop.

Mother sings off-key.

My dad gives a hearty chuckle.

Then there's another sound.

In the sweet, soothing moments of waking up from a restful nap, in-between sleep and being wide-awake, the sound feels life-changing, as though my destiny's been altered. The future feels bright. Brilliant. Glorious.

Possible.

The sound.

Low, deep, and heart-stopping.

Niall's laugh.

Niall whispers to my dad. Then my dad belly laughs.

Now, they're both laughing. Chickadees may as well be swarming the room, dropping candy hearts, and planting chocolate kisses on my forehead. I'm in the hospital version of utopia.

Dad whispers back, "She must be warming up to the idea of working with you and Team Vanguard."

As I fully awake, my face feels wrinkled from lying so heavily on the starchy blanket. The side of my cheek is wet. I was drooling. Perfect. I wipe my lips against the comforter.

Dad continues to laugh. Apparently, I had said Niall's name in my sleep. Oh, no. My eyes are glued shut. Although someone covered me with a thin hospital sheet, I feel naked, because I can't hide from Niall. Once again, there's nowhere to go. I'm stuck. An urgent rescue is needed.

Niall's name?

I sure did say his name.

I wanted him, needed him, dreamed of him.

But the sleepy memory had nothing to do with Team Vanguard or enhancing the company's internet presence. Nope. It had everything to do with a delicious invasion. This time, there may have been a field, high with straw grass, chickadees in heat dotting the sky. I was sitting on a soft blanket, staring at the bluest horizon I've ever seen, wearing nothing but a sheer baby doll nightie. Niall's voice called my name from a distance.

Katie!

Back in the sterile hospital room, something taps my head. My dad's foot brushes against my hair. This is the perfect opportunity to pretend the last few minutes never happened.

"Dad," I say, and hope my voice sounds tired. "Are you trying to kick me off the bed?"

I stretch, then take a very long time pulling myself into a sitting position. While I'm 'waking up', a player hits a double and Niall hoots, my dad boos.

"Why is it so warm in here?" I quietly ask. But I'm not warm at all. The room is quite chilly, although my face is flushed.

I'm not sure what Niall thinks, but now that I'm 'awake', I look in his direction. He's sitting in a low slouch on the chair, with his legs stretched comfortably outward. His eyes aren't on the TV, but they are on…

Me.

"Niall," my dad says, "cancel your hotel reservation and stay at my place while you're in town. That was my preference, anyway. Then Kate won't be alone. Save yourself some money…"

Confused, I make brief eye contact with Niall.

"I usually stay at your dad's when I visit," Niall says, answering the question that's just popped into my head. "In the green room. But this weekend, I got a hotel because your dad thought you'd want to kill me." Niall grins. His tongue pops out from between his teeth.

Dad laughs.

"I don't want to kill you… as much… now," I say and cradle my knees.

Niall's smile is massive, but he'd be smiling even if I had said I wanted to kill him.

"I'll give you both time to catch up," Niall says, standing and stretching. "I'll head back to the hotel and take care of some work and then come back to pick you up." Niall looks in my direction.

And just like that, my afternoon is planned. Niall's itinerary involves a lot of running on his part and driving me around. And he'll be spending the night with me. Alone. At my dad's.

Not wanting to think about that, I assure my dad I'm excited for the grad party and tell him Zakary is driving me. I don't look at Niall when I say this, but I am kind of looking, slightly in his direction. A thrilling sensation fills my stomach when Niall's features alter at the sound of Zakary's name.

Niall says he'll be at a Cubs-White Sox game with Harrison tomorrow afternoon, but he'll be available if I need him. Niall asks if I'll be okay with him leaving the house by eight in the morning. The game doesn't start until four, but he and Harrison are meeting up with friends to tailgate. Dad answers for me and says I should be fine, and he thanks Niall for being there for him—and me—in a pinch. I stare at my folded hands while they talk about whether I'll need Niall or not.

I can't imagine needing him. But when I do, electricity spreads down my pelvis and settles between my thighs. I stretch my legs out. Wiggle my toes. I need—air. I smile like a fool as I slip off the bed. A safe distance away, I pace and fan my face.

My dad says I should stop worrying about him.

Niall's eyes dance.

Dad wants to make sure I don't bail on the grad party, so he shares my cell phone number with Niall. Niall will be my camp counselor tomorrow and ensure I attend all scheduled activities this weekend. After Niall enters my number into his device, my phone beeps.

312-555-1016: Hey, Katie. Niall.

I add Niall's name to my contacts. 'Dream Stealer'. A reply is necessary; his information is inaccurate.

Me: No, Katie here. You must have the wrong number. This is KATE.

After I hit send, I ask Niall to smile. I quickly lift my phone and snap a picture. One of his eyes should be closed, the other looking off to the side, his mouth half-open, but no, when I lay eyes on the picture, all I see is perfection. His smile is devilish, and his eyes hold a visible electric current. I barely gave him any warning. I kind of wish he had worn his dorky glasses today.

"Katie," Niall says.

I look up. He's holding his phone in the air. I stick out my tongue. The phone clicks.

When my dad says, "Kate, really?", I stare at my intertwined fingers.

Dad is teasing me, but I worry he may have seen something. The something I've been feeling. The feeling that has been growing inside of me ever since yesterday. I'm afraid that something is starting to show on the outside.

I quickly change the subject: the gas station donuts. I pace to the counter, back to my dad, and present him with the assorted goodies. He's beyond appreciative and complains that the hospital food has no salt, butter, or sugar. After he eats a donut, he says he has a graduation gift for me. I deflate. He can't give me a graduation gift.

"You can open the present after the party," he says. "But it's not a normal 'gift' you have to unwrap. It's a…" He looks at me expectantly; he wants me to guess.

I play along.

"A pony?" I ask.

"No," he says.

"Money?"

"No?"

I guess other big-ticket items like a new car, a trip, and jewelry, but he says, "No," to each.

Finally, with a growing smile, he says, "Think about when you were younger."

I think. Then, I know. My smile illuminates.

"A scavenger hunt?" I squeal-ask, but then remember Niall is in the room, so I groan. "Dad, I'm not five anymore."

"No, you aren't," he says, "but you still love a good surprise and a little mystery."

I grin foolishly. As usual, he's right.

"The first clue is in your mother's proof copy of *Somewhere Beyond* on the bookshelf in my office." His cheeks glow, and his smile is arched and wide.

"Okay, Dad," I say and play down my overflowing excitement over a mysterious gift hidden inside a magical book that I have access to right now, but am forbidden to open until Sunday night.

It certainly isn't the most glorious thing to have happened to me in forever. But then for a moment, I think I don't deserve the gift… I'm a deceitful liar. A fraud.

I make a silent promise.

I won't search for the present until I graduate, and not a moment sooner. Not until all twenty-seven assignments are submitted, reviewed, graded, and the diploma is in my hand.

"You always loved a good puzzle as a child," Dad says. "Why aren't you leaping up and down with excitement?"

I stand next to his bed and squeeze his hand.

"No peeking until after the party," my dad says. "That's when you officially graduate. Finishing college is a great accomplishment, and you deserve something special for your hard work," he says, resting his head against the elevated bed. "I'm just so relieved you graduated. I was really worried about you for a while there."

"I'll wait." I nod. Internally, guilt eats at me. I've never outright lied to my dad. What kind of person am I becoming?

Group Chat
Saturday, May 28th @ 11:16 a.m.

JUSTPEACHY: I need an update, people. I have been texting all morning. What's the deal with Kate?

JustPeachy: Hello. Kate's not answering my messages. Has anyone seen her?

Slide_OB: I've been with Katie all day. We're at the hospital now with Henry. Sorry, I didn't text earlier. It's been a hectic morning.

FauxyRoxy: Babs said she saw you and Kate earlier outside Triple B's, and she said Kate was pretty distraught.

Slide_OB: Katie's okay, now. A little shaken up after last night, but she will be fine.

Just Peachy: Good. That was a scare. News travels fast in this town, so everyone at the bar has been thinking about Henry. God bless that poor soul. He's going to work himself to death one of these days.

Milly Rodrigo: Glad to hear Kate is ok. Henry, too. Piper is stringing up fairy lights in the bushes. I think she's stuck. I gotta go help her. Keep us posted if you need anything, Niall.

Just Peachy: I can't believe I am saying this, but thank you, Niall, for being there for them.

Slide_OB: No problem.

FauxyRoxy: So, we've covered the formalities. Now down to the gossip. Niall, did you and Cass get into a fight?

Slide_OB: It was a misunderstanding. I thought Kate was in trouble, and I reacted too quickly.

FauxyRoxy: Cass probably deserved it. I saw him, and he was high on something.

ZakAtak: Hey, everyone. I just woke up. Cass was high and drunk. I ended up driving him home from the hospital.

FauxyRoxy: What a messy night.

ZakAtak: Kate was so out of it last night. She is getting worse.

The Pied Piper: Sorry, guys. I'm here. Milly's arguing with the decorators right now.

Fauxy Roxy: I have a controversial thought.

ZakAtak: What is it?

Fauxy Roxy: Kate's a very rational girl. She wouldn't make things up. If she thinks something shady happened, I'm having a hard time doubting her.

ZakAtak: Like what?

Fauxy Roxy: Like maybe murder.

Just Peachy: Let's not get crazy, now.

Fauxy Roxy: I'm just saying, does anyone really know what happened?

Just Peachy: Professor Holliday told us what happened. He had it on video.

Fauxy Roxy: Exactly. Did any of you actually see it? I didn't.

The Pied Piper: Me, either. I guess now that you put it that way, I agree. Milly is going to freak out when she reads these texts.

JustPeachy: I trust Henry and Henry told me what happened.

Fauxy Roxy: We need to see Holliday's video.

Just Peachy: You think Henry and Holliday are lying?

Fauxy Roxy: I'm just saying. Did anyone actually see her fall? What do you all remember about that night?

ZakAtak: The red flag party was supposed to be innocent. Fun. I don't know what went wrong.

The Pied Piper: Too much alcohol.

Just Peachy: Too many repressed feelings.

Slide_OB: I didn't hear the scream, so I assume it happened while I was in Harrison's truck. He and I were both in there.

ZakAtak: Where was everyone else?

Just Peachy: Estelle, Babs, and Professor Holliday were down the road near the switchback path, watching for paranormal activity on the bluffs. Prof had that livestream going. He was confident his audience would finally get a glimpse of Kitty's ghost.

The Pied Piper: Around eleven-thirty, Kate asked me to take her home.

ZakAtak: I was inside with Peaches.

Just Peachy: Confirmed.

The Pied Piper: Cass and Kylie were laughing together. Compulsively. It was so weird. Like they had a dirty little secret. They went off towards the switchback path. They were so… friendly. That night was an anomaly.

FaxyRoxy: This is wild. No one saw it happen.

ZakAtak: Yikes.

Fauxy Roxy: What about after? What does everyone remember?

ZakAtak: Dr. Evers showed up. Once he examined… the body, he drove Kate to the hospital. Her forehead was just gushing blood.

Just Peachy: After she left, we all sat in the parking lot, each one of us freaking out in our own way. After what seemed like hours, we all left at the same time.

The Pied Piper: The next morning, I saw the strange post from Estelle, where she tagged Kylie.

Fauxy Roxy: Right, the quote from Anthony de Mello.

ZakAtak: None of this is helpful.

Fauxy Roxy: Professor Holliday has the video recording. Maybe we need to see it. We should ask him.

The Pied Piper: If he has nothing to hide, then he should be more than willing to show us.

Just Peachy: I want to finish this conversation, but I'm slammed right now. Let's talk tomorrow.

ZakAtak: I know Henry is at the hospital until tomorrow. Can anyone stay with Kate tonight?

Slide_OB: I will.

Just Peachy: Until tomorrow.

Authorized Personnel
Saturday, May 28th @ 5:51 p.m.

AFTER NIALL LEFT, I couldn't stand hearing my dad's kind words, so I too stepped away, needing to stretch my legs and rethink my strategy. After today, finishing my homework assignments will become a priority. But for now, Kylie's words consume me.

Hurry, help, before it's too late.

Don't tell.

What am I supposed to do with that information?

I wander the hospital halls and find myself back on the first floor. Amanda is humming away at her keyboard. She looks up.

"You need some help?" she asks.

And suddenly, I have an idea. I step up to the counter.

"Will this guest pass get me onto all the floors?" I ask. "I'm here to see my dad, Henry Vanguard, but I was—"

"One moment." She pecks her keyboard, chirps, "Oh," and taps her lips. I crane my neck over the counter for a better view of the 'oh' screen.

"Tsk, tsk, tsk," she says and tilts the monitor away from me. "Patient privacy," she says. "We are very strict here at Mayfair Medical. Our records are encrypted, coded, and secure. You'd have an easier time getting into Area 51 than you would getting into these systems."

"Oh," I say, leaning back to give her and the patients' privacy.

"I totally understand and respect that," I say, "I went to Mayfair University, and you wouldn't believe the password protection we had on our student accounts, and that was just for grades. We had to change our passwords like every sixty days."

"Oh," she moans, "we have to change ours every two weeks, but I have a secret…"

"Amanda," I say and put on my sweetest smile, "that sweater is so cute. Did you knit it yourself? Cable knit? What a talent. It is divine."

Amanda blushes.

"Oh, this old thing," she says.

I prop my elbow on the counter and cup my chin.

She tucks a plate of something under the counter.

"Dinner?" I ask.

"My husband makes me a turkey sandwich on rye anytime I work late. And a side of noodle salad. He spoils me." She clicks away on her keyboard.

"I would love to hear your secret for passwords," I say. "I'm so terrible. I always write mine on a Post-it under my mousepad. I'm probably breaking all sorts of rules."

Amanda's cheeks become even redder.

"Me, too," she giggles and knocks the underside of her desk. She scans my visitor pass. "This will get you onto both the second and third floors."

I thank Amanda for the great chat and hope she doesn't have to work much later. She excitedly says her husband will pick her up in 30 minutes. Looks like I have a half hour to kill. I head toward the second floor.

***

Back in my dad's room, we watch Grey's Anatomy. He updates me: so-and-so died, so-and-so cheated, and surprise—she's in love with him. During a commercial, he tells me Zakary's going to bring him home tomorrow, and he's hired a nurse to help at home a few hours each day. He doesn't want me to worry or act as a caregiver. He continues the one-sided conversation, justifying his reasons.

It's for the best, he says.

I want to scream. I want to yell. Why doesn't he trust me to take care of him? Am I any good to him?

Although every fiber in my body wants to start an argument, now is not the time. Instead of flying off the handle, I say that it's a great plan. He thanks me for understanding.

For several minutes, my dad and I sit in a heavy silence. At the end of the episode, my dad coughs, clears his throat, and fumbles with his words.

He says he's very worried…

He cares…

He wants what's best for me…

Earlier today, he overheard me talking to Mother outside the room. Embarrassed, I stand up and look outside. Apparently, Google isn't cutting it anymore. He wants me to see a therapist.

His truth stings.

Mine's going to burn.

Out of my selfish pride, I decided that was the perfect time to tell him that I didn't graduate. Part of me wanted to hurt him as badly as he was hurting me.

I told him the truth about my diploma. I repeated how tough the last seven weeks have been. After I tell him the truth, I assure him I will finish the assignments soon, so my degree is basically just on hold. Before he can reply, I promise to work extra hard and turn in quality work. I do all the talking, and Dad listens. He doesn't interrupt me, and I'm so grateful. He probably understands me better than he's shown; I'm sure he values my honesty. I ramble on much longer than I probably need to. Once the room is silent, I feel relieved.

"I have to be honest," he says.

I let out a sigh. "Please, I need more of that."

"I want you to get better, focus on your health, and those assignments. Until then, I don't want you working at Vanguard—not in any capacity. We'll discuss bringing you back once you're in a better place. For now, you can live at home and focus on your homework."

It's his turn to ramble, but I've stopped listening. As he changes the channel on the TV, I realize his truth is more obvious than ever.

I feel so stupid for not seeing this coming. For not putting two and two together. Back in January, my dad had asked me to go to *Chicago* with him, but I was behind on my homework, so Kylie went in my place. We *switched* places. It's not something we did often. Maybe once or twice a year. And it was only for urgent reasons. But we also got a kick out of it, because no one could tell when she was impersonating me or when I was impersonating her. It was trippy. Anyway, my dad had said he was meeting with a potential client and wanted me to come along and 'sit in the waiting room'. I—Kylie—didn't even have to speak, so the opportunity was perfect. She wore her hair down and played with her phone the entire time, so my dad didn't even notice her blemish-free cheek. That had to be one of the days my dad met with Niall. Maybe even their first meeting? Would things be different if I had gone along that day?

My instincts were right all along. I can't trust anyone. Not even my dad. He had been shopping for my replacement right in front of my face. Kylie's face.

He doesn't want or need me.

I've run out of time.

A tear streams down my cheek. I wipe my face against my sweatshirt.

***

Before long, my dad is fast asleep, so I head back down to visit Amanda. On the first floor, I stop in the reception area. Now that I am officially unemployed, I have nothing better to do but to find out the truth about April 10th.

Amanda is gone.

The room is empty.

Mayfair Medical records. Highly encrypted.

Passwords. Underneath Amanda's desk.

Security cameras sit high in each corner of the room, but as long as I don't set off an alarm… I won't get caught if I slip into her chair and quietly access the highly encrypted records. Maybe these medical records will give me more information about the cause of death? I hurry around the counter and plop into Amanda's chair; it squeaks with my weight, and clunks into the file cabinet behind me. I'm positive the thudding noise echoes throughout the entire hospital, but after several seconds of silence, the room remains… silent.

Relax, Katie.

With my heart beating like a galloping horse, I look underneath the counter. A sheet of paper is taped to the underside of the desk. I mentally note the login information, then hastily type.

Login Failed.

The second time, I type slowly.

Login Failed. One more failed attempt, and you will be locked out.

I double-check Amanda's handwriting. The login and password I'm entering are correct.

Hmm.

Amanda tapes her passwords to the underside of her desk. She eats the same meal for dinner. Amanda is boring. Amanda is predictable. I type the password a second time, but change the last digit from 7 to 8.

Welcome to Mayfair Medical! If you do not have authorization to view these records, you may be penalized to the greatest extent of the law.

On the top of the screen, the cursor beeps in the field labeled 'Last Name'. From a distance, the sound of a woman's laughter echoes down the hall. Shoes softly float against the tiled floor.

A male voice laughs and says, "She fucked me good."

"Well, she should have," the woman says, "she was a hooker. She was obligated."

"She wasn't a hooker; she was a stripper."

Laughter from both now.

I quickly type 'Vanguard' and prepare to hide underneath the counter. The voices are quiet. Whispering. The shoes stop padding. The screen fills with Vanguard family records. I quickly read the list of names on the screen.

The whispering nears.

With no time to pick and choose, I select 'all records', and click 'print'. Once the machine behind me starts beeping and zinging, I lock the computer, then slink off the chair and crawl under the counter. I squat and pull the rolling chair as close to my bended knees as possible. Not seconds later, the murmurs are above me. From underneath the desk, the tip of a mint green Croc clog brushes against my fingertip. I inch my palm closer to my butt.

"Crystal," the male nurse asks, "did you print something?"

"No," Crystal replies.

'Crystal' is my Crystal, the same nurse I had in April, I'm positive.

"Why is that printer going off then?" 'pays for sex' asks.

"Someone from another floor probably printed to the wrong printer," Crystal says. "I don't even know why we have access to this archaic thing, anyway. Who would want to walk all the way down here to print? Plus, it takes like five minutes to print one page."

"I'll grab the sheets," Dollar Bill says. "We can't leave charts out. The cleaning crew will be here soon. We'll shred them."

"Vanguard?" Crystal asks. "Why would anyone print her records?" Crystal's voice lowers. "Did you hear about her?"

"Yeah, she died the weekend before I started."

"Oh, that's right," Crystal says.

"What did you hear?" The male nurse asks.

"It was no accident," Crystal says, "more like a juicy Netflix series."

"Twins are trouble," he says, "that's what I heard."

"Twisted," Crystal says.

The printer zings and beeps in a sickly printer hum.

"I'll unplug it," Crystal says. Her small frame becomes visible. I hold my breath and close my eyes.

"If it wasn't her," he says, "do you think the sister did it?"

"I know she did," Crystal says and doesn't take her eyes off the printer.

"Shut up," he says, "and tell me everything. Let's hit the break room. I'll make cappuccinos. I'm dead. Need caffeine."

I snort quietly; his zombie-robot voice needs work.

Crystal disappears along with my unauthorized documents. Their shoes and murmurs fade down the hall.

Once the voices are gone, I sit for an extra minute. Then I scoot out from my hiding place and slowly peer over the counter. The room is empty. So is the printer.

I searched the sides and the back of the printer for the power switch. On the back of the printer, I tap the 'on' button. The printer wheezes. An error pops up on the screen: *Load paper.*

Ugh!

I scan the counter, gently open the file cabinets, and look inside the credenza drawers. Empty.

The nurses' laughter echoing down the hall is all the confirmation I need: this is a failed mission. Double ugh. I can't do anything right. Before anyone sees me, I rush toward the elevator. Inside, my phone dings. The 'Dream Stealer' has sent a message.

Dream Stealer: Ready?

I don't respond right away. First, I need to check on my dad. Back in his room, the TV is on. *Grey's Anatomy* is playing. The volume is barely audible. The lights are dim.

Me: My dad's sleeping, so if you want to get me now, that's fine.
Me: Thanks.
Dream Stealer: OMW.

I collect my bag, kiss my dad on the cheek, and tuck the hospital blanket underneath his hospital socks. Before I leave, I remove Mother's purple, velvet journal, stationery, and felt-tip pen from the knapsack and place both next to my dad's water bottle. I press my hand lovingly against his forehead.

"Father in heaven," I say, "please protect my earthly dad as he sleeps peacefully and help him fully recover. And please help me so I don't lose any more of my shit."

The Worst of Us
Saturday, May 28th @ 6:45 p.m.

ALONE. SEPARATED. APART. Isolation, take my hand. I'm all yours. If left to my own will—my true self—this is my preferred state of being.

Why?

Well, for many reasons.

For one, social settings require a sense of fashion and sleek hair. And that's just the first stop on the social elevator of disaster. Stop two requires engaging in cordial conversation. Furrow your brow, act interested, remember names. Think that's bad? Floor three is agony. Time to peel off bits of yourself to prop up those around you. And be careful not to use all your pieces, or you won't have anything left for yourself. Oh, and don't forget the fake smile.

Why can't I just be authentic? Maybe the worst version of myself is the best? At least for now.

My worst self and I have lived together quite effortlessly this past spring. Shriveling, shrinking into a perfect nothingness. In May, when I finally returned to the university for the last day of classes, strangers stopped a wilted version of myself in the halls.

Oh, my goodness, are you okay?

I'm sorry, did you really fucking just ask me if I'm okay? Would you be okay?

How horrible!

Really? I thought it was kind of fun.

I'm totally here if you need anything.

When I'm still awake at two in the morning, in a state of full panic, it's cool if I call you?

What a tragedy. And to be so young. We never saw it coming. Had no idea. Did you?

I wanted to scream, "You stupid fucking idiots! Your questions aren't helping; you're making it worse. Stop bringing her up, and maybe I can move on!"

But my only responses were, "Fine," "Okay," and "Not really." And that's what I resorted to just minutes ago. After Niall picked me up from the hospital, I was all, "Fine," "Okay," and "Not really."

Beyond embarrassed, I couldn't bear telling Niall the truth about my dad 'officially' firing me. After we got home, Niall sensed I didn't want company, so he tucked himself inside my dad's study to make a phone call. I heard him talking, laughing, carrying on—being an amazing worker. Part of a team. No one questions his work ethic. After several minutes, he's probably secured clients and cured world hunger, while I've been chewing off a hangnail.

Suddenly, he pops into the kitchen, says he needs to review some contracts at my dad's office. He'll be back in a little bit.

Vanguard Family Builders' office is located in our small downtown, between a stylish boutique and our only trendy coffee shop: The Caffeine Café. Mayfair has been voted Wisconsin's Best Small Town for four consecutive years. We also claim the title of the state's wealthiest city per capita, and we're ranked #1 in the state for top public schools. Due to all this, our housing market has surged. Per Daddy, Mayfair is the best place in southeastern Wisconsin to build your dream home. Contact him for details.

Or Niall.

Not me.

Once I'm alone, I'm free to become the worst version of myself. Although I'd love to crawl into my bed and die, I can't totally give up. Not yet. I could do homework. I've no desire to compute equations or write cohesive sentences. I could do my laundry, but I don't want to go upstairs right now. The first floor feels much safer. Anyway, now that I've discovered Kylie's treasures, my dirty clothes are less of a priority.

And her phone.

In the kitchen, I find an extra charger in the junk drawer and plug in Kylie's cell. When the battery icon starts pulsating, I feel a wave of calm wash over me. Suddenly, I have something else to look forward to. What clues might I discover in her text messages or photos?

Smiling, I move on to the next task: my blanket. After my evening sweat session, I really need to disinfect it. Quickly, I jog to my dad's room, grab the bulky blanket, and carry it through the kitchen. It barely fits in the washing machine. Once it's inside, I pour detergent directly onto the fabric. When I put the soap container back in the cabinet, a blue-and-pink bottle catches my eye. I slide the jug forward and remove the cap.

Kylie's sweet fragrance fills the room.

I've discovered her secret.

To ensure the blanket oozes with my sister, I pour ribbons of pale blue liquid directly into the washing machine. I close the cover and set the cycle to 'bedding'. The soupy mixture sloshes and jerks. I rub my left ring finger and curse myself for being so careless yesterday. I possessively twirl the remaining ring on my right hand.

If Kylie were with me right now, she'd insist I make my famous grilled cheese squares and Mama Bear burgers. The ultimate dish of happiness.

When Niall and I were at the hospital, he offered to drive to the grocery store or a nearby fast-food restaurant to get us something to eat, but it turns out the sterile hospital smell and lingering presence of death made me lose my appetite. He appeased his hunger pains with those bags of chips and candy from the vending machine and the drinks I had bought at the gas station. The early morning breakfast was our last real meal.

Given Niall's hearty appetite and the calories required to maintain that solid ten build, I imagine he's also hungry, so I raid the fridge for ground beef, cheese, and butter. I collect hamburger buns and a loaf of bread from the pantry, and dig through the shelves for seasonings.

At least once a week, my dad requests the homemade version of this dish, so he always keeps a fresh supply of the ingredients handy. But now, with dad's newfound health issues, it's wise that I deplete the artery-clogging supplies before he returns. After I plop the loot on the island, the doorbell rings.

Ding, ding, ding, ding, ding, ding, ding, ding, ding, ding!

At first, I'm startled, but then there's a literal skip in my step. It's not because I'm glad Niall is back. I'm just glad I won't be alone.

I begin to open the door, and for a split second, wonder why Niall didn't just let himself in. He knows the code.

As the door swings inward, several things happen at once. Blood rushes to my head, my legs melt, my stomach expands with fear. Somehow, the parts of my body that are still functioning form an alliance and push against the door.

A lean swimmer's arm prevents the door from closing. The door stops as it crushes against flesh and bone.

"Fuck," Cass yells.

Cass.

Cass, Cass, Cass.

He didn't show up in my *nightmare* last night. He showed up in the alley. *Kylie, is that you? I thought I killed you.*

Cass yelps. The sickening thought that I'm hurting him prevents me from pushing any harder. My grip falters. I stumble backward, tripping onto the rug, and fall onto my butt.

Cass charges inside.

"Damn, Kate," he says. "Why'd you do that? Seriously." He winces and massages his arm. "I'm not gonna hurt you. Why do you keep thinking that? I just wanna talk. That's all."

"Get out, murderer," I spit.

I search the room for something heavy or sharp. The vase of flowers is gone. Fluffy, yellow sunflower decorations surround me. Dammit, Dad, and your sunburst of shabby chic. I spot the lemon lace table runner. If it didn't rip in half first, I could strangle him with it.

"What?" he asks. "Murderer? What are you talking about?"

I try to crab walk away from him, but the cut on my hand has begun to sting again; my arm falters, and I fall onto my side.

"I'm sorry I scared you," Cass says. His arms relax, and his face softens. "And for whatever I did to freak you out. Lemme help you up." He tentatively reaches a hand forward. "Kate, I promise you, I'm not a murderer."

I'm surprised to notice he looks sympathetic and… surprised? He turns away from me and screams, "Dammit!" Then he quickly steps to the right, to the left, and back. And I'm not positive, but I think he's quietly counting to himself.

"Cass," I say with an obvious tremor in my voice, "last night you said, 'I thought I killed you' and you thought you were talking to Kylie." I push myself off the floor and hold my hands rigid against my sides. A speck of maroon seeps through my bandaged hand. "I was super fucked up last night, and kinda forgot we," I motion between the two of us, "ran into each other in the alley, but I remember what you said."

He faces me again and raises his hands in surrender.

"I fucked up," he says. He looks up the stairs, toward the kitchen, then back at me. He lowers his voice and asks, "Are you alone?"

If Cass is the sadistic killer, and I admit to being alone, he might kill me. If he isn't the evil villain in this story, and I let him stay, he might tell me something important. I've got a fifty-fifty chance of being right—and of dying. My luck has to improve at some point.

"Yes," I say. "I'm alone."

A smile spreads across his face, his eyes smile, too. Kylie fell for that lazy cowboy smirk. In college, Cass and Kylie met on the swim team at Mayfair University. Even though Kylie turned Cass down several times, he pursued her. She finally agreed to date him after he showed up under our dorm window, mounted on one of his horses, holding a bouquet of white roses. After campus security gave Cass a ticket, Kylie and he became inseparable. No—I take that back. They became inseparable after Kylie learned Roxy had a crush on him. Kylie loved having things that others wanted. Regardless, Cass and Kylie remained close long after she was banned from the swim team.

Today, his naturally, near-white hair is cut short, which is unusual. He used to wear it long and surfer-boy-like. He's lost the bronzed tan. Instead, pale blue skin surrounds his eyes. After my assessment, my guard drops.

"You didn't try to kill Kylie?" I ask.

"Hell, no," he says, and looks bewildered, but then shakes his head. "I would never hurt her. Look, you need to know some things about Kylie. And… me."

Cass is making zero sense. But I'm intrigued. Beyond curious. What does he want to tell me?

Hurry! Help, before it's too late.

Don't tell.

Cass might know something that will help me help Kylie. Or, maybe he knows what I'm not supposed to tell?

Questioning my judgement, I motion towards the living room. "We can sit in there, and you can tell me whatever you think I need to know. And then, if it's okay, I'd like to ask you some questions about you and Kylie and… April 10th."

"Totally," he says and waves a hand for me to go first.

I shake my head. "You go first."

I mostly trust him, but a teeny part of me is skeptical, so I'd rather not turn my back on him just yet. We walk into the living room. He sits on the large, overstuffed couch closest to the foyer. I take a seat in my dad's navy-blue checkered recliner. The chair that is farthest from him.

"Hey, did that happen last night?" He points at my bandaged hand.

"No, this was from earlier in the day. Yesterday."

"Oh, good," he says.

"So…"

"So," he says and settles into the sofa. "I came home last night."

"Right," I say, "the sabbatical."

"Not quite," he replies.

I frown and tilt my head.

"Lemme explain," he says. He looks at the family of elephants crossing the end table, splashing in an aqua pond. "Lately, my parents haven't been too happy with me. I think they would have preferred I stayed away longer." He rubs the blue seat cover and pounds it with a fist. "Let's just say, last night, I also used unconventional methods to escape reality."

While Cass dated Kylie, he never showed a violent side. I trusted him, and so did Kylie. The longer Cass sits on the chair and acts like… the old Cass, the more I believe him and begin to question my understanding of his words last night and his disappearance over the last few months. And, even more, I'm curious. If Cass wanted to murder me, why didn't he finish me off in the alley? He had every opportunity to do so.

"I didn't hurt Kylie," he repeats. "I've always loved her. She was everything to me."

He massages his arm and cringes.

"Hang on," I say.

I scoot off the chair and take the long way around the couch. In the kitchen, I snag an ice pack from the freezer. Back in the living room, I toss it to him and reclaim my seat.

"Thanks," he says and clenches his teeth when the cold hits his skin. Under his breath, he begins counting. "One, two, three, four, five, six, seven, eight, nine, ten—"

"Cass," I whisper. "Why are you counting?" My guard was momentarily down, but now that Cass is doing his weird counting thing, I'm starting to get creeped out again.

"How's your pops doing?" Cass asks. He lifts his head, seemingly oblivious to my question. Concern washes over his brow.

I nod hesitantly. My dad. I'm not surprised that Cass already knows. Our small town spreads gossip faster than a fourteen-year-old with a 900,000 ClickYap score.

"Actually, really great," I say. "He's lucky. Really lucky. This is a wake-up call for him. I think he finally realizes he needs to take better care of himself." I quietly add, "We all do."

"That's fucking awesome," Cass says. "When I heard he had a stroke… I was just sick. I mean, he seemed to be in pretty good health lately." Cass hunches forward, his elbows resting on his knees. He opens and closes his fist several times. Again, I think I hear him counting to himself. He exhales.

"Last night," he says, "I called you Kylie, and tried to kiss you. That was a jackass move. You looked so much like her in that dress. You looked beautiful. Not that you don't, er, didn't before, do now…" He stares at his hands. "I'm making a mess of this."

In a twisted way, his mistaking me for Kylie is kind of flattering. But at the same time, I'm also a little pissed off because his mistake almost seems like he's cheating on my sister.

"Really, it's fine, Cass. You didn't do anything wrong." I sigh. "The last few weeks have been really messed up, right?"

"Totally," he says. "This probably sounds weird, but I can't move on. I don't remember how to live without her. I know we broke up, but we weren't totally done, at least I didn't think so. Without her, I'm this strange, alternate version of myself. Like the worst possible version."

He's speaking my language. Cass may have acted like an ass last night, but his words release a spring of understanding into my heart.

"It would be nice to talk to someone about her," he says and looks towards me with hope. "I'm not sure you would want to… You know, reminisce and shit. But everyone is so hush-hush. They say, 'move on,' but I can't."

He says now he feels… Everything's so surreal… Kylie will always be his girl... Nothing is the same… With every word, my heart breaks for him. I'm shocked to learn he never actually traveled to Europe or Alaska. That was a cover. The scenic photos he posted on his social media pages were from a vacation he and his dad took after high school. He apologizes for being deceitful.

"Why, though?" I ask. "Why lie?"

"I tried reaching out to you," Cass says. His mouth turns downward. "But you never called me back or replied to any of my messages."

And now, I feel like a complete jerk. How selfish have I been? I'm not the only one destroyed by this tragedy.

"I'm so sorry, Cass," I say. "I don't have a good excuse…"

"I'm not the same man you remember, Kate," he says. "But it's time you know the truth." He relaxes and turns to face me. A large bruise extends from his jaw to his hairline.

"Oh, my goodness, Cass," I say. "What the hell happened to you?" I leap off the cushion and move to sit next to him. I rest my hand on his leg, and I'm about to touch his face, when there's a beep, beep, beep, beep in the hall. The front door clicks open.

Niall's back.

The Possible Version
Saturday, May 28th @ 7:32 p.m.

NIALL'S BROAD SHOULDERS and wide stance consume the hallway. His eyes pierce through Cass, but those multi-colored irises aren't glowing this time; they're nearly black.

"Nice to see you again, Cass," Niall says.

Niall's changed into a new pair of pants; no doubt expensive. Khaki this time. Still molded to his legs. And a bright, white t-shirt. I peer over the couch. Standard white sneakers. I'm in trouble. No—he's in trouble. He shouldn't dress like that in the presence of a chronic spiller.

My hand hovers an inch from Cass's bruise.

"Niall," Cass returns the pleasantries and leans back on the couch.

My hand drops to my lap, and I follow Cass's lead and slouch against the cushions.

"Should you be here?" Niall asks Cass.

Cass shakes his head several times, cracks his knuckles, then pushes himself off the couch. "I'm out," he says. For a moment, I'm confused by the interaction, but then I remember I need Cass. *Need to know what's going on.* I leap up and grip his arm.

"Wait!" I squeal. Cass doesn't acknowledge me, so I clutch his forearm tighter. "Don't leave," I beg. "We're not done talking."

Cass looks down at me.

"Sorry, gotta go." His hand brushes mine. Then he's backing up. "I've no desire to be in the same room as him."

"How are you feeling today, Cass?" Niall asks. "Knock-out? Drop down great? Flat-out fantastic?" There's a hardness to Niall's voice that I've never heard before. The kind laced with distaste and disgust. The unusual sound makes me take a step backward.

Cass scoffs but then turns toward me. "I'm truly glad your dad's doing better," he says.

I release my grip on Cass's arm and hide my trembling hands in my pockets. I desperately want to pull Cass back onto the couch, but now that Niall is here, there's no way Cass will talk. We're not alone.

"What's the problem?" I ask. My eyes dart between Cass and Niall. "Cass, please stay." I sway and fidget with my jeans. I look to Niall.

Niall hasn't moved from the center of the entryway. If anything, he's standing taller and occupying even more space.

"Can't, Kate," Cass says. "Gotta dip. I don't associate with impostors. But go ahead and ask Niall about his connections to your family. Trust me, he's nobody's hero."

My eyes search Niall.

"What is that supposed to mean?" I ask.

"Cass, leave," Niall interrupts. "Now is not the time."

Cass doesn't move but looks at me. "Wanna grab breakfast tomorrow? Before the grad party?"

"Absolutely," I say, and then in a hurry add, "Caffeine Café?"

"Perfect."

"Ten?"

He nods.

But I'm suddenly overcome with emotion and unexpectedly hug Cass. I stand on my tiptoes; my fingertips barely touch behind his neck. The truth. Tomorrow, Cass is going to tell me the truth.

Surprised at my show of affection—Cass and I have only ever jabbed each other in the arm—Cass freezes for a second but just as quickly relaxes and returns the embrace. I don't know if he's hugging me, or if he's imagining I'm Kylie, but his arms feel… good.

"I'm really looking forward to seeing you tomorrow," he whispers in my ear.

"Me, too," I say, and slowly let go.

"How'd you get here?" Niall asks Cass. "There's no car outside."

"Uber," Cass says, looking at me.

"Do you need a ride home?" I ask.

"Nah," Cass says, "I'll start walking, meet the driver. No worries." He rounds the couch. "Tell your pops I said, 'Hey', and I'm glad he's okay."

Cass passes Niall.

"Later," Niall says.

Cass keeps walking and doesn't respond.

Once the front door shuts, my frustration and anger show, but I don't care. "What the hell was that all about?" I screech.

"Be careful with him," Niall says. "I wouldn't say Cass is… dangerous. But he's not good for you."

"Is anyone?" I ask.

"Why was Cass here?" Niall asks.

"Why do you care?"

"I just do."

"You can't always respond to my questions with questions. It's infuriating," I say. "Why do you care?"

"I care about your safety and well-being," Niall says. "And that guy," he points at the door, "is not safe for your well-being."

"Cass is a family friend," I say, exasperated. "He was being nice. You didn't have to scare him off. He came to apologize for last night. I guess we ran into each other in the alley, and I… well, I was super messed up and totally blew things out of proportion—"

"Kate."

"What?" I snip.

Niall's face has lost its edge.

"What is it now?" I ask, my voice unsteady.

"I need to apologize for last night, too," he says, catching me off guard.

"Why?" I examine his face.

"I did something last night," he says.

Oh no. Is Niall going to tell me about his private life? Did he and Roxanne spend the night together? Maybe they didn't even go anywhere. Maybe they took care of their desires at the bottom of the bluffs.

"I don't need to know about your personal life," I say and walk around him into the kitchen. I focus on the open space in front of me. He follows.

"Katie … I punched Cass."

"What?" I spin around.

A splash of guilt and embarrassment covers Niall's face.

"Last night," he says, "when you left me in the garden, I was worried about you. So, I looked everywhere for you. The dining room, behind the bar, and the kitchen. Everywhere. But I couldn't find you. Finally, I went out by the bluffs, and that's when I saw Cass carrying you."

"He was carrying me?" I ask, confused. "But then, why did you hit him?"

"You were whimpering, 'he's gonna murder me'."

"Really?" I ask and cover my face in my hands. "It was a misunderstanding. Cass wasn't trying to kill me."

"At the time, I didn't know that," Niall says quickly. "So, I freaked out. After he set you down, I didn't mean to knock him to the ground. I barely tapped him. The bruise is from when he hit the gravel. After he fell, I thought he was out, so I shook him, but he didn't wake up. That's when I called 911. A crowd gathered around us. But when the EMTs arrived and loaded him onto the stretcher, everyone bolted. I was left babysitting Cass. The medics thought he was just tripping. Turns out he was, and that's why he hit the ground so fast." Niall works a slow smile into his closing statement. "I thought it was because I was so jacked."

"Where did this happen?" I ask.

"The parking lot."

I jog through the bits and pieces of memories from last night, hoping to unlock more details, but nothing comes to the surface. I have zero memory of the 'non-fight'.

"The cops got involved," he says. "I had to give a statement. And you probably don't remember Cass passing out, because you had already run back inside the restaurant. You were looking for your phone. You were anxious to leave."

I rub my hands over my face and feel disgusted for accusing poor, distraught Cass of such outrageous things. This is why I never drink. It seems Cass has turned into a wreck since Kylie's gone. Violence and drugs? What happened to the Cass I knew? He's almost as unrecognizable as myself.

"You don't need to apologize," I say, "I was the one who overreacted and jumped to conclusions. Cass is going through a hard time. He's torn up about Kylie. I feel bad that I never reached out to him. He tried messaging me a bunch, but I was going through my own things, so I never responded. Cass was Kylie's boyfriend for three years. He was part of the family. What is wrong with me?"

I rub my fingertips around my left ring finger.

"Let's blame it on miscommunication," Niall says. "Don't beat yourself up. And as you said, you were caught up in your own grief."

"But what does Cass have against you?" I ask. "Why did he say I should watch out for you?"

Niall stuffs his hands in his pockets and shrugs.

"I know I've only been part of the mix for a few months, but your dad and I have gotten close. Maybe Cass is a little jealous?"

It makes sense. And truly, at this point, Cass appears to be the unstable individual.

"Hungry?" He asks, looking over my shoulder at the counter.

"Since you made breakfast," I say, feeling energized with the opportunity to cook, "I thought I would return the favor and make dinner. Are you hungry?"

"Definitely," he says.

"You're in for a treat," I say and smile. "I'm a pretty amazing fry cook. My dad and Peaches claim I'm like locally, super famous."

I round the kitchen island and check Kylie's phone. It's still charging.

Niall laughs. But it sounds like a nervous laugh. He says he can't wait to see me in my element.

"Come on," he says, playfully, and grabs my hand. "I'll be your sous chef." He leads me to the stove.

I smile, smirk, then frown.

"Put me to work," he demands.

Before I can question his strange behavior, my growling stomach interrupts my thoughts. Needing distance from pulchritudinous eyes, I task Niall with slicing the cheese and buns on the other side of the island.

While he's prepping, I toss my comforter into the dryer, then return to the kitchen. At the counter, we're sitting in our assigned seats from earlier, discussing our favorite sandwich ingredients. Mine is cheese, and more cheese. He teases me, saying it's because I'm from Wisconsin, and our obsession with cow products is disturbing. He prefers burgers, but when it comes to sandwiches, he likes salami or turkey—no, both, and plenty of each. I pat the marbled ground beef and watch his smile grow wider as I say I'll make him a double burger. I move to the stove top and set the heat to medium. Butter chunks sizzle in the pan, and the toast bronzes on the griddle. My body naturally falls into autopilot. Timer set for six minutes. Fatty grease crackles and pops. In a medium-sized mixing bowl, I combine 1 tablespoon of horseradish, 1/2 cup of whole milk, and 1 cup of shredded Colby Jack cheese. Savory garlic and creamy butter fill the air. I turn on the fan above the stove to high; it whirls.

Before I assemble the grilled cheese squares, I ask Niall to turn around, partially joking, partially serious; he can't see my secret ingredients. I can have a few secrets of my own. He reluctantly obeys.

"I wanted to ask you something about yesterday," he says. "It's personal, so if you don't want to answer, don't feel like you have to."

"Sure," I tentatively say and turn the back burner on low. I toss cubes of cheese into a double burner on the stove. "Ask away."

"At the restaurant, I noticed you were wearing two identical rings." He pauses. "One on your right hand, the other on your left."

The cheese begins to melt faster than it should. I lower the temperature setting and add whole milk to the mixture.

"My dad gave Kylie and me matching rings on our twelfth birthday," I say, stirring. "Kind of like promise rings. You know, for us to be honorable teenagers and whatever. Anyway, after Kylie… was gone, my parents entrusted me with her ring."

The cheese mixture is gooey. But not too gooey. I stir for a final time, then remove the pot from the oven and pour the dipping sauce into a ceramic dish.

"Due to my unraveling," I say, "the ring died on the edge of the table."

I flip the patties and assemble Niall's burger tower. I wait for him to say something, anything, because I feel childish right now and… I don't know what I need, but I'm hoping he has it. Or, gives it to me? Finds it?

"Can I get you something to drink?" he asks. "I'll make myself useful."

Relieved to be talking about something other than Kylie, I ask, "You could pour me a glass of Hawaiian punch Kool-Aid? Please. There's a pitcher in the fridge."

Something cool will do. Icey. Sweet.

"Really?" he asks.

"Yeah, and a few ice cubes, please," I answer honestly. "I like it as sugary as possible."

"Of course," he says.

I look over my shoulder, Niall's grinning as he pours the juice.

I cut the grilled cheese into sections. Once the burgers and quartered sandwiches are neatly arranged on two platters, atop a bed of lettuce, sliced red onion, and tomatoes, I carry both to the island and place the plate of double patties in front of Niall.

His eyes smolder when they connect with mine over his plate.

"Dive in," I say. "It tastes better warm." I take a satisfying, distracting gulp of juice.

"They look so good," he says, and holds the burger mid-air. "When I was younger, wait—you can't laugh."

"Wouldn't think of it," I say and rest my free hand over my heart.

"I was the neighborhood babysitter," he says, awaiting my response.

I smile like a goon. I wouldn't think of teasing him… yet.

"Thank you for withholding any commentary," he says and clears his throat. "The kids would live off that stuff." He nods towards the juice. "They'd have permanent Kool-Aid smiles all summer long."

His smile is permanently pulchritudinous.

I lift my cup again and gulp, hoping my lips saturate with color.

"I bet you hated those damn red mustaches on those kids," I say. "Your tidy brain probably screamed at the sight."

Niall shakes his head, then takes a bite of the burger.

"This is amazing," he murmurs and follows up with two more wolf-like chomps. He rolls his eyes and groans. "Best burger ever."

"Thank you," I say. "Watching people devour my food is almost better than eating it."

Watching *him* devour my food is better than eating it.

"I respectfully disagree," he grabs a cheese square, skips the sauce, and tosses it in the air. The bite-sized portion lands flawlessly in his mouth. "These are addicting."

"Glad you like them," I say and add, "show off."

"You may have insane talent at the grill, but I've a mediocre talent." He tosses two more pieces in the air, and both land in his mouth with effortless perfection. "A very useless talent, but a talent nonetheless."

"That was luck." I allow my lips to curl.

"No, seriously," he says, "I've been practicing for years. I can do it like ten times in a row. Watch." He tosses three more pieces in the air. One after the other, they disappear into his open mouth with skill and precision. "And actually," he adds, "you'd think something like popcorn would be easier, but the heavier the object—" Another piece flies through the air, lands. "The better." His fists pump the air.

He looks adorable, like a little kid. I want to walk over and… and what? The comfortable silence, his playful smile, those brilliant eyes. It's all too much. I need to—

"Easy," I say and snag a crust, drown the square in sauce, and toss. On the descent, the heavy object falls, much quicker than anticipated, misses my mouth—of course it misses my mouth—and crashes into my shirt, leaving a streak of cheesy orange in its wake. With no accuracy whatsoever, it splatters onto the floor.

Niall's laughter is booming. Almost contagious.

"Told you," he says. A melody levitates above the table. "This skill takes years to perfect."

While my face turns candy cane red, he slides off the chair, laughing uncontrollably—which makes him even cuter—which makes me even more embarrassed. His burst of joy to my ears is like sugar cubes on my tongue. He unrolls a few sections of paper towel, dampens them underneath the faucet, and hands me the wad.

"Here you go," he says, stifling his laughter.

"Thanks," I say, and skeptically grab the cloth.

He's met me, right? Does he really think I can tackle this infusion of cheese and win? I concentrate and scrub the fabric. But the more I rub, the more the soil penetrates the fabric. Paper towel bits collect on my shirt. Feeling defeated, I look to him for guidance.

"The shirt is ruined," I say. "Look, it's a thousand times worse. Dammit. This was one of Kylie's favorites."

Once his twitching smile has evened, he asks, "Can I try?" A twinkle escapes his eyes, and I'm certain he's not serious. He must be teasing. But now his face looks really serious. He's not laughing. I almost want him to laugh uncontrollably again. I can handle that. But him suggesting that he help me? Touch my shirt? I don't think I could handle that.

"I suppose I should probably go up and change?" I ask, mostly for clarification.

"C'mon," he says and waves a hand for me to follow. He grabs the paper towel roll and walks backward towards the laundry room.

I stand in place until he waves for a second time. If I remain still, I'll only make the situation more awkward than it already is, so I follow. Once in the small room, I wait in silence next to my tumbling comforter.

He opens the cabinet above the washer and shuffles through the cleaning agents. He retrieves an aerosol bottle and turns around.

"Do you mind?" he asks, bottle and towel in hand. The serious expression on his face makes me think only he is skilled enough to handle this insurmountable task.

I nod.

This is business. A serious task. Nothing more.

"I do," I say, and continue to nod.

He laughs again, but I don't understand why. He steps closer. A foot away, he kneels in front of me, then inches forward. I freeze. When he reaches for my shirt, I flinch. My palm bumps into the dryer door. He pauses. He's concentrating, examining the problem. Analyzing. He doesn't look up while he sprays the solution onto the napkin. But I can see a distinct burst of color splash inside his eyes. The smile is gone.

"You, okay?" he whispers.

I unsteadily prop my hands against the machine and say something like, "Sure," or "Yeah."

Actually, I say both.

His hand gently slides beneath the material and holds it flat. He hasn't even touched my skin, but I'm beginning to lose my breath. This cleaning tutorial is wrecking me. And yet, he's unmoved. Content. In his element, cleaning up another mess.

"Believe it or not, this also takes years of experience," he quietly explains and scrubs my shirt. "Like I told you yesterday, if you don't pre-treat right away, well, the clothing might be ruined."

Again, I bob my head in agreement, thinking he's the wisest person I've ever met. I clear my throat, swallow, and watch his hands work with a delicate intimacy. The smudge effortlessly begins to disappear.

With each stroke of his hand, a violent surge brews inside my chest. Boils. Nearly erupts. Maybe he sees the storm coming, or maybe he's concerned with my uneven breathing, because his slight smirk fades and his hands stop moving. He carefully sets the towel and spray on the floor, pushes off the tile, and steps away.

Even though he wasn't propping me up before, now that he's moved, I feel as though I may slide to the floor, like a carelessly thrown cheese square. Effortlessly.

I cling to the dryer for support.

He's retreated; his back against the wall. His pupils have doubled in size, and worried creases slash his forehead.

I understand now.

I think.

Niall is the star varsity player, and I'm benched in Mayfair's t-ball dugout. Out of his league is an understatement. And my thoughts about my potential new boss are grossly inappropriate. I must be high off aerosol fumes because I boldly request answers to the questions that have been sprinting through my mind for the last twenty-four hours.

"Niall," I say. "What's going on? You…"

I nearly lose my confidence, but Kylie whispers: *You deserve to know the truth, Katie.* Her support is all I need to plow through my remaining insecurities.

"You helped me when I passed out at Triple B's," I say. "You took care of me last night. Wrapped my cut, I don't know how many times. You agreed to stay here. Rescued my hair when I threw up. You tease me incessantly, and shower me with an unusual kindness… A flirty vibe follows us everywhere. And I swear, I feel like we've met before. Can you be super honest with me?" I pause and prepare to feel uncomfortable, vulnerable, at his mercy. "I mean it. What's going on?" Any composure in my voice is lost; I'm raw and torn, awaiting his answer.

Niall's eyes turn black, then a pulsating flash of color reappears. A kaleidoscope of pain, regret, and a flicker of hope flies through the grays, blues, and golds.

In the next instant, he's standing in front of me. No—he's everywhere. Like always. His cologne surrounds me. A warm hand squeezes my waist. His chest expands, nearly touching mine. Our mouths, not nearly close enough to kiss, but I swear I can taste him. And he does taste like Pop-Tarts. A sweet, delicious lick of cherry. Decadent. Deep. Warm. Satisfying. Toasty.

I look down. His glorious pants are a mere inch from my pelvis. A lock of my hair falls forward, and he reaches a hand towards my right cheek. I instinctively lift my hand to cover the heat spreading over my skin—my scar—but he's faster and a caring grip catches my hand mid-rise. He folds my hand against his chest.

"Don't," he whispers and gently releases my wavering hand.

His free hand inches underneath my shirt. In a single fluid movement, a strong, complete grip circles my waist. I float onto the dryer. A second later, he pushes my legs apart and consumes the space between. His hands impatiently move to my wrists, guiding them around his neck.

The warmth from his body nears, and my eyes automatically close.

I'm afraid that if they stay open, he'll vanish. A dream. He's only a dream. My heart slams against my chest. Warm lips brush against my right cheek, but insecurity screams louder than my pounding heart. I open my eyes and edge backward. He's real, and his roaming hands are on my hips. Possessively holding me.

My fingertips are touching him, barely grazing his shoulders. The pressure leaves my waist. His hands settle atop the dryer several inches from my thighs.

"I'm sorry," he says. He's examining me. Fixating on me. My lips. "I didn't mean to startle you," he says, "and if you don't want me to kiss you, I won't."

Won't kiss me?

What do I want?

What does he want?

With a tentative movement, my fingers crawl down his arms and rest atop the rough skin on his hands. We seem to stay that way for hours. Neither of us is prepared to make the next move. I know why I'm stalling.

Inhaling.

Exhaling.

Hoping.

Believing.

Is. This. Possible? What do I want?

And I can only imagine why he's still… Is he…

Doubting?

Questioning?

Regretting?

Mistaken?

Could this be possible? What does he want?

Suddenly, his hands are squeezing my ass, dragging me closer to his heavenly body. I pull my hands away from his neck, so I can grip the top of the dryer for support—

"Nope," he whispers, "around my neck."

Scolding, reprimanding, commanding.

In response, my hands trail up his arms and follow his order. My thumbs brush the nape of his Hollywood Hair. A cluster of goosebumps forms underneath. His reaction is all the encouragement I need to cautiously scoot forward. When he hoists me closer, my legs surround him, crushing his lower back. Needing him in my own way.

I moan his name against his neck.

The jealous fantasy I created yesterday, while Roxanne manhandled Niall, pales in comparison to the reality of this man's fiery skin touching mine.

"Please," I say, as I rest my cheek against his collarbone, clinging to him.

His fingers inch under my shirt. His thumbs work their way under the lacy barrier, seeking, finding, massaging. Chills dance across my torso. My body arches against his, and every part of me squeezes him tighter. My moans slow in pace. His touch is overwhelming, and I can't imagine what more I could need from him, because this moment leaves me feeling whole. Put together. Possible. I never knew someone could feel 'possible' or needed to?

BUZZ! BUZZ! BUZZ!

I freeze.

He's kneading me; I'm needing him.

BUZZ! BUZZ! BUZZ!

The dryer.

Niall pulls away from me.

My arms and legs refuse to do the same, because with each passing second, the feeling of possibility fades. But I need to hold on. Wildfires burn my cheeks as Niall tugs my bra back into place. Taking the hint, I self-consciously peel my arms and legs off his body and righten my top.

"May I?" he asks.

My dazed look prompts further explanation. His eyes are liquid. An ocean of color. Drifting. Floating. Sailing away.

"Your shirt," he says, "I can wash it while you grab another."

"Oh," I say and stare down as though I've never seen a shirt before, nor have the slightest idea how to wash one.

It's the restaurant all over again.

When I don't move, he does.

Suddenly, his hands are on me. Again. The hem of my shirt lifts, his fingers take their sweet time brushing up the length of my sides—as though he's savoring this moment—and pause once the cloth reaches my shoulders. He wants me to lift my arms; I remember how. The shirt slips over my head. In a flash of soft pink, my top disappears into the open washing machine.

He steps back and abruptly pulls his t-shirt over his head. In a whoosh, it disappears into the drum. His eyes search mine, and his smile becomes crooked. That's when I realized I had let out an involuntary, "Oh," when he removed his t-shirt.

His hands brace the washing machine behind him, leaving a field of bulging muscles, tanned skin, and opportunity. His pause invites me to openly browse every inch of his exposed body. So much to take in; I take my time.

"The stain remover rubbed off on my shirt," he says. A teasing smile spreads across his face.

The nuances of laundering are unfamiliar to me; therefore, I've no idea if that's even possible or true, so I don't question him. Nor do I care, because the view from atop the dryer is undeniably unlike any I've ever seen. The panoramic views of Lake Michigan are dull in comparison to this scenery. Who needs chirping chickadees feeding from a bougie bird feeder?

Niall turns towards the washer, extracts his shirt, then points at the guilty smear.

I murmur a ridiculous, "Thank you."

He adds laundry detergent and Kylie's blue liquid into the dispenser trays. Of course, he's as wise as my sister and knows all about fabric softener and proper dispenser usage.

To satisfy an urge inside, I watch his every move. He works the dials on the washer. I admire his chiseled arms and toned chest. A gold chain circles his neck. A decorative ring hangs from the necklace. After several moments, I must forget I'm sitting on top of the dryer—without a shirt—because my arms fall, my jaw does the same.

He chooses a setting, second-guesses himself, and chooses another. Instead of starting the washer, he swivels and steps in front of me again, then he takes his time browsing.

Unsure of his plans, tiny somersaults of anticipation flip against my chest. I silently thank Piper for giving me the fantastic bra.

"Did you call me Piper?" he asks, staring at my lips.

I don't even try to explain away my foolishness. Instead, I remember I'm sitting atop the dryer, half-naked, so I cross my arms over my chest.

Seconds later, his hands settle around my waist, and he lifts me onto the floor. I'm inches from his chest, and on the edge of... something new. Something exciting. But this cliff feels safer than any I've ever been near before.

"Since I'm washing a load," he says, "is there anything else you'd like me to toss in?"

His hands release me and slide into his front pockets. The waistband of his jeans drops by a centimeter. A black strip of cotton appears. In that moment, I'm pulled through a tear in the universe, enter a wormhole, pass through space and time, and make the biggest discovery of my twenty-one years. I didn't realize it until now, but Kylie was right. Watching a man do everyday house chores with sublime perfection is the sexiest act on earth. Without a shirt? The sexiest act in the universe. It hides a multitude of sins, and I want Niall more than ever now.

I'm ashamed to admit: I'm ready to toss a stranger my panties.

"We can't…" He reaches forward and tips my chin upward. He looks into my eyes for a second, then shifts his gaze lower, lower, stops, higher, higher. Finally settling on my startled baby blues, he says, "Do this…"

Do this?

Do what?

My laundry?

Doesn't he know how 'possible' I felt? What if… we did more? I'd likely feel invincible. He knows everything about everything, and he must be right. Even so, I ask, "Do what? And why not?"

"We…" He steps back. "It's not an option," he says, "my partnership with your dad is important, and your dad would not be happy if we… Not with my connections to your family." His eyes wander over my face. "It can't happen. This is a mistake. Anyway, I'm not interested in looking for anything serious. My last relationship was…"

This is a mistake?

I'm a mistake.

This possibility is a mistake?

"Devastating," he says. "A nightmare and… I can't."

I'm devastating?

A nightmare?

I knew I was chaotic, but I've never been a nightmare.

"We can never be a thing," he says.

The Game Continues
Thursday, April 7th

FOR ONCE, I'VE scored Harrison a date. Kylie still hasn't mentioned who she's bringing, but I'm positive she's bringing her sister. The two seem crazy close.

Harrison pulls into the Rav4 lot off Eddy Street, a few blocks from Wrigley Field. He parks his Suburban, then gets out and does an actual backflip right there in the parking lot. He's thrilled that I've finally come through for him. We walk toward the Marquee Gate. I walk. Harrison skips beside me and suddenly breaks into some weird, highly embarrassing dance moves. He calls it the 'I'm getting laid today' dance, and even creates an impromptu song to go along with his solo performance.

I message Kylie through ClickYap.

Me: Hey, Harrison and I are outside the Marquee Gate.
Kylie: Harrison! You weren't supposed to tell me who you're bringing! We'll be there in ten.

"Who's she bringing?" Harrison spins in a circle, ends with jazz hands, then gulps from his water bottle.

"It's more fun as a surprise," I say, ignoring his theatrics.

"You've told me, Kylie's standard hot," he says. "And it's a scientific fact that attractive girls only hang out with those at or above their level."

"Your logic is bullet-proof," I say, shaking my head.

"Did Deveraux get in touch with you yet?" he asks.

"Deveraux? Why would I talk to him?"

"Since you left, Lance has only ever referred to you as 'the outside threat'. But Monday, he called you out by name. The room went dead silent. He told everyone he was going to break you. Destroy your business. Take you out of the game."

"He sent me a jump drive," I say.

"What?"

"Jump. Drive."

"What's on it?"

"No idea."

"You didn't look?"

"Why would I?"

"I'm telling you, I'd be a little freaked out if I were you."

"He can't get to me."

"I don't trust him."

"There's nothing Lance or his sweet daddy can do that will bother me, let alone break me," I say. "The clients that leave them have every right to choose their service provider. And considering I charge more than those jerks, clients aren't coming to me because of price. It's service, all day."

"Lance has a serial killer vibe," Harrison says, hoping to convince me. "And that's why you need to see what he sent you."

"If you're so interested," I say, coolly, "have a look. The drive is in my briefcase in the back seat. Go ahead."

From the corner of my eye, a head of platinum yellow captures my attention. I turn my head.

"And there's Kylie," I say, and bob my head to the right.

In a waterfall of blonde hair, short—nearly invisible—denim shorts, and a tight Brewer's tank top, Kylie navigates towards us. She's staring at her phone, lost in another world.

Harrison sees me nod in Kylie's direction and looks over to spot her as well.

"Oh, my fucking—" he begins to say. Harrison coughs up water, sputtering and choking.

"Took your breath away?" I ask, annoyed.

Kylie finally looks up, smiles, and jogs towards us. Once she reaches me, she offers a friendly hug—not even a kiss—and excitedly looks at Harrison, who's composed himself and is now standing next to me.

"My friend knocked back a few spiked teas on the way," Kylie says, "she's hitting the bathroom. She'll be here in a second."

I introduce Harrison and Kylie.

"The pleasure is all mine," Harrison says to Kylie, his expression is curious. "Have we met before?"

Kylie looks from Harrison to me and smiles shyly.

"I don't think so," she says, pointing at his hair. "I'd remember that. Very Odell."

"He's one sexy man," Harrison replies, but presses on. "I swear we've met before… Does Lance Deveraux ring a bell?"

She shakes her head.

Harrison keeps peppering Kylie with questions.

Where did you go to school? Hobbies? Sports? Favorite restaurant? How do I know you? Why are you dating Niall? He's a boring ass.

I take a playful swing—Harrison ducks. "Lived in Mayfair all your life?"

"Yup, unfortunately," she says. "My friends and I wanted to go out of state for college, somewhere by the ocean, but it didn't work out. So, yeah, been stuck there for twenty-one years."

"What about your parents?" Harrison asks. "Siblings? Pets?"

Harrison is the worst at meeting people for the first time. And if he thinks he's met them before, he's the absolute worst. He won't stop until he makes the connection.

"Sorry if he's too much," I tell Kylie. "You can stop anytime."

"No, it's fine," Kylie says. "My dad owns his own business. My mom is an author. No brothers. Just a sister. Actually, I was going to bring her today, but she was hanging out with her ex. And no pets. But my mom has a wild Genet named Doe. It's a freaking wild cat. She's—oh, there's my friend."

Kylie shields her eyes from the sun and points behind us. Not twenty feet away, Roxanne walks towards us, smiling, boobs bouncing.

Alternative Possibility
Saturday, May 28th @ 8:09 p.m.

IN THE SAFETY of the garage, I search for Babs' special seeds, stew, and fume. I kick a bag of potting soil.

I couldn't agree with you more, *Brien.*

Niall wants nothing to do with me? Well, I don't want anything to do with him. Never did. No matter how hard I try to feel nonchalant, I can't help but feel mortified—gut-punched, my cheeks burn with embarrassment. My delusional brain thought that he was kind of into me.

How stupid I've been.

I pull my hair into a knotted bun.

By the time I find the specialty bird food, I realize I won't be able to work professionally with Niall once my dad allows me to come back. (If he lets me come back.) The staircase incident was bad enough, but the laundry room disaster pushed my embarrassment to a whole new level.

I'm a disaster.

We can't be a thing.

As I rip open the bag of seeds, I gasp.

What does this mean for Vanguard long-term? I can *never* work there. The realization hits me like a wave. My heart races.

I'm the reason I can't work at Vanguard. My dad's right, I have to hurry and help myself. With shaking hands, I scan my emails. It's time I get serious about my future. I need a new job. I search my emails for 'Verity'.

She's the only recruiter who didn't balk when I mentioned I hadn't graduated yet. I find the last message she sent and open it. I hit reply.

Dear Miss Verity,

First and foremost, I want to apologize for my delayed response. To be completely honest, I don't have a particularly good excuse—except that I was hesitant to interview with your company because accepting the accounting role would require me to move from my hometown (north of Milwaukee) to Chicago.

After much thought, I have decided that a move is exactly what I need, and I would be thrilled for the opportunity! I understand it's been a while since your last email, so I realize the position might already be filled, but I wanted to at least ask.

I look forward to hearing from you!

Have a great day!

Kate Vanguard

What is wrong with me? *A move is what I need? Delighted for the opportunity?* Did I really use an exclamation point in a business email? Three times?

Ugh.

I'm desperate, and it's making me… peppy.

I press on. For once, I have to be all in. I'll make a decision and follow through to the end, kicking ass every step of the way. Even though it's the weekend, I kick ass and dial Miss Verity's office number. I leave a disturbingly peppy message summarizing the email. After I hang up, I want to stab myself in the eye with one of the used plastic straws in my trash.

Instead, I plop onto the garage steps and let myself feel. A shimmer of something begins to grow inside of me.

Hope?

No, definitely not hope.

Excitement?

Nope. That was manufactured.

Fear?

Yes. Fear.

I'm incredibly scared about my future. How can I leave the only town I've ever called home? Away from everyone I've ever loved? Can I even afford to move? Even if I get the accounting job, how would I pay for an apartment? In Chicago? I have no savings. I have clothes; I could sell them. No, I should donate those. No—I should burn them. I could sell my car. I won't need a vehicle in Chicago; Niall said he uses Uber whenever he can. A few weeks ago, outside Triple B's, some seventeen-year-old with a backwards baseball cap and a nose ring offered me four grand—right then—for my car. I thought he was messing with me, but he said 2010 Golfs are wanted… like my ass. On a whim, I added him on ClickYap, then told him to fuck off. Respectfully.

Hoping the stoner is still interested in buying my car, I message DezNutts on ClickYap.

Kate Vanguard: Any chance you're still interested in my Golf? Cash only. Pick up this week. $4000

DezNutts: Ya. Lemme get the cash together. Can we do Monday? I'll need sum time. 3500

Kate Vanguard: Perfect. $3800 Final offer.

DezNutts: How's that booty?

Kate Vanguard: Fuck off.

Kate Vanguard: Respectfully.

Options are good, as are planning and thinking ahead.

Knowing there's nothing more I can do about my future, I grab a bucket and scoop up some seeds. I take a deep breath—ready to act bored if I see Niall—and open the kitchen door. Inside, the house is quiet. On the counter, there's a slip of paper.

Katie, I'm going for a run down by the lake. Be back in an hour.

Gone? He probably left through the back door because he didn't want to run into me. Although there's a really pretty nature trail behind our subdivision, he headed in the opposite direction. Which is good. I need space from him, so I can think.

I let out a sigh. My eyes scan the kitchen. *Kylie's phone.* Actually, it's perfect that he's left. I can snoop through Kylie's phone in private, as any good sister would. Time to focus on my original mission.

Hurry, help. Before it's too late!

I snag her phone, steady the seeds in my other hand, and head to the living room. Through the sliding glass door, I spot a small bird on the feeder. I quickly unlock the door and peek out, but before I can get a good look, the feathery friend beelines into the forest.

Well, fuck off, then.

I want to be angry, but the view outside calms me. The yard is glowing. The setting sun brushes the trees, casting a bright haze over the field. My dad's backyard borders a family of maple trees. The leaves are full and green this time of year. Prickly grass and weeds cover the soil. My dad refuses to seed or plant flowers and trees until fall. He's firm that landscaping a new yard should wait until after the summer heat subsides. That's what the grass, trees, and flowers prefer.

I walk carefully, so I don't step on a rock or thistle with my bare feet, tossing seeds everywhere. This should do the trick. Once the bucket is empty, I set it inside the door.

In the backyard, my dad has placed a wooden lounging chair about 50 feet from the house. Curiosity leads me away from the house. Although it's getting late, I sit on the wooden slats, lift my eyes, and take in the panoramic view of Lake Michigan.

With my back to the sun, I power on Kylie's phone. The passcode screen flickers. Just as I'm about to lift the phone to my face, I hear a faint noise coming from the woods.

"Hey, Sweetie!"

Group Chat
Saturday, May 28th @ 8:12 p.m.

SLIDE_OB: THIS can't go on any longer. I think we should meet in person. Lying to Kate is not right.

The Pied Piper: Once the grad party is over, Kate's anxiety will die down. We need to give this time.

Milly Rodrigo: Time? How much time? When is enough going to be enough?

ZakAtak: Meeting in person could be a good idea.

JustPeachy: We need a solid plan to move forward. Meeting in person might be the best idea.

ZakAtak: What about at the party tomorrow? We can sneak away for a few minutes.

Milly Rodrigo: Kate will notice.

The Pied Piper: There's going to be so many people there. She won't.

Milly Rodrigo: This is a terrible idea.

Fauxy Roxy: Peaches, while you're Djing you could give a signal when it's a good time to meet.

The Pied Piper: Right! We finalized the playlist, and the only song Kate requested was Disarm by Smashing Pumpkins. That would be the perfect time to get away. Kate will be emotional and distracted. We want her distracted, right?

Milly Rodrigo: Of all the songs she loves, THAT'S what she requested?

ZakAtak: Okay, as soon as that song plays, we rendezvous in Mr. Rodrigo's study, say what we need to say, then go on with our lives and never bring this up again. Everyone cool with Niall being there?

The Pied Piper: Niall wasn't invited to the grad party.

Milly Rodrigo: Kate barely knows him, and we're not friends with him either. It will be weird if he shows up.

ZakAtak: She DOES know him, she just doesn't remember. Sort of.

Milly Rodrigo: And she can't ever find out!

The Pied Piper: Invite him.

Milly Rodrigo: Can't we meet later this summer? I'm not ready.

The Pied Piper: Our plane leaves Monday morning. This weekend is our last chance to talk in person.

ZakAtak: Right, your graduation gift.

The Pied Piper: New Zealand awaits our loose American ways! Milly, how excited are you to spend 24 hours a day with me for eight weeks?!

ZakAtak: A lot can happen between now and when you girls come back. We have to meet tomorrow.

ZakAtak: Niall, you gonna be there?

Slide_OB: I'll figure out a way to come without raising suspicion.

Fauxy Roxy: Tomorrow it is.

Milly Rodrigo: Fine. But no more texting until then. We need to minimize the evidence.

The Pied Piper: You are such a worrywart.

Hamburger
Saturday, May 28th @ 8:23 p.m.

THE CHICKADEE IS taunting me. He or she knows I've been looking for them all spring.

"HAM-BURG-ER-ER-ER-ER-ER!"

Although I'm eager to check Kylie's phone, I'm now more curious about that bird. I sit upright, turning my head toward the woods. I wonder what kind of danger they might sense. A squirrel? Raccoon? Something bigger? The sun is nearly gone behind the trees. In contrast to the twilight sky, the dense forest below is almost pitch black. A cold wind sweeps in from the lake. I shiver.

"HAM-BURG-ER-ER-ER-ER-ER-ER!"

That time, there was an extra 'ER'. A particularly dangerous threat must be lurking in the woods tonight.

I chuckle.

This is the part in every thriller movie where the blonde girl runs into the forest to investigate the noise and loses her top along the way. Then she's murdered.

"HAM-BURG-ER-ER-ER-ER-ER-ER!"

I remind myself that I'm not the helpless girl in a horror film, the fool who dies in the first five minutes. I'm an ordinary person living in boring

Mayfair. My life has fallen apart, yes, and those broken pieces are weighing me down, but I haven't suffocated, yet. And I'm not an idiot.

I can't explain it, but I feel as though once I *see* a chickadee chirp, everything might be okay.

Is that crazy?

"Is that crazy?" I shout to no one.

"Hey, sweetie!" the same chickadee—or maybe another—calls back. She's probably agreeing with me. I'm bat-shit crazy.

"Oh, so you want me to come into the woods and play?" I holler back.

Oh my goodness, is it worse that I've gone from having conversations with dead people to conversations with birds?

"Hey, sweetie!" my little friend sings.

I boldly stand and face the woods. I shake the nerves out of my body and laugh. At this moment, I honestly don't care if I live or die, but I'm not *going* to die just because I want to see a chickadee.

I take a few steps, then a few more, and then even more. As I move further from the house, the weeds grow taller and tickle my fingertips. I'm careful with my steps. The grass is soft, but this part of the yard is wild. Anything could be growing beneath my feet. I curse; I should have worn some shoes.

"HAM-BURG-ER-ER-ER-ER-ER-ER!"

I glance back at the house. In just a few minutes, the sky will be completely dark. I slip Kylie's phone into my pocket and hurry toward the noise.

"HAM-BURG-ER-ER-ER-ER-ER-ER!"

The feeling that I had last night of not giving a fuck, is back and in full force, giving me a false sense of bravery. Any fear of something bad happening is gone; I need to see that damn bird.

"HAM-BURG-ER-ER-ER-ER-ER-ER!"

Like a crazy person, I run towards the sound. I wince when a stick scrapes my pinky toe, but I don't stop.

"HAM-BURG-ER-ER-ER-ER-ER-ER!"

The songbird is so close now.

Within seconds, I'm completely enveloped inside the forest. Just ahead of me runs the nature path. I quietly push through the bushes and wince when I take another step. That had to be a raspberry bush I just stepped on. Determined, I press on. Once on the trail, the ground is soft and covered with baby grass. Above, the stars pour light onto the pathway.

"HAM-BURG-ER-ER-ER-ER-ER-ER!"

On the other side of the trail, just a few feet away, there's a small pine tree. I smile.

And my chickadee.

"HAM-BURG-ER-ER-ER-ER-ER-ER!" She says.

At this point, I decide she's a she.

My heart swells. Not only did I see a chickadee, but she sang. I couldn't be happier.

I lift my hands in the air and twirl.

"See world," I whisper, "I'm winning!"

But then I freeze, worried I might scare her.

Once I finish my victory spin, I notice she hasn't moved.

"HAM-BURG-ER-ER-ER-ER-ER-ER!"

My little friend really wants my attention, so I inch closer. Each step makes me worried the bird will fly away, but she doesn't. When I get close enough, I see that she's perched on top of a nest.

"Aren't you a sweetie," I say, peering more closely.

Inside the nest, there's a white object—an egg? I don't want to invade her privacy, but she's watching me expectantly, as if she wants me to invade.

"Okay, little bird. What do you want me to see?" I lean in. The blob isn't an egg, but a figure.

I frown.

What the...

I jerk back when the chickadee screams, "HAM-BURG-ER-ER-ER-ER-ER-ER!" and flies out of the nest, nearly hitting me. Once I push my heart back inside my chest, I take a closer look. The white object isn't an egg; it's a doll—a tiny figure with platinum blonde hair, dressed in black sweatpants and a white t-shirt. Cautiously, I reach into the nest and pick her up. Studying her, I chuckle, but then quickly frown. She looks like me. I examine her more carefully. On her cheek, there's a mark. A word? My eyes narrow.

"What the fuck?" I whisper. I swear it says: Dye. I squint. That can't be right.

I look around.

Who would leave a miniature Kate in a nest in the woods, behind my dad's house?

My heart begins to thud, and my breathing quickens.

Why am I in the woods?

I *am* the stupid blonde.

The trees seem to close in around me, and the forest is now completely dark. I stuff the figure in my pocket just as I start to feel dizzy. *I need to get out of here.* Facing the faint, distant light coming from my dad's living room, I stumble back into the thick brush I just came from, but this time I do so blindly because the stars have stopped lighting my way.

From behind, somewhere deep in the woods, I hear a thump, thump, thump. Or is that my heartbeat? In a panic, I step forcefully, ready to run, but then something prickly stabs the sole of my foot, and I cry out in pain. Now, hopping in place, I reach for the support of a nearby maple branch. My weight snaps the useless lifeline, and I go tumbling forward.

The thump, thump, thump is closer now, accompanied by heavy breathing. My heart? My breathing? Unable to stop myself, I'm falling face-first onto the forest floor. But before everything goes completely dark, I realize I'm about to be murdered by the same lunatic who murdered—

The Sister
Thursday, April 7th

"WAIT! ISN'T THAT…" Harrison enthusiastically sputters but can't finish his sentence because I backhand his chest. He shoots me a look of pure fascination, mixed with utter pleasure, followed by childlike joy.

Harrison's neck hugs me hard and whispers, "That's the girl you showed me on Instagram. The one you fucked that night. Isn't she Kylie's best friend?"

"Shut up," I whisper back, through gritted teeth.

Kylie—clueless to the interaction between Harrison and me—waves to Roxy and waits for her to join our awkward party of three. The sidewalk becomes my dizzying stage. When Kylie introduces Roxy, Roxy gives zero indication that she and I had shared a night together. *Nice to see you again, Niall. Of course, I remember meeting him, Kylie! It was that night at Triple B's!*

Another layer of 'what the fuck' that I can't handle right now. Let alone for the next three to four hours. Roxanne immediately eats Harrison up like a juicy Johnsonville Stadium brat. On the way inside, Kylie and I make small talk—the only kind we ever have.

Once inside the ballpark, Harrison starts making weird faces at me. While the girls order drinks, he mouths something and points at Kylie. He looks frustrated. I'm having a hard time understanding him. I think it's something about Mr. Vanguard. I'm not talking shop right now, so I ignore Harrison's extra-weirdness. I have to keep my cool and mentally prepare an epic breakup speech.

At least the game turns out to be entertaining. In the bottom of the fifth, Hoerner homers on a line drive to left-center field. Heyward scores. My Cubbies are up by two.

I should be elated, but anxiety claws at my chest, and a heavy dread makes me feel woozy. The worst part of tonight won't be confessing to Kylie that I'm not into her—it'll be accepting that my mystery girl will vanish from my life forever. Any tie or connection to her, severed beyond repair. Her memory feels relentless—it won't just leave, it will haunt me. Whatever she was or wasn't to me, the game is over.

On the drive to the stadium, Harrison and I came up with our own game plan. During the seventh inning stretch, Harrison would take his date to the souvenir shop, and I'd break up with Kylie.

Kylie, you're an amazing girl. You're gorgeous. But I'll be traveling a lot for work soon, and I won't have time for a relationship.

The top of the seventh inning has ended. Harrison flips his baseball cap backward. Roxy swoons. The two walk off to find Roxy 'something sparkly'. Kylie and I sit in silence. I look down at my phone. Harrison has sent me several texts. I ignore them.

Although I haven't said anything yet, guilt eats at me. Even though our 'relationship' hasn't been very substantial, I have a feeling she won't take the news well. Kylie is quietly playing on her phone. I rub my forehead. My heart pounds. I sit; my feet tap. Wong, the Brewers' second baseman, scores. The game is tied.

Roxy and Harrison return—much sooner than expected. The seventh inning stretch is over. The opportunity is lost. Harrison gives me a 'what the fuck?' look. "I texted you," he snaps. I ignore him. He was expecting me to have already broken Kylie's heart. But I can't seem to let her go yet.

Harrison pulls Roxy into his lap. She squirms and giggles. I rub perspiration off my forehead. Kylie scrolls.

Harrison tries multiple times to catch my attention. I ignore him. He even asks if I want to go to the bathroom with him.

The girls laugh.

I flip him off.

In the bottom of the seventh, Happ doubles on a sharp fly ball to the center fielder, Cain. Frazier scores. Contreras scores. My Cubbies are kicking ass. Harrison triumphantly shouts. Roxy hugs him. I sweat. Kylie and I exchange a glance. I think we're both thinking the same thing: Roxy and Harrison are having more fun in these last three hours than the two of us have had in the last two months.

After the game is over, the four of us make our way to the exit. Outside the entrance, Kylie and I say goodbye. Harrison's tongue is planted behind Roxy's tonsils. His hands are on her ass.

Kylie steps back, smirks at me, and looks… beautiful, uncomfortable, and awkward.

"You know," she says, "I always wish I were someone else. Like Roxy or my sister. Everyone loves Roxy. She's so outgoing, so beautiful. And my sister is nothing like Roxy, but she's gorgeous in her own way. She's quiet until she has something important to say or needs to ask some ridiculously fantastic question. Everyone loves her, too. She's a chaotic bolt of lightning one minute, then a stunning rainbow the next. She's so, so amazing."

"Everyone has those feelings," I say. "At least at some point. The desire to have what we can't have can be overwhelming. Or to be someone else. To have what someone else has. Cars, money, looks. It's better to appreciate what you have and who you are."

I wonder what triggered Kylie's introspection.

"The 'looks' part isn't a problem," she says, and emphasizes looks. "Not with my sister and me."

"You look a lot alike?" I ask. I frown. I really don't care if she does or doesn't.

Harrison is hugging Roxy and twirling her around. Roxy screeches when her feet almost collide with a bicyclist.

"Yeah," Kylie says. "Identical."

Roxy playfully drums Harrison's back.

"Wait—what?" I ask. I look at Kylie.

"We're twins," Kylie says, her smile is wide. "Identical. I don't always see the similarity, but others say it's impossible to tell us apart."

Harrison and Roxy's bodies disappear. My brain spins. The deluxe hot dog I had eaten earlier rises to the back of my throat. Acid coats my tongue.

"… and there was this one time—wait, Slide, are you okay? You look really sick. Like you're gonna puke." Kylie takes a step back.

"Yeah, I'm not feeling so well," I say and swallow hard. I raise my voice. "Harrison, you about ready?" Harrison casually tips his head my way. I must look awful, because he quickly unpeels Roxy's legs from around his waist. He jogs over to me, thanks Kylie for the invite, and Kylie and I do another 'head nod' goodbye. After the girls disappear into the crowd, Harrison continues his worried stare.

"Dude," Harrison says. "What the fuck is wrong with you? You look like you've finally seen Soo-Jin's ghost."

A swarm of drunk fans walks in between us. One asshole bumps into me; I trip over an orange traffic cone.

"Bro," Harrison says, grabbing my arm. "What. The fuck. Is wrong?" He steers me behind a parked maintenance vehicle.

"She's real," I answer and slouch against the van.

"Who?"

"The girl."

"What girl?"

"From that night."

"What do you mean?"

"Kylie has a sister."

"So, what? We knew that."

I drag my eyes off the concrete sidewalk and look at Harrison.

"They're identical twins."

"Bro," Harrison says, his mouth drops, and he finally realizes what I just realized. "Now we know why Kylie was so different. Bro, YOU ASKED OUT THE WRONG SISTER!"

The Rescue
Saturday, May 28th @ 9:04 p.m.

OUTSIDE MY WINDOW, the field is alive with fireflies. I stare at them, the room, the fireflies, the room.

What the fuck just happened?

I stretch my arms and wince. I'm sore, but definitely not dead.

Not yet.

I'm in a room that is very pink and looks like my room, but it's so clean. I lean over the side of the bed—I can actually see the floor. My dresser drawers are shut. The photo of me and Kylie is on my nightstand. My oversized comforter is clean and wraps around me.

In the distance, I hear the sound of running water. Someone's in the guest shower. A man is singing a Taylor Swift song really badly. The shower turns off. The singing gets louder.

I giggle.

Niall.

Niall not only came to my rescue outside, but also likely carried me all the way from the trail into the house and upstairs. At some point, he cleaned my room and then tucked me into bed with my clean comforter.

Why is he being so nice?

I rub my temples.

But then groan. My foot stings, and my arms are covered in tiny scratches. I really am the blonde fool in every slasher movie, except I didn't die. I can't even do that right.

A vibration against my thigh tells me someone just texted me. I pull my phone from my pocket. Niall has sent several messages over the past ten minutes.

Dream Stealer: What were you doing in the woods? You scared me to death with that scream.

Dream Stealer: You should be glad that I took your dad's advice and checked out the new running path, because if I hadn't, I never would have known you were back there.

Dream Stealer: I'm not one to get in other people's business, but what were you doing back there this time of night?

Dream Stealer: Sorry, that was me overreacting. You just scared me. I wanted to take you to the hospital, but you said no. When I picked you up, you just clung to me, so I carried you to your room.

Dream Stealer: I cleaned the scratches on your arms and put a new bandage on your hand.

Dream Stealer: Let me know when you're up. I just want to make sure you're okay.

Dream Stealer: Are you hungry?

Dream Stealer: I kind of want ice cream.

I want to laugh at his text. *But we can't do this.* And I'm positive giggling with him is encompassed within 'this', so is eating together.

Dream Stealer: I can see you read my texts, so I know you're alive.

Dream Stealer: My treat. Ice cream from Thirty Below?

I type a 'yes', stop, erase. Re-type. Erase. Decide not to type at all.

Our town's little ice cream shop—the same one that lost out on my extraordinary kitchen skills—is closed eight months out of the year. This weekend is the shop's summer grand re-opening. For the next 120 days, Mayfair residents have direct access to creamy sorbet, frozen yogurt scoops, and countless toppings. Flavor of the week? Death by chocolate.

Warm brownie batter, rich cocoa pudding, sticky-sweet caramel, and marshmallow chunks. And somehow they find room for ice cream. My mouth waters.

Me: Sorry about what happened earlier. I'm so embarrassed.
Dream Stealer: Don't worry about it.
Dream Stealer: What kind of ice cream do you like?
Me: Vanilla. A scoop. Please and thank you.
Me: And just leave it outside my door when you get back.

We can't do this. And I definitely can't have him in my room tonight. That would be a *this* that we can't do.

I hear him leave the guest room and jog down the stairs. I frown because I want to drown in hundreds of useless—yet delightful— chocolate-covered calories. And cherries. I want a heaping bowl overflowing with cherries. I need them after today. But I asked for vanilla… I hate that I'm allowing Niall to influence my behavior.

***

Piper, Milly, Zakary, and Peaches have all messaged, but I'm not in any mood to talk about how I'm not feeling great. Plus, I must look awful. Peaches has sent me four ClickYaps. I take a pic of my forehead and send it to all of them. That should appease them for tonight.

I check my emails.

My breath catches. I have one unread email. I click. Miss Verity has replied.

Dear Miss Vanguard,

Our firm is anxious to speak with you further regarding the open accounting position with our company.

So, so, so glad!!! We want you!!!!!

My boss, Lance Deveraux, was very interested in you after he read your resume. Because he thought so highly of you, I had already contacted your reference, Professor Holliday, and he said you were one of his most gifted students.

With that being said, Lance has given me approval to offer you the job, as long as you can make the move to Chicago asap.

Seriously!!!!!!!!!!!!!!!!!!

Lance is anxious to add a ferocious numbers-savvy member to the team. The attached link includes: the offer letter, the New Employee Form, instructions for accessing our suite, and a list of nearby public parking lots (in case you're driving). Please E-sign and return the offer letter as soon as possible so we can lock in your start date. (I list a tentative start date of this TUESDAY.) Please also fill out the employee form.

I apologize for all the so's and the !!!, but I'm at my ex-best friend's wedding. She's marrying my ex-boyfriend. Waaaah!! WTF, right? Soooo, I am super fucking drank right now!!!! Let's talk wedding presents. I wrapped a King Kong vibrator in Pebble Foil Metallic gift wrapping. The bow is HUGE! Is that a terrible gift? Did I go overboard on the wrapping paper? Am I a terrible friend?!!! TBH my ex's penis was really small. I blame gift selection on insider information!!!

Anyway, can't wait to meet you, Katie-Kat! (It's cool that I call you that, right?!) You and I are going to become the BEST of friends!!! I snooped you on Insta. Sooooo cute! BTW, the only reason this email is somewhat clear is because I had a draft typed up several weeks ago after I called your reference.

I was EXPECTING you to say yes! And it worked! You said yes! Anything with '!!!!' was added tonight, while I was trashed, so I apologize!!! If you have any questions, call me! I've added my personal cell number below.

Sincerely, Verity

I sit upright and hold my phone to my chest. A job offer!? Albeit a poorly written one, and likely not very professional. But this news gives me much-needed hope.

***

After I get the text alert from Niall, I wait a full five minutes before I hop out of bed and peer out my door. A small red, white, and blue bag of delight sits on the floor. I scoop it up, shut the door, and hurry back onto my bed. The ice cream is calling me. I wrap myself in my blanket and open the to-go bag. An extra-large container sits at the bottom, alongside a smaller one. I open the large lid first.

Three hearty scoops of vanilla ice cream topped with… Death by Chocolate? The ice cream is doused in hopes and dreams and everything I've ever wanted. I open the second container. Cherries. They smell like possibility.

Thankfully, there's a plastic spoon in the bag, but a utensil wouldn't be completely necessary, because I'd willingly lick the damn thing like an ice cream cone. I grab my phone with one hand and devour the sundae with the other.

Me: Thank you for the ice cream.
Dream Stealer: You're welcome.
Dream Stealer: Do you mind that I added toppings?
Me: You know the answer.
Me: Vanilla ice cream is sad. Thank u.
Me: All my favorites.
Me: I really appreciate it.
Dream Stealer: Glad you like.
Me: And thank you for my room. It looks so nice. You didn't have to do that.
Dream Stealer: It was not a problem. You are welcome.
Dream Stealer: Tonight was the third time you fainted in front of me. I'm going to start getting a complex.

At first, I smile at Niall's comment. But then I frown so hard my eyebrows hurt. *Third time?* What is he talking about? I fainted at the restaurant and then knocked myself out tonight. That's twice.

As I lick the bowl clean, my thoughts cloud my ability to think logically. *What is he talking about?*

Frustrated that I don't know, I focus on what I do know. Kylie's treasures are in my closet. I have a job offer. The future is still uncertain, but I feel more in charge than ever. Except for…

We can't be a thing.

Boldly, I grab my phone and type.

Me: Please stop doing nice things for me.
Me: It's confusing.
Dream Stealer: Ok.
Me: Thank you.
Dream Stealer: You're welcome.
Dream Stealer: Good night.

Feeling a rush of energy from all the sugar and a new job on the horizon, I raid Kylie's treasures. This time, I'm fearless when I enter the closet. I push open the door and leave the light switch off. Inside, I find a second box of 'Summer wear'. I unpack, then add the clothing to my drawers. Back in the closet, Mother's antique chest calls to me as though it holds ancestral powers. Tempting me—but I'm more terrified Mother would be upset with me for snooping. So instead, I open the bin labeled 'Formal wear'. A black ball gown with tulle lies on top. It's the same dress Kylie wore to Junior prom when she, Zakary, and I went together. Tucked against the side of the heap, I find Kylie's AirPods.

Tonight, for the first time ever, I was going to have to fall asleep alone. But not anymore. After I shower, AirPods in, Mother's happy pills dissolving in my stomach, lights on, I wrap my arms around the prom dress. I glance at my reflection in the mirror. The dress is super tight on me. Tighter than I remember it being on Kylie. And I had a hell of a time zipping the damn thing, but it reminds me of her.

I can't forget about Kylie anymore. At least tonight I won't be able to; I can barely breathe in this thing.

Inhale. *Kylie, please come to me tonight.*

Exhale. *Kylie, tell me how I can help you.*

***

Kylie. She, she, she…pishhhhhhh…
Don't tell!

***

The room is pitch black. The air, hot and smells like freshly installed carpet. I turn my head to the right; an object brushes the tip of my nose. I try to lift my arms, but they're tingling and numb. With short, jerky movements, I outstretch my fingers, clench. A pins and needles sensation runs from my fingertips to my elbow.

The velvet chaise lounge is stiffer than usual tonight. I wiggle my body. Feeling slowly returns to my hands. My fingertips brush the couch. Rough. Like yarn. I pound the surface. Where are the woven ridges lined with discomfort? This can't be my dad's couch.

Push, push, push.

Nothingness surrounds me. Emptiness. A confined darkness. Not the normal closed door—curtains partially opened—bedroom darkness. But a deeper one. Entrapped. Coffin-like.

My hands pat the area.

A sock?

I barely lift my hands before they collide against something solid. I push. I punch. A flat something is above me. Covering me. Containing me.

My heart speeds.

I bolt upright—my head smacks into… the ceiling? My forehead stings, throbs, really throbs. Something drips down my face. I use the back of my hand to wipe. Sticky. Iron. Blood? I pound the hard surface above my head. Flat, flat, hard metal. A frame?

I'm lying on my back.

Under…

A bed?

What am I doing under a bed? In the dark? I inch to my right, but there's a… wall? I inch to the left—a wooden bedpost?

Panic rises with each barrier.

I scream. Then, again. Again. I claw to my left, right, left. Still screaming. Finally, I reach an opening wide enough for my head. Pull, pull, pull. Push, push, push. Fight. Crawl. *Save her.* I heave myself out from under the confining bed and roll onto my chest. Even though I've escaped, air still seems impossible to find. I wheeze. I gasp. In between wheezing and gasping, I'm screaming.

At some point, I think the room becomes less dark, but I can't be certain, because my eyes are tightly shut. I'm locked inside fear. Bound within failure. Gagged with impossibility.

"Kylie! Kylie! Kylie!"

Her name is all around me.

What didn't I do?

What did she do?

She pushed. She pushed. She pushed.

Don't tell! Don't tell!

Kylie pleads.

A cotton candy-light touch lands on my lower back.

"You're safe," a calming voice says. The person wants to know what happened. He rubs my bare shoulders. "I'm not going anywhere," he promises.

My body shakes, convulses, sweats. The person shifts me onto my side and cradles my head in their lap. I lick my lips. Dry. Metallic.

Soft fabric brushes against my cheek. A trembling hand searches my neck, arms, and legs. Looking for something.

"What happened, Katie?" The man wants to know.

What happened?

She, she, she.

"Who are you talking about?" The man asks.

She, she, she.

"I'm so, so sorry," the man whispers. "Everything is my fault. I want to turn back time. Katie, what can I do?"

Niall?

I open my eyes. The pink ceiling stares back. The walls spin, blur. I'm overheating. Imploding. Dying. Then... I cease to exist.

"... hear me? I think you're having a panic attack. Try to slow down your breathing."

I cling to safety, squeezing Niall's warm torso. My cheek presses against his soft t-shirt.

"Can you copy my breath?" he asks. "Follow how I breathe." He guides my hand to his chest. His diaphragm expands. I let my chest expand. His compresses. Mine compresses. Nothingness retreats, like a slow, lazy puddle, eaten up by morning sunbeams. Niall is the sun.

But why is everything still so tight?

"I can't breathe," I finally say. I hold onto Niall tightly with one arm and yank at my shirt with the other. My tank top? What am I wearing? I look down. Air, I need air. Pounding inside my ears. Pressure within my chest. Weakening of my neck muscles… darkness.

"… a panic attack," Niall says. "Hang on."

In a swift movement, I'm firmly pressed against Niall, swaddled in electrifying heat. Completely held. Entirely safe. The ground below disappears, and suddenly, Kylie's beside me. I grip the Downy-scented blanket and tuck my sister against my cheek. My other hand clings to Niall. I inhale the scent from the blanket, but the air refuses to enter. Can't leave? It's stuck. I'm dying.

"Copy me," Niall says firmly.

My fingers find his chest, and I hang onto his every movement. Inhale. Strong fingers grip my body. Exhale. I squeeze his shoulder blade. Repeat. Repeat. Repeat. A calloused hand massages my fingers, my cheek, my arms, caresses my hair.

Breathing slowly becomes easier.

"Damn, Katie," Niall says, "you scared the hell out of me. I was about to call 911."

The air had been thick, indistinguishable, but now I smell luscious fabric softener and husky testosterone. An all-encompassing hug surrounds me, possessing me in the fiercest, most liberating way.

Niall says my forehead is bleeding. But I'm no longer shaking. My breathing is back to normal. But my body feels clammy. Should he call 911? *No.* What do I need? *You, just you.* But then his support and warmth slowly begin to disappear. Niall says he's going to be right back. *No, stay!*

I need him, just as much as I need Kylie.

I sit upright and grip his bicep with one hand, the other presses against his chest and becomes entangled in his necklace.

"I'll stay as long as you want," he whispers and pulls me into his chest, completing our connection. "I was just going to grab something to clean the cut on your forehead."

I reluctantly release him and wrap Kylie around me. In less than a minute, he's back. Feeling foolish once again, I watch as he sits next to me on the bed.

A cool cloth dampens my forehead.

"This will take care of your forehead"—I feel slight pressure above my eyebrow and then the sticky adhesive of a band-aid—"And this will take care of your hand"—He removes the gauze from around my palm and replaces it with fresh material—"Good as new."

"Thank you," I say, more calmly now. Kylie's dress digs into every curve of my body. I tug at the front, under my arms, the cinched waistline.

"It's none of my business," Niall says, "And feel free to tell me to shut up, but do you want me to leave so you can change into something more comfortable?"

Not that I care what Niall thinks, but I do feel compelled to tell him why I'm wearing this dress and why I had a meltdown.

"I wanted to feel close to Kylie," I say, "so I put on her dress. But she's suffocating me." I breathe—need to—but can't. I sit upright.

"Here," he says and stands. "You can wear my t-shirt." He swiftly removes his white cotton tee and places it in my lap. "It's super soft. You'll be swimming in it, but at least you'll be comfortable." He steps away from the bed, and worry flashes across his face. His sunset, oceanic eyes beg me… "I can leave while you change," he says, but doesn't move.

Maintaining eye contact with him, I kneel. I strain to reach the back of my dress. I yank and stretch. Defeated, I rest my hands at my sides. I look to him. He crawls onto the bed and positions himself behind me. He easily slides the zipper down. Cool air hits my back. My skin comes alive. For a moment, he rests his fingers on my shoulders.

"Thank you," I say over my shoulder. I press the top of the dress against my chest.

"I'll give you some privacy," Niall says.

"No—I don't want to be alone," I say.

Before I can even think, he quickly slips his shirt over my head. Automatically, I shrug into the sleeves. I've no idea what his eyes are doing when I carefully slip off the dress.

When I turn to face him, he looks away. Almost as though he's embarrassed.

"Um, I can stay until you fall asleep," he says and scoots to the edge of the bed. He looks at his folded hands. "Can I get you anything?"

I hug my arms around my chest and shiver. I yawn.

Niall yanks down the comforter. He waves for me to lie on the pillow. I crawl to the open space. He covers me, then scoots off the bed.

"I'm good," I say. I turn from him and hug my pillow. "Thank you. But…"

"What?" he asks.

"I'm so…" I begin to say.

So… what?

So, what?

So what am I?

Anger, embarrassment, mistrust, frustration, sadness, fear, guilt, and a thousand other feelings twist and spin around my chest. But more than anything, I'm tired of these feelings. I'm so tired of caring. I don't care that Niall has my job. It was never mine to begin with. I don't care that he's seen me in one embarrassing situation after the next. I don't care that I lost my sister. I don't care that I have to leave Mayfair. I don't care that I've lost Mother. I'm done with caring. What good has it gotten me?

Fired. No degree. Unstable relationships.

So, what!

I'm just going to be.

Me.

I'm so done being anything else.

"Katie," Niall says, "Are you okay?"

In a rush of verbal vomit, I answer, "I am not okay. And that is okay. I am not 'doing well'. And that is okay. I'm not perfect; not even close. I'm not on time for appointments. I have a scar on my cheek. I'm quick-tempered. Curiosity sometimes kills me. But I'm me. And sometimes that's the best I can be. Imperfections are okay. Maybe being me is okay after all?"

I begin to sob quietly into the comforter. Before I know it, Niall is next to me, again, rubbing my back. His fingers brush through my hair. Massage my scalp. He hands me tissues.

I continue rambling. At this point, I'm not sure of everything I've said, but I know it's probably too much.

And even still, Niall lets me… be.

Once I'm done, I murmur a "Thank you."

Niall passes me more tissues.

I wipe snot from my nose and chin, then flip the dampened pillow to the dry side. I sit upright and stare at my crumpled pile of tissues.

"Niall?" I ask. At the same time, he says, "Katie?"

"Yes," we simultaneously say.

We laugh softly.

"You go first," I say.

"I'll stay in here for the night?" he asks. It sounds like a question, but it's a promise. "I can sleep on the floor. I don't mind."

Niall's sitting on the edge of the bed. Just an arm's length away. Shirtless, wearing another pair of those jeans, looking like a god. I stare at his chain necklace and the small ring hanging from it.

"You may as well be comfortable and get under the covers," I say.

"Um… all right," he says.

He stretches, his biceps flex. He yawns.

"I'll go grab a t-shirt and some sweatpants," he says, and pushes off the mattress.

"Please, don't," I say. "Just… stay with me, I don't want to be alone." Before he can argue, I turn away and toss my tissues in the nearby garbage can. "And I trust you, Niall. If you want to sleep in your boxers, or whatever, I'm not worried." My checks, no doubt, are a thousand shades of red.

I wrestle with my pillow, pull the blankets up, back down, kick my feet. I imagine his magical jeans sliding down his magical ass, past his magical thighs.

The jeans crack in the air as he shakes them. He's probably folded them with perfection and set them on the nightstand.

"Can I turn off the light?" he asks.

"Yeah."

The room darkens.

The bed creaks.

The blanket tugs.

Like gravity, Niall's weight on the mattress sucks me towards him. I fight the laws of nature and scoot to my side of the bed.

Niall's gentle, caring hand cautiously finds my waist under the covers. He pulls me close until the small of my back is pressed firmly against his pelvis, my legs become wrapped in his, and my head fits perfectly between his collarbone and jaw. His hand protectively settles outside the blanket on my hip.

"Comfortable now?" he asks.

"Very."

I can hear his steady heartbeat. My erratic heartbeat. His steady breathing. My erratic breathing.

"You probably think I'm crazy," I say.

"Not at all."

"You must."

"You're not crazy, Katie."

"What if I am?"

"Then I'm crazy, too."

"Why are you so kind to me?"

"Because I care about you."

"Why?"

"I'm your friend." His hand moves from the swell of my hip to the curve of my waist, to my shoulder, and back down my thigh. And again. I bite the inside of my lip. He's kind, helpful, and seems to have my best interests in mind. Like a friend.

"You know what?" I ask.

"What, Katie?"

"I don't think anyone is my friend lately. I feel like everyone I love is lying to me. To be honest, I don't even trust myself lately."

"Why would you say that?"

"Well, for starters, I can't remember that night. Like zero memories of the night my…" My voice trails off. "I'm missing twenty-four hours of memories. How does that even happen?"

"Is that why you had the panic attack tonight?" he asks.

"I had a nightmare, a recurring nightmare. And tonight, while I was sleeping, I fell off the bed and somehow rolled underneath. Kylie has been on my mind more than ever. I think that's why I was having such vivid dreams about her."

"That's a lot to deal with," Niall says. "I'm so sorry you're going through this."

"You think I'm crazy?" I ask. "Insane, right?" I let out a nervous breath of air. "I'd think it too if I were you."

"Honestly," he says, low and husky. His warm breath tickles the crown of my head. "I think it's time we level the playing field."

"What?" I ask, nervously.

"Time to make things even."

"What do you mean?"

"It's time I dazzle you with the pilot episode of 'The Most Embarrassing Shit Niall's Ever Done'. And if you think it's terrible, go easy on the creator. It's his first time he's ever had to entertain a stunning woman in a dark bedroom with only his voice."

I belly laugh. Then snort.

"We're taking it way back," he says, massaging my bare forearm, "starting with my childhood. One of my most embarrassing moments. I've never told anyone this before."

"I'm intrigued," I say, giggling.

"I…" He trails off.

"Tell me," I say and playfully sway my hips backward.

"Nope," he says, sternly, "you stay still." His hand clutches my hip. "Yeah, this may not work. Can you hand me one of those pink pillows?"

"Sure…" I scoot forward, grab a pillow, and toss it behind my back.

"Thanks," he says.

I return to my position and giggle. The pillow is strategically placed behind my ass.

"You trust me," he says, "but I've never done this before. I'm not sure I trust myself."

I belly laugh, again.

"You're stalling," I playfully say. "Tell me."

"I had…" he says and pauses.

"A bed wetting problem?" I ask.

"No."

"Hand me down clothes that never fit?"

"Hand me down clothes, yes. But they fit okay."

"What then?"

"Katie, you're really doing this? Making me divulge my secrets?"

"Yes."

"Fine… I had… an imaginary friend."

I laugh.

"Seriously," Niall says. "The kid was real to me. I have distinct memories of Sha—him and I swinging together. The swings were green with metal chains. And when we played trucks, I had a yellow one, and his was silver."

"Did your imaginary friend have a name?" I ask.

"You heard that slip, hey?"

"I did."

"His name was Shay."

"You named your imaginary friend?"

"I did."

We both laugh.

Over the next several hours, Niall shares intimate details about his life with me. Every weird, embarrassing, and sinful thing he's ever done. My stomach aches, and my pillowcase is covered in happy tears.

As my eyelids begin to close, a faint glow from the sun peeks through the curtain. When I finally do fall asleep, it's only after I've laughed until I've cried, and giggled until I've nearly peed my pants. Niall's crazy stories will consume my dreams. I silently thank him for giving me a reason to sleep soundly.

I won't fall tonight.

Not to my death.

I am safe.

But I do fall… utterly, hopelessly, and entirely in love with—

The Daughter
Sunday, April 7ᵗʰ

DRIVING BACK TO Soo-jin's, Harrison says he has something important to tell me. I tell him it can wait.

He says it can't.

I tell him to fuck off.

She's real.

The woman.

My girl.

Nothing else matters.

Harrison says he'll appease me for now and talks me through every possible option and potential outcome… of dating a sibling. Of asking out the wrong woman. Of being a complete idiot.

Perhaps I break up with Kylie, give her some bull-shit excuse, 'accidentally' run into the sister, but then the sister has zero interest in me. Disaster. Break up with Kylie, tell her the truth—I want to date her sister, but the sister refuses, because I made Kylie cry. Disaster.

Or.

The sister isn't interested in me, because she's already in a long-term relationship. She's a lesbian. A nun. A swinger. Polyamorous.

All. Ending. In. Disaster.

Harrison helpfully determines I'm in the worst breakup scenario ever. *How can I win? How do I turn this around?*

"The truth sets you free," Harrison insists, but then counters, "the truth also hurts."

Harrison then drops the atomic bomb of truth on me. He's almost positive that Kylie is Henry Vanguard's *daughter*. He recognized her from the unfortunate vase-shattering meeting. That's why Harrison was trying to catch my attention and texting me during the ballgame. Kylie 1.0 *and* 2.0 are off-limits, regardless of how hot they may be.

Nothing is making any sense. Never—not in a million lifetimes—did I anticipate this reality. The mysterious woman I've been obsessing over for months is real, but she's so untouchable, so out of reach, so utterly impossible to obtain.

I sit in silence the rest of the ride until Harrison tells me he's been texting Roxanne and he's found out her name.

Whose name?

The mystery girl.

The sister's name. And do I want to know?

No.

What good will it do? I can't have her. Ever. Giving her a name will make this situation so much worse.

Harrison drops me off at Soo-jin's. The snow from last night's storm has melted, revealing brown, brittle grass. I trot up the front porch stairs and nearly slip on an ice patch.

Inside, Bennett tackles my leg and shrieks, "Uncle!"

Soo-jin scolds me; I never messaged to say when I'd be home. She wants to know how the double date went. Did Harrison like the girl? Will Harrison ever settle down? Bennett lost his favorite truck again; can I help find it?

The rest of the night, Bennett sits on my lap, crawls on my shoulders, and leaves Nutella fingerprints on my neck. Soo-jin shows me the beta version of the technology she's developed for Henry's home design app.

We devour her homemade Korean barbecue and kimchi. The night would normally be fucking ideal. Normally, I'd fall asleep within minutes of my head hitting the flattened pillow. Normally, I'd be anxious—in a good way—for tomorrow. Excited to win over another client.

After dinner, I lay in bed and type several draft messages to Kylie.

Me: Kylie, we need to break it off, sorry. This is the last time you'll hear from me.

Terrible. I hit enter and move my cursor down. The situation is more than delicate. Mr. Vanguard will be furious if he finds out I dated his daughter. *When* he finds out… I can't keep this from him. But how do I tell him? How do I justify my behavior?

First, I have to take care of Kylie. End it with her. A seamless break-up. What would that even look like? How can I break it off with Kylie without completely destroying my chances with the sister?

Me: Kylie, I need to be completely honest with you. I'm just not into you.

Too honest.

Me: The first night I met you, I never meant to ask you out. Sorry. It was a mistake. A terrible mistake. I meant to ask your sister out that night. Not you.

Me: Your personality is terrible. Nothing like your sister's.

Way too direct. Too raw and stripped, nothing left to hide. What if I offend her so badly that she tells her family all about 'the asshole' who broke her heart? For the next three hours, I come up with one terrible break-up text after the next, a solid ache in my stomach, and a burning pain in my chest. It's magnified a thousand-fold when I finally read through Harrison's earlier text messages. The last one stops my heart.

The Battering Ram: Her name is Kate.

Kylie's Boyfriend
Sunday, May 29th @ 2:30 a.m.

I BOLT UPRIGHT, heart pounding in my chest. Next to me, Niall's arm slides off my hip and falls to the bed. He does not wake when I crawl to the side of the mattress, my mind racing with unease.

What am I doing? Did Niall just weasel his way into my world, forcing me to let down my guard? This is not a rom-com. Death is on the line! A murder needs to be solved. And here I am, getting cozy with my enemy.

Yes, my enemy. Niall is not a murderer, nor is he my friend.

Fuck.

After steadying my nerves, I quickly grab some sweatpants. Careful not to wake Niall, I slip out the door and quietly shut it. I make my way downstairs.

In the quiet kitchen, I devour a box of cold cherry Poptarts and browse through Kylie's phone contents. I spend the first couple of hours scrolling through her photo gallery. Memory after memory floods the screen. I smile, I laugh, I cry.

When the sun begins to rise, I cuddle up on the couch and snoop through her text messages. Of course, I'm the last person to have texted her. The erratic messages I've sent her over the past few months have sat, unanswered. What a bizarre sight to see. We used to be so close, sometimes texting hundreds of times a day. My soul yearns for the past.

On the living room sofa, as a sliver of sunlight slips over Lake Michigan, my eyelids turn heavy, but my search continues. Next, I snoop through her other texts and ClickYap messages.

And I make a very interesting discovery.

During my snooping, I find a plethora of messages between my sister and her 'boyfriend' leading up to April 10th. The initial messages are surprisingly boring. Not necessarily ones that would be exchanged between lovers. The two talk about the weather and other non-sexual topics. But then things get interesting: in the last few messages, the man sounds upset.

We need to break it off, sorry. This is the last time you'll hear from me.
Kylie, I need to be completely honest with you. I'm not that into you.
The first night I met you, I never meant to ask you out. Sorry. It was a mistake. A terrible mistake. I meant to ask out your sister. Not you.
Your personality is terrible—nothing like your sister's.
The dishonesty. Betrayal. How could you? For me to find out this way… I don't even know what to say. How could you?
How could you?

Who is he, and what happened between him and Kylie? And he *meant to ask me out?* This does not make sense.

My heart pounds, and a renewed sense of purpose fills me. I have to *hurry and help* before it's too late.

Could this mystery man be the killer?

I must find Slide_OB and confront him.

Kylie_the_Baddie
Sun, May 29th @ 11:30 a.m.

A MINUTE AGO, I awoke to a ringing doorbell, a rapping on the front door, and Peaches' scream funneling through the open kitchen window, "Kate! Has it happened? Has Hannibal Lecter finally dismembered your body? Girl, tell me your skin is still attached!"

I didn't immediately get off the couch. I couldn't. The ticking clock on the wall says it's no longer morning. I've overslept.

"Girl!" Peaches yells. "Please, please, please, tell me the lotion hasn't been placed in the basket!"

Chuckling to myself, I peel myself off the comfy couch.

"I'm coming!" I jog into the foyer. "I'm up!"

Beep, beep, beep, beep. The front door swings open.

Peaches walks into the foyer carrying a Tupperware tower against his chest, a heaping paper bag of something in one hand, and a large McDonald's soft drink in the other.

"Here," he says, and thrusts the soda in my direction. "You look like shit. What the hell happened to your head? And why do you have scratches on your arms? You need to get your ass in the shower, Zakary's going to be here in less than half an hour. Which means I'm leaving in twenty."

I eagerly suck on the straw. Fizzy, ice-cold liquid tingles my throat.

"Do you know what time it is?" he presses, then gives me crazy eyes.

I suck louder. I do know what time it is. And I do know I missed my coffee date with Cass. Ugh. Now, Cass's truth will elude me for at least the next several hours. But I'm not too worried, I'll corner him at the grad party.

Peaches sets the paper bag on the table and carries the containers into the kitchen. I follow him, groaning and moaning. The cola tastes so good. I thank him multiple times and assure him the cut on my forehead was a stupid accident, and I'm getting in the shower in two seconds.

"These are heart-healthy meals," Peaches says, enunciating 'healthy', "your dad can pop them in the oven and bake. Easy-peasy. Cooking instructions are on top." He pivots, hugs me, then spins in place. "Where the hell did I… oh, there it is!"

He steps into the foyer and returns with a paper bag. "Fresh fruit," he says. "It'll keep in the fridge."

"Why did you make all that noise?" I set the plastic cup down and massage my eyes. The caffeine seeps to the tips of my toes and fingers. "You could've let yourself in."

"Hmm," he says, and taps his fingers on the counter. "Girl, you didn't answer any of my calls, texts, or messages yesterday. And a forehead pic does not count." He picks the phone off the counter. "This thing allows you to communicate with others when you're not in the same room."

"Kylie's phone," I say.

"What?" Peaches asks and looks down at the phone. "You finally found it? Well, what… what are you going to do with it?"

"Niall found it in my car yesterday," I say, matter-of-factly. " Which is super weird, because I swear I'd searched every inch of that thing like a hundred times." I open the fridge and snag the orange juice. After removing the cap, I gulp the rest of its contents.

"Watch this," I say. I reach for the phone.

After I power it on, I bypass the passcode and wait for the facial recognition application to open. I tilt my head, my scarred cheek faces away from the phone. I smile with my best 'Joker smile'. The phone unlocks.

I grin, looking at Peaches. He's surprised.

"We're twins," I say.

"What are you going to do with her phone?" he asks, again.

"Before everything happened, she was dating this guy," I say. I tap on the screen. "I found messages to a 'Slide_OB'. I'm going to find out who he is. Sounds like he knows me. Who could it be? This man knows more about that night. I know it." I shake the phone.

Peaches has gone unusually quiet.

"This could be the missing piece to the puzzle."

"It's her personal property."

"This could be how I find the killer," I say and shake the phone. "She wants me to hurry and help, before it's too late, and now I think—"

Peaches grabs the phone from me and sets it on the counter. He grips my shoulders.

"We are in a time crunch," he says, ushering me towards the stairs. "This pumpkin needs to turn into a princess."

Upstairs, Peaches takes one look at my clean floor and folded comforter and nearly bursts into tears. When I reveal my closet full of Kylie's neatly hung treasures—pressed tops, jeans draped on hangers, shoes in pairs, lining the floor—he actually does.

After I get out of the shower, I see that Peaches has chosen a flowy white baby-doll dress for me. Wrapped in my pink bathrobe, I examine the dress and promptly toss it back inside the closet. White is off-limits. He then chooses a nude satin wrap dress. Better than white. Which is good. And it doesn't cling. Even better. It has pockets. Fucking outstanding. And it's knee-length. So, even if the wind turns on me, no one will get a flash of my ass. That would be embarrassing, but very likely something that could happen to me.

Peaches applies a dusting of concealer to the cut on my forehead, blush to my cheeks, gloss to my lips, and mascara to my lashes. And now, he's gushing over how princess-y I look. So grown up, he purrs. Nothing like a pumpkin.

From the reflection in the mirror, I see myself. Not Kylie so much anymore. I see my scar. Fainter now. I see a Joker smile—still nowhere near as amazing as my dad's. Mother's ethereal beauty. Still not as magnificent as her angelic presence. Not even close.

Although I'm busy 'getting ready', and following Peaches' orders, that doesn't mean I don't notice Niall has washed and neatly folded my white t-shirts, socks, and underwear, and placed them on my dresser. Thinking about him touching my intimate items paints my cheeks scarlet. I turn my back on Peaches and grab the most comfortable pair of panties; Peaches lurks up from behind and smacks my selections out of my hand. He then digs through Kylie's boxes and finds 'a super cute white bra and underwear set—lacy and comfortable'.

Unenthusiastically, I do as I'm told and head to the bathroom. When I return, I inform Peaches that my ass cheeks are hanging out. He tells me to shut my beautiful face and says panty lines are forbidden today. I ask him why anyone would even notice if I was wearing granny panties. Apparently, because of the dress's cut, everyone will be taking a peek at my ass and wondering what's underneath. I fling two throw pillows at him. He ducks just in time.

Minutes later, Peaches shimmies out the front door just as Zakary arrives, ready to cart me to the grad party.

Zakary holds a 'Get well soon' card. I thank him. Zakary looks utterly handsome, dressed in khakis and a seafoam button-down. I wonder if there's really something wrong with the wiring in my brain. Why am I not head over heels in love with this man? Why isn't Zakary head over heels in love with me? Or someone else? I do know, one day Zakary will make someone very happy. It's just not me.

Once inside Zakary's car, I tell him that I can't afford his upper unit anymore. He says he's sad but understands and assures me that he has a waiting list of renters. While he discusses his latest real estate venture— a four-family, he's working on purchasing with Auntie Babs—I'm listening, nodding, and happy for him. But I'm also wondering.

While Zakary tells me about his new tenants, I create a fake ClickYap account: Kylie_the_Baddie and request to add Slide_OB as a friend. Within minutes, he accepts my request.

Kylie_the_Baddie: hey
Slide_OB: Who is this?

If Kylie didn't tell me about this mysterious man she was seeing, there had to be a reason. Either she was embarrassed by the guy or she felt guilty about something. Why else would she hide him from our friends and me?

Today, I will randomly send SLIDE_OB messages from the Kylie_the_Baddie account and see if I can learn anything about the mysterious man. For all I know, he might even be at the party.

Zakary veers onto the Rodrigo's driveway. On each side of the entrance, enormous confetti pink, white, and silver balloon-bouquets float above the column pillars. Full-bloom, strawberry pink tulips erupt from the shamrock green grass on the shoulders of the road.

Tastefully placed 'Congrats Grad' signs—and more sparkly balloons—lead us down the half-mile driveway. At the break in the trees, the blacktop fades into a yellow brick road of sorts, leading to the house.

The three-story home—a golden glow in every window—illuminates against the late afternoon sky. In-ground lights spotlight clusters of peonies, hydrangeas, hedges, and a plethora of other luscious bushes. The home is not a home. It's a sprawling ten-bedroom, eight-bath, brick mansion situated on four acres adjacent Lake Michigan.

"I've been here countless times," Zakary says, "but rounding that corner never gets old. Wow."

"Growing up," I say, "I was so jealous of Piper and Milly. Playdates here were insane. The home theater in the basement, the indoor pool, the outdoor pool, and the canopy beds. So. Much. Fun."

We round the cozy, six-car garage to the evening's make-shift parking lot in the empty horse pasture. Zakary slides next to a Mercedes truck in the designated 'VIP' section. We make our way around the garage and head to the front door. We're not even to the top of the stairs when I hear a squeal from the other side of the door.

The door swings open.

Piper squeaks and hops like a sexy bunny in high heels. She's stunning in a white mini skirt and off-the-shoulder lavender top. Her onyx hair is pulled back in a playful ponytail. She blinks several times, props her hands on her hips, and pops her bubble gum. Drink in hand. Piper's mouth turns into a pout.

"Katie!" She lunges at me and wraps me in a hug. "Can you believe it?" She steps back and wiggles in place. "We made it! Tiiiime to celebrate!" Piper waves a bangle-bracelet hand towards the front of the house. "Wait until you see the back patio," she says. "I will be chatting with both of you later. Right now, I have a very serious honey-baked Brie catastrophe to attend to." She slaps my ass, tells me I look divine, and saunters away.

Almost on cue, as if Milly was waiting just around the corner, she steps into the foyer wearing a sensible, pale pink, fitted summer dress and a thin white sweater. Although she's excited that Zakary and I are here, she doesn't have time to talk either. She must question the caterer. After an intense hug and a pat on my cheek, she rushes after Piper.

Since when do the Rodrigo sisters help each other with cheese-related projects? I'm ready to tackle them both and demand to know why they're acting so strange, but then Zakary collects my hand in his and gently tugs. We stroll down the corridor.

A few years ago, the Rodrigo's updated their elegant hallway into a family showroom. A series of five-foot gilded-framed portraits decorates the walls. Every other year, until Piper and Milly turned eighteen, the family took formal—like real formal—family pictures. The first photo was taken when Piper turned one, and Milly was an infant. Mrs. Rodrigo graced a vibrant red sofa, one arm draped over the back. She wore an off-the-shoulder, full-length, black Grecian gown with a slit sheer up her thigh. I only know the dress was Grecian because Laurel Rodrigo gave Kylie and me a tour of the home numerous times as children and emphasized that detail.

Laurel knew the importance of the three Cs in fashion: cut, color, and cost. JJ Rodrigo, the head of the family, proudly stands behind Laurel, sporting a Dolce & Gabbana suit coat. Baby Milly was wrapped in a silver blanket, tucked on Laurel's lap, while Piper pouted on the couch, arms crossed, tongue sticking out. Apart from Piper's unfortunate grimace, the artwork may have been borrowed straight from Buckingham Palace. Zakary and I laugh at the honest beauty in each canvas.

As we near the great room, excited voices and music pulse through the atmosphere. Electricity, more pink, silver, and white confetti balloons, floral arrangements, and classy 'Congrats Grad' signs decorate the room. Several classmates stop me to give me a hug. Somehow, I lose Zakary.

Hey, girl!

You look gorgeous!

Slay, Kate!

That fit is a total vibe!

The mundane conversation is perfect, because I can discreetly scan the crowd for Cass. He should be here by now. He's not in the living room. I meander out to the patio.

And smile.

Outside, hanging fairy lights lace the trees, and tiki torches line the yard. White tables scatter the area, each doused in pink glitter. Glow-in-the-dark garden pebbles rest underneath trees. Classmates, friends, and acquaintances fill the lawn.

A trendy, elegant bar is positioned adjacent to the DJ station. The same fish-tail braid bartender from Triple B's mixes drinks and offers me a shot. I decline. She hands me an ice-cold crystal glass of water instead. I sip the liquid. Clarity is essential tonight. From his perch, Peaches winks and waves. His headphones are crooked. He's playing Milly's favorites—90s pop. Lots of peppy, over-excited lyrics and positivity.

There must be at least two hundred guests at the party. The dance floor is throbbing with bodies. Piper, drink in hand, grinds on Cousin Bert. And I do wonder if he's actually a cousin or more of a family friend?

Milly stands with a group of underclassmen. When I spot her, I lift my arm to wave, but she quickly shields her face as though the sun's shining, but it's not. It's on the other side of the house.

Why is she ignoring me?

Needing a sense of control, I send my second mysterious message to Slide_OB.

Kylie_the_Baddie: how are you?

Again, the response is almost immediate.

Slide_OB: I'm great. But can you tell me who you are? This is kind of weird.

He's not wrong. This is probably the least sane thing I've done to date. I'm about ready to sit on one of the cozy white chairs when a group of classmates walks by me, and I overhear one of them say, "Cass is here."

Not wanting to miss my opportunity, I rush through the crowd, into the house. I immediately spot Cass's white-blonde hair as he walks down the family photo corridor. I reach the hallway entrance, and he looks up; his arms stretch wide. "Kate," he says, and meets me in the middle. I collide against his embrace.

"Oh, geez," he says, laughing. "Happy to see me? I thought you blew me off?"

"Cass," I say and pull away, "I overslept, that's all. I saw your message when I got up, but this morning's been so crazy... I'm so glad you're here."

He looks down at me. For a second, we're both somber, thinking the same thing: Kylie should be here.

"Can we talk now?" I hesitantly ask.

"Yeah, absolutely," he says, breaking the trance. He looks around. "I'll tell you everything. Everything I've wanted to tell you for weeks."

My heart swells. Simultaneously, I feel selfish for not reaching out to Cass sooner. He points towards Mr. Rodrigo's study. "Wanna talk in there?"

"For sure."

After we're inside the office, Cass closes the door. We stand facing each other. My heart is pounding, my hands are clammy.

"Do you want something to drink—?" I begin to ask, but Cass waves a hand and shakes his head.

"I'm just gonna say it... Kate, I have a mental illness."

"What?" I ask, more confused than ever.

"It's an obsessive-compulsive disorder," he says. "It began after April 10th. The next day—granted, I was hungover as hell—I started having these visions. That I had killed someone. Ran them over with my car. The images were so vivid. They had me freaking out, wondering if I had gotten so fucked up the night before that I hit someone with my car and didn't stop? I drove back to the bluffs. I scanned the sides of the road as I went. Terrified I'd find a dead body on the side of the road. But I didn't find anything. The images in my mind seemed so real, though. I could see a body shattering my windshield. The thud was deafening. Blood spattered the windshield. And it was Kylie."

"What the fu—?" I ask.

"Let me finish," he says. His eyes plead. "I looked everywhere between my place and Triple B's. But I never found the bloody scene, so I came home. The feeling that I had killed Kylie was so real, so I kept driving back. Then I'd come home. Drive back. I went back and forth. Each time I got closer to Triple B's, the panic inside my chest became unbearable. Once I'd get to the parking lot, I'd slam on the brakes, turn around, and speed home. But then return minutes later. The same scene played out. Only after the tenth drive could I convince myself that the images were just hallucinations. When I got back to my parents' place, I took off my seatbelt. Then put it back on. Off. On. I counted each click. Again, panic rose with each click, but by the tenth time, I began to feel calm again and was able to leave my car. At the front door, I typed in the passcode. But once wasn't enough. I had to enter it ten times. Inside, I flipped on the light switch. Turned it off. Ten times. I took off my shoes, put them back on. Ten times. Finally, I passed out in my bed.

"Hours later, I awoke and checked my phone messages. That's when I found out about…what happened. Piper left a message. I was in shock. I had had these visions of killing Kylie… and then this happens. It was so messed up.

"From that day, I began doing everything in tens. The fear was still inside of me, but counting to ten seemed to help. It gave me a feeling of control. When I'd text someone, it had to be in tens. But I still can't get behind the wheel of a car. I'm too terrified that I'll see a person on the side of the road and veer into them on purpose. Almost like a self-fulfilling prophecy. I'm fucked up, Kate."

It takes me what feels like forever to process everything Cass just told me. I'm in shock. I didn't expect this. All this time, I thought he was the murderer, but no. My intuition was all wrong.

I begin to feel as though I'm going insane. But then I wonder… Can I even trust Cass? Maybe he's lying to me? But that suspicion quickly fades. There's pain in his eyes and angst in his broken smile. What would he have to gain by making this up?

"Cass, I'm so sorry," I say, with sincerity. I have to believe him. I have to believe someone.

"Thank you for being brave enough to share this with me."

"The good thing," he says, "is that my parents know about my issues now. I've been staying with them this whole time. Hiding away in their basement. I'm too afraid to go out, unless I'm drunk or stoned. Since they've learned about how much I'm struggling, they've really come along and are supporting me to get the help I need. I'm starting therapy this week. More than ever, I realize I need help. Especially after this weekend. I'm really sorry I scared you at Triple B's. When I saw you, I really thought you were Kylie. And I was drunk and high, so my hallucinations kicked in. Seeing you brought up that old fear that I had killed Kylie. But then when I touched you, I was just so relieved that I hadn't."

"You've got this, Cass," I say.

"I don't want to stay long," he says, looking over his shoulder at the closed door. "My appearance last night caused quite the stir. Not to mention a shit-ton of gossip. And that altercation with Niall didn't help."

"Cass, can I ask you… a few questions?"

"Kate, you've always treated me like a friend. For you, I'm an open book for you. Just please keep what I've told you to yourself. I don't want anyone else to know besides family."

"I promise," I say.

"What else would you like to know?" he asks.

"Tell me everything you remember about the night of April 10th?"

"Even though Peaches invited me to the party," he says, "I wasn't planning on going. But then I got a text from Kylie pretty late that night. She begged me to come. Hang out. Just as friends. I don't remember what time I got there. But I stayed in my car and drank a six-pack of beer before I saw her." He looks at me with embarrassment. "You know I'm still crazy about her," he says, shrugging. "I didn't want to be sober when I saw her. And I knew she was seeing someone else. Or at least that's what she had told me."

"Did she ever mention who it was?" I ask. "Or anything specific about the guy?"

"No. I kinda thought she might have been making up this other guy to make me jealous. She was weirdly secretive about him. And I love that girl, but Kylie never had a problem flaunting her prizes before." He chuckles.

"She really never told me much about him either."

"I don't think it was too serious," he says. "Because when I finally met up with her that night, she said she wanted to get back together. She gave me that red t-shirt."

"Killer cowboy," I say, recollecting earlier in the night when Kylie used a black Sharpie to write that phrase on an extra-large t-shirt.

"Yep," Cass says, "Said I killed her every time she looked at me. Said she still loved me. We went for a walk. Made out. We were getting along just fine, but then she got some texts and got pissed. She stormed off. I was hammered by then, so I went back to my car and passed out in the back seat. The next thing I remember… the sirens. The flashing lights. But I had no idea what they were for. I vaguely remember Piper and Milly taking me home. To this day, I wonder if everything would have been different if I had run after Kylie… tried to figure out why she was so upset.”

I affectionately pat his shoulder.

Hoping he may have additional insight into the events around April 10th, I share the cookie-cutter details I was given. He nods and says those were the same events that Piper shared in the voicemail message she had left him that morning. He offers to play the message. I decline. He doesn't have the pieces of the puzzle I need, so I decide to broach the next subject.

"Why do you and Niall hate each other so much?" I ask. "The tension between you two yesterday was insane."

Cass scoffs.

"I don't want to disrespect your dad," he says. "Mr. Vanguard is a great man, and I won't talk shit about him."

"Well… why did you say that Niall's not good for me?"

Cass's face softens. "I just have a hunch."

"A hunch?"

"It's not my place to say."

"Whose place is it?"

"I just think he's taking advantage of your dad."

Jealousy. That lines up with what Niall thought.

Feeling defeated, I decide to let Cass go. He's tormented in his own way now, and I don't want to add more stress to his situation.

Before Cass leaves, he hugs me and says that if I ever want to talk, he'll make time. He hopes I feel the same way. Of course, I do. I wish him the best with his therapy. As Cass walks away, my phone beeps.

Dream Stealer: I wanted to give you space today.

Me: Thanks.

Dream Stealer: How is the party?

Me: Piper and Milly put in so much work. It's really amazing. So many people came.

Dream Stealer: Harrison and I might leave the game early. Can we stop by?

Me: Sure.
Dream Stealer: Send the address. I'll see you around seven.

The Truth Kills
Sunday, April 10th

YOU KNOW YOU'RE officially an adult when it's ten o'clock on a Saturday night, and you'd rather hang with a sixty-year-old man and his overweight friend than go to the club and pick up women. Although I've carried this sentiment ever since I began dating Jolene, Harrison's only recently acquired the feeling. Today. And he's been acting weird all week.

Kylie has invited me to a party this evening. A party is a good place for a break-up. Right? She'll be drinking. Maybe she won't care? Maybe she will. Maybe she'll freak out? The thing is, I'm not sure if I even want to go. Is breaking up over text really that bad?

No, it's not.

Yes, it is.

It's a horrible idea.

Should I go to the party?

Yes…

No.

What if *she's* there?

Kate.

Katie.

I'm not ready to meet the woman who's been clinging onto every beat of my heart. Filling my dreams every night. Consuming my days with thoughts of what could be?

Kylie sent the invite through ClickYap. I left her message unopened. Just slid the text, so she doesn't even know I've read it. But I'm not sure how to respond. Plus, I still have the draft text messages ready to send. Still not sure which one to send.

I'm unsure of everything lately.

Harrison decided to come with me to Mayfair—moral support and all. So, the two of us are crashing at Henry's tonight. Earlier, Henry smoked pulled pork on his Traeger grill. Dale stopped by. The four of us sat in rickety lawn chairs in the garage—they puffed cigars—we all drank beer and watched the sun set. Up until a few minutes ago, the air had been warm with spring and beginnings.

Now, the temperature has dropped at least twenty degrees. Even still, it's a gorgeous Wisconsin night. Before midnight, a meteor shower is going to light up the sky. There's something electric building in the air tonight.

Maplewood smoke billows inside the garage. A few minutes ago, Henry and Dale went inside to 'check the liquor cabinet selection'. Harrison peels back the label on his beer. One empty bottle sits underneath his chair. Four collect underneath mine, along with an overwhelming urge to message Jolene. Up until now, Harrison has been able to convince me not to. A second ago, Harrison went around the side of the house to 'piss as our ancestors used to'.

That gave me time to type more draft texts.

Not just to Kylie, though.

Me: Jolene, how are you?

We haven't seen each other in four months, and that's the best I can do?

Me: Jo, I've been thinking about you a lot. How are you doing, babe? How's the acting role? I hope you're doing well. I miss you.

Better. Honest. But, too honest? Can you ever be too honest? I should send it. I'm about to, but then Harrison rounds the corner, so I delete it. Inside the garage, he halts when he spots my phone.

"Who are you messaging?" he asks, his wild eyes piercing me.

"No one."

"Jolene?"

"What the fuck does it matter if I'm messaging Jolene?" I spit.

"It just does."

"Stay outta my fucking business."

"You don't know what you're doing."

"You don't know what you're doing," I counter. "You've never even had a serious relationship."

"What do I know?" he says. He puffs out a burst of air. "Hmmm."

I lift my phone—ready to send a message—but Harrison lunges at me, reaching for my phone. I yank my hand back. His force nearly knocks me and the chair backward. I shoulder his chest and dig my heels into the concrete.

"Get the fuck off me!" I yell.

He pushes for a few more seconds, but then slowly backs off.

"Don't do it," he says and abruptly stands upright. "She's not worth it."

"Why do you shit-talk her all the time?"

He grabs his full beer bottle and sits in his chair. He looks directly at me. "She's. A. Bitch."

I bolt from my chair. When we collide, his bottle goes flying and shatters on the ground. The chair tips over. At the last second, I use my hand to shield his head from smashing into the cement. After we land on the ground, he struggles to push me off. I hold him in a bear hug.

"Don't ever say that again," I growl.

"You don't know her!" Harrison screams.

I freeze.

Harrison and I may throw each other around for fun, but we've never raised our voices at each other. This situation is beyond bizarre. I crawl off him and stand. I reach my hand out; he accepts my gesture. I pull him up.

"What the fuck is going on?" I ask.

"If you…" He pauses and lets out a long breath of air. "If you had access to news that would destroy a close friend… would you share it?"

"What do you mean?" I ask. "And you don't have any close friends, so who the fuck are you talking about?"

He stares at the ground.

"What are you talking about?" I ask.

"News that would kill you?"

"Like, if Jolene cheated?"

"Something like that."

"I would want to know."

"What if it was… twisted?"

"I'm not following you."

"What if it could break you?"

"Look at me," I say and flex, "I'm indestructible."

Harrison doesn't smile back.

"Dude," I say, and punch him in the shoulder. "What's with you? You're acting fucking weird."

"Slide… would you really want to know?"

"You're always telling me to dig deep," I say. "Let's go deep."

"Watch the video," he says and taps his phone. He looks up and hands me his device.

"The one from Lance?"

"Yeah, I downloaded it. Look for yourself."

"Okay…"

"I'm gonna, uh, give you some privacy." He walks towards the door. On the stoop, he turns around. "I'll be back in five." The door opens. Henry and Dale's raucous laughter tumbles outside. Harrison steps into the mud room and closes the door behind him.

The screen is paused on a blurry image. A video. I tap the 'play' button. Blackness becomes… a bookshelf? Broken glass on the floor? The view turns panoramic. The screen steadies. The room becomes clear.

Lance's office.

A time stamp appears in the bottom corner. Jan. 24th. The video was taken just a few months ago.

The screen blackens, again. Then, a clear shot of Lance walking in front of the camera and sitting at his desk. A second later, a tall woman in a black dress, nylons, and high heels enters the room.

Jolene?

She walks across the room and sits across from Lance. Her long hair is pulled back in a ponytail. Jolene whispers to Lance. A rap on the door interrupts her.

"Come in," Lance says.

Lance's assistant, Verity, appears.

"Hey, love," Verity says to Lance. "Oh my! So, that man who was here earlier really did throw a vase, then? Shattered the ever-loving… Mmm… Mmm… Mmm… How uncivil. I'll clean this up right away before someone gets hurt."

Shattered vase? This must be the same day Henry went to see Lance. Jolene was in Chicago in January, and didn't tell me?

"The world is full of unstable people," Lance says. "Jolene and I are in the middle of something important, Verity. Can you come back in fifteen? We should be done by then."

"You got it, love," Verity says and gives Jolene a double-take on the way out. "I don't know what is different about you, hun, but you are absolutely glowing. There must be somethin' in that California water. Just breathtaking."

Jolene half-smiles and looks down at her hands.

"Verity?" Lance interrupts.

"Yes, love?"

"Can you reschedule my lunch meeting today? I forgot. I have that dentist appointment."

"Your appointment is tomorrow," she says, "today is only Monday. The twenty-fourth. No need to change anything! Now, I'll leave you two alone." She quietly closes the door.

"Lance," Jolene says, and hangs her head, "what should I do?"

"You have to do what's best for you."

Why is Lance recording this? And without Jolene's permission? Is the asshole going to fuck her and make me watch?

"Should I tell him?" Jolene asks.

"As I said, do what's best for you."

"But what's best for me would break his heart."

"But you're not together anymore—"

"It would wreck him."

"Jolene, I know you better than anyone. You're like family. If you think Niall won't understand, then don't tell him. This is your future. Your life. Do what's best for you."

"You're right," Jolene says. "I'll go through with it. And then I'll tell Niall."

"You don't have to tell him anything," Lance says.

"But this baby is his as much as it's mine."

"…"

"…"

"…"

"…"

"…"

"…"

"…"

"…"

"…"

"…abortion…"

"…"

"…sixteen weeks…"

"…"

"…not even a life…"

"…"

"…feel her move…"

"…"

"…can't do adoption…"

At some point, my hands shake uncontrollably; Harrison's phone slips from my fingers. The screen shatters onto the concrete below. At some point, my knees buckle; I collapse onto the floor. At some point, my bones break. At some point, my fists pound the ground; sticky, red blood smears the floor. At some point, my flesh feels no physical pain. At some point, I've lost all feeling.

At some point… I feel as though I've died.

***

Harrison found me sitting on the garage floor, hands covered in blood. Staring at the ground. Harrison pulled me up and walked me over to the outside hose. He cleaned off my hands, sprayed the garage floor, then told me to go sit on the bumper of his Suburban.

When he returned to the vehicle, he handed me a roll of paper towel. Blood was crusted between my fingernails. My knuckles were raw. Splatters of red covered my jeans and sneakers. The paper towel didn't help much. Harrison and I got in his car. He drove until I stopped sobbing. On a barren side road, he parked.

I don't know how long we sat, but I eventually spoke.

"I should call Jolene," I say.

"I support you," he says.

"She betrayed me. There's no way I can call her."

"I support you."

"I feel like dying."

"I support that feeling but not the action."

"We were in love. She knew what a child would mean to me… our child."

"Love means different things to different people."

"We created something."

"Creation means different things to different people."

"I should have—"

Words are failing me. I have no rights. The baby wasn't mine to keep or discard.

"Do you think she had the baby?" I ask. My eyes plead with Harrison. They search for hope. "She could have given it up for adoption?"

"I think you would have found out," Harrison says. "I watched that video like fifty times. You can very clearly see a little bump in that video. A petite girl could probably hide a pregnancy. But a tall, lean, athletic woman? I doubt that."

"She said 'her'. It was a baby… girl."

"And the two of you," Harrison says, "creating a baby together. That kid would be huge. Like a ten-pound newborn. A monster. There's no way…"

The barren trees begin to trade places. They become one blurry gray, brown, and white mirage. My eyelids flicker. Harrison hands me more crumpled-up paper towels.

Harrison's Proposal
Sunday, May 29th @ 6:56 p.m.

OVER THE LAST few hours, I've been pulled in several directions and have failed to corner Piper or Milly. Without an opportunity to conduct my research, my mind is left wide open with wonderment. Why is Niall coming here? He loves baseball. But he's cutting the game short? The fact that he's coming here doesn't change anything. I'm a mistake. We're not possible. This is a disaster. He's made that abundantly clear.

If I take that job offer in Chicago, I might have the chance to prove everyone wrong.

With my dad no longer needing me at Vanguard, Kylie gone, Mother unreachable, I've no loose ends tying me to Mayfair. It's impossible for me to choke myself.

Is it time I dip a toe into my gloriously terrifying future? If I say yes to Verity, my future becomes certain. The new job will be challenging, and the pay is more than adequate. My new boss—Lance—is undoubtedly a gentleman who runs a professional business. I reviewed the company on Glassdoor; there were only two reviews, and I'm pretty sure Verity posted one of them. She seems to love the company, although she appears to love everything and everyone.

Lance Deveraux Consulting has only been in business for a little over six months. During my search, I found another Chicago consulting firm with a ton of negative reviews… also named Deveraux. But I'm unsure if the two are related.

Since Verity sent the offer letter, Lance Devereaux has emailed me. He thinks I'll be a great fit. He's also mentioned the restraining order, but said he's not worried. But he *is* worried that my chances of securing a job elsewhere may be hindered, so he's very eager for me to say yes to Devereaux Consulting.

Mr. Devereaux is understanding and professional.

I need more of that in my life.

My future is brighter than ever. Me? Kate Vanguard? Scoring a job in Chicago? Niall will probably be happy for me. Maybe even proud. With me being in another state, he'll have the freedom to manage Vanguard sans chaos. Nepotism unnecessary.

I've wandered back outside. The mini sandwiches, appetizers, and candy buffet have been devoured. The event workers toss logs into the fire pit. They strike a lighter and set paper balls on fire. A smoky, summer vibe floats in the air. The breeze picks up, and warm air drifts past me. I can almost taste charred marshmallows and salty hot dogs.

The idyllic scene jars to a halt when a sudden hullabaloo comes from inside the house. I stand on my tiptoes and look towards the patio door. The screen door opens, and a frazzled Milly rushes onto the patio. With an angry tug, she wraps her cardigan around her waist. She's pissed.

I scan the crowd; Piper is nowhere to be found. Unusual. Who else can push Milly's buttons the way Piper does? Who else has an ostentatious, in-your-face personality?

Milly walks backwards. Her voice is raised—I can't tell what she's saying—but she's definitely upset. A jacked figure steps outside. The man shifts his baseball cap backward, revealing bleached hair.

"Babe," the man shouts. "It's not weird at all. We're meant to be."

Even though a sexy R&B song thumps over the speakers, I can hear the man clearly.

"What?" Milly squeals in response and chicken-walks backwards.

"Milly Rodrigo!"

At the end of the patio, he box jumps onto the stone wall border. "You're gonna be my boo!" His arms raise high.

Now, everyone outside is staring at the interaction, looking just as confused as I am. The man spins in a circle and dismounts with a backflip. The stunt ends with a perfect landing. He barely misses the rose bushes. Guests whistle, then clap. Some beg for an encore.

Milly spots me in the crowd and rushes to my side. She grips my arm and tugs me along. Together, we round the house.

"Save me," she cries. She bolts to the front yard. I stumble closely behind.

"What's wrong?"

"That man is a lunatic." We reach the entryway stairs. She yanks open the front door and continues to drag me until we reach the first-floor half bath.

"Who is he?"

"Some guy named Harrison." She pulls me inside and slams the door. The lock clicks.

Harrison? That means Niall—

"He burst through the door," she squawks. "Didn't even bother ringing the doorbell. Or knocking. Acted like he owned the place. He scared me! I was giving a tour of our beautiful family portraits… I had just gotten through the elementary years, and… he… he started talking inappropriately to me." She opens her purse and grips a tube of lipstick.

"What did he say?" I hop on the bathroom counter.

"Well… after he bolted in. He was like, 'Where's Katie?', and I was like, 'Excuuuuuse me?'. Like, who talks like that? He didn't even introduce himself. I told him to leave. And then he stared at me. My tour got really awkward; everyone left because this guy was staring at me. Like he was going to eat me for lunch. Unbelievably rude. I don't even know him! He doesn't even know me!"

"He seems kinda into you—"

"That's the problem! He kept staring. And demanded to know my name. I calmly told him that this was my grad party, too, and you were somewhere in the back. He didn't answer. He kept saying, 'Fuck,' under his breath. Then… he was like 'I'm gonna marry you'. Like what? That's when his friend, uh—Niall, walked inside, insulted him, then the two of them started wrestling. I ran. By the way, Niall is divine." She grins.

Not shocking at all. Milly's story lacks a tragic element, and I'm having a hard time feeling sorry for her. Pure agony. Another man was smitten after one glance.

"Was he rude?" I ask. "I mean, apart from coming inside unannounced and lusting after you?"

"He said I had a hot granny name and wants to know if I have any knee-high stockings?"

A miniature giggle escapes my lips, but I quickly cover it with a fake cough.

"What a disrespectful thing to say!"

I rub the sides of my eyes, but I'm smiling. I press my lips together; if I talk, I'm afraid I'll laugh spontaneously.

"He wants to marry me!" She throws her hands in the air. "I mean, he doesn't even know me. He's love bombing and basing his impression on my hot-grandma name and the fact that I'm dressed like a librarian. He's slinging 'compliments' my way that are anything but." She flings her lipstick into the drawer. "You can't randomly tell people you'll marry them. That's misleading and ruins your credibility. And he wants to sing to me. He's crazy. I can't do this," she says and flings applicators, eye shadow, and other tubes of things I know nothing about onto the counter.

A knock on the door startles us both.

"Milly?" a male voice asks from the other side of the door. "You in there, babe?"

"It's him," she whispers and inches away from the door to the window. "Don't tell him I'm here." She pulls me off the counter and uses me as a shield.

"Hey, uh, Harrison?" I ask. "It's me, Kate. I know we haven't met yet, but, uh—"

Milly vigorously shakes her head 'no' and holds her index finger up to her lips. "Tell him to stop calling me babe."

"Milly's not in here," I say. "And she doesn't want you calling her babe."

"Hey Kate," Harrison says. "Nice to finally meet. I saw Milly come down here. I checked the other rooms, so unless she crawled out a window, she's totally in there. And how would you know she doesn't want me calling her babe, unless she's with you?"

"Fuck," Milly mouths.

"So, he likes you," I whisper. "Big deal. He's not going to bite you."

"I heard that," Harrison says, "and that's not true. I do bite. I'm a very passionate and vigorous lover."

I snort. A shade of red covers Milly's cheeks and chest. She nibbles a manicured fingernail and fans herself with her other hand.

"Milly Rodrigo," I say and poke her in the chest. "You. Like. Him."

"I. Do. Not." She points a finger back at me. "Don't you dare say that."

I suppress another giggle. Milly's lips curve. Her eyes shine.

"Kate, can you open the door?" Harrison asks. "I want to meet you."

"No, you don't," I say, "you want to make vigorous moves on my friend."

"Yeah, you're right." He jingles the doorknob. "But I'm glad you're real."

"What?" I ask.

From the other side of the door, we hear a slapping noise and murmurs. Harrison says, "What the fuck!" Then there's a thud against the wall, more screeching gym shoes, and another explicative.

"Katie?" a voice says.

A bubbling giggle rises in my belly. Milly looks entirely horrified.

"Hey Niall," I say and lean into the door. "You made it."

"Hey, Katie."

"What the hell," Milly says and leers at me. "Katie?"

I pretend to be busy checking the lock on the door.

"I'm really sorry Harrison's being a dick to your friend," Niall says. "Milly, you okay?"

"Milly is fine," I say.

"I'm not fine." Milly raises her voice.

More screeching shoes and murmurs from the hall.

"Hey, Katie?" Niall asks.

"Yeah?"

"I have Harrison in a headlock," he says, "but I won't be able to hold him much longer. Can you let Milly out?"

I reach towards the door.

"Milly," Niall says, "after Katie opens the door, you gotta run."

"I'm opening the door," I announce and unlock, then turn the knob.

In the hall, Niall has Harrison in a bear hug.

Milly bolts past me towards the foyer, shouting, "Thank you, Niall! Truly a pleasure to meet you." At the end, she stops and turns around. "Harrison," she says, waving a pointer finger in the air, "you leave me alone." Her flimsy request is met with a grunt.

"I can't!" Harrison shouts. "We're destined to be together!"

Milly throws frazzled hands in the air and flees around the corner.

"Go easy on her," I say and lean against the door frame. "Milly's like one of those fainting baby goats. If you charge, she might tip over."

Niall releases Harrison. Harrison collects his baseball cap from the floor and stands upright. He smiles at me and outstretches his hands.

"Finally," Harrison says. "I get to meet the famous Katie." He steps forward and bypasses the handshake. His muscular arms circle my back in a welcoming hug.

"Harrison," I say, into his shoulder, "so glad you could come."

"This man—" Harrison leans back, pointing to Niall.

Niall punches Harrison's arm.

"He's a great guy," Harrison says—wincing. "And one day he's gonna be filthy rich, so keep that in mind if you don't think he's attractive enough, or he should work out more." Harrison is walking backwards down the hall.

"I'll let you two catch up," he says, rubbing his hands together, "I have to find… something to eat." His eyebrows raise wickedly.

"Later," Niall says to Harrison. "Don't make me have to kick your ass again."

I stare after Harrison for several seconds, not wanting to look at Niall. Remembering last night. The way he made me giggle. The way he made me feel safe. How I never wanted it to end.

My heart falls and soars all at once. Butterflies expand in my torso. Niall has only been away for a few hours, but it seems like forever. I turn my head to him. His smile devastates me. Those eyes brand me his. My breath, hijacked by a thief—a dream stealer. Unlike Harrison, Niall's changed out of his jersey. He's wearing a black dress shirt and fitted black slacks. The sneakers.

How can I walk away from him?

My smile is slow, timid. His, quick, brazen.

We stay that way. Maybe we don't move, because we both know the ending. We've always known. Nothing could ever come of this. We can't do this. He and I are too different. I'm a tornado headed south. He's an executive always headed north.

"Katie—" Niall begins to speak.

"Niall—" I say.

Our smiles mirror each other.

Maybe we can do this?

Maybe I was wrong?

Is he going to tell me… we're possible?

I'll never know, because just then, British cousin Bert rounds the corner. He loudly greets me and demands to be introduced to 'this wanderlust' guest. Bert heard Niall is traveling to Germany this summer. Bert has many connections in Germany. He gives Niall suggestions on where to stay, sights to see, and the best clubs for singles…

Bert has ruined the moment.

While the two talk, several classmates stop to congratulate me on graduating. I'm eventually pulled away from Niall.

Do you have a job lined up?

I have a couple of things in the works.

Are you staying in Mayfair to work with your dad?

It's a possibility.

Aren't you glad college is over?

So glad.

My accounting study group drags me outside for lemon drop shots. I follow, but refuse the alcohol. I substitute water shots. After what feels like hours, and too many boring conversations to count, a crowd of shouting and singing party-goers envelopes me in a mosh pit. I spot Milly and Harrison off to the side of the house, talking quietly.

Bert and I run into each other again in the kitchen. While I snack on another sugar cookie, Bert raves about Niall's expansive business knowledge. Annoyed with myself, because I'm really starting to like Niall, and that's stupid because there's no way we can be anything more than strangers to each other, I blurt out something idiotic.

"Es tut mir so leid. Ich liebe dich."

Clearly, he knows German, so I'm hoping what I say offends him, and then he stops talking about Niall, or better yet, leaves me alone.

But instead of looking insulted, Bert looks confused.

"Why would you say you're sorry and that you love me?"

And now I'm confused.

"I just said that your business plan sucks and you should be fired."

"Um, no, you didn't," he says. "Es tut mir so leid. Ich liebe dich means I love you and I'm sorry."

My brain turns foggy.

"I—um, I have to go," I say and rush into the crowd.

Why would Niall say that he's sorry and that *he loves me?*

Hip hop music thumps from the speakers. Piper's playlist. Perfect time for me to leave. I work my way through the crowd, but not without receiving several ass slaps. A girl from last year's accounting midterm project grinds against my crotch. She feels up my boobs. Eventually, I untangle her. Nora pops up in front of me from the crowd. She's all smiles and wild dance moves. She grabs my arms and tries to get me to dance with her. But I just feel like throwing up.

"What a wild party!" Nora says and twirls me in a circle.

I pull away from her. She's a killer. Definitely a cat killer. Possible people killer.

At the edge of the dance floor, several of my Advanced Accounting classmates drill me. *Why weren't you at the graduation ceremony? So shocked you didn't make Valedictorian. You were robbed. Jullian did not deserve it! Like WTF?!*

I shrug my shoulders and agree.

Time to find someplace where I can scream properly. I hurry away to Mrs. Rodrigo's flower garden. The music is still loud, but at least no one is humping me. I take a deep breath and capture little snippets of the evening in my memory.

Peaches is jamming away at the DJ booth. Piper, working on a killer hangover. Milly, possibly in love again. Harrison, wrestling with Niall. A pulchritudinous smile. A bizarre German phrase. And maybe that's enough?

I stroll down the rose path. Behind me, a branch cracks. I spin around. *Niall.*

"Hey, you..." He says, quietly. He walks towards me.

"Hey..." I smile, my body floats into the same fog occupying my brain.

The intensity of his presence overpowers me. I freely give in. Time stops. Possibility reveals itself. The future is clear. I see Niall. I see a possibility I never imagined could exist. I see happiness. I see love. In that moment, or maybe those minutes—certainly, we didn't stand that way for hours—I finally feel... whole. Put back together. The magnitude of the situation alarms me.

I take a step back.

I take a breath.

Press my hand to my chest. Now is the time. I have to say something, but when I take another step back, a branch catches on the underside of my dress. I jerk away, but a stinging pain grazes my thigh. I yelp and pinch the fabric on the back of my dress.

Possibility floats away.

"What's the matter?" Niall asks. He moves closer, as though he might reach his arm around my back.

"I think an insect bit me," I say, and squish the material of my dress. "On the back of my leg." I strain my head to see if there's a bug crawling up my leg.

"Oh no." Niall's line of sight meets my hiked-up dress and partially uncovered ass cheek.

I swing to the right.

"A thorn scratched me or… maybe a bug is caught in my skirt," I say, panicked. I hold up the bunched fabric and turn so he can't see my bare ass.

He tilts his head.

I shake a frustrated finger at him.

"Niall, do not make fun of me."

"Wouldn't think of it." His arms lift in surrender.

I shudder. At this very moment, a June bug or something equally vicious might be crawling within the folds of my dress. I cringe. I know what I have to do. I must humiliate myself in the worst way possible. This scenario is a thousand times worse than anything else I've done in the last seventy-two hours. I have to ask Niall to examine my ass.

Niall stares, patiently awaiting my request. Almost as though he knows I've done something ridiculous—something that will give him joy—he shines.

 "Niall," I say and close my eyes. "I think I need your help… again. If I let go of the fabric, I'm afraid that if there is a bug in there, it'll crawl out of the skirt and onto my leg." I stammer for a few seconds, unable to say what I need to say.

"Katie," Niall says, "don't ever feel embarrassed around me."

Either I hold onto my dress for the rest of the night, or I suck it up and ask for Niall's help.

"Whatever you need," he says. "Say the word and consider it done."

I nod and think of the best, most dignified way to ask him to lift my dress and search through the folds for a possible June bug. But there's a problem. My uncovered ass cheeks will be on full display. Damn, Peaches.

"Did you name this dress Peaches?" Niall frowns and points at the dress.

"Niall," I say, frustrated, "I need you to look through the folds of my dress. A bug might be stuck in my skirt. If you find it, kill it immediately. Don't get cute, and show it to me first. Don't chase me with it. Kill it. But…"

"But?" Niall asks.

"I'm wearing what I consider to be non-existent panties, which I didn't purchase. Peaches made me wear them. And that's why this is his fault."

In my time of need, Niall should act like a gentleman—but no—he chuckles. Then, all-out laughs. His ridicule ends with a snort.

"Niall," I beg, "please, help."

"I tend to be more direct," he contemplates. "Let me sum this up: You want me to look under your dress, careful not to stare at your uncovered ass, or at least not to stare longer than necessary, to search for a vicious bug that may or may not exist?"

"Maybe you should close your eyes," I plead, "you know… give me privacy?"

"Nope." He steps behind me. I try to scoot forward, but he grips my hips. "Hold still." He tugs the material out of my hand. A brush of cool air hits my skin. He shakes the dress and—I imagine—examines it very closely. His hand brushes against the outside of my thigh.

"Niall!"

"Got it," he responds triumphantly.

He tugs my skirt down. He moves in front of me.

"Hold out your hand," he says. His eyes flicker. His lips form a slow smile.

I back away. "No… way… I hate bugs. Especially June bugs. And if that is a June bug, I might die."

He opens his palm.

A stick?

"A nettle?" I cry. "It was a stupid prickly stick?"

"For the record," Niall says, "I saw way more than I needed to. But, in the future, if you ever need someone to examine any part of your body, for any reason, I'm in."

My forehead is creased, but I'm grinning at the ridiculousness of the situation.

The music abruptly shifts to an indie-folk ballad. Lovers, seeds, and lore. Although I never gave Peaches a playlist, he knows my taste in music all too well. He's likely to play "Disarm" soon. Such a sad song, such appropriate timing.

"Friday," he says, "when I saw you at the restaurant, I should have said something then."

"Said what?"

"That I knew your dad. If I had introduced myself then, I could have helped you make the connection. Could have warned you about the VP position."

"Would it really have mattered?" I ask. "Plus, you thought my dad had already told me."

"Maybe."

"Why didn't you say something?"

"Honestly?" he asks. "I was nervous."

"Nervous?"

"Yeah."

I hum and look at the neighboring rose bush.

"Katie?" Niall asks, "I want to do this right. Please look at me."

Niall steps closer. The fabric of his shirt clings to his chest, outlining his abs.

I lift my gaze. We make eye contact.

"I'm sorry I was a jackass yesterday at the office," he says. "I teased you, and even when you became upset, I didn't stop. I behaved like a child. I feel to blame for you breaking your ring. My behavior was unprofessional, and I can promise you, I won't ever act like that again. I wish I could turn back time and decline your dad's offer. The position belongs to you. But I want you to know, your dad only has your best interests in mind. I think we all did—do. If nothing else, please remember that?"

I barely hear his final words, because he's maintained eye contact this entire time. His words are genuine. His apology is… perfect.

"With all that being said," he says, "Can you forgive my unprofessional behavior?"

Only Kylie has ever used my apology method on me before. Part of me tries to feel grateful for this, but the confusion still lingers: Niall throws me onto a dryer one moment, and the next seems determined to keep his distance. Now he's apologizing sincerely, and I can't decide how to feel, but I know what to say.

"I forgive you."

"May I?" Niall asks. He reaches for my waist.

Every fiber of my being wants to say no, but the small thread linking Niall and me pulls me forward.

"A dance?" I ask.

"It would be my pleasure."

My arms lift. My fingers reach around his neck. I rest my cheek against his shirt. We swing and sway. Lovers, seeds, and lore… and… So. Much. More.

"So," he asks, "you taught dance?" His warm breath grazes the crown of my head.

"For eight years."

"Do you miss it?"

"I do."

"Will you take it up again?"

"Once I…" My thoughts and voice trail off.

Once I what? I'm leaving tomorrow. My body stops floating. I release my hands from Niall's shoulders and step back. The something more becomes… nothing.

"Why did you tell me you're sorry and that you love me?" I demand.

Niall's cheeks brighten.

"That's… um."

"We can't *do this*, remember?"

"I know but…"

"I'm moving," I say.

"What?" Confusion and immediate panic wrinkle his brow.

"A small firm in Chicago hired me." The moment the words are out of my mouth, my eyes begin to sting. I focus on the buttons on his black shirt.

"Chicago?" he asks. Something drains from his face.

"Yeah," I say. "It just kind of happened. Yesterday, my dad said I need to take a break from Vanguard… So, here I am. Taking a break. Dipping a toe into my bright future. Off to Chicago."

Up until now, I couldn't make eye contact. But I need to own this decision. I look into his eyes.

"I'm leaving tonight," I say.

"Katie," Niall whispers. "We—"

A sudden commotion by the DJ stand halts the music. Bert and Peaches seem to be disagreeing on something. Probably the playlist.

"I was there on April 10th," Niall says.

I look at Niall.

"Where?" I ask. "Wait—what did you say?"

The first three notes of the next song begin to play. The guitar, electric keyboard, mournful, regretting lyrics. The song disarms me. In a hurried movement, Niall unlatches the necklace from around his neck. He shimmies the small ring from the loop.

"I want you to have this," he says. He holds the delicate ring in front of me.

"What?" I ask. "Why?"

"I just do." He cups my hand. "To replace Kylie's ring. On Friday, at your dad's office—I noticed you twirled her ring whenever you became upset. But since her ring is gone… Well, this can replace it."

The simple silver token easily slides onto my left ring finger. The fit, perfection. The feel, heavenly. The connection, indescribable.

"It's beautiful," I say. The ridges swoop, the winged decoration shines. "It must be an antique or heirloom. It's like nothing I've ever owned. Niall, it's… pulchritudinous. Where did you get it?"

The thing that had been growing inside of me has blossomed into a bouquet of love, held up by stems of possibility.

I look up.

Niall's gone.

Group Chat
Sunday, May 29th @ 7:51 p.m.

ZAKARY STANDS INSIDE Mr. Rodrigo's office. He's closed the heavy oak doors, shut the floor-to-ceiling blinds, and propped a chair under the door handle.

ZakAtak: I'm in Mr. Rodrigo's office. Knock three times, and I'll let you in.

The Pied Piper: OMW. But I'm really drunk, so I won't have a filter. It's possible imma fall asleep.

JustPeachy: Hang on. Bert is taking over my DJ stand. Showing him how not to screw up my playlist.

Milly Rodrigo: I can't see my phone, I'm crying.

Fauxy Roxy: On my way.

JustPeachy: Bert's all set, be there in a sec.

Within minutes, five accomplices have joined Zakary in the study. Piper and Milly are seated on the sofa. Zakary and Peaches are seated in the guest chairs in front of the executive desk. Roxy is propped up against the bookshelf. Niall is the last to enter. After closing the door, he protectively stands in front of the lock. The guitar and violin music from outside muffles the guests' laughter, and a heavy sadness overtakes the room.

"Let's get this over with," Piper says, closing her eyes.

Zakary confidently moves to the center of the room. "Kate is distraught," he says, pacing. "Time apparently does not heal all wounds. She's not getting better. She's hearing messages from Kylie. Having visions of dead people. I mean, come on. Leaving her in the literal and figurative dark is not good. But I'm terrified that if she finds out we've all been lying to her, she's gonna hate us. All of us. But can we really lie to her forever? I don't know the answer. But… together, I think we can make the right decision. Before we leave this room, we will collectively decide: to tell or not to tell."

The group of six stays quiet. Five of the accomplices glance at each other. Piper is almost asleep. Milly nudges her.

"I think we should go dance our assess off," Piper says.

"And everyone else?" Zakary asks.

"This may take longer than one song," Peaches says. "I'm texting Bert to play Disarm on a loop until we're done."

"Hey," says a male's voice from the other side of the door, "what are you guys doing in there?"

"Oh, no!" Milly squeaks and hides behind Piper. Piper elbows Milly.

"Shit," Niall says and raises his hands mid-air in apology. "Harrison has my location on his phone."

"Oh, hell," Roxy says, "may as well let him in, we need a tie-breaker anyway."

"No!" Milly says.

"Stop being a baby," Piper says.

"I'm not a bab—"

"Just let Harrison in," Roxy says, "we need that tie-breaker."

Niall quickly opens the door, and Harrison steps inside.

"What the hell," Harrison says, "you all look like you're at a funeral. Or a prison sentence."

Milly moans and uses a tissue to pat underneath her eyes. Harrison rushes over to the couch and squats in front of Milly.

"What's the matter, babe?" Harrison asks.

"You really don't let up, do you?" Milly asks.

"No, babe," Harrison whispers, "not when I know what I want."

"Harrison," Zakary says, "please have a seat and refrain from harassing Milly for like five minutes. We've serious business to handle."

"He shouldn't be here," Milly says.

"Honestly," Peaches says, "he was here April 10th, so it really doesn't matter."

"Harrison?" Milly asks. "I don't remember him being there."

"You were hysterical," Piper says, suddenly wide-awake, "of course you wouldn't remember."

"She was in shock," Roxy says, "it's not uncommon in a situation like that."

"I was with Niall in my truck," Harrison says, and clears his throat, "when everything happened." He rests his hand on Milly's leg.

Milly swats Harrison's hand away.

"Why were you two at Triple B's?" Milly asks, looking from Harrison to Niall.

"We, uh, were in town to see Mr. Vanguard," Harrison says. "Thought we'd have a drink at the bar."

"We should just leave everything the way it is," Milly says, and glares at Harrison. "Everyone should just stop talking about it."

"But Zakary is right," Piper mumbles, "Kate's getting worse."

"Annnnd," Zakary says, "if she knows the truth… I mean, I think eventually she'll be better off."

"I'm sorry," Harrison says. "But to be honest, you all fucked up from the start. Why mastermind this insane lie, anyway?"

"To protect the Vanguard legacy," Peaches says. "The family is a staple in this community."

"At the time," Roxy adds, "it just seemed right. Like the only option. After Holliday told us about what he saw on his camera, we were just so in shock…"

"I regret lying," Piper says, and rests her head on Milly's lap, "and I'm ready to accept the consequences of the truth."

"Guys," Zakary says, "her nightmares are becoming more intense. Eventually, she'll remember. And what happens then? Do we keep lying to her? Let her feel like she's going insane? I mean, what's the end game?"

"She's in a fragile state," Roxy says, "Can she handle the truth right now? Look at everything that's happened to her in the past few months."

"Let's talk about that," Zakary says, "how did Kate happen to get fired from all three of her jobs in the span of a few weeks—"

"We all knew about her getting fired from Triple B's," Peaches says, "to no one's surprise. Her attendance has been spotty lately. But I'm just surprised Bear decided to fire her all of a sudden. But I agree, none of us thought she'd be fired from the dance studio or that Henry was going to pass her up for the VP role."

The room settles in silence.

"Niall," Zakary says, "you must know what happened at Vanguard? Why did Henry change his mind?"

Everyone stares at Niall.

"Without her working at the dance studio," Niall says, "or Triple B's, she'd have more time to concentrate on the small role she had with Vanguard—the one she was still struggling with. Weeks ago, I spoke to Miss Christie and convinced her to let Katie go, then I convinced Bear to do the same. But the decisions were made in Katie's best interest and it was before I knew—"

The room erupts in chaos.

Sheepish
Sunday, May 29th @ 7:57 p.m.

THE OUTBURST I had heard seconds before, when I stood outside Mr. Rodrigo's office, vanishes when I pound my fist against the door.

"Hello?" I shout.

Silence.

"What's going on in there?"

The lock rattles. This time, I kick the door. More silence. I drag a nearby decorative chair across the hall and place it directly below the door frame. I step onto the seat and stretch to reach the ledge. I tap my fingers along the wood.

Bingo.

The spare key.

I hop off the chair and unlock the door.

The heavy oak won't budge at first, but then I press with all my might and the door swings open.

I gasp.

Inside the room, my eyes dart from Piper to Milly, Zakary to Peaches, Harrison to Roxy. Niall. I swing my neck back and forth so many times that I feel dizzy.

"What are you all doing in here?" I ask, my voice trembles.

Roxy is leaning up against the bookshelf. Piper picks at the fabric on the couch. Milly is covering her face with a tissue. Zakary and Peaches look at the floor. Harrison is kneeling as close to Milly as possible, without touching her. They all look guilty.

All eyes turn to Niall.

Niall looks at me. His face is pale.

"But," Peaches says, "how did you get in?"

"The spare key above the door."

"Well," Peaches says, turning towards Piper and Milly, "for heaven's sakes. Why didn't you girls say anything about—"

"Katie—" Niall says, nervously.

"What is going on?" I demand. I swallow hard and inch backward.

"Kate," Peaches says, "we were just—"

"Something is very wrong." My hands fumble behind my back. "Why are you all here?"

Zakary quickly stands. "It's time," he says and rubs his palms against his pants.

"Time for what?" I ask, more confused than ever.

Zakary doesn't answer.

Instead, Peaches points to my right and says, "To tell." Then he points to my left and says, "Not to tell."

"What is going on?" I ask. My knees shake.

Piper stands and moves to my left. Peaches and Roxy follow.

Milly, Harrison, and Zakary move to my right.

"Tell me what?" I ask. A tremor flows through my body.

"A tie," Peaches says to Niall.

"Niall, you're the tie-breaker," Milly adds.

Niall walks towards me and stops a foot away.

"Katie gets to decide," Niall says. "Katie, do you want to know the truth about April 10th?"

No one will look at me. Except Niall. His expression is blank, pained.

"Slide," Harrison says, "This is getting kind of crazy…"

Harrison's words become muffled as my head fills with blood. Harrison is looking at Niall. Harrison just called Niall 'Slide'.

"What did you just say?" I ask Harrison.

"I just think this is a wild situation and we—"

"No," I say. "What did you just call Niall?"

"Um… Slide?"

"Why?"

"Slide O.B. O.B.," I whisper to myself. "O'Brien."

An overwhelming wave of fear washes over my body. *Slide_OB is Niall.* Niall was the mysterious man dating Kylie.

The mirror's reflection across the room catches my attention. In the duplicate version of myself, I see a scarred woman with imperfections. The image stares back. The one without a Joker's smile, the one lacking Mother's ratted hair, the one void of perfection.

I hold my breath.

Sheepish, sheepish, sheepish. She pushed, she pushed, she pushed. Don't tell.

A rush of adrenaline surges through my veins. April 10th… The memory is vivid now. On the bluffs, brilliant stars shine overhead. Silver brush-strokes streak across the sky. Kylie hugs me tightly. She whimpers against my shoulder. "Hurry, help. Before it's too late." Frail hands grip my back. I hold onto her, telling her everything will be okay. Kylie trembles inside the safety of my arms. "Don't tell, don't tell. Katie, please don't tell."

She pushed!

The scream is terrifying. It echoes off the banks repeatedly. Again, and again, and again. I have an overwhelming urge to run; I let go of Kylie… Somehow, my legs start moving. My feet glide down the switchback path.

Down.

"She pushed!" I scream.

Down.

"She pushed!" I scream.

Down.

"She pushed her!" I scream.

As I ascend the stairs, the lake water grows more pungent; the air becomes heavier with dew. The shoreline reveals the truth.

"No, no, no!"

And in that instant, the killer is revealed.

Hastily Sent Text
Sunday, April 10th

HARRISON HAS PARKED his truck on a backcountry road. I'm sitting on the gravel shoulder. Vomit covers the ground in front of me and the tip of my sneaker. I slip my phone from my front pocket.

"Don't talk to her when you're like this," Harrison says. He's leaning against the passenger's door. "Give yourself time to think about what you really want to say."

I quickly type a message to Jolene and send it.

Me: The dishonesty. Betrayal. How could you? For me to find out this way… I don't even know what to say. How could you?

Me: How could you?

Jolene won't reply. She's moved on. I stare at the ground. After several seconds, my phone dings.

Kylie?

I preview her message.

Kylie: So, you found out? I have to ask… how? I was so careful.

Kylie? Why is she messaging me? I click on our conversation. The last person I sent a ClickYap to was… Kylie? I didn't send Jolene that message… I accidentally sent it to Kylie. And all the prior draft messages to Kylie were delivered… and opened just a minute ago.

What have I done?

Me: We need to break it off, sorry. This is the last time you'll hear from me.

Me: Kylie, I need to be completely honest with you. I'm not that into you.

Me: The first night I met you, I never meant to ask you out. Sorry. It was a mistake. A terrible mistake. I meant to ask your sister out that night. Not you.

Me: Your personality is terrible—nothing like your sister's.

Me: The dishonesty. Betrayal. How could you? For me to find out this way… I don't even know what to say. How could you?

Me: How could you?

Every embarrassing message I meant to delete has been sent and opened by Kylie. Plus, I sent her the message I had meant to send to Jolene. What have I done? I reply.

Me: Kylie, I didn't mean to send those to you.

After several minutes, Kylie responds.

Kylie: It doesn't matter.

Me: I'm sorry, I didn't mean to send those to you.

Kylie: Don't lie. Ur mad. You found out. Everyone does eventually.

Me: What? Can we talk in person?

Kylie doesn't respond.

Me: OMW to the party. We need to talk.

Room 202
Sunday - May 29th @ 8:25 p.m.

THE ROOM IS small. The walls are white. If a writer were to write about the room, there wouldn't be much to say. The piece certainly wouldn't win any literary awards or contests in flash fiction. Readers would be left bored, wanting more. They would likely stop reading halfway through.

Room 202.

A subdued, single, white female resides here.

One continuous, concrete, padded wall keeps her safe. An intercom, twenty-two inches above the locked, metal door, alerts her of mealtimes, med times, and bath times. A white clock hangs adjacent to the speaker.

Tick, tick, tick.

The woman often clicks her tongue in unison with the ticking second hand.

Click, click, click.

The woman's face often twitches along with the click.

Twitch, twitch, twitch.

A shatter-proof window faces the parking lot. Outside, the sky is black. Inside, recessed lighting illuminates the ceiling. Furnishings are sparse: a bed, a pillow, a mattress, a blanket. The comforter is made from a special wool (to prevent hanging oneself).

The room has no blind spots.

The woman sometimes feels blind. Feels isn't the right word. She doesn't feel anything anymore. She may as well be blind. Colors elude her. She sees grays and blacks. Sometimes blood-red.

The woman kneels on the padded floor. She presses a pink crayon to paper. Crayola crayons scatter the tiled floor. She's requested a pen, but nurses have refused. A pen, when used with enough force, penetrates flesh. The woman's gorgeous blonde hair is pixie short. Long hair chokes and strangles. Or, can be eaten. Eating hair causes tummy aches.

After April 10th, many visitors came—three to four a day. Eventually, the visitors stopped visiting. No one wants to see someone who doesn't want to be visited. Or who refuses to speak.

The woman's skin stretches taut against bone and visible ribs. At bath time, the nurses scold, "Stick legs aren't very womanly. Eat more!"

The woman doesn't respond.

Although she's free to leave, she stays.

When she's alone, she draws child-like figures. Two girls are playing in a secret room. Two girls are hiding behind a prickly bush. Two girls are eating ice cream cones and giggling. Always two. Always with yellow hair, white faces, and pink dresses. One hundred and fifty-two Crayola colored drawings wallpaper the room.

"How pretty!" The nurses say that they tape the artwork to the padding.

The woman looks closely at today's drawing. It may be her favorite. Two little girls cuddle underneath a pink comforter. Daddy sits on the recliner. He's going to tell a ghostly story.

She was inspired to draw the picture after her visit yesterday. 'Visit' might not be accurate, as she did not speak. Silence protects from unintended truths.

When the woman isn't drawing, she monitors the parking lot.

Piper and Milly visit. Zakary, too. And Babs, Professor Holliday, Bear. Even Niall.

And, of course, Katie.

A chill enters. Her shoulders shake. Light flickers in the window. The crayon stops drawing; the window draws her. She stands, moving sockless feet across the tile. Screech, screech, screech. Bony fingers grip the windowsill.

Her breath catches.

A figure jogs across the parking lot.

Katie.

The woman behind the glass traces the figure. Katie lifts the hem of her nude, satin dress—such a pretty dress, and steps onto the sidewalk. Katie rubs her nose with the fabric. Katie trips. Twice.

Hmmm. Click. Tick. Twitch.

Hmmm. Click. Tick. Twitch.

Hmmm. Click. Tick. Twitch.

Is Katie finally going to tell?

422

Death by Chocolate
Sunday, May 29th @ 8:27 p.m.

IN SIXTH GRADE, my mother was our Wednesday night after-school catechism teacher. During class, she taught the principles of being a devout Catholic. In one lesson, she explained the two types of death: spiritual and physical. To a practicing Catholic, one is more tragic than the other. During the lesson, our class drank sweet lemonade from small plastic cups and shared goldfish crackers.

A physical death happens after the final heartbeat, when the last traces of carbon dioxide, nitrogen, and oxygen escape our lips, and our brain registers its first empyreal memory. Our souls depart the body and travel to heaven or hell. A physical death—unless by suicide—is beyond our control. Then the deceased's soul travels. Where? Well, the destination depends on a person's earthly actions and behaviors. Were you a true Catholic? Were you generous? Judgment-free? Honest? Did you honor the sanctity of life? Volunteer? Give to the poor? Live a life free of sin?

My classmates and I vigorously nodded. Of course, we were always good and obeyed the Ten Commandments. Mother asked if we ever sinned. With wide eyes, we stared ahead. Kylie raised her hand and asked what would happen if we accidentally sinned. Would we automatically go to hell? Kylie said sometimes it was hard to be good. My classmates and

I vigorously nodded. Of course, it was hard to be good when you're thirteen. Mother smiled.

Sinning, she said, didn't immediately send you to hell. No. Sinners had a lifeline. A 'way out' of trouble. And did we want to know what it was?

My classmates and I vigorously nodded. Of course, we wanted to know about a 'free pass'. If, and when, we sinned, we simply had to confess our wrongdoings to Father Peter during confession, repent (a fancy word for 'promise to never do it again'), receive his blessing, and heaven awaits. Did we want to know what would happen if we sinned and did not confess?

My classmates and I vigorously shook our heads 'no'. We were terrified to know what would happen. Mother smiled. She said it was important we understood, then explained the concept of 'spiritual death'. If we sinned and didn't confess and repent, our death would come slowly. First, dishonesty would make our skin crawl. Being dishonest would make us evil. And evil thoughts would cause our minds to twitch. Eventually, our souls would permanently switch. Spiritual death would send us to hell, where we would burn forever.

But… there was good news.

Confess, repent, heaven awaits.

My classmates and I vigorously clapped our hands. We were excited to confess and repent, knowing heaven was our destination.

After the lesson, I raised my hand high in the air. When Mother called on me, I asked if perhaps death by chocolate was more terrifying. Mother giggled, and the class laughed. That was the cue for the assistant teacher to bring out a chocolate mousse birthday cake for Mother with forty-two candles. (It took me only three tries to get the cake perfect.) The class sang "Happy Birthday." Mother blushed and pretended to be surprised. The cake was delicious. I miss Mother.

She always keeps-ept me grounded.

Snuggles-ed with me when I was little.

Brushes-ed my hair when it was too tangled.

She loves-ed me.

My perception was all wrong.

The White Room
Sunday - May 29th @ 8:30 p.m.

TONIGHT, THE DARK sky forms a rectangular shape around Mayfair Medical's solar-paneled, illuminated structure. The fireflies have disappeared. The moon hides behind shadowy clouds. In the parking lot, my hands shake. I open the glove compartment, dig through the contents, and grab a pen and an old receipt. I write frantically. The pen pokes through the paper several times. Blue ink stains my dress.

To my sister, Kylie, you have been my world, but it's time I've found a better distraction to occupy my obsessive personality. I'm taking a new job in Chicago, with Deveraux Consulting. It's time I find my new normal. Find out what I want. No one else can make this decision for me. I'm all in. I will love you forever and forgive you for everything. Good-bye. Love, Katie

I fold the note and crush it in my palm. For a quickly written note, it's not the worst 'Good-bye letter'.

Before I leave my vehicle, I check tonight's Greyhound bus departures from Milwaukee. Looks as though I'll be traveling to Chicago at 3:43 AM tonight—early tomorrow. Leaving Mayfair, family, friends, and Kylie behind.

Diving headfirst into my future.

Hopefully, the water isn't too shallow. Knots form in my stomach. Am I making the right decision?

A little part of me yearns to give everyone I love a proper good-bye, but a larger part knows a public farewell would end in disaster. They'd never let me leave.

Kate, you're not in the right headspace to make a big move!

You'll never survive in a big city like Chicago!

Stay here, with your dad.

Chicago? Chicago! You'll get mugged or murdered!

I message Dez. His teenage shit better be together. I need that money.

Kate Vanguard: Got the cash?

DezNutts: Yo

Kate Vanguard: Is that a yes… or a no?

DezNutts: Yah

Kate Vanguard: Can you meet me tonight at the Milwaukee Greyhound station at midnight? If you arrive by 11:30, I'll knock $300 off the price. $3500 and it's yours.

DezNutts: Cool. I'm in. Seems kinda sus tho. u really that hot blonde with the amazing ass?

Kate Vanguard: Of course, it's me. You asked for my ClickYap. And I've already messaged you.

DezNutts: Cool. I'm not looking for trouble.

Kate Vanguard: I really need you to show up. Are you going to?

DezNutts: Ya

Kate Vanguard: btw, nuts only has one t

DexNutts: No shit?

As I cross the parking lot, I stumble. Twice. I enter the hospital through the main doors. Amanda is working. I compliment her crocheted vest. She thanks me and hands me a tissue. She prints a visitor's badge and sends me to room two-oh-two.

The note dampens against my clammy hand. I climb the stairs to 'Second Floor Up'. In the mental health wing, the nurse leads me to the heavy, locked door. She unlocks the deadbolt.

The smell from inside consumes me.

Crispy, fresh, light.

Fabric softener.

I step inside.

I smile.

"Kylie?"

Will You?
Sunday, May 29th @ 10:32 p.m.

TRIPLE B'S PARKING lot is packed with cars. Laughter and music spill out from the open garage doors. I drive slowly to the back of the restaurant, searching between cars and among lingering couples and groups sitting at picnic tables near the bluffs. Finally, I find your car in the alley. I park alongside you. I expel a sigh of relief. My phone buzzes.

The Battering Ram: YOU GOOD?
Me: Yeah. I just found her car.
The Battering Ram: TRIPLE B'S?
Me: Yep.
The Battering Ram: YOU GOT THIS.

I stuff my phone inside my front pocket and trot through the parking lot. The air is cool. The clouds paint dusk with a smoky, swirling haze. The bluffs stretch to the north and sprawl to the south. Ebony lake water ripples to the east. The wind picks up. A sharp breeze brushes across my cheek.

Where are you, Katie?

You won't be inside the bar—too many people this time of night. I search the empty parking lot again and the alley by the dumpsters. I double-check the beer garden. The picnic area. I spin in circles looking for you.

My mind spins.

What am I supposed to say when I see you? Do I just blurt out, "I can't live without you?" or "I'm nothing without you?" The uncertainty hits me hard. Is there even a chance to win you back?

Back? The truth is, I never even had you. I know I pushed you away, convincing myself that your dad was right. Did I break your heart, or am I just imagining it? Maybe you never felt that way about me. How would I know for sure? I wrestle with this uncertainty, but I know I have to try to convince you that we could defy the odds. I'd even give up the entire state of Wisconsin just to be with you.

I'll quit Vanguard so we can be everything together.

Katie.

Katie.

Katie.

Es tut mir so leid. Ich liebe dich.

I'm.

So.

Sorry.

I.

Love.

You.

Katie.

Katie.

Katie.

Do I tell you the truth about Kylie? How she took what was yours? The attention that was meant for you. The affection that was meant for you. Because she was jealous. Of you. Jealous that a stranger would show such interest in you? That she purposefully took the drinks from Peaches, while you were consoling Milly. That she had zero interest in me. Only an irrational desire to have what was rightfully yours. Katie, will you believe me?

That she admitted to her deceit right before everything terrible happened? Before our destinies were forever altered.

April 10th.

The day that broke me into pieces.

The day that broke you into pieces.

As I jog across the parking lot to the cliff, an eerie sense of déjà vu settles around me. At the drop-off, one hundred feet below, the waters tap the shoreline. A black shadow sits upon the bank. The clouds part. The shadow morphs into…

You.

Katie.

Oh, Katie.

What have I done? What haven't I done? Regret overwhelms me. I keep thinking: Why didn't I just tell you the truth from the start? Would you even forgive me if I did? Could you understand why I kept it inside?

I hike quickly to the switchback path. The same path I took to finally meet you for the first time. To be your hero. Months later, I find you again. To be your everything.

Descending the pathway, my heart pounds, my hands shake, and perspiration drips down my forehead. Bile rises in my throat. I race.

My mind races.

What if you choose to cut me out of your life? What if I can never see you again? Even as a friend or acquaintance? What if you turn me down, but then I'm forced to sit back and watch you live your life? Without me. In the arms of someone else?

Now that I know you're real… I can't give you up. Everywhere I look, I'll see you. The playful—reserved—curve of your lips. The way your hair waterfalls down your back. That wild tendril that always grazes your cheek, hiding—what you call—an imperfection. The way your hips swell, the curve of your breasts. The light that exudes from you, even when you're wildly angry. The way you clumsily—and, yet effortlessly—

succeed at everything you put your mind to. Although you think you're a mess, you're strong, determined, and perfect in every way.

I know exactly what you are.

You're…. the most perfect heartache I've ever had.

The one I want to feel for the rest of my life.

The one I want to put back together daily.

The one I want to protect.

Fight with.

Fight for.

Cherish.

Honor.

Love.

At the bottom of the stairs, my shoes sink into the damp soil.

You.

Fear swells inside of me. My heart laps fate. Can you hear my heart thudding, Katie? I take several steps until I'm next to you, but you don't move. I kneel in the wet sand. My hand traces across your back. You stare ahead into the nothingness. Your cheek is wet and puffy.

"Katie," I whisper and reach for your chin. "I wish time could take me back. I wish I could re-do… everything." My hand brushes your soft skin. "Would you have ever said yes to me? Could things have been different?"

You gently lean your head against my hand. You stay that way for a moment—and for that moment, I feel as though anything can happen. The future is ours to build. No one can take it from—and just as quickly, you pull away and kneel. You face me. In this moment, my entire life is in your hands. I can become everything or nothing.

What will you choose?

Your head lifts. We stare into each other's eyes. The moonlight transforms yellow hair into a blinding crown. Your honesty and truth are all over your face.

I want to grab you, hold you, caress you. Pin you against me. Shield you from everything dangerous. Protect you from… me?

"All this time," you say, "part of me knew Kylie pushed Mother."

As you wipe tears away with one hand, I collect your other hand. You're freezing. I massage warmth back into your fingertips. Kylie's red t-shirt and baggy sweatpants aren't enough to keep you warm. I want to pick you up and… but I can't.

It's not my decision.

"When I woke up at the hospital," you say, "my dad was sobbing. He said Kylie was gone. He didn't need to say anything else. I immediately knew what he meant. For the longest time, Kylie had complained of pressure in her head. Anxiety that would never go away. Sometimes she'd see spots. Have terrible, blinding headaches. She confided in me one night. She thought she was 'one of those crazy people' and she was losing her mind.

"Mother took her to every doctor and specialist our dad could afford. They blamed Kylie's symptoms on poor sleeping habits, too much stress at school, and sports. One day, I overheard our mom on the phone with one of Kylie's doctors. He suggested Kylie was making everything up. Looking for attention. Perceptions aren't always reality, though.

"Tonight, when I visited Kylie and gave her my good-bye letter, I did something… something I shouldn't have done. I logged into her private medical records. Niall, she had seven known concussions. All from swimming. Do you know what kind of damage that can do to the brain? That's why she got banned from the swim team. It was because of health reasons. She wasn't a bad person. She was a broken person. The fears she felt were real to her. She would wake me up at night and say, 'Katie, I'm losing my mind.' I didn't know what to say. I told her she was fine. But what did I know? That night… the night of the red flag party, she and I got into a terrible fight.

"Kylie had a moment of, I guess, insanity. I really don't think she meant to push me… and in the process, Mom stepped in between us. Kylie pushed her instead. But Kylie was angry about something else. She said that she couldn't stand how everyone always chose me over her."

I hang my head. I can't bear to see your pain, your tears, your brokenness. Everything is my fault. But I can't tell you that now.

"It was you, Niall," you say, defeated and broken.

The pain in my gut is unbearable. The throbbing agony within my core becomes nearly overwhelming.

"After the push, Kylie pleaded with me," you say, and dig your fingers into the sand. "'Don't tell!' she begged. Kylie thought Mother would be okay. She told me to run down the path and be with her. 'Hurry,' Kylie said, 'Help before it's too late.' She would stay above and call for help. I ran to be with Mother. But by the time I got to her, she was… gone. Her leg was twisted. Her neck had snapped. Blood poured from her mouth. There was nothing I could do. If Kylie and I hadn't gotten into that fight… Mother would still be here." She looks directly into my eyes. " If you hadn't gotten tangled up in my family, things would be very different today."

You're shaking, sniffling, spinning the ring—my ring.

And, your pain *is* all my fault.

"Katie—"

"No, I need to get this out. I do understand why everyone lied. It was easy. At the time, it made sense. My family and friends were trying to protect the parts of my family that were still intact. It was so easy for them to say Mother died from HCM. When I was at the hospital tonight, after I looked up Kylie's records, I looked up Mother's. We knew she had heart problems. And since Dale's son is Mayfair's Medical Examiner, my dad called in a favor that night. Assistant Evers fudged the death certificate. Illegal, but a very necessary move to keep my family together. Keep Kylie out of jail. He blamed Mother's death on HCM. And Zakary's dad is chief of police, so when he arrived at Triple B's that night, he could easily corroborate the false information."

Your words are coming out in a rush, fumbling over each other, like waves on the shoreline.

"My dad justified his actions because while everyone was in shock about Mother, Kylie drove herself to the mental health clinic. Fell asleep in the parking lot. Then checked herself in the next morning. Since Kylie refused to speak, what better way to hide the truth? And it was perfect, because of my stupid clumsiness, when I tried to run back up to the top of the bluff, I tripped and smashed my head on that rock. Lost my memory… My dad had the perfect plan. I was at the mercy of everyone else. Dad didn't want Kylie to go to jail. Not with Mother gone. We couldn't lose them both. The opportunity arose. And everyone at the party agreed."

You breathe deeply, sniffle, and look directly at me.

"This is so fucked up… But you know the biggest fucking, fucked up part, Niall? Right before I fell, I saw you…"

The butterflies in my stomach swarm and begin eating the lining of my stomach.

"Katie," I say, "I've always wanted you. You were always the one."

"What do you mean, Niall?" Your voice cracks. "You were texting Kylie. You were dating her. And then… when she wasn't available… You came after me?"

"Katie, you have to believe me. It was always you."

You stare out at the inky, black water.

"Back in February," I say, kneeling next to you, "do you remember being at Triple B's with your friends? You were joking around with some guys."

You tilt your head, remembering.

"Peaches brought a kiddie cocktail," I say, "with extra cherries and a vodka chaser to the back room and said it was from 'The One'—"

"I don't know what you're talking about," you say. "But what I know is that Kylie was seeing some guy right before April 10th. Her phone was fully charged when I got home tonight, and I read all the messages from this guy named Slide. He was really pissed at Kylie. And I think he's the reason she was so upset. Then, when I found that 'Slide' is… you."

I try to speak, but you hold up your hand. Everything falls. My world, my heart, my chest.

"And I know why you were here that night," you say, "you and Roxy had a thing—"

"Katie, I wanted you—"

"Stop," you say, and dig your hands into the sand.

"And then you found Kylie's phone in my car. She must have dropped it there when I visited her at the hospital this week. I'm such an idiot. I've been visiting her daily, pouring my heart out to her, and all I get is silence from her. But I guess I understand now. She must be horrified by what she did…"

You pause. I know your heart aches for the old Kylie. The one who was your best friend.

"And then you gave me my phone, knowing that I could possibly find out about the two of you."

Katie, I want to swoop you into my arms and caress you. Kiss every part of your body a thousand times. But what can I say that will make sense—

"I've had hours to think this over," you say, calmly, "and the truth is, Niall, I'm abso-fucking-lutely into you. Ever since you ran your fucking thumb across your stupid lip at the damn bar. That moment had nothing to do with chance and everything to do with destiny. I know it. I've never felt such a deep desire for another human being in all my life. I want you more than anything else in this world. And that's the problem, Niall. I want you more than ANYTHING. More than a sunset, a sunrise, the stars in the sky. Even more than I want what's best for myself. And that's why I'm leaving."

Your words sting. Katie, if you only knew how bad your words sting.

"I have to fix myself first," you say. "Having you around, Niall, is blissful. You fix everything. You save me from all the messes I make. Calm me when I have a nightmare. You make everything better. Even getting bitten by a pretend bug is exhilarating around you. But I can't rely on you for everything. I have to learn how to live on my own. How to clean up after myself. How to handle difficult situations. How to make myself smile. I can't rely on you, Piper, Milly, Peaches, or Zakary to navigate me through life. And Kylie may never be herself again. What happens when no one's around? What am I going to do then?"

"But I don't mind," I say. I tenderly reach for you. "I want to be—"

"No," you say and pull away. "I'm leaving. Tonight. I'm not going to be sloppy seconds. I… I have a job lined up, and I'm moving to Chicago."

You tell me how you've already packed; no one can change your mind. You need a fresh start. You don't want anyone following you.

Not even me.

You hold up a photo. You and Kylie. It's going to be the center of your vision board. Your reminder that truth is more than perception. It's memories (Treasure hunts with Kylie.), words ('Not a chance.'), smells (Fabric softener.), touch (Kylie's hair tickling your face.), and sound (Kylie breathing peacefully on the upper bunk.). Memories have flavor ('Death by Chocolate' ice cream dishes.).

The truth is never black-and-white.

You tell me that you have visions of your mother. Especially when you smell her perfume. And since Nora wears it all the time, memories of your mother are more predominant when Nora's around. You say that you're not embarrassed that you wore the red bridesmaid dress to the Celebration of Life dinner. Estelle would have loved to see you in it. You say you're a little jealous of your dad because he can feel your mother's presence just by thinking about her. He doesn't need perfume.

I beg you to stay for a few more minutes—I need time. Time to tell you how I feel. To offer you everything I have. To give you everything you could ever want—

But you're already gone. Halfway up the switchback path.

438

The Possible Ending
Monday, May 30th @ 12:38 a.m.

DEZNUTTS MET ME in the Greyhound station parking lot—an hour late, and a thousand dollars short—but I'm all in, so I agreed to the new price and tucked the sad stack of hundred-dollar bills inside my duffle bag. Even with the shortage, I'll have enough money to stay at a hotel for at least two weeks, maybe longer if I find a budget motel.

With three hours to spare, I sit inside the terminal on a bench closest to the ticket booth. The entrance doors are directly in front of me. I'd sit farther away from them, but two sketchy-looking men in hoodies sit on the other side of the waiting area. They smell like weed and desperation. My skin crawls with unease, and uncertainty keeps me glued to the seat. The doors automatically hiss open every few minutes when the same homeless man walks past, pushing his grocery cart. With each bypass, a cool burst of air enters the room. I want to dig through my duffle bag and grab my sweatshirt, but I'm afraid the hundred-dollar bills will fall out or be noticed, so I sit with goosebumps on my arms, twirling Niall's ring, clinging to my bag of treasures. The cold air bites me, making me shiver, drawing attention to my growing discomfort.

With my hasty departure, I'm suddenly worried that I've severely under-packed. Inside the nylon bag I've stowed Kylie's two pencil skirts and her button-down blouse, some sweatpants and t-shirts, a hoodie, a pair of dress shoes, Kylie's phone, the framed photo of us, and my cash. I definitely didn't pack enough. I sigh. Nothing can be done about that now.

To stay awake, I scroll through TikTok videos, ignore the text and voicemail messages from Peaches, Piper, Milly, Zakary—even Roxy- and mourn my losses. They want to know where I am. What am I doing? Am I okay? I was smart enough to turn off my location, so they can't find me. And after I told Niall that I never wanted to speak to him again—by the tormented look in his eyes—I knew he would respect my request. He hasn't messaged me once. Each notification triggers a fresh wave of anxiety. Am I doing the right thing?

I want to cry. I wonder what Niall is thinking right now? A small part of me wants to turn around and run back home, another part of me hopes Niall is on his way to rescue me.

I pinch the soft inside of my arm. For once, I am going to rescue myself. As I'm about to power down my cell, I receive a text from an unknown number.

312-555-0666: Kate Vanguard?

Who would message me in the middle of the night?

312-555-0666: Sorry, this is Lance Deveraux. I know it's late, but my plane just landed in Chicago. I'm standing by the baggage claim, scrolling through emails. And I was excited to see that Verity has you scheduled to start with us on Tuesday.

312-555-0666: Sorry, I prolly shouldn't have texted this late. I'm sure you're sound asleep. lol

Lance Deveraux?

312-555-0666: I'm looking forward to meeting you, Kate. And I'm sure the move from a small town is a little unnerving, so if there's ANYTHING I can help you with… recommendations on where to stay, restaurant suggestions, things to do… just ask. Let me be the first to welcome you to Chicago.

Me: Hi, Mr. Deveraux. Yes, this is Kate Vanguard. I'm on the Greyhound to Chicago tonight.

312-555-0666: Hi Kate! You're up!!! Lol

312-555-0666: This late? Where are you staying?

Me: Not sure yet. Planning to reserve something on the way.

312-555-0666: No place to stay yet!? My father has an empty apartment. A few blocks from the office. Fully furnished. He never uses it. Stay there until you find a place of your own. It will be much more comfortable than a hotel.

Me: I appreciate the offer, but I couldn't.

312-555-0666: It's totally fine. I used to crash there before I bought my penthouse condo. I'll text you the address and the door's keycode.

Me: Mr. Deveraux, that's too much.

312-555-0666: Call me, Lance. What time are you coming in? I just got off an international flight. I'm jet-lagged as hell. No way I'm going to sleep. How about I meet you at the bus station? I'll drive you to the complex.

Me: Mr. Deveraux, that's really too much.

312-555-0666: Lance. And don't worry about it. Message me when you're fifteen minutes out. My team is my family.

Me: Thank you, but I can't impose.

312-555-0666: I don't mind.

Me: I am very thankful and appreciate the offer, but I'll be fine.

312-555-0666: You sure?

Me: Truly.

312-555-0666: Well, if you change your mind, just call. I'll most likely be up.

Any concerns I've had about Lance and Deveraux Consulting have been dispelled. My chest loosens as I realize he's generous, honorable, and considerate. Relief and gratitude replace my earlier worries. He's my ally.

Maybe things are finally turning around for me?

I let out a sigh, stand, and stretch. The homeless man passes the front doors. This time, he looks my way and smiles. He pushes his cart and waves. I smile back.

The exhaustion from the day begins to wear on me. I shove my phone in my pocket and sit back down. I slouch in the hard plastic chair and close my eyes. Just for a minute. The bus won't be here for almost two hours. I can rest…

For a little bit…

I mentally make a to-do list. Starting tomorrow, I'll be a focused machine. No more distractions. The past is in the past. The ghosts have shown themselves. Nothing can haunt me anymore. I can concentrate on completing my school assignments, securing my degree, and overachieving my ass off at my new job.

Although… I do have one loose end that could potentially strangle me.

Niall.

One lovely and unmistakably memorable weekend. The memory is bittersweet—equal parts comfort and regret. I know these thoughts will lull me to sleep for months to come as much as they will haunt me. When I think about last night, my heart races with longing and sadness—leaving me smiling like a goon one moment and crying so hard the next that I'm paralyzed, unable to breathe, move, or speak. The duality of loss and desire aches in my chest.

We can't be a thing.

This cognitive dissonance will follow me everywhere and through… eternity? Will something new ever take its place? How could something new replace this thing that's been growing inside of me? This thing with jagged edges, soft curves, and explosive ridges. What could possibly fill it… But him?

A glorious future?

A new job?

No—nothing.

The space will remain empty. My chest aches with the hollow sense of loss nothing seems able to fill.

I will remain empty.

But I mustn't let this affect my future.

Confidently, I will move forward.

Filling the space with a new future.

For once, I've made a decision, and I will follow it through. The time Niall and I spent together—not only last night, but over the past two days—will be a lovely memory. A frustrating inconvenience. An annoying presence. A breath-catching vision. A possibility that could never exist, happen, or be, therefore an utter impossibility.

Chicago is my future home.

Maybe even my destiny?

For once, I've selected my own path, and I will move forward with a sense of purpose. Kylie's not here to tell me what she thinks I should do. My dad's already chosen Niall for the VP role—and daddy takes his business relationships very seriously, so I won't complain any longer or fight his new Vanguard vision. And my dad's gotten himself a home nurse. He doesn't need me. Tomorrow, Piper and Milly leave for their vacation. They'll soon be having too much fun to even think about me. Clearly, Zakary is too preoccupied with managing his multi-unit apartment complexes to enable any more of my unhealthy behaviors. Peaches fired me; his opinion of me is evident.

The decision is made. But in a way, the decision was made for me. So, is it even my decision?

Feeling a strange sense of calm—the kind of calm I haven't felt since before Mother's death—I allow myself to dream. Of Mom. The smell of her perfume. The way she loved learning and digging into a mystery. Of Kylie. The old Kylie. The one who will be the focus of my vision board. The one who loves adventures, swimming, her friends… and me. The one whose love for me is unending. Who would do anything for me? I just know she's going to be normal again… someday. I wish I could help her—

Crash!

My eyes snap open. I've goosebumps on my arms, a wet line of drool down the side of my mouth, and panic in my chest.

Outside the doors, the homeless man is kneeling next to his scattered possessions.

I brush my tongue over my top teeth, stretch, and check my phone.

The bus will be here in five minutes.

I bolt upright, sling my duffel bag over my shoulder, and stride outside. The homeless man crouches low, pale knees sharp under baggy sweats, picking up scattered rags, battered tin cans, and flattened, rain-stained cardboard. I brace to cover my nose, expecting sour grime, but instead, a crisp, spicy hint of expensive cologne lingers in the air. Close up, his face is young—clean lines, stubble shadow, dark hair unkempt. It unsettles me, makes me question what I missed before.

He smiles at me.

I have a minute to spare. I can help.

I drop to my knees and start gently tossing items into the cart. When I'm grabbing the last aluminum soda can, the strap of my bag tugs against my shoulder. I turn. The wayward man is gripping my bag, pulling as hard as he can. I yank back, but I'm so caught off guard with what's happening that I lose my balance and stumble backward. The straps float away as the derelict runs down the sidewalk to the neighboring alley.

I chase after him, but when I round the corner, the man has disappeared. In the middle of the alley, I find the framed photo of Kylie and me. The glass is broken. Kylie's phone, even more cracked and dented, lies next to it. Everything else is gone. Everything.

The money.

From the street, the heavy hum of a diesel engine passes behind me.

I race after the bus, waving my arms. Just when I'm certain, the driver hasn't noticed me, the engine grinds to a halt. The side doors open. I run inside. The driver smiles.

"I thought we had one more passenger," the sweet old man says. "C'mon aboard."

I force a grin, hand him my ticket, and head to the back. Once safely seated, I slide my phone from my back pocket.

Me: Mr. Deveraux?

312-555-0666: Lance. And what can I do for you, Kate?

Me: I'm so sorry to do this to you. But I've changed my mind. Can I please stay at your dad's?

312-555-0666: Of course. I'll meet you at the bus station. And you are not a bother at all.

Me: Money is kind of tight right now. I'm not sure how much rent I can afford.

312-555-0666: First month is on me.

I smile big, admire the intricate detail in Niall's ring, and dip a toe into my glorious future.

446

Double Take
Book 2

Sometime Later

IF THE EYES tell a story, his debut novel is a psychological thriller with the most terrifying plot twist imaginable. Through slits of freezing rain, he must feel the weight of my petrified stare; his head jerks in my direction, and he lurches like a leashed pit bull. A devil's orange jumpsuit makes him appear larger than life. A fifteen-foot chain link fence, 7000-volt electric wire, ten guards, and the length of a football field separate us. The iron shackles, handcuffs, and four guards slow his movements. Even still, he lumbers towards me. My foot slips in the wet grass; fear pools around me, washes over me.

He nearly destroyed me…

I thought I knew him…

Those vibrant eyes are as familiar as the ridges on my scar. Burning tears drip into the crease of my lips. I wrap my freezing arms around my waist and clutch the drenched, muddied wedding dress. "Dammit, Milly," I whisper. "This is why I don't do white…"

The guards, smaller in stature, muscle the man towards the slate-gray doors. I maintain a life stare, watching this man lose his freedom. I must witness it with my own eyes until he's safely locked inside the state penitentiary. Maybe then, the nightmares will end?

"KATIE!" The man's growl macerates my heart, nearly shattering bone.

His solid upper body strains against the officers. Biceps bulge under coarse fabric. A guard stumbles. An orange arm swings and collides with the guard's chest. The man is strong and fast, we've established that, but a maximum-security prison has batons, tasers, and marksmen with rifles.

After several moments, the man goes down—not without a fight—face-first into the puddling mud.

Gratitude

Razor Thin began as an overwhelming and constant idea. A feeling in my heart that begged to be expressed on paper and shared with the world. It's the story of a broken girl whose only chance at rescue depended on her own sheer will. Katie's story is my story. It's probably yours, too.

This novel wouldn't have been possible without the unconditional support and honesty of my family, friends, and beta readers.

Thank you...

To my very first beta readers: Heather, Jackie, Dolores, and my mama. Heather, Jackie, and my mama said my first draft was 'really good'. (Liars!) Every new writer needs a few friends like them. They gave me the courage to believe I could be the next Colleen Hoover. Thanks to one of my besties, Dolores, a former librarian—who read the same version—I learned that the first draft was 'a little rough'. Every writer needs a brutally honest friend like Dolores. I credit much of my success to her. She encouraged me to keep revising and to bring her the next draft.

To my first Fran Fans: Amanda C., Kelly T., Allie L., Sarah T., Celeste S., Erika B., Teri C., Annette A., Michele M., Anna G., and Julie S. Thank you for patiently cheering me on as I agonized over the last 50 pages. I couldn't have finished the novel without you!

To my friends who liked, loved, and commented on my social media posts about Razor Thin. These lovely people insisted on waiting to read

Razor Thin until it was published: Crystal T., Lauren D., Jin M., Alyssa Z., & Gina K. Thank you for your friendship. You believed in me, even when I didn't believe in myself.

To Hannah Linder, of Hannah Linder Creations. This book cover is amazing! Your artistic talent blows my mind. You took my confused words, copied and pasted sample covers, and created a hypnotic, captivating masterpiece. (Chef's kiss.)

To Amanda Claas. The Fran Fans social media presence has grown into a fun space to nerd out on all things Niall and Kate. You played a key role in developing this site. Thank you so much for your enthusiasm in building www.AmyFrances.com and the private Facebook group. Thank you for being one of my biggest fans as a beta reader and for providing fantastic feedback and critique.

And to you, the reader. Thank you from the bottom of my heart to the tips of my toes. I'm over the planet Pluto, happy that you took a chance on a silly, sassy, small-town indie author. You're the reason I write—to connect with you during this journey called life, through all the ups and downs, heartbreaks, and mysteries. Life is just one big psychological thriller. We can't put it down or look away, even when it gets scary. Keep turning those pages, watch for that plot twist, and stay tuned for the seemingly happy ending.

Follow me as I struggle, strive, hit rock bottom, succeed, and soar. www.AmyFrances.com

About the Author

Growing up in Land O' Lakes, WI, a self-proclaimed book nerd, Amy would geek out at any Scholastic Book Fair, earning an embarrassing number of free books and pizza. This passion followed her through adulthood. Whenever changing addresses, the first item on her to-do list? Register for a library card.

In July of 2019, after a reading slump, a good friend challenged Amy to write a book. At first, she was like, "Whaaaaaaaaaat?"

Then she wondered if she could.

Then she was like, "Yeeeeeeeeees!"

Soon, she began devouring YouTube videos and Audibles, buying books online, and checking out creative writing books from the local library. (Go Germantown!) She even started dissecting her favorite novels (*Twilight* in the house!), and spent every free moment writing what she calls 'terrible stories'.

Now, over 20 beta readers from around the country, and some across the pond, say *Razor Thin* is as good as any best-selling novel!

Recently, she approached a local writing friend to have her manuscript formally edited. After the published author read the first five pages, the published author said, "Amy! You don't need me!" But for real… if you find any errors, please message Amy directly. www.AmyFrances.com

Contrary to what her three beautiful children think (she's super mom), she is only human.

Thanks to months of editing (reading printed copies, listening to the novel via the lovely Word app, collecting beta reader feedback, and reading the manuscript aloud), *Razor Thin* flows like any polished thriller.

As a child, Amy read *The Babysitter's Club*, *Sweet Valley High*, *The Chronicles of Narnia*, Christopher Pike, and R.L. Stine. In high school, while cleaning the local library on Sunday evenings, she 'borrowed' spicy historical romances (by Jude Deveraux and Catherine Coulter), and returned them the following week. As an adult, she's loved classics like *The Giver* and *Slaughter House Five*. Currently, she enjoys reading psychological thrillers with wicked plot twists. Some of her recent favorites? *Big Little Lies*, *The Silent Patient*, and *Atonement*. Her all-time favorite book? *Twilight!* There's just something about handsome strangers and dark romances.

Presently, Amy is keeping readers in suspense while she writes book 2 in her *Razor Thin* series: *Double Take*.

While Amy's not writing, or thinking about writing, you'll find her at home, in a quaint Wisconsin town, chasing her family around the living room, demanding Chapstick kisses or snuggling with Milly (who looks suspiciously like an Aussie Doodle, but is, in fact, entirely human).

www.ingramcontent.com/pod-product-compliance
Lightning Source LLC
Chambersburg PA
CBHW061418150726
47987CB00001B/13